Praise for *Deadly Odds*

"… Original and a first rate thriller."

—Phillip Margolin, *New York Times* bestselling author of *Woman with a Gun*

"With Allen Wyler you get thrills and a dash of humor combined in a high-tech plot written by a guy who knows what he's talking about. I love his books and *Deadly Odds* was the best one yet."

—Mike Lawson, award-winning author of the Joe DeMarco series

Praise for *Dead End Deal*

"A wild journey … cutting-edge science, greed, corruption, and political intrigue, you won't be able to put it down."

—D.P. Lyle, award-winning author of *Hot Lights, Cold Steel*

"… a medical thriller of the highest order."

—Jon Land, bestselling author of *Strong at the Break*

"The gritty, graphic details of cutting-edge surgical procedures, capped with an exciting conclusion, should keep fans of the genre riveted."

—*Publishers Weekly*

Praise for *Deadly Errors*

"… a fast-paced thriller that reawakens your scariest misgivings … an unsettling backstage tour through the labyrinth of … the American hospital."

—Darryl Poniscan, author of *The Last Detail*

"… a wild and satisfying read."

—John J. Nance, author of *Pandora's Clock* and *Fire Flight*

cutter's trial

A novel by

allen wyler

This is a work of fiction. All characters and events portrayed in this novel are either fictitious or are used fictitiously.

CUTTER'S TRIAL
Astor + Blue Editions
 Published in the United States by:

Astor + Blue Editions
New York, NY 10036
www.astorandblue.com

Publisher's Cataloging-In-Publication Data

WYLER, ALLEN. CUTTER'S TRIAL. —1st ed.

ISBN: 978-1-941286-14-2 (paperback)
ISBN: 978-1-941286-16-6 (epdf)
ISBN: 978-1-941286-15-9 (epub)

1. Thriller—Medical—Fiction 2. Doctor on trial for mercy killing—Fiction 3. Legal—Fiction 4. Political—Fiction 5. Family drama—Fiction 6. Religion & Morality—Fiction 7. South I. Title

Jacket Cover Design: Ervin Serrano

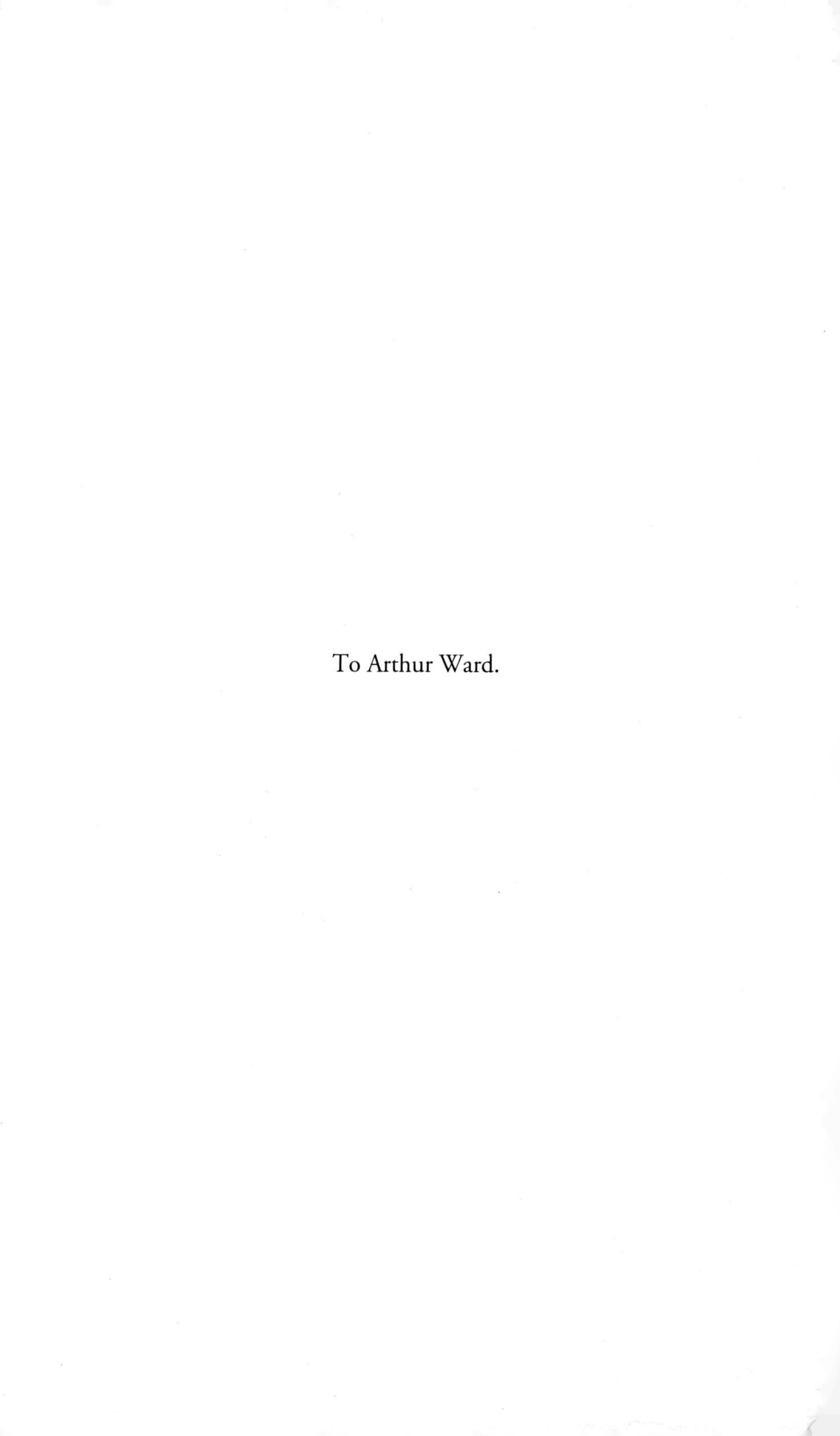

To Arthur Ward.

1

"ISN'T IT TRUE, DOCTOR, that you murdered Meredith Costello?"

And there it was: The Question. Time stopped, as if God pressed "pause" for Alex Cutter's universe. Every courtroom detail suddenly became ultra sharp: the American and state flags to either side of the judge's black robe, dirt coating the outside windows, the metallic, mold-tinged smell of air conditioning, the jurors' eyes on him, the observers scattered throughout the viewing gallery. Alex's breath caught. Two beats passed before time began creeping forward again.

How did I ever get to this point?

THE BEGINNING: 10 years earlier, 1981

"You seriously going to stick around this place?" Gordon Malden, the other graduating resident, asked with bemused incredulity. Malden held a sweating longneck pale ale while choreographing his words with both hands, either ignoring or unaware of the beer flying out the spout. Speaking with his hands was a characteristic that made him particularly amusing to watch during teaching conferences. The more the professors boxed him into a corner, the more herky-jerky and wild his movements became, reminding Alex of an amateur puppet show.

The private dining room of Parker's, an upscale steakhouse, was filled with professors, the two graduating residents, and spouses, the group milling about as they enjoyed the cocktail hour.

Alex felt defensive for having to explain his decision yet again. Besides, all the present faculty, with the exception of Baxter, had stayed on as faculty after residency. None of them showed any signs of Two Banjo country inbreeding. Still, the common wisdom held that the big boys leave while the babies stay close to the womb.

"I am. I start tomorrow. Why?"

Gordon glanced around, as if making sure no one eavesdropped. "The senior partner in my new group said to tell you if you're interested, they'd love to have you come with me. We'd be a package." He chuckled. "I told him how tight-assed you are in surgery, and he loved that. Said you'd make a great addition to the group. He'll be ready to bail in about two years, meaning we'd bump up in seniority when it comes time to hire his replacement. And that made me think of Guyton. Timing would be just about right for his graduation. We could make a tight little group, the three of us, all like-minded partners." Gordy took a long pull off the beer. "What do you think? Not too late to change your mind."

Alex was flattered, but private practice was out of the question. "Thanks for the offer, but I'm staying." He took a sip of cabernet. Resident folklore had it that wine flowed at these dinners, turning conversation into drawn out speeches and sodden reminiscences. He intended to pace himself.

"If you don't mind me asking, why stick around? I mean, isn't it going to be a bit awkward?" Gordy checked the fluid level of his beer before draining the dregs.

"Awkward?"

Gordy set the empty on a serving tray. "You know … today you're *the boy*, tomorrow you're *one of them*. Just can't see how the magical transformation's going to work. You know damn well Ogden, Baxter, and Heart will always consider you their little scut jockey. You'll be hanging onto the bottom rung of the feces ladder." He glanced around for a waiter.

Alex laughed. Not so much at the words as the comical way they were delivered, hands flying.

Gordy signaled a drink waiter for another beer. "Why subject yourself to that kind of humiliation?"

Alex had asked himself the same question numerous times since Dr. Waters—the departmental chair—first proposed he stay on as an assistant professor. "That's easy. My research. You know Eberholt Foltz just moved to Utah?"

"Hadn't heard."

One and a half years of the residency was devoted to research under the mentorship of a faculty member. Gordy had done his with an anatomist on an electron microscope project. Alex had worked on developing the technique of using tissue culture to study brain tumor cells.

"Waters gave me his lab. Karen Fitch will stay on, so I don't have to start the search for a lab tech. She knows the lab and knows my work, so there's no down time to get a new lab up and running, which is what would happen at a new place. I just submitted a grant to NIH. Waters said until I'm funded, the department will support me."

Gordon shook his head. "No offense, Alex, but how much will you make as an assistant professor?"

Alex blushed. Assistant professors took home a fraction of what guys like Gordy would be pulling down as a junior partner in a practice. "I guarantee it's not as much as you." *Something you know already*. "But the department covers my malpractice, and they'll contribute to my TIAA-CREF account," Alex said, referring to the retirement plan a majority of universities used.

Gordy raised both hands in surrender. "Fine, sounds like you're committed. Just wanted to make sure you were aware of the offer. It's a booming practice with lots of room to grow. Yeah, yeah, I know … Idaho is Idaho, but Boise is growing and we could build into the premier practice in the area. You could always come back to the coast for vacations." He chugged the second beer, then set the empty on a nearby table. "Looks like people are picking their seats. Time to collect our wives before one of us gets stuck next to Baxter Rabbit."

Laughing, Alex went to find Lisa.

The ring of cutlery against crystal brought the slightly intoxicated conversation down to a few dying whispers as everyone's eyes went to the head of the table where Waters stood. Joyce, his tall, angular Smith College wife, sat on his left. Waters wore grey flannel slacks and a blue, double-breasted blazer with the Yale emblem proudly displayed on the breast pocket. Alex had seen him drag out that jacket only once before, and that, come to think of it, had also been a university event. Everyone's attention now captured, Waters cleared his throat.

"It's with a curious mix of joy and sorrow that we convene these annual dinners in honor of our graduating residents. Speaking purely for the faculty—because I can't speak for you two characters," he glanced at Gordon and Alex, triggering the obligatory chuckle from the others, "—these dinners bring a deep sense of pride at seeing well-trained neurosurgeons take their place in the honored heritage of our specialty. At the same time, we experience tremendous sorrow that comes from parting between dear friends. A separation made more acute by having spent five years of tireless work in the intimacy of the surgical theater, sharing the emotional highs and lows inherent to practicing our art. It is with these conflicting emotions we honor Gordon Malden and Alex Cutter with a toast." Waters raised his glass of cabernet as Baxter slurred, "Hear, hear!"

Joyce, Waters's wife, stood, raising her glass. "I propose a toast to Lisa and Joan, who, through it all, kept the home fires burning brightly in support of their husbands. I'm not sure our new graduates have a true understanding of the hardships we wives experience through the difficult residency years, the long hours spent alone. Here's to the women who made these men what they are today."

Another toast.

"Let's hear from the newly anointed neurosurgeons," Baxter shouted.

Waters swept a palm toward Gordon before sitting down.

Gordon stood, fresh bottle of beer in hand. "I'll make this mercifully short. If any of you happen to find yourself in Boise, look me up. My door is always open. That is, assuming I can break away from my practice long enough to take you out for a beer. Looks like I'm going to be extremely busy there. Thank you everyone." With a nod to Waters, he sat down.

All eyes turned to Alex.

Tentatively, Alex pushed up from his chair. He was completely unprepared, his mind scrambling for something appropriate to say as a niggling voice in the depths of his consciousness reprimanded him for being woefully unprepared. The room grew still, distant restaurant sounds filtering in from outside their private dining room. The warm glow of wine amplified the emotional impact of ending fifteen years of grueling competition. Four years of premed, struggling for grades and references good enough to garner med school admission. Four intense years of med school, working against even tougher competition for grades that could open the doors to a top internship, which in turn might allow entrance into one of the less-than-one-hundred residency spots nationally. He and Gordy had been the two candidates chosen from more than a hundred applicants that year. Finally, a grueling five-year residency. This nonstop treadmill of work would end abruptly in a few minutes, like hitting a brick wall at sixty miles per hour. He thought of how proud his mother would be, had she lived to witness this moment. Then, for lack of any words, and to prevent these intense emotions from swamping him, he raised his glass. "I want to thank all of you for the privilege of fulfilling my life's dream. Here's to you!"

"Jesus, Alex, you didn't prepare *any*thing? No acceptance speech?" Lisa laughed, shaking her head in exaggerated dismay as they pulled out of the parking lot. "Didn't you know it would be expected tonight?"

Alex's face burned, embarrassed yet again. "I thought I had prepared a few words," he lied to save face. "But when I stood up in front of that group, I blanked."

She put her hand over his. "I'm sure they understand. They've all been through it before."

He braked the Audi at a red light and turned up the radio slightly in hopes of changing the subject. In the rearview mirror, the headlights of a car approached and stopped a few feet behind them.

Lisa said, "You notice the way Baxter was sucking down that bottle of Château Margaux? I'm surprised Waters let him get away with that. That bottle must've set the department back a small fortune. Can't imagine how much the dinner cost. Does Waters pay for those out of departmental funds? I mean, you guys don't pony up for them out of your own pockets, do you?"

That was one of the soon-to-be-revealed mysteries. He doubted he'd be charged for this evening's dinner, but the absurdity of the thought caused him to laugh. "I have no idea. Guess I'll find out next year." A surge of pride hit from the mental image of sitting among the faculty at next year's graduation dinner. He watched the second hand on the dashboard clock as it ticked from 11:59 to 12:00. "Hey, look. It's after midnight. As of this moment I'm an assistant professor of neurosurgery."

She squeezed his hand. "I'm proud of you."

The light changed to green. "Hey, tomorrow's our first day without either of us having to go to work. In fact, the whole weekend's free." Seemed too good to be true, and now that he thought about it, intimidating, like being a prisoner released from a fifteen-year sentence. "What should we do?"

Lisa blew a long, slow breath through pursed lips, slumped back in the bucket seat, and remained silent several seconds as if soaking up the reality. "For starters, how about we sleep forty-eight hours nonstop. I need to get used to the phone not ringing at any hour of the night."

"Yeah, sleep would be good. Great idea." This past year—his tour as chief resident—he pulled continuous call every hour of every day for the entire 365. Barbaric. Senseless. Six months at University Hospital followed by six months covering the "downtown service" of the VA and county hospitals. Coastal County housed the region's Level 1 trauma center. But that was this residency's structure. As chief resident, he backed up the junior residents taking first call, handling every problem that came in. If a major issue developed—such as taking a patient to the OR—he cleared it with the attending physician on call. His judgment and performance would be subsequently critiqued by the professor the next day on rounds. Driving slowly down the street now, the exhausting year of constant stress and chronic sleep deprivation came crashing down on him.

It's over! Done with.

Two more blocks and they'd be home. The thought of climbing into bed without having to worry about the phone ringing seemed too good to be true.

2

"OKAY, I'LL TAKE IT from here," Alex told the chief resident who just opened the dura—the tough protective membrane that adheres to the undersurface of the skull and protects the brain. The resident shot him a disapproving glare, triggering a momentary pang of guilt for taking over so soon, especially on a case so seemingly routine. Alex's first urge was to apologize, to explain this was his first case as an attending physician, that as a resident he never appreciated the difference. Sure, residents work extremely hard. But working hard by putting in long, tiring hours was not close to the emotional stress that came from assuming total responsibility for the patient's life: an enormous distinction that went unappreciated during his residency.

Explain it to him? No. Best to move on, especially the way the brain appeared, swollen and angry.

High-intensity surgical lights radiated heat, making Alex sweat, an occasional drop slithering from his armpits down his chest, soaking the elastic band of his Fruit of the Looms. The 2.5x power loupes he wore for magnification pressed against the bridge of his nose, producing two aching footprints. A second resident, the newbie, stood to the side watching them, not daring to say a word for fear of showing his inexperience.

Alex glanced over the surgical drape to the anesthesiologist. "Give him twenty-five of mannitol," he said. Given through the IV, the mannitol would suck water from the brain tissue, which would then be peed out by the kidneys. "Brain's tighter than a tick." He turned to the junior resident. "What does *dura* mean?"

The young man appeared startled at being asked a question. "Not sure."

"Means tough, strong, *dura*ble. Way I figure, the membrane got its name when Hippocrates was doing his first head dissection. As he was cutting it, he said, 'Man, this is one tough mother!' So the scribe, being the diligent worker he was, wrote down 'tough mother.' So that's what it's been called ever since: the dura mater." The membrane open now, he turned to the chief resident. "Where's the tumor?"

The left side of the patient's skull was exposed in the center of the surgical drapes, a horseshoe-shaped incision of scalp pealed back, a four-inch square of removed skull safely protected in saline-soaked cotton towels on the overhead table with the rest of the surgical instruments. The "skull flap" would be reattached to the skull with wire during the closure, eventually growing together like a bone fracture. A square flap of dura had been opened on three sides, hinged, and held in place with small sutures. Inside this opening, the brain surface glistened from the saline gently squirted over it to prevent drying under the intense surgical lights. But the brain was beginning to bulge out of the opening, pushed by edema and extra mass caused by the tumor. One small area on the surface looked discolored and inflamed.

"There," said the resident, pointing to the discolored portion. "This one's relative easy to spot because it comes all the way to the surface."

"Right." Alex felt rather foolish playing the professor role, but hey, you had to start sooner or later. "This being the left side of the brain of a right-handed person makes it …?"

"His speech-dominant hemisphere," the chief answered with an obvious hint of boredom.

Alex noticed the first-year resident hanging on every word. For him this was all new material to be learned as quickly as possible because there was just so much to absorb. "Okay, given that, how do we remove this tumor without damaging the speech cortex?"

"We know from our pre-op exam the patient is presently intact neurologically," the chief explained, getting into teaching mode for the sake of his junior resident. "On the CT, the tumor looks like a glioma." Which is a tumor of the brain's supportive tissue instead of the nerve cells. "As long as we stay within the tumor and don't get into normal brain, we should be able to gut this without damaging the functional brain."

"Exactly right." Alex looked to the junior resident. "Okay, so how do we do that?"

"Very carefully."

Alex laughed at the stock answer and nodded for the chief to answer.

"After we take biopsies, we use very gentle suction. In these tumors the tissue is softer and more vascular than normal brain, so it can be sucked out bit by bit until we see more normal-appearing tissue. And being able recognize this is where experience comes in."

Alex laid saline-soaked rectangular strips of cotton—called cottonoids—over the non-involved brain to keep it moist and protected from their instruments. "A fifteen Bard Park, please," Alex told the scrub nurse, satisfied the tumor was now ready to be removed. A carbon steel scalpel made by the Bard Parker company, the number fifteen indicated the blade size and shape.

Using the very tip of the scalpel, Alex gently cut a half-inch incision in the glistening pia, the brain's thin outer membrane. As soon as the cut was made, soft, swollen tumor tissue began oozing out of the small incision like toothpaste from a tube. He began carefully sucking away the mushy tumor with a small-bore suction, allowing the pressure in the brain to keep squeezing the tumor out without having to handle or manipulate the surrounding brain. His right hand controlled the sucker while his left hand held a small Malis forceps that could cauterize blood vessels caught between the tips when he stepped on a foot pedal. After several minutes, the pressure inside the brain lessened, allowing Alex to open the pia more.

"Call pathology for a frozen section," Alex called to the circulating nurse filling out paperwork. Using forceps with a cupped tip, he plucked out ten small globs of tumor, making certain to sample as many areas of it as possible.

Satisfied, Alex then removed bits of tissue to send to his lab where he'd try to grow the tumor cells in a tissue culture. He believed the only way to solve the mysterious cause of these tumors was to be able to control their growth under laboratory conditions.

"What do you think?" he asked the chief, still trying to console him for having stolen the case.

The resident shook his head sadly. "I think he's totally hosed. I'm betting glioblastoma."

"Looks like a GBM," said the pathologist, confirming the chief resident's hypothesis. The scrub-clad woman poked her head inside the OR doors, holding a mask in place with her hand.

Shit. Alex gave an acknowledging nod. "Thanks. I'll be by later to take a look." To the scrub nurse, he said, "Okay, I need to take more samples for my lab." Turning to the new resident, he asked, "Know what I do in the lab?"

"No sir."

"I'm trying to learn what makes these damn things grow and become malignant tumors. Unlike some tissue—bone marrow, for example—that's always reproducing, glia remain fairly static and neurons don't reproduce at all. So the question is, what kick-starts these cells into growing? And once that happens, what makes them turn malignant? Any guesses?"

"Seriously?"

Alex used the cup forceps to pluck out his last sample, and handed it and the instrument off to the scrub nurse. "Yes, seriously."

"I have no idea."

Alex chuckled. "Nor do I. But I do have one theory I'm working on. Know what a stem cell is?"

The junior resident shot his chief a hey-don't-leave-me-dangling look. The senior resident simply ignored him. Getting "pimped" was part of the game. "Not really," he finally answered.

"Well, look it up. They were only discovered recently and are still being understood. But they do occur in the brain. I suspect they're the cause of these tumors. Why? Because they have the ability to turn into many different tissues. That why they're called *stem* cells. They're the stem from which you can produce just about any cell in the body. I need to find what sets them off to go nuts."

Alex worked swiftly and carefully, saying nothing. He focused intensely on every move, the responsibility of shepherding the patient through surgery unscathed weighing heavily on him.

"Ask you a question?" the chief said, breaking Alex's concentration.

"What?"

"What made you get interested in GBMs? I mean, they've got to be the most depressing tumor I can think of."

Alex paused, deciding whether or not to tell him. "My mother died from one."

3

"I'll check the duck," Alex said, rubbing the soles of his shoes back and forth on the doormat, "if you pop the cork on the wine. Bottle's on the counter." He was still sucking wind from the mile-and-a-half hike back from the stadium, the last quarter mile up a steep, winding street to their neighborhood. It was a glorious autumn Saturday of muted reds, browns, and oranges, the air crisp and slightly biting, tingling his earlobes and the tip of his nose. A perfect football day. Even better because their team won.

"Deal." Lisa followed suit with her shoes.

Alex passed through the small dining room and on into the kitchen, then out to the back porch and the barbecue. He loved the red lacquered cooker. Bought it at a hardware store as a graduation present. The bottom compartment held charcoal briquettes, the middle section held a pan of water, the top had the grill over which the red dome sat. Cooking was controlled either by frequent monitoring or by simply starting with a limited amount of fuel. He preferred the latter option. After lighting the briquettes he would insert the water pan and then the grill with whatever meat needed cooking. No matter how long the football game lasted, by the time they returned home the food would be cooked to perfection with a lovely smoky flavor. He removed the lid to inspect the duck. Perfect—a crisp golden-brown skin. Even better, it was still warm.

After setting the duck on the kitchen counter, Alex returned to the front closet to hang his jacket, his face still stinging pleasantly in the cozy warmth after several hours exposed to chilly fall air. Lisa returned to the kitchen. "Sorry, I didn't open the wine yet—had to make a pit stop."

"That's fine, I'll do it." He picked up the bottle to start peeling away the foil, and Lisa took one of two chairs at the small bistro table to watch. "Great game."

Lisa issued a derisive snort. "You say that about every game we win, regardless of how many penalties or mistakes they make. But I have to agree. Certainly was exciting. That ending … wow."

Foil off, he began screwing the worm into the cork. "Oh man, tied at the start of the fourth quarter. Wasn't sure they'd be able to pull it off."

"That punt return was what saved us. Special teams have done it all year long. Not the offense or defense, but special teams." A rabid NFL fan, she wasn't as keen on college ball as he was. Still, she could hold up her end of a postgame conversation.

"Well, the punt return and the defensive play in the final ten minutes. Jesus, thought I was going to stroke out those final seconds." He sniffed the cork, nodded approval, and poured two glasses of cabernet, which he brought to the table. Lisa waited for him to sit before she raised her glass in a toast. "Health and happiness."

"Health and happiness." They clinked and sipped, making no effort to dive straight into conversation, just enjoying the beginning of a wonderful fall Saturday evening. He loved these well-worn-jeans-and-sweatshirt moments with Lisa.

Alex sat cross-chaired, back against the wall, admiring the small kitchen of a home someone had classified as Dutch Colonial. He couldn't define the style. It had three bedrooms, two and a half baths, and an unfinished basement. A good "starter home." His first. Shortly after moving in, he'd replaced the linoleum kitchen floor with pre-stained parquet squares. Not a perfect job by any standard, but it was work he felt proud of. A butcher block occupied the center of the room and held a wood salad bowl, salt and pepper set, and knife block.

"You know, right now life seems too good to be true. Does it seem that way to you?"

Lisa nodded. "Yeah, it does."

He swept a hand left to right. "This home, our lives … I just feel so content. Just look at today: we walked to the football game and back while dinner cooked on the smoker. Tonight we'll stay in and watch a movie. I'm an assistant professor at a good university. We're both making some money and have our health. What's not to like?"

Lisa hesitated for a moment, then spoke up. "Well, there's one thing that could be better."

"Oh? What?"

She cocked her head as she collected her thoughts. "I just wish we had more time for evenings like this, just the two of us. I don't really understand why you need to spend so many nights in the lab."

He reached across the table, took her hand. "I love you. You know that don't you?"

She nodded.

He'd explained it all before: the junior man gets stuck with the crap the senior partners are sick of—rounds at the VA Hospital Tuesdays and Thursdays that included the outpatient clinic. Not only did the commute burn an hour and a half, but dealing with the bottomless pit of red tape from VA career bureaucrats was hair-tearingly frustrating.

"Things will get better. Once I get my grant I'll be able to hire another lab tech, and that'll relieve some of the pressure. Soon as that happens, my productivity will improve to where I can advertise for a postdoc. Things will get better. I guarantee it."

Lisa sighed. "Heard anything from NIH yet?"

The contented glow vaporized. He snapped back to reality. For the past several hours he'd been blissfully distracted from the issue.

"No."

"Have you talked to Dr. Waters about it?" Lisa was still finding it difficult to refer to him as "Art." Only recently had Alex broken the habit of calling him "Dr. Waters."

"Yesterday, as a matter of fact. He was pretty frank about things, said if I hadn't heard by now, chances were it didn't pass study section." Study section was the group of scientists who reviewed and prioritized grant applications.

"What does that mean for your lab?"

The anxiety eating away at his gut these past few weeks returned, a deep, uncomfortable distress bordering on pain. "Until I'm funded,

I'll have to scale back my work. Art says I have to take over a hundred percent of the trauma center coverage."

"But you've been so productive in the lab." She was frowning now. "How can they do that to you?"

He downed his wine and poured fresh glasses. "No problem understanding that, Sweetie. My salary is based on lab effort, not clinical work like the other surgeons. If I can't support myself on grants, I have to earn it clinically. All the other guys have established practices, so I can't compete at the U hospital. Well, I could over time, but for right now I can't. The only solution is to cover the trauma center." A funk settled over him at the thought of having to spend his time in the OR instead of the lab. More than once, he considered going back to school for a PhD to allow him to devote all of his time to research instead of continuing this schizophrenic division of responsibilities.

"Actually," he continued, "I start taking call Monday." He'd not mentioned this before for fear of spoiling the weekend. Recently, he'd begun to view himself as a failure. Winners had grant support. Losers had nothing. Twice now, he had served as an ad hoc NIH reviewer, so he had insight into this classic catch-22 conundrum: grants were awarded to seasoned researchers with proven track records, leaving unfunded scientists like himself in the cold. How the hell were you expected to develop a track record if you couldn't support a lab?

4

"HUMMUS AGAIN?" ALEX ASKED Karen Fitch, his lab tech.

Karen responded with a self-conscious laugh, her habitual reaction to most questions. She pushed strands of scraggly, shoulder-length black hair behind her ear. "Why do you ask?"

Alex, Karen, and Steve Stein, a local student slated to begin Vanderbilt Medical School in ten days, were sitting in the lab having a lunch break.

His turn to laugh. "Seems like hummus and pita bread are all you've eaten for lunch these past two weeks. This a new diet?"

Karen, a tall, big-boned free spirit, constantly dove into various special diets reputed to contain undocumented naturopathic benefits. After perhaps a month or so, her focus would shift in a sort of dietary Brownian movement. Last month she ate only sardine sandwiches on whole grain bread, one of which she shared with Alex and Steve. He had to admit it tasted wonderful, but a month of nothing but sardines seemed a bit, well, over the top.

She returned to grinding garbanzo beans with the lab's mortar and pestle, adding in a splash of extra virgin olive oil and some spices. Her kitchen was the lab's sheet metal countertop. She routinely bought the beans and other ingredients at a co-op known for predominately organic fare. "Hummus is healthy. You should eat it instead of that greasy fried chicken every day."

"Already have. You gave me a taste last week. I have to admit, you do a great job with the hummus and bread. Where'd you get the recipe?" He knew she baked breads from a hundred percent organic ingredients.

She perched on a lab stool, her six-foot frame hunched over the counter, knees angled to the right to keep from banging against the shelves. She stopped grinding and plunked her elbows on the countertop, her eyes glazing into a thousand-yard stare. "I was on my ultimate world trip." Recently everything had become "ultimate": the ultimate New Year, ultimate birthday, ultimate sardine sandwich. "We'd worked our way through India and were in the Middle East when we stopped at this *kibbutz* in Israel. Did I tell you about my year at the *kibbutz*?"

He brought his brown-bag lunch to the counter and took the neighboring stool, with Steve to his right munching a PB&J on white bread—a choice Karen rode him about constantly, yet good-naturedly. "You mentioned it briefly one time but never told me the full story."

"Well you're not getting the full story now, or ever. There's not enough time for the ultimate version." Another laugh. "Perhaps one of these afternoons when it's slow. Anyway, this one really amazing Israeli cook taught me the recipe from scratch. I watched her work, and when she finished, she offered me a serving. It was the most delicious food I'd eaten in months. So," she shrugged, "I tried to remember the exact recipe, but of course, couldn't. This is close enough. You like it?"

From his brown paper bag, Alex withdrew his daily lunch: two pieces of fried chicken and an orange. "I do. It's very good." It wasn't simply a gratuitous compliment. She was an amazingly good cook.

Steve chimed in. "Sure is healthier than your greasy chicken. How can you eat that? It's so … unhealthy." Steve glanced at Karen for support.

Alex couldn't tell if Steve was joking or not, but laughed anyway. True. Every Sunday he stopped at Safeway for a ten-piece bag of frozen fried chicken and five oranges. Sunday afternoon he baked the chicken, sorted the pieces into five equal portions—each of which he wrapped in aluminum foil—then assembled and stored five sack lunches in the refrigerator. On his way out the door each morning he grabbed a sack, giving Lisa more time to get ready for work.

"I can't argue with you on that," he said. "Just seems like so much trouble to go through every day."

Karen stopped mashing beans to face him, beaming. "Trouble? Not at all. Dishes I make with my own hands,"—she held them up as if mystical instruments—"that I create from raw ingredients taste so much incredibly better than store-bought food. I made the bread too. Did you know that?"

"Yes, that's why I asked how you do it. You only mentioned the hummus recipe, though. Where did you learn to bake bread like that?"

Another distant stare settled over her eyes. "We trekked as far as Africa—have I told you this part of the story before?"

He raised a just-a-minute finger, then swallowed. "No."

"About a month after we left India, we were trekking across Africa," she said as if it had been a leisurely stroll on a picturesque park trail, "when I saw this incredible woman baking bread in an outside oven fueled by wood scraps. She was making the bread her family would eat that day. We stopped and watched her. Ended up staying in the village overnight, and the next day she showed me every step of how to prepare it."

Alex opened his small carton of milk. "Remind me again; who was the girl you were with?"

"Oh, just a girlfriend," she said dismissively. "On my eighteenth birthday we decided to walk around the globe, staying close as possible to the equator." She blushed. "Silly, huh? But it's what we both wanted to do at the time. The ultimate adventure."

"Why?" Steve asked.

With a laugh, she brushed some graying hair away from her bright eyes. Most days her unruly strands remained turbaned under whatever silk scarf matched her colorful sarongs. Other days she opted for shapeless mid-ankle dresses in bold batik prints. She always wore sandals, never shaved her legs, and smelled vaguely of musk and patchouli oil.

"It was either do the trek or have to figure out a way to convince Clem I wouldn't start premed at Stanford so I could graduate with honors and head off to some prestigious medical school—of his choosing—on the East Coast. I chose the easier path."

Ah, a new wrinkle to the engrossing life story she parceled out in segments, like today. "Your father expected you to attend medical school?"

"You bet. And believe me, if I'd done it, I would've had to ascend to the same lofty heights of recognition as he." She went back to preparing the hummus.

Alex pulled off a hunk of golden-brown chicken skin to eat. "You sure about that?" He popped the piece of skin into his mouth.

"World-famous hematologists have world-famous expectations for their only child to fulfill. I didn't want to compete with him, because I knew that's exactly what would've happened. He has this bizarre way of bringing out the worst in me when it comes to these things. In case you haven't realized it, I'm not a competitive person. Besides, I'm perfectly happy with my life as is."

He believed her.

"But you ended up in medicine anyway," Steve said. "Maybe not a physician, but as a researcher."

She paused, pestle in hand. "Purely happenstance is all, not by intent. I ended up broke in Boston, so I took a job as a lab tech." A quick shrug, as if this explained everything. "Now I'm here. Wasn't as if I planned it that way. It's just the way things were destined, I guess."

"And your father? How does he accept you not being a doctor?" Alex asked.

Pestle still in hand, she scratched the tip of her nose with the back of her wrist. "He's too busy with his second wife and new family to worry about me. Besides," she said with a slight flick of her head, "it's in the past."

Ah, another one of her wisdoms: what's past is past. Move on.

Alex swallowed. "You never mentioned how far you got on this trek."

She banged the pestle against the crucible rim, knocking off excess hummus. "Never finished making it through Africa."

Another new episode. Her adventures fascinated him, perhaps because her life had been—and undoubtedly would be—so different from his linear, goal-directed career. "Because?"

Karen blushed and glanced at Steve, as if he were an outsider. Although she insulated herself from most awkward situations with nervous laughter, she now displayed frank embarrassment. "I met this boy …"

"Go on." He popped another tear of fried chicken skin into his mouth. Lisa harped at him for eating the skin, claiming it to be the unhealthiest part of the chicken. She was probably right, but it tasted too damn good to ignore.

Karen returned to work, probably to avoid eye contact as her blush intensified. "Happened in Israel; he was part of the kibbutz I just mentioned. We became very attached to one another."

Clearly an understatement. "And?"

"Well, Carrie wouldn't continue trekking without me, and she realized I wasn't planning on leaving the kibbutz any time soon, so she flew back home and enrolled at Berkeley. That's it. End of our ultimate journey."

"And you?"

Karen poured more olive oil into the bean mash. "His family didn't approve of me for obvious religious reasons—and I wasn't going to convert to Judaism—so they gave him an ultimatum. There, family is tighter than love, I guess. Or maybe his love wasn't as strong as I wanted it to be. Anyway, I ended up in Europe and eventually Boston. I got the job in Beneke's lab, and you know the rest of the story."

Alex was about ready to pop the other hunk of chicken skin in his mouth when Art Waters came through the open lab door. "Morning, Karen, Steve, Alex."

Before anyone could answer, Waters addressed Alex. "We're on our way to lunch. Why don't you join us?"

Alex pointed to his brown paper sack and the wrinkled aluminum foil holding the remains of his chicken. "Thanks, but I have mine here."

"I see that. But Alex, you're faculty now, not a resident. You need to break bread with us, make an effort to become part of the group. It doesn't do you any good to stay holed up in your lab every day all day."

"I drop into the conference room on free afternoons." The surgeons who weren't tied up in the OR or otherwise engaged habitually congregated for forty-five minutes or so in the conference room to gossip over coffee.

"I know you do, but I really would like you to start joining us for lunch." Waters seldom threatened or gave orders, but this sounded like more than a simple wish.

Alex nodded. "Thanks."

Waters said his goodbyes and left.

After a few moments of silence, Karen said, "He's right, you know."

"I know."

"Why don't you? You can afford it now; it's not like you're still on resident salary."

Alex set down the chicken leg. "It's not the money. It's the time. Now that I have to drive across town to the trauma center for afternoon rounds, I can't afford to spend an hour talking department politics with them." As it was, he was already returning to the lab two or three nights a week after heading home for dinner.

"I understand." Karen paused with a knowing smile, making him believe she did understand. "On the other hand, you're never going to be one of them if you don't start playing the role. That's all it is, you know—role playing." She turned to Steve, raised her eyebrows a moment before laughing. "You're going to have to start doing the same thing when you enter med school."

Alex felt trapped. He was already overcommitted, and his NIH grant had once again been denied funding. He was in serious jeopardy of losing the lab to a full-time researcher, someone with the funds to keep it productively staffed and generating publications rather than just limping along with one lab tech and a catch-as-catch-can investigator. Appetite now ruined, Alex balled the remaining chicken in the foil and tossed it into the trash can. "I better get back to work."

5

The telephone rang again, rousting Alex from sound, dreamless sleep. "Hello?"

"Doctor Cutter, sorry to call you at this hour, but we got a through-and-through GSW, probably fairly large caliber by the hole it made, maybe .38. Anyway, we're taking her to the OR now." We, meaning the chief and a junior resident. Alex recognized the resident's voice and knew the call came from the trauma center.

"Be right in." The bedside clock showed 1:37 a.m. For a few beats, he felt an overwhelming urge to snuggle back down in the warm bed and work on dispensing the heavy fatigue that cloaked him endlessly these days. Taking a hundred percent of the trauma center call was the price the senior partners exacted for keeping his lab limping along until he could win enough funding to justify devoting a fixed percentage of his time to research.

He hustled through the automatic ER doors at 1:58 a.m. and detoured to the small basement coffee shop—closed this hour of morning—where one wall was lined with vending machines. He slipped three quarters in the coin chute, then made sure the cardboard cup dropped vertically into the serving slot for the jets to squirt in hot chocolate—his reward for being up at this ungodly hour. He drank the tepid liquid while changing into scrubs, then closed and secured the locker before taking the stairs down to the operating rooms.

The skull X-rays looked terrible, the entrance wound obvious by the round, jagged skull defect. A cone-shaped trajectory of bullet and bone fragments expanded from one side to the other through the brain, a chunk of skull blown out the exit wound, radiating spider web cracks from the jagged edges. The two residents were working furiously to prep and drape the patient now that the anesthesiologist had her ready for surgery, which was probably unnecessary from the looks of the skull films. "Want me to scrub?" Alex asked the chief.

The senior resident turned, apparently unaware Alex had entered. "Not unless you feel a burning desire. Pretty straightforward. She's a goner anyway."

"Agreed. Tell me what happened."

"Twenty-eight-year-old black female picked up at Manville Terrace," he said, naming a low-income housing project nearby. "Story is she bought the gun for her boyfriend as a birthday present. He was in the other room showing his homeys his quick draw when the gun accidently fired. Bullet went through a wall, hit her. She was allegedly watching TV in the next room. That's all we know. Medics did a scoop and run."

Alex looked at the junior resident. "What's her prognosis?" Now eight months into his first clinical year, this rotation on trauma service provided more independent responsibility for the resident than the heavily supervised university rotation.

"Through-and-throughs—especially at this caliber—are universally fatal."

"Then why bother to waste the taxpayer's money by operating on her?"

The resident continued assisting his chief while he responded. "Reasonable question. One that's debated. One argument is that since they're going to die anyway, why not just put a bandage over the wound and stick them in the corner until they officially die. Guess that's still done in some places. There's not as much data on civilian GSWs, so most of what we do is based on military work. But the problem is, civilian wounds are different. Usually military wounds are from higher-velocity bullets or low-velocity frags. Anyway, the current thought is to remove all foreign material from the brain and close the wounds, since no one knows for sure how long the patient's going to live."

Alex was impressed. The kid had obviously been studying. "If the patient's going to die regardless of what we do, why bother operating at all?" he said, referring to bone and bullet fragments as well as in-driven hair and skin.

"Because even though the bullet is probably sterilized from the heat of the blast, it drives skin and hair and other contaminants into the brain. The bone and bullet frags are signposts for where the contamination is. Best to clean out what you can easily get away with and close up the wound. Better to die having been given the best chance rather than to die having done nothing."

"Very good," Alex said, truly impressed and proud of the resident's knowledge. Then to the chief, "I'll write the operative note." Recorded in the patient's chart, the operative note documented vital information such as who was present and what was done. Following surgery the resident would dictate a more complete note for the record, but in the meantime, the handwritten note would let staff know where things stood.

After writing the chart note, Alex spent fifteen minutes perched on a stainless steel stool as he watched the residents work. He decided to watch for perhaps another fifteen minutes before heading home, the accumulative fatigue of three consecutive nights of interrupted sleep weighing down his eyelids as he watched. His mind drifted to the patient, and he wondered what her story was. Divorced, married, widowed? Any children? The family breadwinner? A hooker or a secretary? Sad, the thought of someone losing their mother. Although he identified and empathized with that loss, he felt an unnerving detachment from the pathos playing out before him. He thought about that, too, questioning why he felt so detached from these trauma cases but not the elective ones.

For one thing, in contrast to elective cases, he and the patients weren't in the OR as a matter of choice. And he certainly could not be held responsible for their ultimately grim outcome. The only reasons to supervise the residents—who were gaining valuable experience by doing the surgery—were to ensure an acceptable level of quality and to satisfy federal and state billing requirements. When Waters had the job—before assigning it to Alex—he would simply drop by the trauma center once a week and sit in the billing office to countersign all the residents' operative notes and progress notes of patients discharged during the previous week. Once the charts were signed, the bills would be submitted as if Waters had actually provided the service. But the laws had tightened as a result of Medicare reform, making it now a felony to bill for such phantom services. Because the residents weren't actually licensed neurosurgeons, they could not bill for their services. And neither the university nor the department were eager to leave such a huge chunk of money on the table. Still, over 75 percent of the services billed at the trauma center were never paid.

Wearily, Alex pushed off the stool and caught the eye of the chief resident. "Heading home now. See you for afternoon rounds."

6

ALEX WALKED INTO THE conference room, poured a cup of coffee, and plunked down in one of the four chairs around the break table. Geoff and Baxter, two full professors, seemed to be enjoying a spirited debate at the table. Baxter routinely had intermittent bouts of blinking as he talked, as if dust had blown in his eyes. Years ago—no one was sure when—one of the residents nicknamed him Baxter Rabbit, and that had been his nickname ever since.

Geoff amused himself playing his coin game, arranging pocket change in ascending size: dimes, pennies, nickels, quarters. It was an annoying habit of his during rounds. His other one was to rock back and forth from the balls to the heels of his feet.

Baxter turned to Alex. "We're discussing that patient of yours at County, the gunshot wound. How long she been on the respirator now?" Alex had presented the case for the second week in a row during the Monday afternoon Morbidity and Mortality teaching conference.

Alex had to think for a moment, the seemingly indistinguishable days melding into one another. "Two and a half weeks now."

"Tough problem." Baxter shook his head sadly. "Had my share of those. Puts you in a lose-lose situation. Administration's on your back to free up the ICU bed, but her family refuses to take her off the respirator by claiming she's still alive."

"In the meantime," Ogden added, "her hospital bill just keeps growing bigger and bigger. Have any idea what it's up to now?"

Alex had no idea for sure. "Last time I checked it was past a half a million."

Baxter blew a long whistle.

"She have insurance?" Ogden asked.

"Nope," he answered, shaking his head.

"Which means we, the taxpayers, end up paying her bills."

Alex was sick of the issue. He was caught in the middle—just as Baxter said—between two opposing forces. Although the patient unequivocally met all criteria for being brain dead, her parents refused to let Alex discontinue the respirator. They claimed she was still alive because her heart still beat. It was nonsense.

"Remind me," Baxter said, "what steps did you use to determine brain death?"

"The usual." In fact, he had more than enough evidence to indicate her brain was totally devastated. He held up an index finger. "She has a large-caliber through-and-through trajectory." This meant the brain centers for consciousness had been completely destroyed. The second finger popped up. "There's no evidence of any function on her neuro exam." The third finger. "She can't breathe on her own." And then the final finger. "She's had three flat-line EEGs separated by twenty-four hours."

Baxter used a spoon to stir his coffee. "More than enough evidence."

"You explained all this to the family?" Ogden asked.

Jesus, give me some credit. "Several times. Their lawyer—a real Al Sharpton type—is claiming we want to kill her because she's black, that if she were white, we'd have no problem 'keeping her alive,'" he said, using finger quotes in the air.

Ogden dumped the coins back into his pocket. "Glad she's your case, not mine."

Alex wanted to move on to his reason for being here. "I'm applying for AANS membership. May I use you two as references?"

Ogden cocked his head. "You can't be a member; you haven't passed your boards yet." Board certification came from passing both a written and oral examination, and the oral part couldn't be attempted until the applicant had been in practice for two years.

Geoff dug the coins out of his pocket and started playing with them again. "What's the hurry? Why not wait until you have more experience under your belt?"

"Because I want—" He stopped short, embarrassed to admit he sought the validation of being board certified.

"He wants to show the world he's qualified," Baxter said.

Geoff raised his eyebrows. "You have your eye on Art's chair?"

The suggestion floored him. "You nuts? Where did that come from?" Alex couldn't imagine the department without Waters at the helm. He had built it from the ground up, starting when the newly formed medical school consisted of two Quonset huts on the edge of campus. Legend had it that Waters was the second faculty member to be hired, second only to the dean. This would always be Waters's department.

"Want a word of advice?" Baxter offered. "Best way to pass the orals is to do exactly what you've been trained to do during teaching rounds. The examiners aren't looking for right or wrong answers. They want to find out how you approach clinical problems. The best strategy is to tell them everything you're thinking. Don't stop talking until you're pretty sure you've said every word on your mind and then some. Don't hide your knowledge. Right, Geoff?"

Geoff kept mixing the coins, then rearranging them. One iteration after the other. Without looking up from his hand, he said, "Know Karl Borne?"

It took Alex a moment to attach a person to the name. "Sorta. But not all that well. He was chief the year I started. We didn't rotate together—only saw him at conferences. Why?"

Geoff scrambled the coins again. "Heard about his experience on the boards?"

"Experien*ces*," Baxter said.

"We all like Karl." Geoff shook his head sadly. "Man's a good neurosurgeon. But when we asked him questions on rounds, he'd defer to one of the other residents. Made them think—and I'm sure this was the case—that he knew the answer and was just giving them a chance to shine. We never forced him to answer," he said, casting a glance at Baxter, "making us partly to blame. So when he took his orals, he clammed up, just wouldn't answer. The examiners tried to get him to answer, but the harder they tried, the more he clammed up. Flunked it. To this date, he's this program's only graduate to never pass orals. We were all horrified. We even brought him back for a day of special coaching and thought we'd gotten him over the hump, but when he took them the second time, same thing happened. Never tried after that. Said he refused to submit to that degree of humiliation again. It's a shame, too, because he's a good clinician. Right, Baxter?"

Baxter blinked twice. "Agreed."

"So you guys will write me recommendations?" Alex said, looking from one to the other.

"You bet," Geoff said.

"We will," seconded Baxter.

"Thanks." Alex withdrew sheets of paper from a manila folder and handed one to each of them. "Here is the info. I'd appreciate it if you'll dictate them this afternoon so they can go out in the morning mail."

Geoff gave his trademark silly grin, exposing acres of glistening gums and tartar caked between his front teeth. Baxter folded his copy lengthwise to slip in his white coat. Standing to leave, Alex looked both men in the eye. "Today, right?" Baxter nodded. Geoff just grinned.

7

"I'M IN THE KITCHEN."

"Be right there." Alex hung his coat in the hall closet under the stairs to the second floor and headed into the kitchen where Lisa sat at the bistro table sipping a glass of white wine, looking very upset.

"Bad day?" he asked while removing a wine glass from the cupboard.

She finger-combed her hair then shook it out. "Laura called."

He knew of two Lauras in her life: her sister and a friend. "Your sister?"

"What other Laura is there?"

Whoa. Not good, whatever was upsetting her. Long ago he'd learned that when she showed this mood, he should simply allow her to raise the problem on her own terms rather than prying it out of her. He picked up the wine bottle to pour a glass and was surprised at how light it felt. He held it up to check the level. Three quarters gone. Not good at all. "Go on with your story."

"She called about Mom."

He poured some wine and set the bottle on the table. "What's wrong?"

"You probably don't remember me mentioning the chronic cough she developed, but it became progressively worse, so she saw her doctor. Turns out it's lung cancer."

Ah shit. He wanted to reach across the table to take her hand, but knew she'd pull away. She got like that when depressed or upset or both. "I'm sorry. Has it been staged yet? Know any more details?"

"She said it's too advanced for them to consider surgery, so her only options are radiation or chemotherapy—one or the other, but not both. Laura wants me to come home soon as possible." She dumped the remainder of the wine into her glass.

"I'm so sorry, Sweetie. Of course you'll go. Have you booked a flight yet?"

She shook her head. "No. I wanted to talk to you first."

He didn't see any need for discussion. "What's to talk about? You're going."

"Will you come with me?"

He considered that a moment. "How long?"

"Christ, Alex, how should I know? However long it takes."

"I don't know how soon I can get away. I'll have to arrange coverage. Why don't we get you back there first, and I'll come soon as I can."

She flashed exasperation. "But I want you *there* to explain things. You know how I am about medical things."

"Honey, I'll see what I can do. It's going to be difficult getting someone to cover the trauma center. That's the best I can say right now." Feeling trapped, he sipped wine and waited. She was rotating her wine glass by the stem now, making little screeching sounds as the glass rubbed the marble.

"Why don't you open another bottle?" she said at last, clearly not making it optional. "We can have a little while I heat up the chicken."

"Okay."

He removed the one remaining bottle from the small countertop wine rack. As he stripped foil from the neck, he heard a sigh. Not just any sigh, but her proprietary *I'm-fed-up-with-this sigh.*

"Know the one thing I resent the most in our marriage?" she asked.

Okay, here we go.

Without a word, Alex screwed the opener into the cork. This was her classic gambit. Nothing he could say or do at this point would alter the ensuing argument. Often, when frustrated or angry—especially when fueled by wine—she had an urge to beat up on him, as if him serving as an emotional punching bag was a given in the "for better or worse" clause of their marriage vows. Didn't mean he liked it.

When he refused to take the bait, she continued. "That you've never loved Mom. Not like Dan does. He still sends her a Christmas card every year."

Working on prying the cork out, he wondered if Dan—Lisa's first husband—really loved Donna or if Lisa just used this phrase to try to make him feel guilty for his lack of connection with her mother. Did it make a damn bit of difference? It was something that would never be reconciled.

"Why *don't* you like her?" Lisa asked.

Alex turned toward her, bottle and corkscrew in hand. How many times had they discussed this? "Look Sweetie, I don't *dis*like her. For whatever reason, we've never been able to resonate. If I try to talk with her, she clams up. What am I supposed to do?"

"She's extremely passive, Alex. *Extremely* passive. She never takes the lead on anything. You know that. But you don't like passive women. You don't respect passive women. You only like strong women, just like your *Mommy*."

Okay, there it was. Squelching a retaliatory zinger, he popped the cork, perhaps with a bit more force than necessary. "Being passive and non-communicative are two entirely different things. She won't say much more than yes or no to anything I say. What more do you expect me to do? You just said it; she's passive. I can't change that."

She glared at him. "For one thing, you could try to be a bit more understanding. Maybe if you did, you'd be able to accept her."

They were on a path traveled too many times where he was the villain and Donna was the victim. He debated the wisdom of pouring her any more wine, but decided hiding it would only inflame her even more. So, without a word, he brought the cabernet to the table.

"We've been over this, Alex. The reason she can't talk with you is you intimidate her. We grew up poor. My father was a farmer. There's never been a doctor or lawyer or any other professional in our family. The only doctor we knew was the vet. She doesn't know what to say to you. She's afraid of saying the wrong thing and that you'll laugh at her and think she's stupid and uneducated. She's a smart woman, Alex.

Maybe not university educated, but smart in other ways. Is that so hard for you to understand?"

Best strategy now, he decided, was to change the subject. He poured more wine and hoped for the best. "Let's try to think of a way to get you home soon as possible."

8

"WELCOME BACK," GEOFF SAID as Alex entered the conference room. Baxter, Ogden, and Waters sat at the square table in the break room. The other half of the room contained a large conference table, separated from the coffee area by an accordion divider that was presently closed. Muted voices could be heard from the other side, most likely from a secretarial staff meeting underway.

"Thanks." Alex went straight to the coffee pot, found his cup on the drain board, and poured it half full.

"How did it go?" asked Baxter.

Alex took the remaining chair. "I feel good about it," he said, then laughed at a memory. "Got off the plane and went out to the curb for a cab. The guy in line right in front of me was holding a thick neurosurgery text, so I asked if he was there for the boards. He was, so I suggested we share a cab to the hotel. On the trip in, I asked if he wanted to have dinner, but he said he was getting room service so he could spend the night cramming. Can you believe that? Cramming? I mean, if you don't know the material by then, one night of reading a textbook isn't going to help. Besides, how can you expect to cover the entire field?"

"You didn't study that night?" Baxter asked with a sarcastic chuckle.

Alex smiled. "I bought a paperback—*Marathon Man*—at the airport. You know, something to read on the flight. Stayed up half the night to finish it. Had breakfast with him the next morning. I was one of the lucky ones who were assigned the morning group, so soon as I finished breakfast, I went upstairs to the exam. I finished up before noon and was able to catch an earlier flight back."

"Any section give you problems?" Waters asked. The orals contained three one-hour sections: cranial neurosurgery, spinal/peripheral nerve surgery, and neurology. Individual candidates rotated from one room to the next every fifty-five minutes. Each session contained two examiners with one observer to monitor the process.

"No, not really—don't think I dug myself any holes."

"How about the neurology section?"

Alex shrugged. "Seemed to go okay. Turned out I only had one case: a fifty-five-year-old male with tingling in his feet. The neurologist who presented the patient asks, 'What would you do now?' I say, 'Take a history.' He says, 'Go ahead, take it.' So I started in asking him questions. Went on and on and on like this until I'm down to two probable diagnoses, cervical spondylosis with cord impingement or Vitamin B12 deficiency. The neurosurgeon—I forget his name—was a real bear, too. When we reached that point, he asks, 'What do you do now?' I said, 'Draw a B12 level and then give the patient a shot of B12. I'd have him return in a week for follow-up.' The neurologist says, 'You wouldn't just take him to the OR to decompress that spine? It looks like hell,' and he points at the X-rays. He says it as if I just buggered his dog, so I think maybe I just blew it. But I decided to stick with my answer, especially this being the neurology section. I told them it wouldn't hurt to wait for a week before offering the patient surgery. I hoped they'd tell me if I got it right, but just then we ran out of time. I was floored. We spent the entire hour on just that one case. Couldn't believe it."

Waters smiled while checking his watch, slapped his thighs, and stood. "Have a conference call in three minutes. NIH. I'll leave you three to your war stories." He looked at Alex. "I suspect that was the right diagnosis. You were correct: in the neurology section they're most likely to discuss a nonsurgical case. They wanted to find out if you could tell the difference between those two diseases since they mimic one another so closely. The board isn't in the business of certifying a bunch of scalpel-happy cutters. I suspect you did just fine."

After Waters left the room, Geoff spoke up. "Going to be a much different department without him around."

Alex did a double take. "Why? He going somewhere?"

Geoff glanced at Baxter, then back to Alex. "You don't know? He just turned sixty-five. That's the mandatory retirement age for professors here. You can stay on in emeritus status for two years, but only at the pleasure of the new chair. After that, you're required to leave."

Was that a note of anticipation in Geoff's voice? Alex studied him and saw no sign of sadness or regret. "But he trained you and brought you onto the faculty."

"So?" Geoff glanced at Baxter with a bemused expression.

Baxter chimed in. "Those are the rules here. For good reason, too. It allows room for younger people like you. This place isn't like some schools where junior people are forced to play Dead Man's Boots until a position opens up."

Showing even more of his glistening gums, Geoff smiled and added, "Dean already formed a search committee." Throwing it out there casually.

Baxter and Geoff waited for the words to sink in, as if reading Alex's mind. Stunned by their callous disregard for the man who'd brought them up through the ranks, Alex remained speechless.

"You realize, of course, you'll probably be interviewed by the search committee," Baxter added.

Alex was having difficulty paying attention to the conversation now. "No, I didn't."

"Count on it," Geoff said. "They're bound to ask questions about the department, where you think it should be in five or so years. These days, a department like ours—with a strong heritage of clinician research—simply can't be sustained. Deans are facing severe financial difficulties, especially when having to support non-revenue-generating departments like anatomy or physiology. They're forced to use their clinical departments to generate income. So, of course, this means the dean will be tempted to look outside the present faculty for someone who doesn't hold research with the same respect as Waters has. Faculty such as yourself will be vulnerable. Right, Baxter?"

"Absolutely." He nodded emphatically. "So when you interview with them, expect to be asked if any of us would make a good replacement." Baxter locked eyes with Alex. "Or are you considering tossing your hat in the ring?" Blink, blink.

Alex recoiled. "You serious?" When neither man answered, he realized they were. "Of course not. I'm too inexperienced. Why would I even think of that?"

Smiling, Geoff nodded approval. "That's what I thought. Point is, both Baxter and I are being considered. We encourage you to be extremely circumspect in everything you say during your interview. Think about your lab and all it means to you. Think about how we—the present faculty—cover your salary so you can continue to apply for grant support. Think about how both Baxter and I would maintain the status quo if either one of us became chair."

Jesus, a campaign speech.

Baxter chimed in. "You don't have any outside candidate in mind, do you?"

Outside candidate? Of course not. He hadn't even wrapped his mind around the idea of Waters not being there. A foreboding sprouted deep in his gut. As Baxter just pointed out, he was the only nontenured faculty member, making him vulnerable. Why hadn't he factored in Waters's age when considering this job? Too late now.

He realized they were waiting for an answer. To what? Oh yeah—did he have an outside candidate in mind?

"No. If you'll excuse me,..." He needed to be alone and think.

9

"Afternoon, Dr. Cutter." Nancy, Geoff's secretary, nodded to him as he passed her desk on the way to the departmental mailboxes.

"Afternoon, Nancy. How goes it?" He retrieved the handful of mail, memos, and sundry messages that had accumulated since the day before.

She rolled a fresh sheet of white paper into her typewriter. "It's Friday, so life is good."

Back in his office, he began sorting mail, tossing junk into the wastebasket. Two items immediately caught his attention—a letter from NIH and a headline in the American Association of Neurological Surgeons (AANS) newsletter: "Welcome Our New Members." The article listed all new members. Eagerly, Alex scanned the list for his name.

Not there.

After a stunned moment, he scanned the list again. Still not there. His gut tightened with anxiety. A simple mistake, an oversight?

Or …

Had he been rejected?

Wouldn't AANS headquarters notify him if that happened?

Okay, so what could've possibly gone wrong? He ticked off the steps he'd taken: he submitted the completed application via FedEx, and its arrival had been confirmed. Check. The application had been filled out correctly. Check. He passed his boards. Check. He obtained the required number of recommendations from AANS members. Hmm …

The vague noxious feeling in his stomach intensified, making him nauseous.

He leaned back, gulped a few deep breaths to collect himself, then leaned over and opened the door. Rip, the secretary he shared with Baxter, sat in the cramped reception area just outside their offices, wishbone earphone in place, typing away on her IBM Selectric. He paused to settle his nerves. "Hey Rip, got a minute?"

She stopped typing, left foot automatically releasing the dictation pedal, and removed the earphones. "You bet. What can I do for you?"

"You remember typing a letter of recommendation from Baxter in support of my AANS application?"

She thought a moment, then turned to a file drawer. "Must've been six weeks or so. Have it right here. Want to see it?"

He held up a palm. "Whoa, no, that's confidential. But tell me something."

She pulled a sheet of onionskin from the files and held it up. "Don't think he'd mind. He was very supportive."

Alex smiled. "You just answered my question. Thanks. Sorry to interrupt your concentration." Her nickname "Rip" came from an ability to rip through dictation at incredible speeds, her entire demeanor efficient: placid expression, eyes closed, fingers flying across the electric typewriter. She exhibited an uncanny ability to know when reaching the bottom of a page without bothering to look. When she caught up on Baxter and Alex's work, she cheerfully picked up other dictation from the secretarial pool.

"Anything else? Long as I'm taking a break, might as well grab a cup of coffee. Want one?"

"No thanks." His was stomach now too upset for caffeine, or anything else for that matter. Had to be Geoff. Just fucking had to be. Waters's secretary had given Alex a carbon copy of his letter. Same with Jack Harris—the chief resident Alex's first year—now practicing in Portland. Of the four supporting letters, three were verified. Unless, of course, something else had gone wrong. What that could be, he had no idea.

Blowing another slow breath, he shut the door again and tried to relax sufficiently to make a phone call. A moment later, he dialed AANS headquarters in Chicago.

"May I help you?"

Alex stared out the window, the outside coat of grime more noticeable than usual. "I'd like to speak to the secretary in charge of membership, please."

"One moment, I'll transfer."

Muzak.

"Membership, Maureen speaking."

"Hello. My name's Alex Cutter. Six weeks ago I applied for membership. Today I saw the latest bulletin and noticed my name isn't listed. Is this a mistake or did something happen to my application?"

She answered without hesitation. "No, Doctor Cutter, there is no mistake. Your application wasn't forwarded to the membership committee because it wasn't complete."

Not complete? The words reverberated through his mind like a tuning fork. Geoff. Had to be.

"I'm not sure I understand. I submitted everything along with four letters of support. What was incomplete?"

"That's the problem. Not all your letters were received."

"Oh?" He knew, but just had to ask. "Which one is missing?"

"Dr. Ogden's."

"Excuse me, I don't want to sound difficult, but why wasn't I notified?"

"Dr. Cutter, there can be any number of reasons a member might not endorse a candidate. I'm sure you understand. It's for this reason we prefer to not notify the applicant. We did, however, send Dr. Ogden two reminders, both stressing how vital his letter was for your application. We never received a reply."

"What do I do now? Is there any way to keep my application active until I can arrange for another letter of recommendation?"

"I can certainly do that, but you realize, of course, your application will not be reconsidered until the membership committee reconvenes in six months."

Six months.

Alex slumped in his chair, trying to mask heavy disappointment from his voice. "I understand. That would be wonderful if you would do that. I'll have another letter in your office within two weeks. Thank you."

"Anything else I can help you with?"

You've got to be kidding! "No, thanks. You've been very helpful."

Alex fought the urge to throw the goddamn phone against the wall, gently dropping it into the cradle instead. *Think.* What had he done to provoke sabotage from Geoff? Perhaps this was all a mistake, and it wasn't his fault. Yet, an instinct hovering just below the brink of consciousness knew Geoff had intentionally torpedoed him. *Why?*

Alex stood in Geoff's open office doorway. "You busy?"

Geoff glanced up from his typically cluttered desk in the center of his typically cluttered office; books, journals, and unfiled papers were stacked to the point of tumbling over, filling every available horizontal surface. Alex wondered yet again how the hell he found anything. Amazingly, Geoff always seemed able to pull the rabbit from the hat. Might take a few minutes, or even days, but he apparently had the key to this random access filing system solidly embedded in his memory. Geoff slowly removed his glasses and pinched the bridge of his nose. He blinked. "Yes?"

Alex closed the door for privacy. "Remember I asked if you'd write a letter to the AANS supporting me?"

Out came the coins. Geoff eyed his hand, busily organizing them. "Yes."

Aw man, guilty! "You agreed to write it."

"Yes."

"But you didn't."

Geoff glanced out the window. "I've been too busy."

The words enraged Alex. Five minutes. Tops. Insert dictation belt, press button, dictate letter, hand belt to secretary. Done. Five fucking minutes was generous.

"Then why didn't you tell me that in the first place? Why didn't you just say, 'I don't have time'?"

With a snarky smile Geoff finally looked up. "I'm very busy, Dr. Cutter. In addition to my departmental commitments, I serve on several AANS committees. And, I might add, I serve on the editorial board of *Neurosurgery*. This all takes time. You need to realize this."

Alex wanted to scream. "But you knew all that when you agreed to write the letter."

Geoff returned to sorting the coins. "I suppose so."

"You *fucking* suppose so?" Alex stopped. No sense rehashing what had already been said.

Face puckered like a prune, Geoff dumped the coins back into his pocket and picked up his pen. "If we're done with this conversation, I need to get back to work."

Livid, Alex fought the urge to sweep a few stacks of papers and journals off the desk. *Don't be juvenile.* Geoff continued to ignore him.

Fuming, Alex sat in his office with the door closed, staring out the window, no longer aware of the grime coating the outside. He was trying to quell his anger but couldn't get his mind off of Ogden. *Why? What have I ever done to him?*

He noticed the unopened letter on his desk from NIH. With trembling fingers, he opened it:

GRANT: INVESTIGATION OF STEM CELLS IN CNS NEOPLASIA

PI: ALEX CUTTER, MD

PRIORITY SCORE: 250

FUNDING CUT OFF: 200

Better score than last time, but still not good enough to be funded. The lower the score, the higher the priority. *Just fucking perfect! There anything else that can make this day worse?*

A knock on the door.

"Yes?"

Rip's muffled voice came through the door. "Dr. Cutter, clinic just called. You have patients waiting."

Slowly, Alex pushed out of the chair, shrugged on his white coat, and trudged from his office. This time the hallway walls appeared dinged and scarred, the scuffed linoleum in need of buffing.

10

"I'M IN THE KITCHEN," Lisa called out as he came through the front door. Alex paused for a moment, then hung his coat in the hall closet before heading to the kitchen where he found Lisa reading *Vanity Fair*.

She glanced at him, did a double take. "Uh-oh, bad day?"

"Really bad." He pulled two glasses from the cupboard and started to open a bottle of cabernet as he told her first about the Geoff Ogden brouhaha, then about his grant's priority score.

When he finished, she said, "Oh Alex, I'm sorry. What do you do now?"

He explained to her that the AANS agreed to keep his application active and that he'd already arranged for another letter of recommendation. And as far as his research went, he would submit a revised grant application taking into account the criticisms of the study section. Starting tomorrow, he planned to devote evenings and weekends to the revision so it could be submitted in time for the next review cycle. The longer his lab went unfunded, the more tenuous his departmental funding would be, especially if there was any chance that Geoff Ogden might become the new chair.

She didn't seem pleased with the plan. "Guess that means instead of working nights in your lab, you'll be working on the grant."

He nodded. "Well, at least I can do some of this at home, but this is the treadmill that comes from trying to support yourself on grant money. Half the time you're doing your research and the other half you're scrambling for funding. One day, if I keep at it and get funded, I'll be able to apply for a five-year grant instead of just two."

"Always the optimist. But that's assuming you get funded to begin with."

"Well, there's that too."

They sat in silence for a while until Lisa spoke up. "This Ogden thing. Why would he do something like that?"

Good question. "I have no idea." Alex shook his head in dismay. "It's not like he's so busy he can't find two minutes to dictate a damn letter."

Lisa paused. "Maybe you should've gone elsewhere. Maybe you're not taken seriously here because you were their resident."

He rubbed the back of his neck, trying to loosen up the muscles so tightly knotted. "You know how many times I've thought about that, but you know what? Everyone except Baxter trained here, and look where they are: full professors, every last one of them."

"Yes, but if you think about it, only Baxter has a real research program going."

"Good point, but that doesn't change my funding predicament. I just have to buckle down and work harder. I've even thought about going back for a PhD. That way I could do research full time. Trouble is, we haven't even paid off my students loans yet. We'd be back to where we're accumulating debt again, and I'm getting too old to not be solvent."

"You really serious about being a full-time lab rat? Somehow I can't see you giving up medicine for research no matter how much you think you might want it."

"I know. Besides, going the research route is just too daunting. I'd have to secure a postdoc position somewhere, meaning I wouldn't be able to do my own work for years. I can't see losing all the time it would require, especially now that I believe I'm really onto something with the stem cells. I can't give that up now. It all boils down to not really having a choice."

He could see something else was bothering her, something she hadn't yet mentioned, and it triggered a pang of guilt for being so self-absorbed that he missed it until just now. "Something wrong?"

She poured them both more wine. "More bad news. Mom."

"Why? What's going on?"

She paused to sip. "I have to fly back to Lincoln."

Uh-oh. "Why, what happened?"

Lisa folded her hands in her lap, an unconscious habit when giving bad news. "She's really going down hill rapidly. Laura says she might not last two weeks."

Aw shit. He reached across the table, offering his hand to her. "Well then, fly back. I'll call the airlines now and make a reservation. You can fly out tomorrow. Take as long as you need."

She didn't take the offered hand. "I don't think I can get the time off work again."

"Sure you can. What can they say? It's your mom we're talking about. They'll understand. This is important."

Alex could see the tension pulling at the corners of her eyes. "I took ten days off last month to fly back. I'm worried they'll fire me if I take any more time off."

"Hey, let them. You could get another job in a blink, especially with your background. The point is, family is more important than work. Laura needs support and you need to see Mom. There's no other option. Ted will understand; he'll give you the time off. There, it's settled: I'll call United and book a ticket for day after tomorrow."

11

EVERY MONDAY AFTERNOON THREE hours were devoted to teaching conferences. It started with the 2 p.m. Radiology session and was followed by Morbidity and Mortality, in which complications and deaths throughout the preceding week were discussed in detail. In addition, all scheduled elective surgeries for the week were reviewed, emphasizing the indications for each. This last conference usually dragged on for as long as the professors wished to pontificate, confining their serfs to soporific CO_2 levels as the evening's scut work continued to pile up, making it impossible for an off-call resident to head home at a reasonable hour. For the on-call residents who had to drive back across town to the trauma center, their workday would not end until late evening, if at all.

At the Radiology conference, residents and professors sat in rows of five metal folding chairs, the faculty in the front with the residents behind, allowing them to step out of the room to answer frequent pages. The room's only light emanated from the X-ray panels, casting eerie shadows that sometimes gave the presenting resident a Bela Lugosi flair.

Neuroradiology professor Larry Harris slid a CT scan onto the multipanel screen and asked the group, "Can anyone tell me what this is?"

Without really thinking—for the picture, strange as it appeared, could logically only be one thing—Alex blurted, "A vein of Galen aneurysm in an infant."

Dead silence. Harris seemed shocked at the answer. After a few beats, he asked, "What made you pull that one out of your hat?"

Alex had to stop, back up, and think about his shoot-from-the-hip conclusion. "Well, the shape and thickness of the skull along with the open sutures make the patient an infant, probably a newborn." He went into detail, as the point of the conferences was to provide in-depth explanations to teach residents logical clinical associations. "The abnormality is located in the midline, exactly where the venous sinus are. This lesion is large and contrast enhances, which indicates it's filled with blood. The smooth, linear, discrete borders and the enlargement at confluence support it being a vascular structure. Lastly, the mesial edge is perfectly straight, suggesting it abuts the Falx"—the membrane that separated the two hemispheres. "Keeping those things in mind, the only reasonable diagnosis would be a vein of Galen aneurysm." Then again, he realized, it could be something really off-the-wall weird, like a bizarre vascular tumor. But he seriously doubted that.

Harris nodded approval. "Very good, Dr. Cutter. Impressive. Especially since this is the first one I've seen on CT." The professor pointed to a first-year radiology resident. "Hansen, what's the prognosis?"

Hansen's horrified face blanked. "Uh, don't know, sir."

Harris turned to the pediatric neurosurgeon. "John?"

John Luciano, a boisterous surgeon from the Bronx, boomed out in his New York accent, "Typically these kiddos die of heart failure before anything can be done. But commonly nothing can be done because there's no known way to effectively treat them."

Harris replaced that image with two views of a different skull. "McGinnis, what's this X-ray show?"

And so it went.

12

"HAVE A SEAT, DR. Cutter," offered the assistant dean.

Alex chose the chair at the end of the small, glossy mahogany conference table, the room insufferably stuffy, the warm air spiced with the bitter smell of coffee that surely had been on the hot plate way too long. Four professors, two with their white shirtsleeves rolled up and ties loosened, lab coats draped haphazardly over the backs of their chairs, stared at Alex as if he was the star witness in a murder trial. The one female, a biophysicist with gray hair and big glasses, was the one Alex was least familiar with.

"Thank you for taking time from your schedule to discuss this important matter of Dr. Waters's replacement. Would you like some coffee, a glass of water?"

He would've loved some coffee, but this stuff smelled like toxic waste, the sheen on the surface making it even scarier. He envisioned the fluid eating through the Pyrex pot and then continuing on through the floor. "No thanks, I'm good."

"Well then," said the spokesperson, "let's get on with it. Please tell us the strengths and weaknesses of the department." Three of the interviewers sat back almost in unison, pens readied over notepads.

Alex cleared his throat. "The department's overwhelming strength is a strong culture of academics. By this I mean Dr. Waters provided us with a clear departmental mission. That has been to teach and conduct impeccably honest research. It's very much the same as the NIH's program to produce teacher investigators." He paused, marveling at his off-the-cuff pithy summation of a complex dynamic. "The only weakness—if it can be considered one—is, unlike other departments, our emphasis is on quality research instead of high patient throughput."

The chair of the committee nodded sagely. "I'd like to explore that particular issue a bit, if I may. If the goal of a department is to train neurosurgeons, isn't a high clinical volume desirable?"

Certainly a loaded question, Alex thought as he paused to consider his answer. "True, but only if the mission of the residency is to produce cutting neurosurgeons. Although the country does need neurosurgeons, it also needs teacher-scientists if we are to have any hope of advancing the art. This rare species can only come from a department devoted to producing *academic* clinicians." He felt passion moving his words in much the same way as a senator delivering a campaign speech. "We produce tomorrow's leaders. Competent clinicians who, in addition to practicing medicine, have the investigatory skills necessary to raise our art to the next level. Enough residencies already exist to turn out a steady supply of surgeons, but only a handful produce true academicians." He felt as if Waters was patting him on the shoulder saying, "Atta boy!"

"Very admirable, Dr. Cutter," interjected the biophysicist. Alex thought her name was Linda Lehman—or something close to that—but wasn't sure, and he couldn't read her name tag. "But the hard reality of this day and age is that particular idealistic philosophy had merit years ago when the feds had enough money to pour funding into biomedical research. Recently, and in the foreseeable future, Congress's health funding has stayed constant, which means that after factoring in inflation, the money allocated for research is actually shrinking. Bottom line is that medical schools—especially state schools like ours—find themselves in a deficit. Which means that clinical departments, like yours, must generate the dollars needed to keep the school afloat. We can't, and shouldn't, rely so heavily on grants and contracts that can dry up faster than the Mohave Desert. Or do you have another opinion on how to solve such fiscal problems?"

This was a hot button for many of the clinicians. "In other words," Alex answered, "it's the job of the surgical departments—and not tax dollars—to support the overhead and salaries of non-revenue-generating departments in a state medical school?"

She smiled. "Bluntly speaking, yes."

Alex felt his muscles tense. At the moment, an argument would be counterproductive. "It all comes down to one thing: if the state wants a medical school, tax dollars should fund it, not the surgeons whose primary job is to train more doctors and to do research."

"Yes, but we're getting off into the weeds with this discussion," the chair broke in. "I'd prefer you address the initial question: If the primary goal of a medical school is to train physicians and surgeons, isn't it in our best interests to do just that?"

The biophysicist held up her hand to indicate she wasn't finished. "If your department is primarily concerned with research, how can you possibly expose your residents to enough clinical material to produce competent graduates?"

Alex saw his position rapidly eroding. Clearly, the committee had decided where to focus their search, and it was toward a strong clinician. They were now simply going through the motions of asking for the input of the current faculty. "With the exception of some very tricky surgeries—aneurysms or AVMs for example—neurosurgery is, to be blunt, quite rote. It's piecework. How many subdural hematomas does a resident need to remove before being competent at that? Ten? Fifty? A hundred? Speaking strictly for me, my fifteenth didn't teach me anything more than did my tenth. On the other hand, learning to design a research protocol has taught me a lot about critical thinking. I submit that critical thinking benefits a neurosurgeon more than does purely manual skills." He knew his argument fell on deaf ears, but felt compelled to give it anyway.

The one to the chair's right, an older professor Alex recognized as a thoracic surgeon, said, "I don't agree with you, Alex. Things happen on the wards and in the operating room, sometimes strange things, and they always seem to pop up at the damndest times. Having to deal with them and get the patient through unscathed provides a richness of clinical experience that simply can't be taught from a textbook or lecture. We learn from *doing* and *observing*. Seeing an attending handle tricky, sometimes novel, situations that arise when least expected is an invaluable learning experience. Or do you disagree?" The older man's bushy eyebrows rose, accentuating the question.

Another loaded question, one he'd be a fool to disagree with. Alex nodded. "You have a good point." He wanted to circle back to his original argument but knew it'd be beating a moribund horse. If there was one thing Waters had instilled in him, it was intellectual honesty. That was the most important facet of Waters's training program. He hated the thought of a hard-driving clinician destroying such an important aspect of the established culture.

"As much as I find this conversation stimulating," the chair said, "we're held hostage to our schedule. Sadly I must move this interview along. Are there any members of the present faculty you believe to be a suitable replacement for Doctor Waters?"

He thought of Ogden's desire to take command. "No, sir."

"Is there anyone on the present faculty you would not want to see become the new chair?"

Thank you, Jesus! "Yes, sir. Doctor Ogden."

The chairman's eyebrows arched again. "Oh? Why is this?"

"A chairman needs to be the strongest team player on the faculty. If he isn't, he won't get the best performance from the others. Doctor Ogden is not a team player." He believed this to be true.

One of the committee members began tapping a pen on his notepad. "Isn't Dr. Ogden well respected in national neurosurgery circles?"

"Yes, but only because his older brother—who's very well connected—has promoted him." Alex doubted his words would make much difference, but you never knew,...

"There any outside candidate you'd recommend?" the chair asked.

"I haven't really given it much thought." True. "Sorry, I guess that doesn't reflect well on my preparedness for this meeting, but I'm still having a hard time wrapping my head around the idea of Dr. Waters not being chairman."

The hematologist asked, "How about you? Are you looking for the job?"

Alex chuckled. "No way."

The chair nodded sagely. "How about Richard Weiner; do you know him?"

"Dick?" he said, surprised. He considered that a moment. Young, aggressive, a surgeon who also ran a research project. In fact, very similar research to his own. "Yeah, sure, I know him. We share the same research interests."

"Your thoughts about Dr. Weiner?"

Alex's immediate thought was Dick was too junior to handle the tenured full professors in the department. It would certainly be a struggle, especially to deal with Baxter and Ogden. "He's only marginally more senior than I."

"Yes, but would he be a good replacement?"

"I don't have any firsthand experience with his administrative capabilities. I guess I'll have to pass on that." A foreboding morphed in Alex's gut. Clearly, the committee was considering Weiner a hot contender. And if he got the job …

Couldn't possibly happen. Dick's way too junior.

Right?

"Thank you for your time, Dr. Cutter."

13

"What things do you think can be improved within the department?" Dick Weiner asked Alex, the two of them sitting across from each other at a noisy downtown restaurant frequented by business people catching a quick but elegant lunch. Weiner, a short, plump, prematurely bald man with a ski-slope nose and thick fingers, had been pumping Alex for inside department information for the last ninety minutes, making Alex feel awkward and a bit like Benedict Arnold.

"I don't want to see things changed," Alex replied.

"Oh, c'mon." Weiner waved his palm in a "no, no, no" gesture. "I've seen the numbers. Because you cover the trauma center, you're the single biggest earner in the group. In spite of that, you're taking home the smallest paycheck, just about a fourth of what Baxter pulls down. How you feel about that?"

Easy answer. "I'm not doing this for the money. If I were, I'd be in private practice with a friend in Boise."

Weiner sipped his ice tea. "Wow, sounds like you've got something against private practice."

Alex shifted on the seat cushion, partly because he'd been sitting in one place for ninety minutes, partly because Weiner kept trying to pry personal information from him. He didn't like it. "Private practice is okay," he said. "It's just not for me. I love my research."

Weiner jiggled the ice in his empty glass. "You ever done any private practice?"

Where was this going? Besides, Dick undoubtedly knew the answer. "No."

Weiner nodded, the lights from the wall sconce reflecting off his oily scalp. "You like the job here? Other than your lab?"

"Boy, there's no good way to answer that. I say no, I look like an idiot for staying. I say yes, I look like an idiot for working for peanuts. Like I said, the reason I'm here is because of my research. I had the lab going when I graduated, so there was no start-up time."

Weiner copped a glance at his watch. "Looks to me like you're saddled with all the shit jobs in the department. Covering the VA, covering trauma call, working the charity clinic. How much trauma call you take?"

A sore point for sure, and Weiner probably knew that answer, too. Why bother asking? "All of it, unless I'm out of town."

Weiner laughed and shook his head woefully. "How's that working for you? I find it hard to believe a lab rat like you wants to take all that trauma call."

Good point. "Can't say I love that, but the department pays my salary until I get funded." He was curious to know how Weiner got his lab funded but thought asking might come across as sour grapes.

"How often you make rounds there?"

"Every day at the trauma center, once a week at the VA."

Weiner sat back and laughed again. "Every day? No way. You like that?"

"It's a hassle," Alex admitted. "By the time I finish up at the U, I have to fight traffic to get across town. Only good thing is the traffic's pretty much played out by the time I head home. Still, it's a thrash."

"And all those tenured full professors won't help? That type of work beneath them?"

The words made Alex feel even more like an idiot. As uncomfortable as this conversation was making him, he wasn't about to badmouth colleagues to Weiner. "Not really."

"How's that? Give me an example."

"As you probably know, we discuss the week's OR schedule at Monday conference. If a case shows up—an aneurysm for example—that's someone else's subspecialty, it's transferred to whichever surgeon does that work at the U."

Weiner snorted. "In other words, they cherry-pick the good cases and leave you all the crap. That about sum it up?"

That stung. "I wouldn't really put it that way, Dick."

"Oh yeah? Then how would you put it?"

"We all have subspecialties. Mine's brain tumors. Baxter's is vascular—"

Weiner cut him off. "Yeah, yeah, yeah, I know all that crap. My point in all this is those clowns refuse to roll up their sleeves and cover that service unless there's a case they want. Then it gets transferred to the almighty U so they don't have to sully themselves with driving downtown. That's exactly the kind of shit that drives the administration at County crazy insane. On top of that, everyone—meaning Coastal-County *and* the U—loses money each time they pull that. Those holier-than-thou full professors are shafting the system, Alex. Don't you get it?"

Enough. "What's your point?"

"Just so we have things in perspective, everyone but you is a full professor with tenure."

"So?"

"They're at the top of the university's salary range."

"Again, so what?"

"So, none of them are going anywhere. Why should they? They have no incentive to leave. They're getting paid top dollar to sit around their offices and drink coffee every afternoon and do the minimum amount of work. And frankly, who'd want to hire them? Not one of those clowns knows how to work. They're all deadwood."

"Again, I don't see your point."

Weiner smiled. "Believe me, if I take over the department, those fat cats aren't going to be living as they do now. I know exactly how many cases they're doing. No other department in the world allows surgeons get away with the shit they're pulling." Weiner shook his head with a look of disgust. "Believe me, things are going to change. And I can tell you this, you'll be the first one to benefit." His expression turned serious. "Will you back me on this?"

Alex found the question deeply unsettling. "I'm not sure what you mean by that."

"You'll get a vote on who replaces Waters. Will you support me?"

Alex didn't answer.

"Let me be very clear, Alex. You back me, I'll guarantee I'll fund your lab until you get a grant. Not only that, I'll make sure you have the time to actually set foot in your lab for more than a couple minutes at a time. Since you and I would be the youngest members of the department, we can make a good team. I'll appoint you vice-chair. How does that sound to you?"

Alex mentally compared Weiner to the other two viable candidates, both as senior as Baxter and Ogden, both currently at prestigious East Coast universities. If Weiner would guarantee to support his lab, well, why not vote for him? Baxter and Ogden would vote for themselves, and Waters couldn't vote. Depending on how the search committee felt, Weiner might just get it in spite of his age. Certainly things would drastically change from the Camelot environment of the Waters years. Was that bad? Weiner put out his hand to shake. Alex took it. "Yes, I'll support you."

If Waters had to step down, wouldn't it be better to have a research-oriented surgeon take over?

14

"... AND IT IS UNTO Jesus Christ our Lord ..."

Alex sat on butt-numbing oak, spacing out and doing his best to ignore the nauseating combination of scents that filled the room: mourning lilies, perfume, body odor, and—from someone—the rank odor of a silent fart. The sermon, Alex believed, contained far too much fire and brimstone and threats of spit-roasting in eternal hell if the congregation didn't accept Jesus into their hearts as lord and master. He hated this sort of crap. First of all, he believed funerals were to honor the deceased, not to threaten and intimidate the mourners. Although he believed in God, it wasn't Jesus Christ. Neither did he believe the man named Jesus who walked the earth had necessarily been God's son. Because of these doubts, he found the self-righteous fundamentalists obnoxious and sanctimonious in their insistence on having "The Answers." No one knew all "The Answers." Not by a long shot.

Lincoln: the capitol and the second-most populous city in Nebraska after Omaha. A series of exits off Interstate 80 fed a flat grid of streets with a population of almost a quarter million. The kind of city, he suspected, that its salt-of-the-earth inhabitants regarded as "a great place to raise a family." His preference was the West Coast. But now that he thought about it, he'd never lived anywhere else, so what did he know? He'd spent two quarters of medical school on a surgical clerkship at Middlesex Hospital in downtown London, but the remainder of his life had been confined to within fifty miles of the Pacific Ocean.

Just before the funeral service began, he'd glanced around and was shocked at the congregants' homogeneity: one hundred percent white—probably law-abiding—people who he bet referred to themselves as "folk." Good, God-fearing, hard-working "folk." Not that there was anything wrong with that, but he found it a little too *Leave It to Beaver*-ish for his tastes, preferring an ethnic mix, especially when it came to food. Although they'd only been in town twenty-four hours, the only ethnic restaurants he'd seen were a few Chinese joints featuring all-you-can-eat lunch buffets. Then again, perhaps he was completely wrong, and this really was the perfect place to live and raise a family. He sort of doubted it.

Lisa dabbed a tissue to her eyes, staining the Kleenex with mascara. With a muffled sniff, she discreetly pushed the sodden tissue under the cuff of her left sleeve. He wished there was some way to comfort her but knew from personal experience that the loss of a parent is inconsolable. He would simply support her as best he could, but that job was made harder by the fact he'd not been close to her mother.

The funeral made him think of his own mother, of how terrible her disease, glioblastoma, had been and how it compelled him—as melodramatic as it sounded—to search for a cure. It had been heartbreaking to stand helplessly as she lost more and more brain function. Through it all, she remained cognitively intact, aware of exactly what was happening, imprisoned in a body she couldn't control. And that was the worst part. Countless times he'd wished for a way to lessen her suffering. Toward the end he talked to her doctor about giving her more morphine in the hope of dulling her senses, but the doctor refused, saying she showed no signs of pain. "But what about her mental pain?" he'd asked. The doctor gave him some theological mumbo jumbo that made no sense. Some Hippocratic babble about do no harm. But what harm had the doctor done by steadfastly keeping her heart beating when her brain had long ceased to function? Now, as a doctor specializing in such tumors, he practiced from the heart, ignoring any religious hindrances.

The black-clad congregation rose en masse at the organ's introductory chords. Alex dutifully opened the hymnal and found the correct page but made no attempt to even lip synch the plodding, senseless lyrics. He never had been able to carry a tune, so why try now? Occasionally he sang along to familiar songs in the privacy of his car, but even that was only on the best of days. Hymns were another mystery of life. What was their *raison d'être*?

Hymn over, the mourners returned to their seats, and the preacher once again began to drone on.

Burial was another difference between Lisa's family and his. His family chose cremation, their ashes—sometimes illegally—scattered over the beloved coast. His mother and father had been released into the waters of San Francisco Bay, his mother off the north shore. The concept of decaying in a box underground seemed, well…

Alex discreetly nudged up the cuff to his white shirt for a glance at his Seiko. Forty-five minutes now, and they still hadn't reached the halfway point of the service. He shifted weight again on the hard oak, letting his mind wander to happier thoughts.

15

BAXTER AND GEOFF WERE talking intensely in hushed tones at the small conference-room table when Alex entered, heading to the coffee maker. Baxter turned to him. “Heard the news?”

“What news?” Alex started pouring a cup.

Baxter’s face became pained. “The dean just announced our new chair.”

Alex quickly checked Geoff’s face. Neither one of them appeared happy, so undoubtedly neither had been The Chosen One. He replaced the pot on the hot plate. “Who?”

“Come sit down first,” Baxter demanded.

Alex took the chair directly across from Baxter, putting Geoff on his right.

“Richard Weiner,” Geoff said with just enough venom to be perceptible.

Alex suppressed a smile. It came as a welcome relief to know Ogden didn’t get the position. Baxter would’ve been a better choice. Marginally.

“Guess where he intends to set up shop.” Baxter said.

“He’s not planning to move into Dr. Waters’s office, is he?” Alex asked, surprised.

“Get this; he talked Coastal County administration into gutting the entire top floor of the old building to convert it into an office suite. A *suite*, for God’s sake.”

Alex glanced from one man to the other, searching for any telltale sign that a huge joke lurked behind the statement. They were dead serious.

"No kidding," Baxter said, reading Alex's thoughts. Baxter nodded for emphasis. "Word has it, they're going whole hog on the renovation. Wood paneling, designer carpets, designer colors. No one's sure what kind of package Weiner negotiated from the dean and administration, but it had to be massive. I've never heard of this kind of money being spent on that place."

The original hospital, like most county hospitals during the pre-Medicare/Medicaid days, was built to serve uninsured patients—a municipal "charity" hospital. In addition to the actual hospital facilities, the building housed other county health-related offices such as the medical examiner and public health officials. In contrast to plush private hospitals with their base of wealthy donors and paying patients, its fiscal health depended solely on tax revenues. With the emergence of regionalized trauma centers serviced by Medic One responders, a spiffy new trauma center had been built contiguous with the original 1930s art deco building. The complex now served as a major teaching hospital for the local university, a standard symbiotic relationship between a state school and a municipal hospital. This parasitic affiliation provided an easy source of round-the-clock physician coverage for mere pennies on the dollar. But when tax revenues remained flat in periods of soaring costs, the county and university ran into budgetary deficits, forcing them to cut costs. Since both institutions received various state monies, it made fiscal sense to contract medical personnel from the university, which, in turn, forced the medical school to assume primary responsibility for patient medical care. This was delegated, in large part, to residents.

"Okaaay… but if he's over there, what happens to Dr. Waters's office?" Alex asked, a bit perplexed. The thought crossed his mind that if Weiner was true to his word and made him second-in-command, it might become his office. *Interesting.*

Geoff shrugged. "Remains empty. And that's another bit of news: Weiner won't grant Art professor emeritus status. Word has it he wants him physically off campus soon as humanly possible."

Baxter crossed his legs, smoothing the crease of the black slacks he wore daily. "He'd get rid of us too—*if* he could. But he can't. We're tenured." Baxter glanced at Alex. "You, on the other hand, little lamb, are as vulnerable as a newborn in an incubator. I suggest you begin sending out feelers to see what openings are available."

Jesus, Baxter looked serious too. "Why would he want to get rid of me? I don't make the same salary you do." He remembered Weiner's rant about how the others were pulling down the top spots in the salary range.

Baxter shook his head. "Don't be naive, Alex. I've seen this happen elsewhere. This is exactly what we predicted would occur if an outsider assumed control. He'll want to clean shop and replace all of us with his own people. Part of that, I guarantee you, will be to make our lives so miserable we'll want to move. But Geoff and I aren't going anywhere, are we Geoff." It was a statement, not a question.

Arms folded defiantly across his chest, an expanse of glistening gums exposed, Geoff nodded. "We're staying right here. We're tenured. He can't do diddly-squat to us."

"*And*," Baxter said with an imperious wave, "we'll sit right here and torment him by simply doing our thing."

Silence.

Baxter continued. "He's making a huge mistake by moving administrative downtown. When the cat's away, the mice will play." He flashed a knowing smile across the table to Geoff, who appeared to know exactly what the threat implied. "We can keep on doing our thing here at the university while the money in our TIAA-CREF just keeps on accumulating, ka-chink ka-chink." There was a mischievous twinkle in his eye. "Nope, no way is Herr Doctor Weiner going to get us out of here."

"That's right," Ogden seconded. Baxter's words made sense. New chairman meant a new culture. Hadn't Weiner said as much? But Weiner had given Alex his word. Then again, now that he thought about it, he had nothing in writing. Weiner could do exactly as he pleased. Suddenly, the coffee burned like acid in his stomach.

16

"PATIENT IS A FIFTY-FIVE-YEAR-OLD Caucasian female." the resident flipped the switch to illuminate one panel of the viewing screen on which several CT scans hung. "Story is, she screamed, grabbed her head, and immediately lost consciousness. Her husband called 911. When the paramedics found her, she was a Glasgow nine." The Glasgow Coma Scale was a standardized measure of global brain function that ranged from three, coma, to fifteen for normal. It's an easy way for paramedics and other medical personnel to quickly transfer a pithy assessment of neurologic function from one person to another.

Sensing motion to his right, Alex glanced in that direction. Dick Weiner had just entered the conference and was motioning a resident in the front row to vacate his seat. The resident stood, Dick sat, and the resident presenting the case continued reciting the patient history. When the resident finished, Weiner turned to a first-year resident. "What's the diagnosis?"

"Subarachnoid hemorrhage. From the distribution of blood on the scan, it's probably an aneurysm of the left middle cerebral artery."

Weiner cocked a finger-gun and shot the resident. "Correct." He pointed to a junior resident. "How do we treat it?"

The resident glanced beseechingly at a senior resident in hopes of a bail-out, but since Weiner's arrival, residents quickly learned to not aid colleagues when being grilled.

Weiner leaned toward the resident, getting right into his face. "*Well?* We don't have all day, Olson." He held the position, inches from the kid's face, glowering intently into his eyes.

Olson swallowed. "It's fair to say the treatment is debatable and—"

"*Debatable?* Wrong!" Dick swiveled ninety degrees, arm across the back of the chair to scan the others in the room. "There is only one—I repeat, *one*—way to treat these patients." His voice grew louder. "From this point on, any SAH who arrives in the ER will be immediately squirted"—administrating an X-ray angiogram to show blood vessels—"and if it demonstrates an aneurysm, that patient will go straight to the OR and the aneurysm clipped. This is departmental policy." He spun around to the resident again. "Stand the fuck up, Olson, you're not done yet."

The room became stone-cold still, pulsing with tension. Weiner slowly rose from his chair to stand beside the view box. "Why operate immediately, Olson?"

The resident paused, either wanting to think or as a way to deal with the intimidation. "To prevent rebleeding?"

Weiner shook his head. "I'm asking the questions. Answer me."

Olson swallowed. "To prevent a second bleed."

"Bullshit, Olson. That's the reason *any* aneurysm is clipped, regardless of whether it's done early or late. Try again. You're not sitting down till we finish this case; I don't care if it takes the rest of the goddamn night."

By now Olson appeared mute, so Baxter piped in. "Acute surgery removes the aneurysm so that any vasospasm can be treated, which results from the irritant effects of blood against the *out*side of the vessels. You can't do this if the aneurysm hasn't been treated."

Weiner's face grew red. "Goddamnit! I asked Olson, not you."

Baxter ignored him. "Vasospasm"—a narrowing of the blood vessels—"evolves within the first seventy-two hours of a bleed and carries a mortality rate of well over 50 percent. However, the residents should know that there are very valid arguments *against* such an aggressive approach. There are no objective data to support the concept that early surgery is superior to delayed surgery."

Weiner's eyes burned at Baxter like lasers. "Sit down, Olson." The room remained ominously silent. Alex saw a satisfied smile flicker across Baxter's lips. Weiner was pacing in front of the X-ray viewing panel, the knuckles of his fists white at his sides. After composing himself, he cleared his throat. "An agreement has been reached with Coastal County and the county-wide emergency services that all 911 responses suspected to be subarachnoid hemorrhages will be taken directly to the trauma center regardless of the family's wishes. This is in the patients' best interests. Should, for some unanticipated reason, such a patient arrive at the university ER, I want that patient transferred immediately to the trauma center where they will be handled appropriately."

"I want the residents to know there are no AANS guidelines for the treatment of aneurysm patients," Baxter added.

Weiner jabbed a finger at Baxter. "Fuck guidelines. This protocol has the patients' best interests in mind." He swept his palm toward the university faculty. "You can continue treating patients incorrectly, but I guaran-fucking-tee you if I find that any faculty operated any kind of vascular abnormality at University Hospital, they will have their operating room privileges revoked." Baxter was the only surgeon in the group who specialized in vascular work, so the threat was obviously directed at him.

"This is *my* department, not Waters's. Waters was a pussy when it came to surgery. He trained decades ago and never kept up. Waters wasn't a neurosurgeon. He was nothing but an administrator. I checked his cases for the last five years, and you can count them on one finger. It's a damn travesty he was allowed to maintain OR privileges here. This is *my* department now, and I'll damn well see to it every resident is trained my way. Conference adjourned. I want the faculty upstairs in the conference room in five minutes." Still seething, Weiner stormed from the room before anyone else moved.

With the accordion wall closed to separate the conference side from the coffee klatch half of the room, Baxter, Geoff, Alex, and others waited for Weiner's arrival in silence, glum from having to deal with another of Weiner's tirades. Alex wasn't sure about the others, but anxiety churned his gut. Since arriving, Weiner's behavior toward the university-based faculty—Alex included—had been capricious, unpredictable, and vengeful. Everyone at the table seemed wrapped up in their own thoughts rather than entering into the usual chitchat. Alex wondered if they knew something he didn't or if they perhaps worried the conference room might be bugged. He shrugged off that idea as pure paranoia. *Weiner wouldn't do that … would he?*

Appearing relaxed—in a passive-aggressive way—Baxter and Geoff sat quietly at the table, Geoff engrossed in his coin thing, Baxter doodling on a yellow legal pad.

The hall door flew open; Weiner strutted in like a Gestapo captain. Like many men pushing five foot nine, he fought for additional millimeters of height with a militaristic posture. *All he needs is a swagger stick* , Alex thought. He halted at the end of the table, door still ajar, the harsh fluorescent ceiling light glistening off his oily scalp. Weiner slowly scanned each faculty member, sending a look of frank contempt. Once he had assured himself of everyone's attention, he announced, "Roger Delaney is now vice-chair of this department. His office will be adjacent to mine at the trauma center. When duties require him to be here, he'll use Waters's old office."

Without thinking, Alex asked, "Who's Delaney?"

Weiner shot him a withering glare. "My previous chief resident. He graduated a month ago."

Geoff was smiling, eyes never wavering from his coins. "That's not the way we do things, Dick."

Weiner glared at Geoff. "Yeah? Well, fuck that. We do things my way now. Meeting adjourned." He spun around and was out the door.

Alex jumped from his seat and squeezed past Baxter, hurrying to catch Weiner before he made it to the elevator. "Hey Dick, wait. Need to talk with you."

Weiner motioned him into the deserted administrative offices. "In there." He marched through the reception area into Waters's vacant office. Once Alex entered, Weiner slammed the door and glared. Alex found the emptiness of the office disorienting. The only sign of Waters was the old black phone on his desk.

"What do you want?" Weiner's hands cupped both hips, pushing back his white coat in a pose reminiscent of Hitler.

Why am I being attacked? "What's going on?"

"What do you mean, '*What's going on?* You need hearing aids?"

When Weiner didn't continue, Alex said, "Yes, I heard, but I'm not sure what happens to me now."

"You're out of the trauma center now. That's what you wanted, wasn't it, to stop taking every night call? Well, don't piss and moan. You got what you wished for."

"The trauma center generates ninety percent of my billings."

"So fucking what?" Weiner shrugged. "Not my problem. Find another job."

"What about my lab? Our agreement? Me being second-in-command?"

Weiner shifted weight impatiently. "Why didn't you take the job in Cleveland?"

Surprise. "You know about that?" Two days after the dean officially appointed Weiner, Alex received a call from the chair at a Midwest university, asking him to come back to look at a job. Both Baxter and Geoff encouraged him to at least visit, but he declined because, with Weiner coming on board, he anticipated being able to return to the lab.

"Do I know about it?" Weiner snorted. "Hell, I gave Ajay your name, said you were looking."

Looking? Alex suddenly felt nauseous. He swallowed.

"Well? Why didn't you accept the offer? It was a good one."

A laundry list of reasons flashed past, all of them beside the point. "It wasn't the right job."

"Bullshit. You'll never find the right job because, let's be frank about it, you like it too much here. You're just like the rest of that deadwood; you don't want to move. Well, guess what, Cutter? You damned well better get your head around it, because in six weeks you're out of here. As of now I'm cleaning house, and you're the first to go. Roger has your spot now, and he plans to be settled here by the end of next month. And let me tell you, when I finish, every damn one of Waters's minions will be out on their ass. Six weeks, Cutter. Fair warning."

Shock morphed to anger. "We had a deal. You promised me a place."

Wide-eyed, Weiner glanced around. "A deal? A *deal*? What fucking deal?" he yelled, his face now livid.

Alex swallowed.

Weiner put his face inches from Alex's. "Guess what? Gets better."

When Alex didn't answer, he continued. "Starting tomorrow, I'm the principle investigator on your grant. So don't bother coming to the lab anymore. Use the time to hunt for a job."

"You can't do that. That's *my* grant. After I find a new job, I'll transfer it." The grant award had just been announced the previous week, ending months of hard work and rejection. It was inconceivable to lose it.

Dick shook his head as if Alex's words were totally inappropriate. "No you won't. It's a done deal. I talked with NIH today and explained the situation—that you're leaving and I'm prepared to assume the PI role. This conversation's finished, Cutter. I'm behind in my schedule as it is, so leave already."

Is it even possible? Too late in the day to check with Grants and Contracts. Bastard can't do this. Can he?

"We are *not* done," Alex sputtered. "That grant was awarded to me."

Eyes narrow and hard, Weiner again pushed his nose inches from Alex. "News flash, Cutter. NIH awards grants to institutions, not people. For cases in which the institution believes the PI has diminished capabilities to conduct the granted research, the institutional administration may assign PI responsibilities to whomever it deems fit." Weiner spoke the lines as if memorized from a procedural paragraph. "End of discussion." He pointed to the door. "Out!"

Still reeling, Alex entered the empty hall across from the door to the deserted conference room, the accordion room divider once again opened, the usually glowing red switch of the coffee maker black and cold. For a confused moment, he stood, not knowing where to go or what to do. Without a word, Weiner shouldered past, heading straight for the fire door to the stairwell, then was gone.

I was used. Manipulated. A fool.

Feeling sorry for himself, he remained in place, paralyzed, unable to decide what to do or where to go. *Home. Go home. Talk to Lisa about it; see if she has ideas.*

He sensed someone watching him and glanced up to see Raj, a fourth-year resident, at the end of the hall near the elevator alcove. He wasn't in the mood for conversation but couldn't just ignore him.

"May I have a word with you, Doctor Cutter?"

Alex nodded and started numbly toward the resident. Raj opened his mouth to say more, but Alex raised his hand, stopping him. Could his earlier flippant thought actually be correct? Did Weiner have rooms bugged? Was that why he denied any agreement in Waters's deserted office? What seemed ludicrous an hour ago suddenly seemed very possible. "If you don't mind, let's talk in the basement."

"Good idea." Raj appeared relieved at the suggestion, which only reinforced Alex's paranoia.

A thought hit. "Before we go, I need to pick up a few papers from the lab."

Alex trotted to the lab, unlocked the door, and went straight to the cabinet holding his lab books and data. Without checking to verify the bundle contained all of the files, he scooped them into the briefcase he used for shuttling work back and forth from home. Finished, he locked the door and led Raj to the elevators.

They rode in silence, Alex unsure if the resident was really nervous of being overheard or just wary because of his boiling anger. The door rattled open at level B1 to an echoing, musty-smelling underground hall to the five-level parking garage. Alex stopped. "Okay, what do you want to discuss?"

Raj shifted from foot to foot, scanning the immediate area. They appeared to be alone. "Have a problem downtown," he said, referring to the county and VA hospital combination.

Alex nodded for him to continue. Raj glanced toward the steel fire door again. "Doctor Weiner's been running two rooms most of the time," he said, voice barely above a whisper now.

An alarm rang in the back of his mind. *Don't say anything incriminating.*

Jesus, what's happening to me?

He chose the most neutral answer that flashed to mind. "Costal County administration wants him to build the caseload. Sounds like he's doing just that."

Raj's eyes continued to scan their surroundings. Still whispering, he said, "Yeah, I get that part. That's not the issue." Raj paused to lick his lips. "Thing is, he's doing things that, uh, make us all nervous."

Raj appeared as genuinely paranoid as Alex felt. This wasn't just an act.

"For example?"

"He's ma … fac … ing cas …"

"Say again? I can't hear you."

Raj cleared his throat, stepped closer. "He's manufacturing cases."

"What do you mean?"

"Okay, for example, a simple, linear, nondisplaced skull fracture comes in. Used to be we'd scan the patient, make sure there wasn't any clot under it, and observe it for twenty-four hours. We'd never operate on it and—best I can tell from reading the literature—there's no reason to do so. But now he makes us take them to the OR to plate the fracture." This meant anchoring metal struts across the fracture line with small screws to hold the fracture in place to heal.

"He has us write up the case as a depressed fracture"—where a fragment of skull is pushed below the inner surface into the brain—"so he can bill the surgery as a depressed fracture."

Ah, so this was how Dick had tripled the number of neurosurgical cases overnight. This explained a lot.

"Give you another example," Raj continued, now apparently more at ease. "Last week a subarachnoid comes in. Okay, fine, we squirt her, see the aneurysm, take her to surgery, and clip it. Soon as she's out of the OR we take her back to angiography and squirt her again. Weiner says the clip isn't across the aneurysm—which is simply wrong. It was. So back she goes to the OR. We reopen the crani but don't do squat for fifteen minutes, then close her up. Back we go to angio. Same thing. Back to the OR. Three times now. Finally he goes, 'Okay, we're done.' He bills for all three surgeries, but the clip never changed; it was just fine in the first place."

Alex still didn't say a word.

"This is felony fraud, Doctor Cutter. He's forcing us to be accomplices."

Alex massaged the back of his neck, the muscles tight with anxiety. "Couldn't agree more."

"If we question him, he goes ballistic, like you saw him do today in conference. Oh my God, yesterday? He laid into Waller like you wouldn't believe, tore him a gaping new one, said he had to stay another year to graduate." Waller was a chief resident only months away from graduating.

Anger boiled up inside. The contract residents stipulate five years. However, in actuality residents were allowed to graduate only if the residency director certified them as adequately trained.

Raj shifted his feet, talking quickly. "We like being busy and all, but this is over the top. He insists on being notified about every ER call we get. I'm talking real time. So, if something trivial comes in—like the fracture I just mentioned—he operates it. Did another one of those yesterday. And if he's running another case when a patient comes in, he tells us to go ahead and start the case in another room—but most the time he never sets foot in the OR. When that happens, he has us document him as being there. We're all scared shitless of being busted for felony fraud. It'd ruin our careers before we even start."

Sure would. They'd lose their licenses. The FBI would have a field day with Weiner if they found out. But what could he do? Nothing. Well, he could be a whistle-blower, but only at the risk of getting Raj or other residents arrested, fired, or both. Alex took a deep breath and closed his eyes, still massaging his neck. "Aw, Jesus. When you dictate the op report, who do you say were the surgeon and assistants?"

Raj was back to a whisper. "We have specific instructions to put him as attending surgeon, present and scrubbed."

"And you do that?"

Raj gave desperate shrug. "Like we have a choice? Look what just happened to Waller. I sure as hell don't want to stick around another year. Would you?"

"Good point. What about the nurse's records?"

Raj laughed derisively. "They're more afraid of him than we are. Okay, let's say one of them blows the whistle. How they going to prove it? Who are the investigators going to believe? And with the administration so happy about the increased billings, he's their golden boy."

Alex began to massage his aching temples. "Why tell me this?"

"What do you mean? You ran that service. We thought maybe, you know …"

"I could talk to Weiner about it?"

Raj shrugged. "Yeah, I guess. Something like that."

What a mess. He didn't dare to directly intervene but felt compelled to help the residents. How, he had no idea. "At the moment I'm in no position to do a thing. Certainly, I can't talk to Weiner about it."

Raj appeared annoyed. "What about *us*? What're we supposed to do?"

"Let me think about it. At the moment, there's nothing you guys can do other than keep a detailed record of every case he falsifies. All the details. These things seem to have a way of working out. Like you said, you can't go to the administration for obvious reasons; he's doing exactly what they hired him to do."

Raj's eyes widened in fear. "You're not going to mention this to him, are you?"

"No, of course not. I'd never do that to you guys." An idea germinated. "For now, keep your powder dry and make it through the next year and a half. In the meantime, I'll work on it."

"Says he never promised me a thing." Alex sipped his martini. His anger caused his hands to shake, making it difficult to pick up the glass without spilling the contents. The restaurant smell of grilled meat and spices, usually pleasant, was making him nauseous. Kitchen clatter, the other muted voices, and the music from the recessed overhead speakers competed with their attempts to keep their voices down for privacy. This restaurant was theirs for special occasions, good and bad. They had celebrated their engagement here. But tonight was far from celebratory.

Lisa was playing with the toothpick-skewered olive in her drink. "What do we do now?"

"Far as I can see, I have two options: try to start a private practice here in town or look for another university to hire me. Either way, my research will have to stop. Least until I can get settled." Research would be out of the question if he opted for private practice. Strange, he'd just been awarded his first grant, but now that dream seemed elusive as ever, the timing ironically perverse.

The waiter walked over, pen in hand. "You folks ready to order?"

Alex nodded for Lisa.

"I'll have the fried oysters."

"And you, sir?"

"The sautéed chicken livers," he said, knowing he'd be unable to eat a bite.

17

Alex pulled into the basement parking lot early the next morning with plans to call friends outside Weiner's sphere of political influence, which had expanded significantly since being awarded the chairmanship of such a prestigious department. Academic job hunting could be difficult and politically tricky.

This time of morning the halls were empty, something he was grateful for. At his office, he inserted the key into the lock. It wouldn't turn. He double-checked. Yes, the correct key. Tried again. Same thing. A sick feeling rippled through his gut. He backtracked to his lab to try that key. Didn't work either. One lock might be a mechanical error. Two locks indicated intent. *Fucking Weiner.*

As he turned the corner on the way back toward his office, he saw Nancy, a staff secretary, unlock the main office door. "Morning, Nancy," he called, suppressing his anger. "Forgot my keys. Would you pleases unlock my office for me?"

She busied herself dumping her own keys into an oversized purse, avoiding eye contact. "Sorry, can't do that."

He nodded slowly. "What's going on?"

Without looking him in the face, she turned and crossed the hall to unlock the two doors to the conference/break room. "Not sure what you mean."

"The locks to my office and lab have been changed. Know anything about that?" He immediately regretted putting her in the middle of a bad situation. With no place to go, he followed her into the break room as she started the day's first pot of coffee.

From the hall a booming voice called, "Cutter, I want to talk to you."

He recognized the voice before looking. Weiner filled the entryway. "In my office." Weiner headed for Dr. Waters's empty office.

"Close the door," Weiner ordered, his back to the windows that overlooked a massive parking lot, the football stadium in the distance. Reminding Alex of pleasanter times.

Alex closed the door but kept his hand on the knob. The conversation, he knew, would be short. With a smug expression, Weiner leaned casually against the windows, hands in the pockets of his white coat. "I reassigned your office and secretary."

Alex didn't want to give Weiner the satisfaction of seeing his anger.

"You have the office next to the conference room." Weiner's hand came out of his pocket to toss Alex a key. "Here."

Reflexively, Alex grabbed for it and missed but made no effort to pick it up. "What office is that?"

"First door to the left of the conference room. Can't miss it—straight out the office and across the hall." Weiner was grinning now.

Puzzled, Alex mentally replayed the sentence, visualizing the location. "The janitorial closet?"

Weiner shot a finger gun at Alex's head. "Bingo."

Enough. "Why you doing this, Dick?"

"Hold on, gets better. I reassigned your priority time"—designated OR time—"to Delaney."

Alex stopped listening. He needed to be on the phone job hunting. Dick won. Anything would be better than this.

He noticed Weiner waiting for an answer. He didn't know what he'd asked, so Alex cleared his throat and changed tactics. "Why single me out, Dick? I supported you with the search committee. I don't get it. Explain it to me."

Weiner approached, poking a finger at Alex's face. "You deaf or just fucking stupid? This is *my* department. And I *will* change it. The only way to do that is for everyone to understand I mean business. Guess what? You're leading by example." Weiner waved his hand dismissively. "I'm done with this conversation. But before you leave, here's one more revelation: your patients have been reassigned to Delaney."

Alex was dumbfounded. "Why my patients? Why not Baxter or Geoff?"

"Seriously?"

"I'm asking."

"Jesus Christ! Think about it. News flash, Cutter: they're harder to get rid of. Told you once and I won't tell you again. I need your spot for Delaney." He pointed to the door. "Out of the fucking office. Now."

Alex was relieved to find the elevator empty, allowing him to avoid the embarrassment of a face-to-face encounter with anyone. By now everybody in the department knew he was fired, that his entire world had just been incinerated. He was left with a mortgage, two car payments, and absolutely nothing to show for all his research. The depth of his rage frightened even him, the flint and tinder sufficient to spark violent acts.

Alex drove to a large city park. There, he aimlessly strolled jogging trails while ruminating through his options. Beg for a job with one of the local groups? That'd be difficult for two reasons. A smoldering adversarial chasm historically existed between the academicians and private surgeons, fueled in part by Waters's not-so-subtle Ivy League style. Being a state school, most faculty salaries were paid by tax dollars, causing the private surgeons to claim this represented unfair, tax-supported competition. The far right-wingers claimed it verged on communism. On the flip side, the academicians were expected to fulfill multiple academic obligations other than practice, making it impossible to devote the same amount of time to competing for patients. Of more direct economic relevance was that university physicians were required by law to accept all patients regardless of insurance—which a majority of the time came to zilch. This was the foundation for their accusation that the private surgeons cherry-picked the well-insured cases, referring to them only the unfunded or high-risk ones. Each side had valid points, but it distilled down to one thing: Alex would have difficulty finding an established group to accept him.

Starting a solo practice would be daunting. In addition to his current debt, he'd need to secure a multi-million-dollar line of credit to pay overhead—such as a fifty-thousand-dollar malpractice insurance premium—until his practice became profitable. In a city saturated with neurosurgeons, his best shot would be to find a less-desirable suburban hospital with unsophisticated operating rooms and staff. He'd have no choice but to do craniotomies in an OR used by all surgeons. He cringed at the thought of opening a head in an OR used earlier that day to remove an infected appendix.

By late morning he was walked-out, depressed, and ready to head home. He dreaded telling Lisa the bad news, but perhaps she'd help him see an overlooked possibility, maybe even be willing to help start a practice if that's what they decided. One of her strong attributes was a rock-solid business sense.

Stop by the store and ask her to leave early?

No. He would be more productive spending the afternoon job hunting.

At his desk, thumbing absentmindedly through a medical journal, the telephone rang. He debated whether to answer it. Friends knew neither he nor Lisa would be home at this hour. Another ring.

He slapped down the journal. "Cutter here."

"Hey Alex, Jim Reynolds."

Who? "Yes?"

"James Reynolds," he repeated, clarifying his position as neurosurgery chair at a southern university. "Heard you might be fixin' to relocate."

"How'd you hear that? Weiner tell you?"

"What? Oh, no. Was talking to Bob Chang at a meeting last week. Bob mentioned you'd interviewed in Cleveland but turned it down. We need to fill us a position, so thought I might oughta run it by you, see if you were interested."

Suspicious, yet desperately wanting something positive, Alex leaned back in his chair. "What do you have in mind?" After hanging up, Alex opened a copy of the AANS membership list and jotted down the phone numbers of Paul Tunny and John Krause, fellow residents who, like many of Waters's graduates, had gone on to academic careers, both friends he could trust for honest, unbiased opinions. For the first time in two days, a glimmer of hope motivated him.

18

"GAWD, WHAT A ROYAL asshole," Lisa muttered, referring to Weiner, just before taking her first a sip of the Junipero martinis. For the second night in a row, they were at their favorite restaurant. Neither wanted to cook, and moreover, Alex felt the need to get out of the house. The restaurant felt comfortable, a touchstone of normalcy.

Alex nodded and did the same, savoring the juniper botanical. "Nothing like Junipero." He'd decided to hold off mentioning Reynolds's phone call until she had a moment to relax from work. They had left the house soon as she returned home, and he'd just finished telling her of the embarrassment of being delegated, quite literally, to a broom closet.

She sighed and leaned back against the booth. "What do we do now?"

"For the moment, nothing. I need to scout around for a job. I was too upset to make any real calls. I thought about trying to set up a private practice so we wouldn't have to move, but I just can't bring myself to seriously consider it."

She spooned a few ice cubes from her water glass into the martini, a trick they both used to dilute it some.

"I did get an interesting phone call shortly after I got home."

"Oh?" She replaced the spoon on the linen napkin, the restaurant din and piped-in music making it a little hard to hear again in spite of being in a booth.

He told her of Reynolds's pitch to fly there for a job interview.

She wrinkled her nose. "You said no, didn't you?"

He spooned a few ice cubes into his drink. "Actually, I agreed to come."

She sat back against the booth, hands in her lap. "Really? I'm surprised."

"Why?"

"Well, for starters, it's in the *South*. You'd seriously consider living there?"

"I know, I know … but the way I see it, I can't be very choosy at the moment. Considering our finances, my highest priority is finding a job. The longer I stay unemployed, the deeper in debt we'll be. Besides, there's no harm looking. Chances are I won't take it, but hey, who knows?"

She nodded. "Good point."

"And say I do take it. Once our lives stabilize and the pressure's off, I can start to nose around seriously for something more ideal. But you never can tell, maybe we'll discover it's our dream place. Neither one of us has set foot in a southern city other than New Orleans, and that was only a couple of days at a convention." He picked up his martini. "Who knows? We might like it."

"Okay, granted, but think about this: we're both non-church-going liberal democrats. The place you're talking about is the heart of the Bible Belt. We'd be surrounded by right-wing Christian conservatives. You ready to deal with that?"

Having already considered this, he nodded agreement. "Every word you say is true, but we may be getting ahead of ourselves. I haven't even looked at the job. In fact, he was pretty vague about the details, so I'm not exactly sure what the job actually entails. After I hung up and thought about it, I got the distinct impression his intent is to get me down there and take a look at me before he decides what he wants to offer. But hey, it's university-based and has a residency. From everything I've heard, Reynolds is a straight shooter and well connected politically. Might be a good temporary job. You never know, sometimes these things work out for the best. And as I said, what do I have to lose by looking? Besides, I'll get frequent flyer miles."

She laughed and spooned a few more ice cubes into her drink. "When are you going?"

"Day after tomorrow. My flight's already booked."

19

"NOT THAT IT MATTERS, but Waters built a reputation for academic excellence. What makes you ready to leave that place?" Reynolds asked. He was wearing smudged, slightly askew glasses, bright red suspenders, a rumpled navy suit, and a bad comb-over. Alex guessed him to be in his mid-fifties.

Alex's flight had connected through Chicago O'Hare after a two-hour layover, getting him to his destination a few minutes after 6:30 p.m. Reynolds had met him at the airport and driven them straight to Justine's, a New Orleans-style restaurant in the heart of the city. They were now at a small table in a private side room, isolated from the clatter of cutlery and the din of muted conversations. In contrast to Alex's accustomed West Coast casualness, the men here seemed to dress in sports coats or suits and the women in dresses. For the flight, Alex had chosen a blue blazer and grey slacks but hadn't bothered with a tie, which he now regretted. It remained in the trunk of Reynolds's car, still packed in his suitcase.

Alex decided nothing would be gained from trivializing his situation, so he gave Reynolds a candid accounting of Weiner's tactics, including setting up the Cleveland interview.

"Can't say I'm surprised," Reynolds said when Alex had finished. "Know Dan Richards?"

Took Alex a moment to register the name. "I know *of* him, but don't know him personally."

"Well, Richards and Weiner are big buddies. When Dan took the job upstate, he inherited a huge raft of trouble. The faculty started to fight him on every single thing he tried to change. He eventually prevailed, but not after a massive amount of bloodletting. Know for a fact that Weiner stopped off there to visit Dan on his way out to your place. Suspect they sat up a couple nights with Dan detailing all the problems and how he ended up handling them. That could have something to do with his behavior now. But stealing your grant?" Reynolds shook his head. "Mm, mm, mm, that is low. Never heard of such a thing." Reynolds paused. "If you don't mind me asking, what was it made you turn down the Cleveland job?"

Again, Alex saw no downside to being honest. "First, I wouldn't have a lab. Second, although whoever takes the job will have a university appointment, the actual job is to cover the VA full time. I hate working in the VA system."

Reynolds straightened slightly. "Really? Why's that?"

Uh-oh. A blunder? This was, after all, the South. Home of numerous prestigious military academies, an area of the country in which military service was considered a noble, desirable career. *Oh well, in for a pound …* "The idea of providing medical care to veterans can't be faulted. They've earned it. But the system itself sucks. I don't want to be part of that, is all."

"Understood." Reynolds adjusted his glasses slightly, but they remained a bit off-center. "Appreciate your candor. Which brings me to my next question: What are your goals? Where do you want to be career-wise in, say, five years?"

Alex didn't hesitate. "Ideally? To cure glioblastoma. I know that's unrealistic. But I sure want to give it my best shot."

"Trying for something real simple, huh?" Reynolds let out a sarcastic laugh. "People been struggling to crack that miserable goddamn disease for decades now without one thing to show for it. What makes you think you can do something no one else been able to do?"

"Isn't that how progress is made? On the shoulders of others?"

Reynolds considered that a moment. "True. But what are you doing that others haven't done?"

"Several things. I'm making progress, but I'd rather not discuss it in detail."

"Paranoid, huh? Afraid of me stealing your secrets?"

Sounded ridiculous to put it that way, but … "Unfortunately, that's happened all too often in science. After all, Weiner locked me out of my lab and took my grant."

Reynolds laughed. "True, but I know all about your NIH grants. I served on Council." Council was the NIH group that determined funding levels. "Which means I know you're telling *some*one what you're up to."

"Not entirely," Alex admitted. "Perhaps that's one of the reasons it took me so long to actually get an award." He shook his head, feeling sorry for himself. "I was just getting started again when this happened."

Reynolds busied himself with using the linen napkin to clean his glasses. "I find it sorta interesting that Weiner snatched your grant right out from under you. Especially seeing how y'all are doing pretty much the same thing."

Alex hadn't considered that angle. He rolled that around in his mind a moment. Didn't make sense. "You saying he planned on stealing my research?"

"No." Reynolds slipped on his glasses back on. "But once he was out there and you were exposed, well, why not? Easy pickings."

Alex's anger flared at the thought. Lisa always claimed he was too trusting and that he always expected the best from people—which, in reality, seldom happened.

After a moment of silence, Reynolds poured more Bordeaux into both of their glasses. "I like your candor, Alex, so let me be candid too. The job I called about is also a VA one. What are you now, assistant professor?"

"I am." He felt a heavy pang of disappointment he hadn't expected. He liked Reynolds and was beginning to be hopeful about a potential job. All this way for nothing. And as much as he needed a job, covering the VA wasn't going to cut it.

"Y'all come down here, I'll ask the dean to make you associate prof. Be a feather in your cap."

"I see." He paused. "At least we're being totally honest with each other. But I don't think I can do that."

Reynolds flipped a dismissive wave. "If y'all excuse me a moment, I need to make a call." He pushed back from the table and disappeared into another room.

Reynolds returned minutes later grinning faintly. "Just had me a talk with Garrison Majors, senior partner in the Scranton Majors clinic. What're the chances you could stick around an extra day?"

Alex wasn't sure he saw the point of staying. "I don't mean any disrespect, Dr. Reynolds, but I can't see a reason to stay if we're talking about a VA job."

Reynolds smiled. "See, that's just it. I'm thinking we might just have a place for y'all in the clinic. You know how we're structured here?"

Alex's mood brightened. "I don't have the foggiest. Tell me."

"I'm sure you know most of this, but let me take you through the history. When neurosurgery was in its infancy, about half the training programs were run out of private practices instead of universities. This one here started when Pappy Scranton finished training with Walter Dandy. Being from the area, it was natural for him to return and set up practice. Back then there wasn't another neurosurgeon within a couple hundred miles, so he was busy as hell the first day he hung out his shingle. With so much work to do, he started taking on general surgeons who wanted to learn a bit about neurosurgery. Didn't have a damn thing to do with the university back then. Then several years ago the powers within organized neurosurgery decided it was time to phase out training programs that weren't university-based. Only way the clinic could keep its program was for us to make nice with the dean. On account of me being the residency director, the dean made me full professor and department chair. But see, I'm also a senior partner in the clinic. Way it works, my university salary goes straight to the clinic, but my real paycheck comes *from* the clinic. I'm residency director, but Garrison Majors is the clinic CEO. Old Garrison was Scranton's handpicked successor. With me so far?"

Seemed straightforward. "I am."

"The medical center here has three hospitals: Baptist Central, the VA, and the county hospital, which is a Level 1 trauma center. Clinic docs admit their patients to Baptist Central, but the residency covers all three hospitals. Seeing how y'all want to keep your research going, I'm going raise the ante and sweet-talk the dean into bringing you on as full professor with tenure. But if we decide on this approach, y'all gonna have to stick around an extra day on account of the people who need to interview you. Interested?"

Interested? Overwhelmed was more appropriate. He couldn't believe it: an academic job with private practice income. "Let me make sure I understand the deal you just described; I'll be a university professor in private practice?"

"That's right. But let me clarify something. New clinic members are hired as a salaried employee for one year to make sure everyone's happy with the situation. When your year's up, if everything goes well, you'll become a full clinic partner eligible for profit sharing."

Later that evening, Alex telephoned Lisa from his hotel room to explain the details of the potential job. She quickly agreed that staying a day extra was well worth it to explore the opportunity, but they both worried things sounded too good to be true.

Lying in bed, hands knitted under his head, Alex stared at the ceiling and replayed his discussion with Reynolds. He knew he should try to get sleep before tomorrow's interviews, but the strange surroundings and the excitement of the offer kept him awake. Also gnawing on his mind was a niggling suspicion that Reynolds was right, that Weiner used his power to steal his lab out from under him. Had Weiner discovered the missing data? And what would happen when he did? Had he broken any laws by taking it from the lab? At the time, he didn't think of these questions, reacting solely by instinct to protect his data. There would be repercussions, he was certain of that. But what? And how would that affect this new job?

20

"WHAT'RE YOUR INITIAL IMPRESSIONS?" Garrison Majors asked.

Alex, Garrison, and Reynolds were back at the same table at Justine's. Apparently it was touted to be one of the best dining facilities in town, second only to the Chickasaw Country Club, which, Reynolds explained, couldn't accommodate a reservation on such short notice.

"I'm definitely intrigued with the situation." An understatement, as it sounded too good to be true.

"In that case, I assume you're okay with staying one more day?" Garrison said. "Reason is, I lined up a real estate agent to take you 'round to see a few homes."

Alex glanced at his watch. "No problem. I just need to check with the airline, see if I can change my ticket."

"I had Claude look into that already," Reynolds said, referring to his university secretary, "Got y'all set up, assuming you're willing to stay."

Alex marveled at their efficiency. "Okay then. Looks like I'll be here another day."

Garrison smiled and raised his wine glass to toast. "To a wise decision."

After the customary clink, Reynolds said, "Talked with Dean Summers after you left him. Man agreed to appoint you full professor but said your CV has to be reviewed by the promotions committee if he's gonna give you tenure. That shouldn't be a problem. I'll talk with a couple friends on the committee to make sure there're no issues. Once y'all come here, I'll submit your credentials to the residency review committee, have you appointed vice program director. Suspect with your academic background there won't be any problems with that either. Lastly, had me a talk with Steve Saito, chair of Cell Biology. He's more than happy to give you a clinical professor appointment in his shop where you can share a lab with one of his junior people."

Alex tried to recall the proximity of Baptist Central to the main campus and the building that housed Cell Biology, which, if memory served, was a block further than Neurosurgery's one-secretary, two-office suite in which Reynolds ran the residency and conducted university business. Keeping a separate—although redundant—office in a university building offered a layer of protection and a firewall to support the claim of a university-based residency.

"That's wonderful." Alex was very pleased. Things were working out better than anticipated.

Garrison added, "Let me take a moment to explain how coverage works. The clinic admits patients to two hospitals: Baptist Central and Baptist West. Residents cover Central but not West. That means when you're on call, you'll cover all hospitals—including Baptist West. That's the bad news. The good news is, given the number of surgeons we have, you'll pull call roughly every ten nights, depending on if someone's on vacation. If, for any reason, you need to take a night off, you're responsible for swapping with another partner and for notifying the exchange." Referring to the after-hours answering service for the clinic. "Call schedule gets published a month ahead of time. Once it's out, you're responsible for any change. How does night call sound?"

"Not bad at all. I expected worse." And he did too. After his stint covering every night call at Costal County, this seemed like nirvana.

Reynolds smiled and seemed about to say something when Alex continued. "I can begin revising my NIH grant when I get home. Who's the Grants and Contracts person at Baptist?"

Reynolds shot Garrison a glance. He nodded for Reynolds to answer. "That won't work. Baptist doesn't accept federal funding of any sort, certainly not from NIH."

Alex blinked. Had he heard correctly? "What? Why not?"

"That policy," Reynolds said, "was established years back, before World War II. Baptist's hospital system was originally started to serve church members and church members only. They refused to treat non-church members regularly. Even when some pretty pathetic cases showed up on their doorstep. Since then, their mission has expanded, but they still remain selective in who they treat. If they accept just one penny of federal money, they'd be required by law to take *all* comers, if you get my drift. 'Cause of this, they refuse any and all federal assistance."

"Okay, so what if the grant was awarded to the university?"

"Might work, but we'd have to make damn sure no one from Baptist gets a dime. Might be difficult if you have to ally with someone from their system, but it should be workable."

Alex sat back in his chair digesting the myriad details just discussed.

"In the morning," Garrison said, "Betsy Henry, the wife of a general surgeon who died of lung cancer few years back, is gonna pick you up at nine. She's blocked out the entire day to take you 'round to see places. She's our go-to girl for relocating docs to the area. Told her all about y'all, so she's anxious to meet you. Also, she's licking her chops to get Miss Lisa involved in some Women's Auxiliary projects."

21

"This next neighborhood is The Gardens. It's a more established neighborhood than what you just saw … mmm, less in transition, you might say." Betsy Henry—a diminutive dynamo in her early sixties with salt and pepper hair stacked and pinned to the back of her head—wore a string of yellow pearls big enough to choke a hippo. They clashed with the lanyard for her orange reading glasses. She had on a floral patterned dress with a frilly white lace collar hugging her neck, hiding age lines. She breezed along Central Avenue in her forest-green Mercedes, five miles over the speed limit.

Alex figured her use of the word *transition* was real estate speak for gentrification. They just toured a residential area in an old section of the city characterized by gone-to-seed mansions selling at rock-bottom prices to young professionals eager to restore them to their past glory. Alex neither had the time nor inclination to get involved in a renovation, preferring instead a turnkey, move-in-ready home.

Alex kept a city map open on his lap to learn streets and start the arduous process of familiarizing himself with general geography. He was also keeping track of the distance from neighborhoods to the medical center, an important issue for taking night call. A contiguous series of ratty, tired businesses—fast-food franchises, 7-Elevens, discount gas stations—lined both sides of the wide street, interspersed with residential stretches of peeling clapboard homes with cluttered, dead yards and an occasional refrigerator on a front porch. Overwhelmingly African American, from the people he saw walking the streets.

Betty slowed and turned right into a short asphalt road, driving up to a brick guardhouse that stood between two sections of a ten-foot-high brick wall. A uniformed guard behind the lower half of a Dutch door stood as Betty pulled alongside and rolled down her window.

"Howdy Miz Henry. Fixing to show today?"

"Yes, George. Should be about an hour, give or take."

"Yes, ma'am." He nodded as the gate began to slide open.

"A nice feature of this neighborhood," Betty said, slowly accelerating to twenty miles per hour, "is security. As you can see, it's a gated community with random patrols day and night. You'll appreciate that aspect when you're at the hospital all hours of the night and your bride is home alone. When you leave for vacation, the guard service will stop by to pick up mail and newspapers and walk the perimeter of the house. All of this is extremely comforting."

Considering the economically depressed neighborhoods they just drove through, Alex figured these winding, oak-lined roads with substantial homes and manicured landscapes would be the first choice of any burglar in search of high-yield items. "You live here?"

"No, but I'm in and out frequently enough that the guards know me. I've sold many a home in this neighborhood over the years, all to physicians." She seemed pleased with herself.

She parked next to an emerald lawn with parallel boxwood hedges on either side of the brick walk that led to a brick portico with balancing white columns. The one-story house had a large peaked roof. "I believe you'll like this place."

"What're your thoughts?" Betty asked as they strolled slowly back to her car.

"It tops all the others we've seen so far." He liked the location: equidistant between Baptist Central and Baptist West, the two opposite directions he'd drive if called out at night. This house was certainly much nicer than their present home. It quickly became clear the housing dollar went much further than in their present location, but he wasn't so keen on living in a gated community. It seemed a bit pretentious. "I'll have these pictures developed soon as I get home," he said, holding up the disposable Kodak camera he'd purchased that morning at the hotel gift shop. "If Lisa likes the house, we'll fly back so she can see it in person. I expect to have an answer by Friday."

22

"WHAT DO YOU THINK?" Alex asked Lisa.

Lisa pushed up off her haunches after inspecting the long cupboard space under the master bathroom twin sinks and vanity. "Plenty of storage, that's for sure. More than we'll ever need." She brushed off her hands. "Can see why you zeroed in on this place. Certainly is spacious."

He was pleased she approved of his selection. "You agree we should buy it?" He was prepared to make a full-price offer to ensure they got the house. Buying the home long-distance would present unique problems.

She surveyed the bathroom one more time. "I do. Let's go tell Betty."

"Good choice," Betty said, her words echoing slightly off bare living room surfaces. The home carried a faint smell of mildew, probably from months of being uninhabited and closed up without benefit of air conditioning. "A perfectly respectable neighborhood for a young doctor and his wife. An additional benefit y'all will appreciate is being only a couple miles from First Pres."

"First Pres?" asked Lisa, raising her eyebrows questioningly.

Betty reached out, touched her arm in a motherly gesture. "Oh Miss Lisa, sorry. Keep forgetting y'all are new to town. It's just that everybody refers to First Presbyterian as First Pres. That's where y'all will want to attend Sunday services and midweek Bible study."

Interesting. "Why's that?" Alex asked.

Betty seemed shocked to be asked, as if some things were self-evident. "Well, 'cause that's where all the socially prominent folk—the ones you'll want to be on a first-name basis with—attend." She flashed them a satisfied smile, as if this golden nugget of information was just one additional benefit of choosing her as their real estate agent.

Lisa raised an eyebrow at Alex, demurring to him.

Betty obviously caught the exchange. "Y'all *are* Christian, aren't you?"

Again Lisa nodded for Alex to answer. He hesitated, momentarily taken aback by the in-your-face question. Although mentally prepared to encounter more overt religiosity than what they were used to back home, the assumption triggered resentment. *Ignore it. Move on.*

"We were married in an Episcopal church," he said. True. But only because they decided a traditional ceremony bestowed a solemnity to marriage vows that a simple civil ceremony could not. Even so, it had been a modest service attended only by close family members and a few friends.

Laughing, Betty patted Lisa's arm again. "Oh, well, Episcopalians count too, dear. After all, we're all God's children. Us Christians, that is."

Did that mean Buddhists, Muslims, and all other non-Christians were summarily excluded from the God's Children Club? Again, he said nothing.

The momentary tension gone, Betty continued. "And be sure y'all attend First Pres Bible study, 'cause that's where you really get to know your kind of people."

Your kind of people? What the hell is that supposed to mean?

From the corner of his eye, he caught Lisa roll her eyes.

"Y'all don't even have to be Presbyterian to attend. We embrace all Christian denominations same way we accept all our southern teams. No discrimination there." She let out a short laugh. "Y'all should see us during football season. Lord have mercy! If Ole Miss, 'Bama, the Vols—any of our teams—play an outsider, we all get together and root for us rebels. Go Ole Miss! Go Vols! Have us a good old time with that." She seemed momentarily engrossed in a memory, perhaps of days when her husband lived. Then, just as quickly, she snapped back. "Y'all love football, don't ya?" Not opening it for debate, but as if validating their bona fides for buying in The Gardens.

What a strange conversation.

"We do," he said truthfully, stopping short of adding he preferred collegiate games while Lisa preferred the NFL. Not wanting to chitchat with Betty any longer than necessary, Alex glanced through the window at the manicured landscape. "I'll need to buy a lawn mower and hedging sheers."

"For heaven's sake, what for?" Betty asked, aghast. "Y'all can't possibly think of doing your own yard work. That just wouldn't be proper for a young professional. I have an excellent yard man. He's black, but he's one of them you can trust. I'll pass along his number soon as y'all move in. You tell him Betty told you to call, and I guarantee he'll do y'all proud."

Lisa must have seen Alex fighting back a remark, for she gave him an almost imperceptible headshake.

With a sigh, Alex relaxed into the soft leather wingback, his eyes wandering the rich wood paneling and a series of gilt-framed paintings of what probably represented an English fox hunt: traditionally dressed riders atop horses, hounds at their hoofs, rolling green hills in the background. A waxing and waning hint of rich cigar smoke floated in the air. Small, traditional brass wall sconces with green shades cast soft, vertical swaths of light on the dark wood. Plush, soft carpet underfoot.

Too amped from house buying, Lisa and Alex decided it'd be fruitless to retire to their hotel room, so they decided instead to enjoy a glass of wine in the lobby bar and rehash the events of the day. Earlier that evening they'd dined at Justine's again with Garrison and Anne Majors.

"You notice that none of the houses we saw was contemporary?" Alex said.

"I did. Everything here is so traditional. All the furniture, too. Not a piece of ours will fit in here."

"I know." He disliked the "cutesy homey" touches so prevalent in the houses they'd toured. Plaques with "Bar" printed in 1880s-style lettering above wet bars, or the "God Bless This Home" embroideries. Then there was all the brass: lamps, free-standing toilet paper holders, door handles, cabinet pulls, on and on. He and Lisa favored contemporary styles in brushed nickel or stainless steel. "And what's with all the claw-foot bathtubs? Doesn't anyone take a shower?"

"Guess they use the bathtub for that."

"How does that work?" He held up a hand. "Yeah, I know. You pull the shower curtain around the tub, but still—a ton of water must splash on the floor."

She laughed, inspecting her wine, rocking the glass to check the "legs." "That's one of the things I like about the new house; it has a couple showers."

"Yeah, but they're still just tubs with three walls around them rather than a real shower stall. Did you notice none of them have a light? I stepped in and pulled the curtain closed, and it was like being in the black hole of Calcutta."

"I know, I know." She rolled her eyes. "Notice the kitchen wallpaper?" She stuck a finger in her open mouth. "That's the first thing to go."

Alex nodded. "How about the knotty pine in the study? I'll paint over that with a neutral color, maybe a taupe." He'd been considering ways of making the interior more open and inviting.

"Almost every piece of furniture other than our bed will have to be replaced sooner or later."

Yikes. "That can come later. Before we do anything, we need to settle in and see what we can do with what we already have." The thought of what it would cost to furnish their new home was unnerving. Since being fired, his priorities had changed dramatically. Now, his foremost goal was to completely free them from any debt. Once he'd done that, he'd begin to build a nest egg. Never again would he be placed in such a financially vulnerable position. Now, financial freedom trumped all other career goals.

"You okay with all this?" he asked. "Buying the house and moving here?"

Lisa swirled the wine around the interior of her glass, then held it up to the light to inspect its color. "Think so. Guess we'll find out soon enough. Speaking of which … what'd you think of Betty?"

He wondered if this was queuing up to be an I-told-you-so moment. "Not sure exactly what you're asking. She found us a house, so that's okay. Why?"

"You know what I'm talking about—the whole being-a-Christian thing. I saw your reaction."

He had admittedly been saddened by their conversation with Betty. "Guess you were right the first time we discussed this. This is the Bible Belt, so guess I should've expected something like that. But I wasn't prepared to hear it so strongly. Thought maybe in this day and age, things would be different. Obviously that's not the case. Doesn't mean I like it."

Lisa watched another woman walk out of the bar, probably critiquing her dress. "I know. I found it off-putting too. I mean, what would she have done if I said we were Muslim or Buddhist?"

Alex chuckled. "Probably would've stroked."

"Does this mean we're going to have to become SEC fans?"

"If we want to fit in."

"Could be awkward if, say, Ole Miss plays a PAC 8 team."

She was right, Alex knew. No matter how long they might live here, they'd remain loyal to their West Coast teams. "Guess we just don't invite anyone over to watch the game."

"True."

Alex raised his glass in a toast. "To new beginnings." And for the first time, he wondered if Weiner may have done him a favor by forcing him from the nest. Perhaps. But the way it had been done, the deceit, could never be forgiven. Some day, in some way, he would return the favor.

"To us and a fresh start." Their glasses clinked.

23

"Dinner's ready," Alex called after pushing through the back door with a red-and-white box of fried chicken and slaw from a fast-food chain off Central Avenue, only a couple miles from their new home. He heard the clatter of Natalia's nails on hardwood as she scrambled for traction, and visualized her puppy paws going all-out, her body staying stationary. She came skidding around the corner, followed a moment later by Lisa. Lisa's work shirt was paint spattered, but her jeans seemed to have avoided even one smear. She wiped her hands on a rag before stuffing it back into her rear pocket. Alex knelt down to give Nat some behind-the-ear scratches. In return she gave him several wet doggie kisses. He opened the door for her to go out into the back yard.

"Great timing. Just finished the window trim."

Alex set the boxed chicken on the table while Lisa brought two glasses from a cabinet. "Real plates or paper?" Before the moving truck arrived, they'd been using paper plates.

Both of them dropped into chairs at the kitchen table, exhausted. According to plan, they had arrived three days before the moving truck's scheduled delivery. They'd devoted the intervening days to stripping wallpaper and painting rooms. Nights were spent in Dr. Garrison Major's guesthouse. At the risk of offending their gracious hosts, they declined to dine with them for fear of being an imposition and a nuisance. Plus, they wanted to orient as quickly as possible to the new city before Alex became swamped with work. Alex believed if you were forced to find restaurants and stores, you learned the geography more quickly.

The moving truck had arrived that morning, and by afternoon they'd assembled their bed and unpacked just enough clothes and kitchenwares to make the house livable until they could completely unpack. The other goal for the day had been to finish painting. By the next morning all the fresh surfaces would be dry and the house aired out. Tonight would be their first in the new home, a milestone marking the beginning of a new life for them.

"We'll use paper," Lisa replied. "The thought of cleaning up dishes makes me ill. In fact, once we finish dinner, I think I'm going to fill the tub and soak for an hour or two. My muscles haven't ached so much since that aerobics class I took. Did you remember to pick up a bottle of wine?"

"Does the Pope shit in the woods?" He triumphantly produced a bottle of cabernet from one of the bags. "I did. But they didn't have much I recognized. We're going to have to scout out a good wine store."

He filled the two glasses with tap water, brought them to the table, and grabbed two wine glasses from a moving box while Lisa opened the container of slaw. They divvied up the two plastic forks and napkins that came with the chicken. Famished, he grabbed a chicken leg and started in.

They ate ravenously, not bothering with the nicety of dinner conversation. With most of the chicken and a good portion of the slaw devoured, Lisa sat back to lick her fingers. "Boy, was I a piggy at the trough! Didn't realize how hungry I was until I caught a whiff of the food."

Alex licked his fingers too. "Oh man! Make that two piggies at the trough."

They leaned back in their chairs and laughed. After a moment of silence, Alex started in on the corkscrew. "One more week before I officially start. I was toying with the idea of driving in tomorrow afternoon to attend teaching conference, learn how they run things here. You mind?"

She dabbed her lips again with the napkin. "Not at all. That actually works out well because Betty invited me to a luncheon at a friend's home. I was going to ask if you mind being on your own for a few hours." She glanced around, then continued. "Slowly we're getting things in shape. Wouldn't hurt if we both get a break from this place. At least now we know about that Kroger." The supermarket anchored a small mall about a half mile outside the Central Avenue gates to The Garden.

The phone rang and Alex picked it up.

"Alex?"

He didn't recognize the voice. "Yes?"

"What the fuck did you do with the data in your lab?"

Ah, Dick Weiner. Alex hesitated. *How to answer*... He wouldn't put it past Weiner to be recording the call. Besides, there was no upside to admitting anything. "What data?"

"You know exactly what I'm talking about. All the lab books. Karen claims they were in the lab the day before you left."

"Are you suggesting I took them?"

"Who else would do that?"

"If you remember, you changed the locks to my office and my lab. How the hell could I get them?" When in doubt, deny, deny, deny.

That seemed to slow Dick up. "Fair warning, Cutter. Return them."

"Or what?"

Weiner hung up.

Alex found the Baptist Central main auditorium after several minutes of wandering the first-floor halls. Two of the six doors remained open, so he slipped in silently. Alex figured the room could comfortably seat two hundred people. He chose a seat toward the back, settled in, and glanced around. The wedge-shaped room with dark, wood-paneled walls funneled to a small stage on which sat a multi-panel X-ray view box. The first two rows of seats were occupied with residents, nurses, and a handful of attending physicians. Reynolds sat on the center aisle with Garrison directly behind him.

A resident slapped the last of a series of CTs in the blackened view box, then flipped on the switch to light one panel before turning to the group. "Next case is a forty-five-year-old, right-handed black female with a history of bilateral, bitemporal headaches."

After the resident finished presenting the patient's history, Reynolds turned to scan the audience for candidates to question, noticed Alex in the back of the room, and said, "Dr. Cutter, come on up here next to me. Group, I want y'all to meet Dr. Cutter, the surgeon who I mentioned is fixin' to join us."

Embarrassed at the attention, Alex walked down to the front row. As he was just about to sit, Reynolds said, "Before y'all sit down, Alex, take a look at that scan and tell us your thoughts on this patient and how y'all would handle it."

Alex stepped closer to the view box and flicked on all the panels, backlighting the CTs that included a normal series alongside a contrast-enhanced series. Contrast enhancement occurs when an X-ray opaque material is infused into the blood stream to help visualize the vessels. Normally, the contrast agent remains in the vessels, but inflammation from tumors or infection allows it to cross into brain tissue, making the abnormalities much more apparent. Alex suspected Reynolds was using the opportunity to evaluate his clinical judgment. Being trained by Waters, and given Waters's reputation as a conservative surgeon, Reynolds undoubtedly wanted to assess the level of Alex's conservatism.

Alex tapped his index finger on the obvious tumor. "This tumor is likely a meningioma for the following reasons," he said, slipping into teaching mode. "First, it seems to originate from the falx as seen by the flat surface here along the falx." He pointed with his index finger. "The bulk of the mass pushes into the mesial frontal lobe. In a woman this young, you need to worry that it might be more aggressive than meningiomas usually found in older females. As you can see by the contrast enhancement," moving his finger to the same view in the enhanced series, "slight edema is in the brain immediately adjacent to the tumor. This isn't a good sign."

He turned to the group. "There are two—actually three—ways to deal with these tumors. First, watch and wait. Repeat the scans every six months to see if it grows. The downside is you're wasting time if it *is* aggressive. The bigger the tumor, the more difficult the removal and the less likely the odds of achieving total resection. It's important to keep in mind that these tumors can only be cured by total resection.

The second option is to radiate it. The downside, of course, is that radiation won't produce a cure, because they don't shrink and go away. And, of course, there's always the risk that the radiation will only piss it off." A few of the residents chuckled at that. "That happens, you've made things worse. The third option is to go after a total removal now while the chances of cure are best. Bottom line is that if this were my mother, I'd push for surgery."

"I agree," Reynolds said with a vigorous nod. "But before you sit down, tell us your approach."

Alex studied the scans more, absentmindedly pinching the back of his neck, visualizing how best to get at the entire tumor.

"I'd position her in the lateral decubitus position," he said, indicating her side. "I want the right hemisphere down. I'd incline the table slightly with the head above the feet and have a lumbar drain in place. I wouldn't open the drain until I was ready to open the dura. My bone flap would cross the sagittal sinus." This was a large vein running front to back in the dura between the hemispheres. "Cutting the bone flap across that sinus is the riskiest part of the operation, because if you accidentally open that puppy, you could be in a world of hurt. Stay out of it. Once I started to open the dura, I'd begin to drain off spinal fluid to allow me to retract the frontal lobe with as little pressure as possible. In fact, the whole point of having her on her side is to let gravity retract it for you. I'd preserve the sagittal sinus if possible, but since you're in the anterior third of the sinus, if absolutely forced to, you can sacrifice it. But *only* if absolutely necessary."

Reynolds smiled, his hand on his chin. "Lateral decubitus position. Never would've considered that. We'd usually put the patient brow up with the head rotated away from the side of the tumor. Lateral decubitus position … hmm!" He turned to the residents. "Good suggestion. Y'all need to think about what Dr. Cutter just said. Might be better than what we're doing."

Alex sat down, glowing from Reynolds's words of endorsement. This wouldn't happen where he came from, especially with Weiner now in command. There, he was a non-entity, the junior faculty member. Here, he now felt the stature of being a professor and surgeon, capable of expressing new thoughts and bringing fresh skills to a deeply inbred training program. This move might become one of the best things to happen to his career. He glowed.

After conference, he walked out of the auditorium with Reynolds. At a T in the hall, Reynolds stopped at the bank of elevators. "Going upstairs to check on a couple post-ops. Great to have you here, Alex."

"I have a question for you. Know of any squash courts in town?"

"Squash?" Reynolds rubbed his chin. "There're a couple over at the University Club. I have a membership, so y'all let me know if you want me to sponsor you. Garrison has one, too, so I'm sure he'll be happy to support you."

Wonderful. He wanted to begin a routine of regular exercise again, assuming he'd be able to wedge it into his busy schedule, whatever that turned out to be. "Take you up on the offer soon as we get more settled and I have time. Appreciate it."

Reynolds seemed to remember something. "I appreciate the fact you're not officially working yet, but I have several matters in need of settling. You mind dropping by the office tomorrow?"

The only things he had on his plate for the next day were several honey-dos around the house, getting some final touches done while he still had his days to himself. An excuse to break away would be welcome. "No problem. What time?"

"Late morning works best for me, say between ten and eleven? Tomorrow's my day at the university office, and I'll make sure to be available round about then."

"I volunteered for the decorations committee for their annual black-tie affair," Lisa said with as much enthusiasm as Alex had heard in years. "I did it more as an act of self-preservation than desire. What they really want are volunteers for the procurement committee. I did that once before and *hated* it. I just don't feel comfortable walking into businesses and asking for donations, especially being new in town and not knowing a soul."

They were in the TV room with the news on but the volume turned low, enjoying a glass of chardonnay before another take-out dinner of fried chicken and slaw. Tomorrow one of his many tasks was to rehabilitate the gas barbeque in the back yard. It sat under a large oak tree and was covered with pollen, sap, and debris. By the looks of it, it hadn't been used in a year or more. On the drive back from the conference, he noticed a barbeque dealer on Central Avenue so planned to stop in on his return trip after meeting with Reynolds tomorrow.

"Think you'll enjoy working on that?" he asked Lisa.

"Yes, but I was *so* embarrassed. I showed up in my denim skirt, which would've been okay back home. All the other woman were in dresses. I felt *totally* out of place. I need new clothes if I'm going to be going out. Nothing I have fits in here." She paused to sip wine. "Oh, how'd your meeting with Reynolds go?"

"Great. I finally feel like a real professor instead of a senior resident. It's forcing me to think the move might actually be good for me. For you too, from the sounds of it." He checked their glasses. "One more small glass before we eat?"

"Sure. Why not. Oh, I tell you, I was *sooo* embarrassed today."

24

The candy-cane-striped arm swung up, allowing Alex to drive into the large, six-floor concrete parking behemoth serving Baptist Central. As he worked his way up looking for a parking space, Alex learned the first three floors were reserved for physicians. He made a mental note to ask Reynolds about obtaining a parking card to open the gate. After scouring every floor without luck, he eventually found one narrow space on the roof between two Ford pickups. Both trucks were decorated with confederate flag decals on the rear cab window. One had the silhouette of a kid pissing on a Chevy emblem. Nice. Almost immediately upon driving back into the blazing sun, he could feel heat radiating through the car roof. The car would be a pizza oven by the time he returned. In self-defense, he cracked the front windows and sunroof but knew that would help only minimally. He squeezed out of the door hoping one of the pickups would be gone by the time he returned.

He discovered a stairwell to the left of the two elevators and decided to walk to ground level in an attempt to learn as much as possible about navigating the massive medical complex before officially starting. Too lazy to walk the half block to the intersection, he waited at the curb for a break in traffic, sprinted across the street to the campus, and wandered the pleasant, tree-lined paths until finally recognizing the building that housed Reynolds's academic office. Claude, Reynolds's secretary, sat behind her desk typing on an IBM Selectric, the door to her boss's office closed. A cigarette burned in an ashtray next to the typewriter. She glanced up with a guilty smile when he entered. "I'll see if he's available," she said and picked up the phone.

"Settlin' in?" Reynolds set his pen down and leaned on the armrest of his desk chair, tie loosened, shirtsleeves rolled up, glasses smudged as usual.

"Pretty much. I'm ready to start on Monday, that's for sure. I miss work, to tell you the truth." The room carried the faint odor of stale cigarette smoke, but he spied no ashtray.

"Can't"—pronouncing it *cain't*—"tell you how happy I am to have y'all here. Going to be wonderful for the residents to get more academic input. You're exactly the person to do that. Believe I mentioned to you previously, the residency review committee dinged us for not having a strong enough teaching program. I'm counting on y'all to remedy that.

"Having said all that," Reynolds continued, "the most important item to be discussed today is which level of resident you want. Given that we graduate two a year, you'll be assigned residents for six months at a stretch. This means that one or two of the private guys won't receive coverage any longer, but reckon that's just tough titty. You better believe we can expect some howling from whoever we decide to cut. Long as I can remember, some of them been just using our boys for their convenience, having them assist on cases and cover the ER. Most of 'em haven't paid a lick of attention to our boys' education.

"I have the fifth-year guys assigned to me. Advantage to that is it gives me more flexibility in having them open and close my cases. Might wanna consider doing the same."

Reynolds finally stopped talking and Alex took the cue. Luckily, he'd anticipated this question and given it some serious consideration. "I prefer to have the first-year residents with me."

Brow furrowed, Reynolds leaned forward, forearms on the desk. "Y'all serious?"

When Alex didn't answer, he said, "Means you'll have to watch 'em like a hawk. Know that, don't you? Sure y'all don't want a more experienced set of hands with you?"

He felt obliged to defend his decision. "Way I see it, their first year is the most formative. Get them when they're fresh and you can mold them. Get them when they think they know it all and just want to get out on their own, you're not as effective. If our goal is to change the program orientation, we'll have a better shot at success if I get them fresh."

Reynolds sat back again, steepled fingers tapping his bottom lip. He stayed this way a moment before a smile played at the corners of his mouth. "See your point. Huh! Smart. Damn smart. Must admit, you've got a point. I'll give you that. Okay then, that's settled." Reynolds flipped a page on the notepad to his right. "Next order of business. How about your research?"

Another topic Alex had been considering since accepting the job. "I'm presently working on a grant submission. Soon as I get settled in the clinic, I'll arrange a sit-down with Steve," he said, referring to the chairman of Cell Biology, "and get a better feel for the lab situation. Figure I'll do things similarly to the past and work with tissue from patients. I'll see what their tissue culture capabilities are."

Reynolds spent a few moments making notes. "Agree. That makes the most sense."

Alex knew it wasn't quite what Reynolds wanted to hear, but it was the best he could do at the present time. Now for the good news. "Do the residents have a journal club?" He suspected they didn't.

Reynolds started swiveling his chair side to side. "Nope."

"Well then, that's the first thing I'll do. We'll meet monthly at my place, say 7:00 p.m. I'll have Lisa supply munchies for the guys. I'm thinking first Wednesday of the month in order to avoid conflicts with year-end holidays."

Reynolds slapped the desk. "Good! At least we got us something tangible to show the RRC next time they come snooping around."

Alex was pleased to make his first contribution to the residency. "Glad it meets with your approval. I'll set it up next week." A brief pause. "I have a delicate question for you."

Reynolds's face became serious again.

Alex's concern was how to broach the subject without ruffling Reynolds's ego. He decided a direct approach was his best bet. "I'm vice-chair of the department, am I not?"

"You are."

"What does that mean as far as my authority?" He worried that some personalities might have difficulty sharing or delegating control if they've been the only one in charge, especially as long as Reynolds had.

Reynolds laughed. "Y'all got nothing to worry about on that issue; I'm not your friend Weiner. I'm just tickled you're here to take some responsibility off my shoulders. Thing you need to realize about this place is there's good and bad points of being inextricably linked to private practice like we are. The big negative is most of the surgeons who benefit from resident coverage don't give a hoot about teaching. Like I said earlier, all's they want's a warm body to help"—pronouncing it *hep*—"in the OR and see patients in the ER. The quid pro quo is we benefit from an increased caseload. By the time our boys graduate, there's not much they haven't seen or done. But getting back to your question, I want y'all to take as much responsibility as possible without running into conflicts. I need you in control of things when I'm out of town. Which happens to be too damn much of the time. That answer your question?"

Alex was relieved to have aired the topic. The more he got to know Reynolds, the more he liked his straightforward, no-nonsense approach. Reynolds might not have Waters's Ivy League smoothness, but the man was certainly far less conniving than Weiner. "Thanks. Was hoping to hear that."

Alex was about to broach the parking issue when Reynolds said, "Garrison wants a word when we're done. Know how to find the clinic from here? Want me to have Claude walk you over?" The meeting was clearly finished.

"No thanks, I think I can find it. If not, I'll learn. Have to do that sooner or later. Might as well be sooner." He stood and extended his hand.

Reynolds did likewise. "Again, good to have you on board."

Alex waited for a break in traffic before sprinting across the wide, busy street, then walked back to the Baptist Central parking garage where he took the second-floor sky bridge to the professional office building. More familiar with the sights and landmarks now, he made fewer wrong turns and quickly found the elevator to the fifth-floor clinic.

The elevator opened into a hall that connected the waiting room on the left with the doctors' offices and exam rooms on the right in an H configuration. The clinic took up the entire floor. He approached two receptionists at the front desk of the packed waiting room, introduced himself, and said Dr. Majors wanted to see him.

"Oh, yes Doctor Cutter. He's expecting you. Please follow me." She led him through the elevator area into the clinic, then down that hall to Garrison's office, the maze of halls also more familiar this time. "Have a seat. I'll let Doctor know you're here."

Alex remained standing to inspect the room. Unlike Reynolds's utilitarian university office, Garrison's office contained darkly stained mahogany bookshelves, a heavy matching desk, and two maroon leather wingback chairs with a matching desk chair. This style of interior decorating, he was learning, seemed typical for the region. He preferred contemporary furniture, but it was nowhere to be seen, either in the medical complex or in the houses he had toured with Betty. He took a closer look at Garrison's vanity wall, inspecting the assortment of diplomas and pictures. Clearly, he flew airplanes. One picture showed him in front of the engine of a red-and-white biplane. Closer inspection revealed the plane matched the model proudly displayed on a corner of the desk.

"Morning, Alex." Dressed in green scrubs and a white lab coat, Garrison lumbered into the room. A few inches over six feet, with thinning gray hair and a paunch accentuated by his hunched shoulders, he displayed a disarming folksy demeanor that Alex suspected served him well in managing both clinic and patients.

"Didn't know you fly planes," Alex said, offering his hand.

"That's my Pitts you're looking at. Real beauty, my pride and joy. I'll be happy to take you up sometime. I fly competitive aerobatics with her. Another pilot and I own her, which is the only way to make one of those things affordable. I share another half interest in a four-seat

Cessna which we lease to the clinic for flying to out-clinics each week, but more about that later." Garrison habitually hooked his right index finger over the white surgical mask dangling from his neck, pulling it this way and that and playing with the ties, wrapping and unwrapping it around his finger.

The thought of recreational flying, with or without Garrison, left Alex cold. He had no problem flying commercial airlines but had long ago decided hobby flying was dangerous. Especially for physicians who typically overestimated their ability to do just about anything, including navigate through insane weather. "Reynolds said you wanted to see me?"

Just then a short, crew-cut man approximately Alex's age came hustling through the doorway. Garrison nodded at him. "Hey Dave." Then to Alex: "Wanted Dave Ray to stop by to meet you. He's our business manger. Once you and I finish up, he can walk you through several matters."

Dave Ray extended his hand. "Nice to meet you, Doc. Heard a lot a good things about you."

Alex hated that particular social platitude, believing it unnecessary. Odds were he hadn't heard a thing, because there wasn't anything to hear. "Nice meeting you too, Dave."

"C'mon, let me show you around." Garrison started for the door.

The tour ended in an office with a desk, chairs, and a bookcase in the exact style as Garrison's but with empty walls and shelves. A small secretarial alcove separated this from a mirror-image office. "This here's your office," Dave said. "You and Marty Berger share Kasey Williams for a secretary. We staff one typist for every two docs. She must be on break at the moment."

Garrison spoke up. "I've assigned my nurse, Linda Brown, to cover you till we hire a suitable one for you. It'll take you time to build up to full speed, but in the meantime we'll keep you busy seeing Any Doctors.

Alex turned from looking out the window. "Any Doctors? What's that?"

Garrison chuckled. "Every day we get a bunch of patients who walk in or call without an appointment. Girls at the front desk ask 'em, 'You okay seeing any doctor?' That explain it?"

Ah, the unscheduled walk-ins, the bane of maintaining a timely schedule, especially if, like so many physicians, you don't leave time for add-ons.

"Yes."

"Each day the Any Docs are divvied up between whoever's got clinic that day," Garrison explained.

"Since most our docs run a full schedule," Dave added, "or even overbook, these walk-ins can become a real pain to work in. So you might oughta be prepared to have busy days right from the get-go. We see anyone who walks in regardless of whether or not they've been seen at the clinic before. Until you get your own caseload, we'll assign you all the walk-ins. I can guarantee the other guys are going to love you for that. Sometimes these patients can be pretty gol-darn difficult to deal with."

"You can start bringing in your personal items any time you want," Dave added, handing him a key and a swipe card. "This here's the key to the office, and this card gets you in and out the parking lot. Be careful to not lose it."

Dave looked to Garrison. "That's it for me. You?"

Garrison nodded. "Good, 'cause Ellen Bowen wants to talk with him when we're done. I'll take him on over." Then to Alex, "Ellen's the OR nurse manager."

Ellen Bowen, a plump, cherub-faced woman in scrubs, had her brown hair tucked into a bouffant surgical hat. She sat at her desk in a small, glass-enclosed office at the intersection of two halls. Garrison explained that the two dedicated neurosurgery operating rooms were opposite one another at the far end of the hall. ORs dedicated to single specialties provided numerous advantages, including greater flexibility in case scheduling.

Soon as Ellen saw them approach, she stood and opened the door. "Come on in, Doctor Cutter. Oh, you're allowed to join us too, Doctor Majors," she said, obviously joking. "Have a seat."

The cramped office held one desk and two chairs with barely enough room to keep your knees from banging into something. The adjoining glass walls provided a panoramic of the intersecting corridors and a straight shot down the hall to their ORs. Alex noticed the office bookshelves were stocked with three-ring binders from suppliers of various surgical instruments as well as the Baptist Hospital Procedure Manual.

"Getting settled in?" she asked when they were seated.

"Pretty much. Still unpacking, but we have it well under control, enough to get by, anyway. The other stuff isn't essential. Looking forward to starting work."

"And we're looking forward to having you here." She smiled.

Garrison stood. "I'll let you two talk business while I go finish clinic. You can find your way out?"

"I'll show him," Ellen offered.

With Garrison gone, she launched into business. "Reason I wanted to talk is to finalize your card." A surgeon's "card" listed preferences for routine instruments used in various types of cases: glove size, preferred sutures, routine instrument, and so forth. "Roberta was kind enough to fax me a copy of your craniotomy tray." Roberta, Ellen's counterpart from his old job, sent her a list of the instruments routinely used for opening a head. "So I believe we have that under control. There are a few other items I'd like to nail down. What's your glove size?"

Requesting this level of detail was impressive and not something done at the university hospital he left. "Seven and a half."

"Regulars or browns?" she asked, referring to the dark brown hypoallergenic gloves favored by some surgeons.

"Browns."

Alex realized being catered to with such deference was strangely refreshing, especially having spent his career thus far in the shadows of others. Yet he also found it somewhat embarrassing and the allure of being accustomed to such treatment frightening. Too much of this could transform a well-intended person into the stereotypical prima donna personality screenwriters loved to portray: megalomaniacs prone to throwing OR hissy fits while expecting red-carpet privileges at all times.

They had just about finished with Ellen's checklist when a thin, scrub-clad male tapped the window. Ellen motioned him in, explaining, "This here's Chuck Steven. Asked him to drop in, schedule permitting. Chuck is our neuro specialist. Chuck, this is Doctor Cutter."

Alex stood to shake hands. The scrub tech appeared to be in his mid-thirties with sun-damaged, acne-scarred cheeks and a face that managed to look serious and affable at the same time. A surgery cap covered his hair and a mask dangled from his neck.

Chuck launched straight into a Q&A session. "Any particular preference on how you want your cases handled, Doc?"

"Not really, other than I'm a stickler for maintaining sterile technique," Alex said. "My only real 'quirk,'" he said with finger quotes, "is to double glove during the openings. Then, soon as the bone flap's out, I re-glove and use a wet lap pad for wiping down the new one. Oh, and I use a ton of irrigation during cases." Although double gloving restricted finger movement slightly, the highest chance of breaking sterility occurred while opening the head.

After five more minutes of chitchat, they finished. Chuck needed to set up his next case, and Alex was anxious to find his way back to his pizza-oven car. Several projects still needed completion, especially refurbishing the grill since Lisa was expecting him to grill steaks for dinner.

As he worked his way to the second floor and the sky bridge back to the office building and parking lot, he paused to savor this new sense of professional happiness. Finally, after years of training and a stint in professional no man's land, he'd become his own man. No doubt Dick Weiner used and manipulated him, then discarded him. But if there could ever be a happy ending to that story, this might just be it. He hoped Lisa would adapt as well.

25

"Good morning, I'm Doctor Cutter," Alex said, entering the small exam room furnished with one exam table, two rolling stools, and a wall-mounted, fold-down charting desk. A man in his late fifties or early sixties sat in the chair opposite the desk.

"Hi, Doc, Bart Jorgenson." The man offered a meaty hand but didn't rise from the chair.

After shaking hands, Alex set the patient's chart—a manila folder only a few pages thick—on the chart desk and took a seat on the remaining rolling stool. "What brings you in today?" This was his fourth Any Doctor patient for the morning.

"Well, got me this dang prickly numbness," he answered, pointing to his feet.

Alex opened the manila chart to check the man's age on the front sheet. Yep. Sixty-two, pretty much the age he appeared to be. Alex tore a sheet of clinic notes from a tablet and jotted "CC-feet numbness," the *CC* standing for "chief complaint."

"Both feet or just one?" An important first step to narrowing the problem.

"Both."

Alex made a note of this. "Have any pain with the numbness?"

"Nope. Just burning numbness. Doggone thing bothers the heck outta me, 'cause when I rub it, I don't get no satisfaction." These last words brought a faint smile to the man's lips.

"Rolling Stones fan, huh?" Alex said, making another note. "How long's it been bothering you?"

"'Bout six months, give or take. Sorta hard to know for sure on account of it coming on so doggone slow."

The symptoms reminded Alex of peripheral neuropathy, a disorder affecting the nerves. "Any other medical problems you're being treated for? Diabetes, vascular problems?" Both were commonly associated with neuropathy.

The patient shook his head. "Nope."

Alex continued to take the man's history, the whole time thinking, *Naw, couldn't be.* But with each new detail, one specific diagnosis stood out as the top contender of all possible causes. History finished, Alex started in on the physical exam, testing the man's ability to feel pinpricks, light touch, and vibration from his toes to his thighs. The sensory loss appeared in a classic "stocking distribution" over both of the patient's feet and ankles, another telltale sign of peripheral neuropathy. His next job would be to find the root cause of the problem. Most peripheral neuropathies, he knew, were secondary to metabolic problems.

Alex handed the man his shoes and socks, then busied himself checking off various blood studies on a pink lab sheet.

"What you reckon is my problem, Doc?" The man pulled on a sock.

"I need some tests to be certain, but after we draw your blood, I'm going to have the nurse give you a shot of vitamin B12."

He stopped tying his shoelaces to look questioningly at Alex. "Vitamins? You're going to treat me with vitamins? Hell's bells, I can just pick me up some a' them at a Rite Aid an' save money."

Alex shook his head. "It needs to be a shot to make certain the vitamins get into your system. You might not be absorbing as much B12 as you need."

Minutes later he led the patient to the nurses' desk and handed the paperwork to the first available nurse. "Mr. Jorgensen needs this blood draw, and then give him three hundred micrograms of B12 IM. But in that specific order." It wouldn't do to give him the B12 first.

Before seeing the next Any Doctor, he detoured to his office to dictate a note, confident for having diagnosed his first case of peripheral neuropathy secondary to vitamin B12 deficiency, a condition he'd read about but never actually seen. Ironically, this was the same problem he faced in his oral boards. If the lab work confirmed the diagnosis, he'd ask a gastroenterologist to work up the reason for the B12 deficiency. Once these issues were settled, he'd send the patient back to his primary care physician with a treatment plan.

For a moment he savored the impact a correct diagnosis would have on the patient and his family, mildly amazed at this feeling of satisfaction for having diagnosed the problem. He hadn't really experienced this at his old job and was struck by how much more significant and personal it felt in contrast to chronicling another data point in the lab. Lab research seemed so detached and sterile in comparison. Not that clinical medicine lessened his drive for research, but it brought a different type of professional joy. Hopefully he'd just altered the course of a disease in another human. With renewed vigor he picked up the next Any Doctor chart.

That afternoon Alex purposely arrived at the auditorium five minutes in front of the 4:00 p.m. conference, his first teaching conference as vice program director of the residency. He intended to lead by example. A handful of residents were already chatting in the first two rows when he slid into his front row place, leaving the aisle seat on his right for Reynolds. Now with a say as to how these conferences ran, he intended to make sure they began and finished on time. He wanted the residents to consider them a high priority and believed that teachers who arrived late for conferences set a bad example, demeaning the importance of teaching.

At precisely 4:00 p.m.—in spite of Reynolds's absence—he announced, "Four o'clock, time to get going. But before we hear the first case, I have an announcement. I'm instituting journal club. It'll be held the first Wednesday of each month at my home, seven p.m. Snacks will be provided so that those of you who don't have time to grab dinner won't die of starvation. You can expect to receive your assigned articles in the next few days. Okay, who's got the first case?"

A midlevel resident approached the view box and illuminated a CT scan. "First case is a,..."

Alex settled in, listening closely to the presentation. As the professor, he was expected to solve any case a resident might throw his way, and with a program having this much clinical activity, curveballs and doozies were probably common.

Five minutes later, Reynolds slipped silently into his seat. Alex glanced at him, worried he might have offended him by starting conference before he arrived. Reynolds smiled with a nod, as if to say, "Perfect." A wave of relief swept over Alex.

Halfway through conference Alex surveyed the group again, realized all the residents were now present, and took the opportunity to announce, "I want to chat with the seniors after conference, so please stick around." He nodded for the resident to continue.

Reynolds glanced at his watch. "Don't believe we have time for another case. Conference adjourned."

Alex stood and caught Reynolds's eye. "Want to stick around, hear what I have to say to the residents?" The last thing he needed was for Reynolds to suspect he was working with the residents behind his back. This thought made him realize just how gun-shy and paranoid the ordeal with Weiner had left him.

"Naw, y'all go on. Need to get on back to the farm. Victoria's got some honey-dos waiting on me." Reynolds clapped Alex on his shoulder. "This have to do with what we discussed last week?"

"Exactly."

Reynolds winked and gave Alex a collegial punch to the shoulder. "Atta boy!"

With no other meeting scheduled to follow in the auditorium, Alex and the four seniors decided to stay put.

"I want to hear," Alex began, "how you guys view the teaching in this program. What do you see as strengths and weaknesses? Anything you tell me remains absolutely confidential." He made direct eye contact with each of them as he spoke. "Mark, why don't you start?" Alex picked him for no other reason than he remembered his name. He'd learn the others' names in time.

Mark glanced at the other three, obviously uncertain or uneasy about how much to divulge—a sure sign they still considered Alex an outsider. Hesitantly, Mark said, "The amount of call sucks."

Alex laughed. "That's par for the course. I'm asking about the teaching."

The others seemed content with continuing to let Mark be the group spokesman. "What teaching?"

The others snickered.

"Okay, let me be specific. How much teaching you guys get in the OR and on rounds? How well do the attendings educate you? Where do you see need for improvement?"

Another round of glances were exchanged.

"Reynolds tries," Mark answered tentatively. "But he's gone so much of the time ... and when he's here, he's so busy. The only time we actually learn from him is during our chief-year rotation on his service. There's the Monday conference, but that's not one-on-one. Garrison tries, I guess, but he's so busy running the clinic and operating that he's not around or available all that much."

The other three residents nodded agreement.

"How about other faculty?" This was the point Alex was really interested in. Someone would lose resident coverage, and Alex wanted to cut the least effective teacher.

"They're a joke," another resident said. "All they want's a warm body to hold a retractor or suck during a case. Only teaching we hear is, 'retract here' or 'suck here.' That's not teaching."

Pretty much what Alex expected. Nonacademic programs often suffered from a dearth of structured teaching. Larger surgical throughput counterbalanced that to an extent, but volume could only be effective if residents actually learned from those cases.

"Let's talk about the OR then. How much they let you do?"

"Depends on the surgeon," another resident offered, the group becoming more responsive now. "Some let us do a lot, others don't even let us open or close. Most of the time we're nothing but slave labor."

Another resident muttered, "Tote them bales, boy." The others laughed. Alex took a blank piece of clinic notepaper from his white coat and a pen from his breast pocket. "Let's go through the attending you cover and grade them." He'd suggested this approach to Reynolds during their talk last week. Reynolds liked the idea of making the residents responsible for determining which two private surgeons would be weeded from coverage. His actions, Alex realized, would generate resentment from the affected surgeons. But hey, you couldn't please everyone all the time.

26

Alex stood at his desk dictating a note on a patient when Dave Ray knocked on the doorjamb and walked in. Alex held up a just-a-minute finger while finishing his clinic note. He popped the cassette from the small, black Sony recorder and replaced it with a clean one. Instead of piling up a day's worth of dictation for his secretary, Kasey, he kept a supply of clean tapes in a bin on the desk, handing off a dictated clinic note after each patient. Once Kasey transcribed the tape, she rewound and degaussed it and dumped it on back in the bin. An advantage to this method was that it allowed Kasey to ask questions while the visit was still fresh in his memory.

"What's up?" Alex asked.

"Since you're not at full speed yet, thought we might be able to get us some tennis time in this afternoon, say five o'clock?" Then as an afterthought, "You do play, don't you?"

Alex glanced at the remaining schedule. "Five thirty too late for you?"

Dave smiled. "Naw, that works. There's a set of courts out on Poplar 'bout two miles north of your place. We can meet there. Think you can find it okay?"

He vaguely remembered noticing the courts during one of his exploratory drives through the areas adjacent The Gardens. "Should be able to."

"You seem to be settling in just fine. Like working at the clinic?"

Alex loaded a new tape into his recorder. "Things are running great. Much more efficient than my old job." Which was unbelievably true. The difference in efficiency between the university and clinic was mind-boggling.

Dave glanced at the degrees Alex had placed on the wall during the weekend. "Getting enough support? Lacking for anything?"

"No, I'm good. Have everything I need, except for surgical cases. I suspect those will come in time."

Dave nodded vigorously. "Count on it. A couple more months and you'll be so busy you won't have the luxury of afternoon tennis. You need anything, let me know. Got us a good set-up here. Those of us in administration do everything possible so the docs do what y'all do best, which is take care of patients. It frees you guys from doing what we do best, which is run the clinic. Makes for a win-win relationship." He knitted his fingers together in a sign of symbiosis.

Curious statement. "All right then, see you there."

"Oh, one other thing. You hear about Robert?"

Alex still hadn't learned all the partners' names well enough to flash on who Dave referred to. "Who?"

"Robert Sands. Does our pediatrics."

Alex vaguely remembered meeting him. Because Robert spent his time at the children's hospital, Alex saw him only at clinic meetings. "No. What?"

"Aw man … really a sad situation. Man can't do surgery anymore. *Ever.* In fact, we're thinking we're gonna have to stop him from seeing patients. Essentially, he's finished. Forced retirement."

Alex was shocked. The man he remembered was approximately his age. "Why? What happened?"

"Guess that means you ain't seen him lately. Man's low sick with a bad case of hep C. We're all figuring it's from sticking himself with a needle last month while working on a kid over at the trauma center." Dave shook his head in sorrow. "Damn shame, real damn shame. Man's a world-class surgeon."

Once infected with the hepatitis virus, always infected, just like HIV. "Jesus, he's young, too. Right?"

"About same age as you. Hired him six months before y'all."

Kasey popped in as Dave was leaving and handed two sheets of striped lab results to Alex. "Thought you might like to see this. The patient you ordered the B12 shots for?"

He quickly scanned the sheets, one listing hematology results, the other listing blood chemistries, any abnormal values in bold font. Several abnormalities were obvious: the white cell nuclei were multi-lobed, and the size of the red cells was excessively large, both findings typical of pernicious anemia. The other sheet verified the suspected B12 deficiency as the cause. A tingling elation snaked through Alex. *Nailed it!*

"Kasey," he said, handing the lab results back to her, "please have him scheduled to see a gastroenterologist. I'll fill out a consult sheet."

"Who you want him to see?"

Alex realized he had no idea. He glanced across the hall at Berger's office, but Martin was out. "Ask Garrison's secretary who he refers to. That should work."

Before turning his attention to the next Any Doctor, he quickly filled out the GI consult. Sitting back in his chair, he momentarily savored the glow of hitting a home run in his first at-bat, how different this felt to the hypothetical case on his orals. That one had been just that: hypothetical. This one, however, was startlingly real. He'd caught the problem before it could cause irreparable damage. This was *real* medicine, not some abstract, detached mental exercise in a test tube or under the microscope. Then again, the comparison wasn't really warranted. Practicing medicine and doing research were totally different endeavors, each yielding their own unique satisfaction. Which reminded him, he was behind on getting his lab activity running again.

He glanced at the half-written NIH application on his desk. Instead of tennis, he should be working on the grant. *Call Dave and cancel? No, I deserve a break.* The pace of clinic was faster than anything he had yet experienced, and certainly faster and denser than he'd expected.

Alex grabbed the phone before the second ring finished. He squinted at the bedside clock. 1:03 a.m. Rolling onto his left side, his back to Lisa, he said softly, "Alex Cutter."

"Sorry to call so early in the morning, Doctor. This is the Baptist West paging operator. Dr. Singh on Six West would like to speak with you. May I connect you?"

"You on call this evening?"

Yeah, but it's morning. "Yes." Alex sat with his legs over the edge of the bed now, a ballpoint and notepad in hand.

"Have a patient needs seeing ASAP. How long before you can get here?" Singh's words carried a tinge of panic.

Depends. "What's the problem?"

"Nurse found my patient unresponsive about an hour ago and called me. I came in to evaluate him but don't have a clue what's going on or what to do for him. I need help."

"Be there soon as I can." Alex mentally ran a list of things Singh could do while he was in transit. "Any recent imaging on the patient?"

"No."

"Then have them do a CT scan." Having never set foot in the building, he wasn't sure how long it would take to find them. "Which floor is the patient on?"

Years ago Alex discovered the comfort of wearing scrubs to bed. The nights he was on call, he brought a fresh set from the hospital and returned the old set the next morning. When he got called in for emergencies like this, it allowed him to get out the door a couple minutes faster.

He hung up the phone. Lisa—long since used to nighttime interruptions—was back asleep. He believed some of the calls no longer woke her. Noiselessly, he eased the bathroom door shut, rinsed his face, grabbed his electric razor, and headed for his car.

The empty streets allowed him to drive a bit above his usual speed as he headed west on Central, catching a long string of green traffic lights and even blowing through a red light after first checking for cops.

Driving left-handed, he worked on knocking down his stubble with the electric razor. Not a perfect shave by any stretch, but at least he wouldn't look quite so ratty.

Twenty minutes later he pulled into the parking lot outside the ER, killed the engine, and jumped out of the car, slipping on his white coat as he headed toward the automatic sliding glass doors. An armed security guard in the ER directed him to an elevator bank that would take him to the sixth floor.

He hurried down the dim hall toward the brightly lit nursing station where a middle-aged man with dark skin and gray hair stood talking in hushed tones to two nurses in blue scrubs. The man—literally wringing his hands—wore a tie-less white shirt, dark slacks, and a rumpled sports coat.

"Dr. Cutter?" the man asked with obvious relief. "Ajay Singh."

After shaking hands, Alex wiped the sweat from Singh's palm on his scrubs. "Tell me about your patient."

"This way," Singh said, pointing over Alex's shoulder. "We can talk as we walk." He started hurriedly down the hall. "I admitted him this afternoon from my office. He had a temp of 103, said he felt awful the night before. He looked dehydrated and sick enough that I decided to hospitalize him straightaway. I ordered codeine for his headache and some routine blood work and, because of the temp, the usual cultures. I started him on IV fluids, but in spite of it he seemed to get worse. When the nurses checked him"—he paused to look at his watch—"an hour and a half ago, they couldn't arouse him." As they entered a room, Singh pointed to a patient on his back, both eyes tightly shut.

Alex watched the patient for a few moments to get a gestalt impression. The man *looked* sick. The next thing he noticed was Cheyne-Stokes respirations, a waxing and waning breathing pattern indicative of decreased consciousness. This finding immediately decreased the odds of a psychological cause for the coma.

"What's his first name?" Alex asked no one in particular.

"Ethan."

Alex placed his hand on the man's shoulder and immediately felt the heat. "Yikes, he's burning up. Hey, Ethan!" he shouted, rocking the man's shoulder. "Wake up!"

The patient grimaced, both arms flexing at the elbows, hands fisted, eyes clamped shut—a classic posture associated with organic coma. The limb symmetry indicated both sides of the brain were equally affected. At this point Alex knew any further attempt to assess the patient's orientation would be impossible, so he turned to evaluating the cranial nerves. Normal eye function requires precise coordination of half of the twelve cranial nerves, making the eye exam the most important part of the neurological evaluation. Alex tried to open the upper lids, but the patient resisted. Alex tried harder. The patient responded again by flexing his limbs and clamping his eyelids together. Applying even more force, Alex was able to open the eyes enough to glimpse the pupils, equal in size. He tried to rock the head side to side, but the patient's neck wouldn't move. That gave Alex two critical findings: photophobia and nucal rigidity. In other words, light on the retina was painful, and his neck was stiff from irritation to the meninges. Together, these two pieces of information indicated bad news.

"Aw man," Alex muttered. "He has meningitis."

"What?" Singh asked anxiously.

"This whole picture," Alex said with a nod at the patient, "indicates meningitis. At his age, most likely cause is subarachnoid hemorrhage. But the history of onset doesn't fit."

Could it possibly be? Just like that case at Coastal County?

Alex looked to the nurse. "We need to set up for an LP." Then to Singh, he said, "He get the scan?"

He nodded. "He just returned when you arrived."

"Good. Before we pop a needle in his back, I need to check the scan to make sure we're not dealing with something weird like a mass up there," he said, pointing to the patient's head. A common mistake generalists made was to perform a lumbar puncture on a patient harboring a brain mass from a tumor or abscess, because removing spinal fluid lowers the lumbar spinal pressure, causing the increased cranial pressure to squeeze the brain out the base of the skull with disastrous results. More than a few patients had been inadvertently killed as a result.

"What do you see?" Singh asked Alex.

This question always amazed Alex, because CT scans seemed self-evident, clearly showing the brain, its various cavities, and the skull. There was nothing subtle about the anatomy. Then again, he supposed he was used to reading them. He wondered how well he'd do looking at a CT of the abdomen.

"Good news, bad news. Good news is we're not dealing with a mass, so we can probably get away with an LP. But the bad news is the brain's tight as hell." The entire brain appeared swollen from edema, the internal chambers collapsed, increasing the risk of a lumbar puncture.

Alex asked Singh, "You want to do it?" Offering Singh the chance to do the LP would allow him to bill for it. Alex suspected he wouldn't want to touch it, shifting all the risk back on Alex.

Singh waved his hand. "No, no, please, you do it."

"Better get going then." Alex headed for the door, thinking about the radiologist who would read the scan later that day—perhaps while enjoying her cup of morning coffee—and then bill for an interpretation rendered hours after the information had been processed and acted upon. This sort of after-the-fact analysis irritated Alex. If the radiologists wanted to charge for those readings, they should have dragged their asses out of their warm, comfortable beds to provide the service when it really mattered.

While they were downstairs viewing the CT scan, the floor nurses had wisely called for backup so that by the time Alex and Singh returned, a male nurse was waiting in the room, ready to help. On the over-bed table, the blue plastic water jug and box of Kleenex had been replaced with a disposable LP tray in the unopened cardboard packing box. "What size gloves, Doctor?" the floor nurse asked.

"Seven and a half."

"Prep solution?"

"Betadine."

"Bed's already flat," the male nurse said from the opposite side of the bed.

Alex slipped the pillow from under the patient's head and handed it to the male nurse who knew enough to fold it and place it between the patient's knees. Alex moved a chair next to the bed, removed the clear plastic wrapper from the LP package, and slipped out the sterile wrapped tray. "Ready?" he asked the nurse.

"Yep."

Alex motioned to Singh. "Get on the other side to help hold. He's not going to like what I'm about to do."

"Okay, on the count of three," Alex said once everyone was in position. "One, two, three." Using the draw sheet, Alex rolled the patient onto his right side then quickly pulled him toward the edge of the bed, positioning the patient's back parallel to the edge. The nurse and Singh held the patient in this position. "Don't move his legs until I'm ready, okay?"

"Roger that, sir."

Another ex-corpsman. Carefully, Alex pulled off the coverings to expose the molded sterile plastic tray of disposable plastic parts. He opened the gloves and slipped them on as the floor nurse poured Betadine solution into the prep-tray compartment, saturating three sponges. Alex painted the lower spine area with the solution, dropping each contaminated sponge into the wastebasket rather than back in the sterile tray.

Alex placed the sterile paper drape over the man's hips so the hole in the center was over the lower lumbar spine. Using the drape as a sterile barrier, he felt for the edge of the hip and adjusted the position of the hole slightly. As the Betadine continued to dry, he replaced the prep gloves with real surgical gloves for a better sense of feel.

With his left hand he felt for the space between spines, found what he wanted, and told the nurse, "Go ahead, curl him up with his knees as close to his chin as possible. We're only going to get one shot at this." Flexing the back opened up the space between the spines so the needle could pass more easily, but it would still be extremely painful.

"Get the head," the nurse said to Singh as he wrapped his muscular arm behind the man's pillowed knees. The nurse pulled the knees toward the head.

With his left thumb and forefinger straddling the desired space, Alex adjusted the angle of the long spinal needle to the correct trajectory, said, "Hold him," and pushed the needle through the skin. Reacting to the pain, the man tried to straighten, but the nurse and Singh held him in position.

"No local?" the nurse asked, surprised.

"Hurts worse than what I just did. And takes longer." With the long needle halfway in, Alex paused to sight along the patient's spine once more, double-checking the trajectory, making sure it was perfectly perpendicular to the spine. Satisfied, he continued to slowly advance the needle deeper, feeling each level of resistance the tip encountered, mentally visualizing the anatomy as the bevel approached the spinal canal. The tip grazed bone as it moved deeper, suddenly unimpeded, meaning he just passed into the proper space and was only millimeters from the target. Next, he felt slight resistance and gently tapped the needle a millimeter farther. He felt a slight pop as the bevel punched through the tough dura and entered the spinal canal. A perfect pass.

Alex readied the manometer and stopcock, withdrew the needle stylus, and quickly attached the pressure-measuring device to the end. "Hold the top of the manometer, please."

The floor nurse reached over Alex's shoulder to hold the top.

Left hand holding everything snug in case the patient moved unexpectedly, Alex opened the stopcock. "We'll do this slowly," he said to no one in particular.

Ugly, grayish viscous fluid began to slowly fill the manometer. "Ah, Jesus,... will you look at this. Nothing but pus." Fluid this thick would make an accurate pressure reading impossible.

"Call Infectious Disease," he said to the floor nurse. "Tell them to get someone up here STAT because we have a flaming case of meningitis. Ask them for a list of all the cultures they want." Most likely they were dealing with a bacterial infection, but you never could be sure. Whatever the problem, it looked like shit.

At this point Alex's job was essentially done. With the pressure measurement useless, he simply drained several CCs of the viscous fluid into three sterile collection tubes before withdrawing the needle. "Okay, we're done."

At 3:37 a.m. Alex set the brake and killed the engine. He sat in the silent car decompressing from mixed emotions. On one hand he felt exhilaration from slam-dunking the diagnosis. Only once before had he actually seen fulminate infective meningitis—an unconscious street person brought to the county hospital without a history. That time he performed the LP because an astute senior resident ordered him to do so. On the other hand he felt sorry for the man at Baptist West who could end up permanently damaged from a terrible disease. He tried to buoy his spirits by reassuring himself things would definitely be worse if he hadn't done the LP, but that helped only slightly.

Perhaps he'd been wrong about private practice. Diagnosing problems with life-saving implications brought such a different sense of satisfaction than research. Probably, he realized, because each case became a self-contained story with an obvious ending. Research seemed to have no such well-defined conclusions, most lab days simply generating more work and more questions. In comparison, these little case-by-case triumphs felt meaningfully tangible. In spite of being dead-dog tired, he decided to devote at least two hours the following evening to his grant submission.

He slipped from the car and made his way silently back to bed. Morning would come too soon.

27

"Got a moment?" Reynolds asked Alex as the Monday conference was breaking up.

Alex stood, waited for Reynolds to vacate the aisle seat. "Sure. What's up?"

Reynolds motioned for him to continue up the aisle with him toward the exits. "Got a cerebellar tumor scheduled for the morning but just learned I need to fly up to Bethesda on Navy Reserve business. Mind taking it for me?"

Two weeks had passed and still no surgical cases. This would be Alex's first surgery here, and he was anxious to begin this facet of practice. It seemed too long since his last case. "Yeah, sure. As long as your patient doesn't mind."

"Mind? Hell, that nigger's not going to know any difference. Just walk in the room and tell her you're the surgeon. Got her as a referral from a doc who doesn't send me much, so I know he doesn't give a lick either."

Alex recoiled at the use of the word *nigger* but said nothing. He immediately felt ashamed for his silence. His hesitancy, he realized, was from still being gun-shy after the Weiner experience. Last thing he wanted to do was piss off his chairman.

Reynolds must have read his mind, for he punched Alex's shoulder good-naturedly. "Don't like the word *nigger*, huh? Alls I can tell y'all is to get used to it. Us southerners don't mean nothing bad by it, 'cause niggers are niggers. Always have been, always will be. Hell, even niggers call each other niggers. It's something y'all are just gonna have to learn to tolerate."

Doubt it. Besides, a white man calling someone a nigger isn't quite the same thing.

"What's the patient's name?"

"Latisha Alexander, East 715. Y'all have a 7:30 start. Appreciate you taking her for me. Hadn't planned on this trip, just suddenly popped up is all." They passed through the doors into the hospital lobby where a young African American male in scrubs and bouffant surgical cap hummed while steering a floor buffer back and forth across the marble.

Alex jotted her name on one of the three-by-five note cards he stored in his breast pocket for exactly this purpose. "Naval Reserve, huh? Didn't know you served."

"Yep. If I stick with it another four years—which I have every intention of doing—I'll make admiral. Do that, figure I can retire. I can fix you up too if you want. Make some extra money while you're at it. Easy money. University and the clinic are required by law to give you the time, so it's one sweet deal. 'Sides, you don't have to do a damn thing except your monthly weekends and a couple weeks a summer. Reckon you might oughta look into it."

Alex wondered why Reynolds needed extra money on top of his clinic salary. Not only was he pulling down great money at the hospital, but Alex learned from Betty that Reynolds's wife sold real estate in the neighboring suburbs. "Thanks for the offer, but don't think I'm the military type."

"Hey, your loss. Offer's good if you change your mind. Okay, gotta get back to the farm. Owe you one for taking her for me."

Chart in hand, Alex knocked on the open door to the patient's room. "Ms. Alexander?"

A thin, dark African American woman lay in bed facing the TV, a hefty, lighter-skinned man in the chair to her right. She jerked at the sound, her head snapping around toward him. "Yes?"

He approached the bed, dragging the other chair with him. "I'm Dr. Cutter. I'll be your surgeon tomorrow. Dr. Reynolds was called out of town unexpectedly and asked if I'd substitute for him, assuming, of course, that it's okay with you. If not, I'm sure he'd be more than happy to reschedule for a time when he's back. May I sit down?"

"Any questions?" Alex asked, having spent the past twenty minutes explaining the surgery to the couple, who appeared scared shitless. He always hated this part because there was little he could do to assuage a patient's anxiety. He placed the consent form—which he'd filled out before coming into the room—on the sky-blue plastic chart binder. Next step would be for her sign.

She glanced from the consent form to Alex's eyes. "Only one."

"Yes?"

"Will you pray with us?"

Not used to this request, he had to actually think about his answer. "Yes, of course." *Whatever helps give you peace.*

She extended her left hand to him and her right hand to her husband. Not knowing what to do next, Alex simply held her hand and bowed his head. The husband reached out to hold Alex's left hand, forcing Alex to lean awkwardly across the bed, straining his back. It was Latisha who spoke first. "Heavenly Father, please watch over us,..."

As he listened to her words, he wondered, *Is her God listening?* If so, is he or she—if the deity possessed such a thing as gender—aware of his conflicted beliefs? Of how self-serving and hypocritical his charade of praying was? Instead of genuinely asking God to bless the surgery, he was merely trying to put this couple at ease. A pang of guilt hit. *Don't be ridiculous. You're doing the right thing. You can never be faulted for that.*

Can you?

28

"Cheers!"

Alex, Lisa, and Andrew and Diana Canter clinked wine glasses.

"Glad we're finally able to get together and be properly introduced," Andrew said. "Having been neighbors now for what, four weeks?" The Canters—who lived directly across the street—had introduced themselves the day the moving van pulled up to the curb in front of Alex and Lisa's house. The two couples had tried to schedule a dinner out ever since, but Andrew's job required business travel and Alex had night call, leaving this evening their first opportunity to socialize.

Lisa laughed. "Something like that."

They were at Ridley's, a basement barbecue joint off a downtown alley. Not much in the way of atmosphere, but the place had a regional reputation for killer ribs featuring a spicy dry rub instead of the more common wet sauce. Years of barbecue smoke, beer, and sweat filled the air with a musky but pleasant odor, attesting to the dive's long-standing popularity.

"How do you like the new job?" Andrew inquired. Both Canters spoke with British accents.

"So far so good, but we're still in the honeymoon phase. I'm sure that sooner or later something will come up to dampen my enthusiasm." He considered bringing up Reynolds's racist comments but decided against it. "Long as you brought up the subject of work, I'm sorry to say this will need to be a short evening. My debut surgery is scheduled for first thing in the morning. I want to be there early so I can make sure things are set up the way I like." He disliked talking about his work, so he redirected the conversion toward Andrew. "I'm sorry, but I don't think I know what it is you do." He vaguely recollected something about Proctor and Gamble.

"I'm a chemist by training, but now I manage people. The plant I'm presently assigned to is a division of Proctor and Gamble, which explains my need to be constantly running back and forth to Cincinnati. That's where our corporate headquarters are located."

"Ah, that does explain it. Where are you from originally?"

Diana chuckled. "Our accents give away that we're not natives?"

Alex nodded with a laugh.

Andrew was playing with the square packets of hand wipes from the table supply, perfectly aligning them in a stack, then spreading them out again. "A small town in England, actually." Pronouncing it *act-sley*. "I'd be shocked if you've ever heard of it, so I won't bother supplying a name. Suffice it to say, it's about a hundred kilometers northwest of London, if that's of any help."

"And the reason you're here in the States?" Alex remembered that P&G was an international company.

"Been with the company my entire career. Started straight out of Cambridge and have been a good soldier ever since, moving whenever and wherever they wished to post me. Probably still have one or two relocations before I retire. Just happen to be here in the U.S. at present."

Alex loved hearing what other people did in their jobs. "And what does a chemist-turned-manager do?"

Andrew smiled politely. "When a plant is having issues of various types, I am sent to sort them out. I reckon that qualifies me as a fixer of sorts, although there is no real job description. Not very glamorous, but it keeps a paycheck coming."

Alex and Lisa exchanged glances, making Alex wonder if she had the same question on her mind as he did. "How long have you lived here?"

Andrew thought about that a moment. "Over a year now."

"How do you like it?" Lisa asked, picking up on Alex's direction.

Andrew hesitated a beat. "Just fine."

"No culture shock?" Lisa probed. "It has been for us. We're West Coast people."

"Yes, well," Andrew said with a glance at his wife, "every place has its own unique culture, this being no exception. However, I must admit we have met a lot of nice people here. I'm sure you will too as you settle in, the neighbor boy included."

"Richie? The kid who sneaks around the neighborhood in camouflage and climbs over our fence with his pellet gun?"

"Mmhmm, that's him."

Andrew's words were guarded, leaving Alex to suspect he hadn't reached his level of upper management without honing some very strong diplomatic skills. Most likely, the Canters didn't feel comfortable divulging personal opinions to complete strangers. Perhaps they never would. One never knew what might filter back through the grapevine and cause embarrassment. Alex had hoped for an opportunity to discuss race relations in this city. So far, no African American he'd encountered had said a word about it. He sensed smoldering unrest among them and wondered how prevalent it was.

How could it not be present?

Guilt still nagged him for not voicing an objection to Reynolds's use of *nigger*. But he rationalized his silence by thinking he needed to establish himself before taking a stand on such politically loaded issues. He found his heightened sensitivity to such diplomacy both necessary and disgusting.

Diana rescued the pause in conversation. "And Lisa, what sorts of things are you interested in doing? Are you involved with any volunteering?"

"I worked at the university bookstore before we came here but don't work presently. Not sure if I'll look for a job. I've been asked to do some volunteer work, and that, hopefully, will keep me busy enough. I've grown very fond of being able to have options and control my time. It's a luxury."

Diana smiled, as if pleased with the answer. "We have a lovely book club that I'd be pleased to have you join—that is, if you're into that sort of thing. I find several of the ladies quite interesting."

"Yes, I'd like to try it."

Interesting. Lisa had never been one for luncheons or book clubs or other girly-girl activities.

"You folks ready to order?" asked their waiter, who'd been eyeing them since serving their wine.

29

For the 7:30 a.m. start, Alex arrived in the surgeons' lounge by 7:00 and went straight into the men's locker room without bothering with a cup of coffee from the three fresh pots on the counter hotplates. There he changed into scrubs, selected his style of mask, and pulled a bouffant-style cap over his head instead of the traditional surgeon's cap which became too hot during cases. Now dressed, he went to his locker and grabbed the mitered wooden box containing his loupes. He closed the narrow door, spun the combination once, and verified the lock was secure. Every now and then surgeons who didn't secure their lockers discovered valuables stolen.

He poked his head into Ellen's office. She was sitting at her desk, white Styrofoam cup in hand, talking to another scrub-clad woman. "Did Dr. Reynolds mention I'll be doing his case this morning?"

She glanced up and smiled. "Yep. His office called yesterday. Room East Three—straight down the hall, last room on the left. We pulled the patient's X-rays. They should be in your room already."

Your room. He liked the sound of that, made him feel respected as a surgeon again. Much better than at the university where OR personnel fostered the attitude of doing surgeons a favor by even bothering to acknowledge them. "Thanks."

Alex shouldered through the heavy swinging doors into the OR. His arms immediately sprouted goose bumps from the chilly, metallic-tasting conditioned air. One scrub nurse and one circulating nurse were busily counting instruments while a third nurse was filling out forms. An anesthesiologist was putting together an induction tray on his anesthesia cart as a black Sony boom box to the left of the tray softly played Bob Seger's "Hollywood Nights." A stack of CD cases was on the floor next to the cart. The scrub nurse glanced up. "Can I help you?"

"Yeah, I'm Doctor Cutter. I'll be doing the case today."

The scrub nurse nodded. "Hi again, Doc. I'm Chuck and this here's Susan," he said with a thick drawl. He pointed to the third nurse now spinning the large locking wheel of the autoclave door. "Roberta is just helping us set up. She's leaving as soon as we get started."

He remembered Chuck from his first meeting with Ellen but had already forgotten the other names, his mind too distracted by making sure the room was as he wanted it. He intended on making this case go perfectly. He believed that first impressions heavily colored subsequent interactions and wanted make known his attention to detail. He also believed that not paying attention to detail greased the skids for complications, and the longer you postponed the inevitable complication, the better your reputation. God help the surgeon who had a disaster in his first case at a new hospital.

The anesthesiologist waved hello. "Hi, I'm Bob Cole, your gas passer today." He wore an untied patient gown over his scrubs for extra warmth. A powder-blue surgical mask partially obscured a beard of closely cropped white hair. Twinkly eyes suggested a smile under the mask. Perhaps it was his choice of music or the way in which he introduced himself or the combination, but at once Alex felt a familiar resonance toward him.

"Bob Seger and the Silver Bullet Band. Love that CD. In fact, love most everything he's recorded," Alex said, walking over to the X-ray folder.

"Then we're going to get along just fine. That is, unless you want to hear whiny girl songs. Don't have any of those."

Alex picked up the folder to double-check the patient name and hospital number. "Good. Don't like them either. Give me Motown and Blues and that 'Old Time Rock and Roll.'"

"I'm also happy to turn it off if you want silence."

"You kidding? Can't drive if I can't jive."

Cole laughed and resumed organizing various syringes on the tray, filling them with the drugs used to put the patient to sleep. "Don't usually see surgeons until start time. Even then, some show up late. Anything special you want on this case?" "Night Moves" began, another of Alex's favorites.

"No. Just here to watch you guys set up, this being my first case here. But it's also something I've always done. Superstitious behavior, I guess." He felt a twinge of embarrassment from the admission and worried the OR staff might interpret his behavior as a vote of no confidence in their ability or as an attempt to micromanage their jobs. But he didn't apologize. If all went well, he wouldn't feel compelled to be here as early for the next case. He began sorting out which films to display on the X-ray panels.

"Anything special I need to know about for the case?" Cole asked.

"Yeah. You'll want a central line in her. We're going into the posterior fossa tumor with the patient in the sitting position." Then to the circulator, "I want a lumbar drain for the case." Alex nodded at the boom box. "'Working on mysteries without any clues.' That's got to be one of his best lines."

Cole dropped a drug vial into a drawer on the red anesthesia cart and locked the door. "He really captures the mood and mind of being a teenage male. At least that's the way his songs seem to me."

Just then the main OR door swung open as another scrub-clad male entered. "Doctor Cutter, Lawrence Drew. I'm assigned to be your official scut jockey from now until January." Alex recognized him as one of the first-year residents in the previous day's conference.

A circulator answered the OR phone and spoke a moment before putting a hand over the mouthpiece. "We're ready when you are," he said to Alex.

Alex glanced at Cole and raised his eyebrows. Cole nodded.

"Where you from, Larry?"

Lawrence and Alex stood at the stainless steel scrub sink, hands and forearms thickly lathered in rust-colored Betadine soap, Alex working the disposable plastic sponge over the surface of each finger in his habitually methodical manner. He wore his 3.0x magnifying loupes with the upper edge of his surgical mask taped securely over the bridge of his nose and cheeks to keep from fogging the loupe lenses.

"It's Lawrence, sir, and Birmingham's my hometown."

Finished with his left hand, Alex started in on his right. "I assume you mean Alabama and not Michigan."

"Yes, sir."

Alex wasn't used to people being addressed as "sir" and "ma'am" but had to admit it had a nice ring to it. "What are your plans once you finish up the program?"

"Man, that's a long time from now." Lawrence laughed as he worked the lather over his left pinkie. "Dad's a neurosurgeon back home. Wants me to join him, so reckon I might just do that. Why d'you ask?"

"Curious, is all." So far, no resident he questioned voiced the slightest inclination to pursue research or teaching. Alex kneed on the water valve to begin his arm rinse and bent over the sink. He kept his elbows below hand-level so water—which isn't sterile—drained from his hands down to his elbows instead of the reverse. Instead of sterilizing skin—which is impossible—these presurgery scrubs were intended only to minimize bacteria that live there.

Alex accepted a sterile towel from the scrub nurse and began to dry his hands, fingers first, then worked back toward his elbows, not bothering to dry past his mid forearms for fear of contaminating the towel and then his hands. His damp arms would dry in the surgical gown. "What's the biggest risk when using the sitting position?"

The resident was also drying his hands. "Subdural hematoma?"

"Nope. Air embolism," Alex said. "Next question: How does that happen?" He tossed the damp towel into the linen bin.

"Not sure, sir. Tell me."

Alex shook his head. "No, you tell *me*. Think about it a moment. If the patient is sitting, where is the heart in relation to the head?" Alex slipped his arms into the surgical gown the scrub nurse held open for him, gloved, then waited for the circulator to tie the back of the gown closed. Finished gowning, he stepped away from the scrub nurse so Lawrence could repeat the process.

"Guess it's below the head."

Alex smoothed his gloves over his fingers before holding out his hand for a saline-soaked lap pad. He would use it to clean any residual powder from them. "And that makes the venous pressure in the head what?"

Lawrence gave an understanding nod. "Guess it's negative. Hadn't thought of it till now."

"And what big venous structure will we work right next to?"

"Okay, I get it. Air embolism." Lawrence tied his gown also.

"And how will we know if that happens?" Before Lawrence could answer, Alex said to Chuck, "We can move in the overhead now," referring to a large instrument table with a platform for Chuck to stand on so he could hand tools down to Alex instead of working at his side where there was no room.

"Not sure, sir." Lawrence watched as Alex and Chuck jockeyed the table into position.

"Bob?" Alex asked the anesthesiologist. "Want to answer that one for him?"

"I have a Doppler stethoscope taped to his chest, right over the heart. It lets us hear any air sucked into his heart, because it causes what's called a 'windmill murmur.' That's pretty hard to miss. Once you hear it—and I hope you never get the chance—you'll never forget it." Bob turned up the volume of the Doppler for a moment so they could listen to the rhythmic whoosh of blood pulsing through the heart chambers.

"What do we do if we hear it?" Alex asked the resident.

Lawrence shrugged. "I don't know."

Alex stopped work. "How many months you been a resident?"

"Five."

Then you should know the answer. Then again, this was a prime example of why he chose to work with the most junior residents. "This time you get a free pass. Next time we discuss this you better have the right answer. Chuck, you know what to do?"

"Nope." Chuck continued organizing instruments in a stainless steel tray.

Alex smoothed out the sterile drapes, preparing the area they'd operate in. "First thing is to pack the wound to stop the air leak. Next we drop the patient into the horizontal position and turn them on their *left* side. Why the left side?"

Took Lawrence a moment to figure it out. "To keep the air in the atrium?"

"Bingo. Then what do we do, Bob?"

He answered without the slightest hesitation. "Use the central line I placed at the start of the case to suck out the air before it can embolize to the lungs or if the patient has a septal heart defect, on to the brain." A septal heart defect allows blood to short-circuit from the right to left sides of the heart and then up the carotid artery to the brain.

Alex smiled to himself. Lawrence was actually learning important information before the case began. "I can't emphasize this next point enough; the most important things to learn in your first year are the complications that can occur in each case you do. Know exactly what can go wrong and how to handle it, and you'll never be caught flat-footed. Most residents come into a training program with the mindset that good hands make good surgeons, but they're wrong. Knowing how to stay out of trouble and how to react if you *do* unfortunately get into trouble is what makes a truly excellent surgeon. Any fool can take a patient to surgery. The trick is getting them through the case with only a scar as evidence of your footprint."

Chuck said to Lawrence, "See? Momma didn't raise no fool."

With the patient draped and ready, Alex looked Lawrence in the eye. "Way I do this, the first time we scrub together I show you how I want things done. Then, next case, you do as much as you make me feel comfortable with, etc., etc., until you rotate off my service. Meaning, how much of the case you actually end up doing is determined by your ability. Got it?"

"Think so."

"Ready Chuck?"

"Roger that, sir."

Alex held out his hand. "All right, time to flash the healing steel."

Minutes later, the skin from the middle of the neck straight up to the back of the head was being held open with retractors, exposing the white surface of the skull. The cut edges of the skin were crimped with clips to stop blood from oozing during the surgery. The ligament in the middle of the neck that fused together the muscles of both sides contained little blood supply, so it was spread apart with hardly any bleeding. "Ever put in a burr hole?" Alex asked Lawrence.

"Yes."

"With a hand drill?"

"A what?"

Alex said to Chuck, "Cushing perforator, please." He turned back to Lawrence. "You need to know how to open a head without power tools. Archaic as that sounds, you never know when you might find yourself in a situation that forces you to use them. It's a good skill to know. I'll do the first one, you do the second." He felt the cold heft of the stainless steel drill placed securely in his hand, the instrument similar to the brace and bit carpenters use for cutting dowel holes.

As they were closing, sewing the muscles back together, Alex said to Lawrence, "Got a question for you." Alex was laying down one-handed knots—a skill he'd perfected during his surgery internship—one knot right after the other as quickly as possible. Chuck loaded the empty needle holders as soon as Alex returned them, rotating between two needle holders, while Lawrence snipped away the excess thread a few millimeters above each knot as soon as Alex finished tying one.

"What?"

"What would you say if I told you Humpty Dumpty was pushed?"

The only sound in the room now was Cole's boom box. After a moment Lawrence said, "This a joke?"

Alex kept working, one knot after the other, quickly closing on the skin now. "Just answer the question."

Lawrence cut another suture. "It's a trick question, right?"

Forceps in his left hand, Alex accepted another needle holder from Chuck. "It's a question. What's your answer?" With the forceps holding the edge of skin, he laid in one side of the suture then moved to the opposite side.

"I don't know. Can't think of anything to say, sir."

Cole chuckled. "Is it a conspiracy theory question?"

Alex pushed the needle through the opposite skin edge, jerked the needle from the thread, and started to tie the last knot.

Lawrence glanced at the wall clock. "You had a muffuletta yet?"

"No, what's that?" He decided to let Lawrence off the hook with the Humpty Dumpty question. For now. Last deep skin suture now finished, he had only the top surface of skin to close, which he proceeded to do with staples.

"It's a very special sandwich. Started in New Orleans originally, I think. Since we're fixing to finish up 'bout lunchtime, thought we could run cross the street and get us a couple. What say, you up for it? Can't live down here without trying one."

Lawrence and Alex sat on a weathered, rotting picnic bench ravenously devouring their sandwiches, the bright sun hot against their backs, drying their damp cotton scrub shirts. Alex had never tasted a sandwich with such a flavorful mix of meats, olives, and cheese. He was washing his down with a can of diet Pepsi while Lawrence opted for high-octane Dr. Pepper. Alex watched a ridiculously raised Ford F-100—with fifty megawatts of lights over the cab and confederate flag on the tailgate—park at Shoney's next door, country music blaring from the open cab windows.

"Get you a Moon Pie for dessert, you'll be right at home," Lawrence said.

Alex licked his fingers. "I'm so damn stuffed I couldn't think of possibly eating anything else. What's a Moon Pie?"

"Man, you ain't had you a Pie?" he said with an increasing accent. "What planet y'all from?"

Alex used a wad of napkins to dry his fingers. "C'mon, let's go check on our patient. Should be waking up about now."

30

"You're building quite a reputation," Linda Brown, Garrison's nurse, told Alex as they rounded the corner onto 7 West, the neurology and neurosurgery floor.

"Reputation?" Alex asked, unsure if this was good or bad. "What? With whom?"

"Among the residents," she replied with a good-natured lilt.

He stopped. "Hold on. You can't just say something like that and not explain it. This good or bad?"

She smiled at his obvious concern. "They say you like to teach and seem pretty good at it, too." She hesitated, as if there was more to say but wasn't sure how to phrase it.

"Go on, spit it out."

"For them it's good, of course. But you might oughta be a tad cautious."

Cautious? Why? "What do you mean? This is a teaching program; that's my job. I'm glad they regard me in that way. It's what I'm supposed to do."

She glanced down the hall, as if checking who might overhear their conversation. "Keep in mind there are other egos involved. Other faculty. Some of them might see you as a threat. Understand what I'm saying?" Linda was born and raised in Kentucky and spoke with an accent Alex now recognized as noticeably different from those who were natives here. When he first arrived, all accents seemed similar—people saying *Ah* for *I*, for example—but he'd since started to develop an ear for the numerous variations. It had so many more nuances than the generic West Coast accent that seemed so normal to him. He wondered if his accent grated on southern ears as much as theirs did on his.

"Faculty?" *Huh.* "A threat?"

"I'm sure you know your coming here had a few negative repercussions on a couple of them. Resident coverage, for one. Reynolds cut Harry Rosen loose. He's not your greatest fan now. In fact, you might say he's a tad pissed over it. Once people start talking, feelings become polarized. There might be some clinic members who come to resent your hold over the residents."

Alex massaged the back of his neck and exhaled a long, deep breath. He knew this might happen, at least in theory. Having Linda confirm it made him nervous. Then again, what could Rosen do to him? Probably not much. Unless he had some juice with people like Garrison. But other clinic members? Well, that could become a problem. But Garrison should be on his side, right?

"Let me ask you, what kind of political pull does Rosen have?"

"Not much. Fact is, he's not well liked."

Comforting. But still … He glanced up at the acoustic ceiling tiles. Linda had become a trusted source of medical center gossip. On the other hand, he suspected her ears were wired directly to Garrison's. The ghosts of paranoia seeded by Weiner rose again. Part of him sensed Garrison could be trusted. Another part warned to trust no one. He hated the ambiguity.

"Thanks for the advice. Now let's finish rounds."

Alex had been back in the office for about a half hour when Garrison knocked at his door. "Got a minute?"

"Sure. What's up?"

Instead of ambling into the office, Garrison remained at the door. "I'm assigning you to cover Tuesday out-clinics. Understand how that works?"

Alex shook his head. He'd heard the term from the nurses but hadn't asked for any details. Now, with a practice developing, he was being assigned fewer Any Doctors while simultaneously being integrated into other clinic responsibilities.

"Two days a week we fly out to towns about a hundred miles or so away. See folks in another doc's office during their day off. Helps them meet overhead while it gives us a place to see patients. Any patient needs a work-up, we schedule it back here at Baptist or the clinic. Helps drum up business and hold on to our referrals. Also gives those towns some neurosurgical coverage. Everybody wins. Starting tomorrow, you're scheduled for Tuesdays. Two Clinic Tuesdays, we call 'em 'cause we see patients in one town in the morning and another in the afternoon, then fly back on home. Meet us out at the commercial aviation terminal by 6:30 a.m. That's the commercial terminal, not the one folks fly in and out of. Know where that is?"

"At the airport, I suppose."

"Yep, except instead of going to the main terminal, you take the side road away from it. There's signs to help you find it."

Alex wasn't a big fan of small airplanes. "Who's flying?"

Garrison smiled. "That would be me. That's the Cessna I told you about. My partner and I lease it back to the clinic for these out-clinic trips. Say, long as we're on the subject, you might oughta come out to the Arlington airfield Saturday. I'm flying in an aerobatics competition. Might just get you interested in taking it up. Would love to teach you a few things while we're in the cockpit Tuesdays. Might as well be doing something during those flights other than mashing hemorrhoids."

Fuck!

Alex opened the chart on his next patient and immediately recognized the name: Bart Jorgensen, the man with the B12 deficiency neuropathy. He'd been practicing long enough now to be seeing long-term return patients, and Bart was one he really looked forward to following. He pushed open the door and stepped in the exam room.

"Hey, Bart, how you doing?"

The man grinned broadly. "Just fine, Doc, just fine. Tingling in my feet's all gone now, and I reckon the sensation's a hundred percent." He sounded as happy as his smile was broad.

Minutes later, exam finished and the patient discharged from his care, Alex dictated a letter summarizing the diagnosis and treatment plan to Bart's physician. He recommended Bart see him every couple weeks for vitamin B injections. The gastroenterologist had diagnosed and treated chronic gastritis as the cause of the vitamin deficiency, so the case had been amazingly textbook. Four months ago he never would have believed such personal satisfaction could come from diagnosing and treating medical neurological problems outside of surgery. In retrospect, becoming a doctor had always been his only motivation for working so damn hard to enter and graduate med school. As a youngster he'd never considered research as a calling. But all that had changed once his mother's illness became apparent. No one knew anything about those awful tumors other than they were universally fatal and untreatable. As pleased as he was to be honing his clinical skills, he also yearned to be back working in the lab. He took some satisfaction with the small amount of research he was managing in collaboration with Cell Biology, but it was not nearly what he would prefer. Every day now, it seemed his clinic responsibilities increased, making it more difficult to eke out any time at all in the lab.

10:12 p.m. Instead of watching television with Lisa, Alex holed up in his study putting finishing touches on his NIH grant application. Tomorrow he'd have Claude FedEx it to Bethesda to make the deadline for the next round of evaluations. Getting his research back on track would be the one missing facet of having the perfect practice: clinical activities, teaching, and research. As more time passed, he also worried about his work becoming trumped by other labs. The previous week, a competitor lab had published a paper in *Science* claiming two of Alex's prior findings were valid. If Alex didn't get his research back on track soon, other researchers would leave him in the scientific dust. He sat back in the chair to massage his aching neck muscles. Although he couldn't see how, there had to be a way to carve out more lab time.

31

"HEY, JIM, HOW WAS Bethesda?" Heading back to the office after rounding on the post-op patient, Alex saw Reynolds walking his way from the opposite end of the sky bridge.

Reynolds stopped and polished his smudged glasses with a tail of his white shirt. "Good trip. Great bunch of guys up there. Think you'd really mesh well with 'em if you have a change of heart. I know you didn't think much of the idea last time we talked, but I reckon you've had time to think on it for a spell now. Offer's good—just say the word, I could get you in with a nice commission." Reynolds inspected the lens, but the only difference Alex could see was a new pattern to the smudge.

"Thanks for the offer, but I just don't have time for the Reserves." *Well, partly true.* Honestly, the hassle didn't seem worth the few extra dollars. Besides, any extra time should be devoted to research. "Was hoping to run into you so I could tell you about your patient I operated, the cerebellar tumor? Surgery went fine but the tumor's a lung met. Not a smoker either." He had less empathy for smokers who developed cancer and felt a twinge of shame for harboring such a prejudice. "We rescanned her and it appears to be the only one, but still, not good for her. Had oncology work her up, and they couldn't find any other mets either. But you know how that goes; they're there, sure as hell."

Reynolds glanced at his watch as if anxious to be somewhere. "Yep, heard all about it. Thanks again for doing her."

Alex's suspicion gelled: Reynolds hadn't really needed the extra time to catch his Bethesda flight. The only reason he asked Alex to do the case for him was to evaluate his surgical ability. In all likelihood, he had the residents give him a detailed report. Did he pass the test? He suspected he had.

"She's coming into the clinic later today if you want to stop by to see her."

Reynolds palmed his thinning comb-over, patting it back in place. "Naw, no need to see her. Only saw her once before. Hell, she probably doesn't remember my name. Besides, what she needs now is a good oncologist, not a neurosurgeon." Reynolds seemed to think of something that trumped his pressing engagement. "I mention to you Val's running for town council?"

Alex needed a second to realize Val was Reynolds's wife, Valarie, a certified, grade-A southern belle with newly developed political aspirations. "Don't remember hearing you mention it."

"Yep. Has her a good chance to win, too. Speaking of which, we're hosting a fundraiser Saturday after next out at the farm in support of the upcoming senate race. Like y'all to come. Be a good chance for Val to get to know your pretty bride better. Can I count on y'all?"

Uh-oh. Alex scrambled for an acceptable excuse to decline. He hated politics and did everything possible to steer clear of any involvement. More importantly, Reynolds's invitation seemed nothing more than a weakly disguised solicitation for money. On the other hand, Reynolds was his boss, and there was the old saying about biting the hand ...

"Thanks for asking, but we already have plans for that night," Alex lied. "Tell you what, how about I make a small contribution to the campaign?" He saw this as the best way to control the monetary damage. "Just let me know where to send the check."

"Good man. My girl will drop off the information at your office. Your Republican Party membership current?"

Shit! Why do people automatically assume doctors are card-carrying Republicans? Admit the truth or spin another little white lie? Months ago, when his world crashed down on him, Alex pondered how men like Waters, Weiner, and Reynolds rose to be leaders in organized neurosurgery. Well, standing here in front of him was a living lesson: men like Reynolds ascended political ladders through active organizational involvement, the same way Alex established his scientific reputation by publishing in journals and presenting at meetings. This simple concept only now came sharply into focus, the corollary being this: leaders promote colleagues who share their attributes and vision, and Alex—certainly this early in his tenure—intended to stay on Reynolds's good side to avoid another Weiner disaster.

"Truthfully? It isn't." Which, taken literally, wasn't actually a flat-out lie. "I'll take care of it right away."

Reynolds punched his shoulder. "Good man." Another glance at his watch. "Wish I had more time to talk, but I'm running late."

"Before you go, you know I submitted the grant?"

"Yep. Claude told me. Glad to hear it."

Alex continued toward the hospital, thinking the first thing he should do when he reached the office was to ask Kasey to obtain the necessary form to join the local Republican Party. Chances were Reynolds wouldn't check, but if for some insane reason he did, Alex didn't want to be caught lying. Signing up would make him feeling duplicitous and slimy, but he was stuck in a lose-lose situation. Then again, sometimes you had to do distasteful things to stay in the good graces of those to whom you are beholden.

Right?

Right.

Probably wouldn't hurt to sign Lisa up too.

32

"HE CAN'T POSSIBLY THINK you want to learn to fly. Or does he?" Lisa asked from the passenger seat. She held a map on her lap, open and folded to the section for Arlington—a small town some twenty miles to the east—and its airfield.

"Already told him a couple times I wasn't interested." He adjusted the visor to block out the glare from the blazing sun. He supposed the clear sky and lack of wind made for ideal flying weather, especially for aerobatics, but hey, what did he know? Next to nothing when it came to flying.

She turned toward him. "Then why did you order that computer program?"

"*Flight Simulator*?"

"Yes."

"Looked like it'd be kind of fun," he admitted sheepishly. "Didn't cost much." The new version of Microsoft's DOS-based game had just been released for Windows 3.1. Alex bought it as a way to familiarize himself with flying so he wouldn't look totally stupid in Garrison's eyes. "Besides, I can at least show him I didn't categorically reject the idea. He seems to be pretty gung ho on the subject."

"And we're driving all the way out here for what reason exactly?"

Farmland stretched as far as the eye could see to either side of the straight, two-lane highway, thick, green clumps of kudzu spiraling up wood telephone poles and power line towers and engulfing Burma Shave signs. Kudzu: another idea that sounded good at the time but ended up having nasty, unintended consequences.

"I could give you some inane answer, but the unvarnished truth is we're doing it to suck up. He is, after all, clinic CEO, which makes him my other boss."

The airfield was a large, flat, grassy field with one cracked cement landing strip and a Quonset hut at the terminus of the approach road. Brightly painted planes were parked at haphazard angles along the side of the runway with people milling around chatting and inspecting the machines. As soon as Alex killed the car motor, he could hear an airplane overhead. A handful of spectators peered skyward, hands shielding eyes from the baking sun. Alex looked down the runway and recognized what looked like Garrison's red and white Pitts from the picture so proudly displayed on his desk.

"That could be his plane over there," he said, pointing.

As they approached the aircraft, Alex spotted Garrison in suntans, a brown leather, fleece-lined aviator jacket, and a leather cap with goggles atop. If it wasn't for Garrison's slumped posture, he would have been the dashing image of the World War I flying ace. Alex waved and yelled a greeting.

Glancing their direction, Garrison's face broke into a broad grin. He extended his hand to Alex. "Glad y'all could come on out. I'm up next, so y'all's timing couldn't be better to see me in action." Garrison spoke with enthusiasm Alex hadn't heard from him before. He nodded at Lisa as if she were an afterthought in a mano-a-mano discussion.

"Looking forward to it," Alex said. *Tell me I really didn't just say that.*

Just then, Linda Brown approached. She wore tight jeans, a denim shirt, and a Dallas Cowboys ball cap with her ponytail sticking out the back. Out of her usual white uniform, Alex didn't immediately recognize her. *Interesting seeing her here.*

The four of them stood staring at each other for an awkward moment until Alex said, "Linda, I'd like you to meet my wife, Lisa. Lisa, Linda. Linda's the nurse I've told you so much about." Was the invitation to come watch the flying accidental or intentional? Was Garrison sharing something about his relationship with Linda? He knew the two were professionally close, but socially? Hmm.

Lisa flashed Alex an inquisitive expression, turned to Linda with hand extended. "Glad to meet you. Alex says you've really made his transition much easier than he expected. Thank you."

Garrison was beginning to get antsy, patting his pockets and glancing around as if he'd lost something. He muttered to no one in particular, "Damn, forgot my ChapStick."

Linda snaked fingers into the front pocket of her tight jeans. "Brought it for you," she said, handing a tube to him. Garrison quickly applied the lip balm, capped the tube, and started to hand it back to her.

"No, keep it. I'll get it from you later."

He zipped up his jacket. "All right then, better get ready." He pointed at an area next to the Quonset hut. "Best place to watch is over yonder."

Ninety minutes and a mild sunburn later, Alex and Lisa retraced their route back to town, Alex driving again, Lisa navigating. After a prolonged silence, Lisa said, "Something's going on between them."

"Between who?" He realized how lame that had to sound, but for some undefined reason, he felt slightly defensive of Garrison.

"Oh, for God's sake, Alex. *Garrison* and *Linda*. Who else would I be talking about?"

Point taken. Still, he hated personal intrigue. If they had something going on, well ... "None of our business."

"Maybe, maybe not. But have no doubt he's messing around with her. Question is, why would he ask you to come out if he knew she'd be there? Or does he seriously think we can't see what's going on? I don't get it."

Alex decelerated as they came up behind a faded red Chevy pickup stacked high with bales of livestock hay, fenders dented from years of abuse. As soon as they came to a straight section of road, he'd pass it. "Honey, what he chooses to do outside the office doesn't affect me. But I kind of have to admit, if I were married to Anne, I'd probably fool around, too."

She stabbed a finger against his ribs. "Not nice, bad puppy! But *Linda*? I mean why fool around someone you *work* with? That's a classic recipe for disaster. And why her? She really doesn't have a lot going for her in the looks department."

"Jesus, speak about bad puppies! Not nice at all. To tell you the truth, she's a real sweetheart. Besides, he probably doesn't have the time, personality, or inclination to look elsewhere. They've been working together for God-knows-how-long and probably have grown quite close. Just makes you wonder what's going on in the Majors's household. Obviously they have problems."

"Obviously. But look out, Alex. I'm telling you—this isn't good for you or the clinic. He's vulnerable."

"How so?"

"You have to be kidding me, right?"

33

Tuesday morning Alex pulled into the airfield lot and parked next to Garrison's lime green Chevy station wagon. Alex doubted many people would go out of their way to drive one of those, but for some strange reason it seemed to fit Garrison's personality. This part of the airport serviced private planes and charters; the big terminal for commercial airlines could be seen a half mile away. Having not been given specific instructions on where to go or what to look for, he could've easily missed the single-story rectangular hunk of fading red clapboard that served as the terminal. The wall facing the small asphalt parking lot displayed various signs advertising charter and maintenance services: Bardall, Penzoil, Mid South Charters. His dash clock showed 6:25. Five minutes early.

He opened the door into a tired lobby of five ratty leather armchairs, a cracked brown leather couch, and a wall map of the region with concentrically expanding mileage rings centered on the airfield. A chipped faux-walnut laminate counter separated the waiting area from two equally second-hand empty desks. Linda Brown and one other familiar clinic nurse were waiting by the door to the runway. Linda noticed him and smiled. "He's outside doing the preflight. We should be ready to take off in two, three minutes, so if you need to use the bathroom, better do it now. Hope you're prepared for a long day. These always are."

Alex nodded. These Tuesday trips would chew up one more weekday that he preferred be spent on research. But his paycheck came from the clinic, so …

At ten thousand feet with Garrison at the controls and Alex riding shotgun, the nurses in the back two seats, Garrison said over the headphones, "Why don't you take her for a bit?" This sounded like a statement not up for negotiation. Was he serious? A bolt of terror struck as Garrison lifted his hands from the control yoke and pointed for Alex to assume the slave controls.

"Go ahead," Garrison said, grinning. "Steers just like a car, except you got foot controls too. But don't worry about those none, I'll handle that part for now. Oh, a word of advice: don't lean into the yoke. That's a normal tendency to do. Keep it neutral."

Alex didn't touch the damn controls and wasn't about to start. "No, hey, wait a sec. I don't have the slightest idea what I'm doing."

The plane continued to fly with both sets of controls abandoned, the sight making Alex nauseous.

Garrison pointed to the compass on the front panel. "Just keep a heading of 320."

Gingerly, Alex took hold of the yoke with his fingertips but kept his feet as far from the pedals as possible.

"Don't look at the ground. Just look straight ahead or at the altimeter and compass."

After five terrorizing minutes Alex couldn't handle the gut-churning anxiety any longer. And if Garrison didn't like it, too bad. "Can't do it. I'm getting dizzy." True. He was feeling the same weird empty-stomach butterflies as when atop a high building or bridge. In concert with the dizziness was an odd suicidal urge to jump. If the clinic required him to fly this trip every Tuesday simply to scrounge up a few extra patients, then he'd make damn sure to build such a vibrant surgical practice that the clinic would choose to keep him in the OR instead of doing this shit. He resented Garrison's repeated attempts to interest him in flying, especially by forcing him to take control of the plane.

"Sweetie, I'm home," Alex called out as he came through the back door from the carport. 7:30 p.m. He'd walked out this same door at 6:00 a.m. and was now exhausted.

Minutes later, after changing into jeans and a T-shirt, he and Lisa sat at the kitchen table enjoying a glass of wine and exchanging accounts of their day. Lisa liked her involvement in the two organizations she volunteered for and had developed friendships with several other women. They both, Alex reflected, were living very different lives from what they'd left. He thought back to the leisurely pace of academics where his long hours in the lab paled in comparison to the present grind. And although he enjoyed the challenge of building a practice, he still missed the intellectual challenge of research. The phone rang. Alex glanced at Lisa. With no inpatients that night and not being on call, he'd anticipated a relaxing evening of mindless television. With a feeling of dread, he reached for the telephone. "Cutter here."

"Doctor Cutter, Steve Stein."

"Can I have a word with you, Jim?" Luckily, Alex caught Reynolds in the lounge between cases, sitting with two scrub-clad men, Reynolds howling as if one of them had just cracked the funniest joke in the history of the world.

Couches and chairs lined three of the four walls, the fourth wall featuring a built-in counter on which sat a three-burner coffee maker with all pots miraculously and constantly full of freshly brewed coffee during the usual surgery day. These bountiful pots were, Alex believed, the eighth wonder of the world. He suspected that whoever was in charge of surgery made sure fresh coffee was available twenty-four hours a day as a courtesy to the surgeons. The diagonal corner from the hall door featured a large TV perpetually tuned to CNN. Weekday mornings, before the day's first cases kicked off, two large boxes of maple bars, doughnuts, and other sugary treats mysteriously appeared—another perk that didn't exist at his previous practice. The university didn't bother with things like that because the university surgeons were held captive to the system, having no other place to operate. Here, surgeons could just as easily practice at the methodist hospital across town. "Please your customer" being a prime rule for running any business.

"Yeah, sure," Reynolds said, then turned to the others. "Y'all've met Alex Cutter? Alex, this here's Johnny Kirk and his brother Ralph, two world-class heart surgeons. Alex's my new second-in-command." Smiling, they nodded at each other as Reynolds pushed wearily off the worn leather couch.

They took their conversation out to the hallway that separated the hospital's two wings like the center of a large H. Reynolds removed his glasses to polish them with his green scrub shirt. "What's on your mind?"

"Got called last night from a kid who worked in my lab during summer breaks. Good kid, did good work. Ended up at Vanderbilt for med school. Stayed on for a straight surgical internship with a verbal assurance of being their pick for the neurosurgery residency when his internship finished. Then Pendergrass, the chairman at the time, retired for health reasons, and the dean brought in McNamee from Hopkins."

"I know." Reynolds held up his glasses to inspect in the overhead fluorescents. "Surprised the hell out of everyone. Dan Sugar was the heir apparent for the job. Reckon it's sorta reminiscent of what happened at your old place."

"The long and short of it is the kid was passed over for a guy McNamee brought with him."

Reynolds anticipated the punch line. "That program's accredited for only one slot a year."

Alex nodded. "Stein called me at home last night for advice. I was thinking that with Slater"—a first-year resident—"being fired last month, we might want to consider bringing him on." Night call depended so heavily on a full complement of residents that unexpected holes in the rotation rippled back on all of them, producing hardships.

"Room's ready, Dr. Reynolds," a nurse called from down the hall. Reynolds returned a just-a-minute signal and slipped his glasses back on. "What'd you tell him?"

"Said I'd talk to you about it."

Reynolds tossed his old, balled-up mask at the wastebasket and started to tie a new one around his neck. "See if he can get on down here Friday. We'll have a couple of the seniors give him a sniff test, see what they think. After all, the residents are the ones who'll work with him. We sure could use another good resident. Good thinking."

"I can't thank you enough, Doctor Cutter. I'll never forget this."

Alex was leading Stein back through the maze of halls and stairs to the garage where he had parked when he rolled into town in the middle of the night. The hospital maintained small, utilitarian hotel rooms in one of the three professional office towers for family members in need of lodging. Alex had arranged one for Stein with instructions to meet for breakfast in the cafeteria.

"Glad it worked out for you. How soon you think it'll take to close up your apartment and move here?"

Stein scratched his prematurely balding head. "May have to forfeit the deposit, but I'll come soon as I can. Don't have much other than my clothes and a guitar. The place came furnished. Late next week, I suppose."

"Don't worry about the deposit. I'll reimburse you." He suspected Stein, like most med students, was in the hole several hundred thousand dollars in student loans.

They pushed through the aluminum and glass doors from the sky bridge into the parking garage, the abrupt switch from the A/C chill to hot, thick humidity as acute as running into a wall. Having arrived at such an early hour, Stein scored a prime spot on the second floor where the "Doctors Only" slots ended. Stein stopped next to a faded red Toyota beater. "This one's mine." For a moment the tired young man stood, one hand on the driver's door, the other at his side, overnight bag in hand. He seemed to wrestle with finding his words. Finally he said, "Thanks again, Doctor Cutter."

"Hey, you're doing everyone a favor, especially the junior residents. You'll patch a hole in the rotation. Doubt you'll hear any complaints about that."

Stein unlocked the door, wearily tossed his bag into the passenger seat, and sighed. "Better start back. Long drive and lots of work to do."

Alex shook his hand, pleased at seeing a friend from his previous life. He felt a connectedness to the kid that was more than just memories of times shared in the lab. For whatever reason, he lacked the same degree of resonance with people from the South. The contrast made him aware of his doubts of ever being able to adapt to this culture.

"Good. See you in a week."

34

"I NEVER REALIZED THERE were so many ways to prepare catfish," Lisa said. "We never had it before coming here."

It was Friday evening; Alex, Lisa, Garrison, Anne, and the Canters sat at a round table with a white linen tablecloth in the University Club dining room. Every Friday, Alex learned, the club offered a themed buffet, and that evening was Catfish Night. Large stainless-steel serving dishes filled a buffet table with seven different catfish preparations: barbecue, teriyaki, fried, Cajun, on and on.

"They're very tasty fish, long as you don't have to see their heads," Diana Canter said.

"Ugly devils, they are," Andrew added.

"You're a member here," Alex said to Andrew. "How long did you have to wait before you were allowed to join? I submitted my application over two months ago and still haven't heard a word from whoever handles memberships. I've called and left messages, but not one of my inquiries have been returned." He popped the last bite of Cajun catfish into his mouth.

Andrew delicately set down his fork on his plate and clasped his hands together as if preparing to say something earth-shaking. "Have you been interviewed by the membership committee yet?"

Just then, out of nowhere, Anne announced rather loudly, "Right now, this very moment, I could go outside, get in my car, and drive straight off a cliff, and no one would give a damn." Her heavily bagged eyes stared at a distant point beyond the wall behind Alex.

Uneasy silence came over the table as all eyes turned to her. She dropped her dejected gaze to her untouched plate of catfish and drained the double Johnny Walker Red in her right hand.

She serious? He glanced at Garrison, who simply continued to rock the ice in his glass of scotch back and forth, seemingly unconcerned and as inscrutable as ever. Lisa shot Alex a told-you-so glance.

Andrew cleared his throat. "Yes, well, the way it works here is you must have a member—either Garrison or myself, but Garrison's been around the longest, so he's the natural one for the task—to host you here in the men's bar two or three consecutive Thursdays. Thursday evenings are when the membership committee convenes for a bit of conviviality. Protocol is for him to introduce you so you may chat them up, tell them a bit about yourself. If they decide they like you, you're invited to hand over an outrageous initiation fee. This is how the application process works. Right, Garrison?"

Lisa, still staring at Anne, began to say something when Alex almost imperceptibly shook his head. He asked Andrew, "How is a person supposed to know this?"

Andrew made a face. "I assume you're to know this from being told so by your sponsoring members. Serves as an internal selection process of sorts."

"I'll bring you down next week if you like," Garrison quickly volunteered.

"Wait a sec." Alex held up his hand. "What does this place have to do with the university?"

Andrew laughed. "Seriously? Absolutely nothing. Why?"

For a moment Alex was slack jawed. "Well, the name is the University Club."

Andrew paused to sip water. "Only because an applicant is required to hold a university degree as a prerequisite for membership consideration. Nothing more, nothing less."

This made no sense. "Because?"

Andrew nodded for Garrison to answer.

"The club originated in a, uh, political period much different than now," Garrison said. "By requiring a university degree, a segment of society was automatically excluded from membership. Well, I guess excluded is a harsh word, but I can't think of any other way to explain it at the moment." Garrison seemed to struggle for the right words, perhaps aware the others at the table might be a tad more socially liberal than the club's forefathers.

"You mean African Americans?"

Garrison nodded. "Well, them too."

"Them *too*? Who else isn't allowed membership?" Alex asked in shock, now wondering if squash remained a sufficient reason to join.

"Jews aren't allowed in either," Garrison said matter-of-factly.

"Are you serious?" Alex saw Lisa roll her eyes.

Lisa held up her hand. "Wait a minute, back up. I want to ask about the 'men's bar,'" she said, using finger quotes. "What's that all about?"

Garrison smiled, perhaps aware he was about to ruffle her feathers further. "Women aren't allowed in here except for the Friday dinners, like we're having now. Otherwise ..." he simply held up both palms in an I-didn't-make-the-rule gesture.

"And the point of that silly rule is?" she asked.

"The way it was explained to me," Andrew said, "is that this area provides a sanctuary, a place where a man is able to enjoy a drink with fellow members without worry of being disturbed."

"You're—"

Andrew continued, "Should a wife call looking for her husband, the bartender—who knows every member by name—will hold up the phone for all to see and call the man's name. If said man wishes to not be disturbed, he'll not say a word. The bartender will then tell the wife he's not here." He raised his eyebrows as if to be held innocent of the misogynous attitude of the club's Board of Governors. Alex was having difficulty deciding whether Andrew bought into the idea or was being sufficiently diplomatic to thwart any blowback to his executive position with Proctor and Gamble. Did the Canters join purely to satisfy social commitments required of him at work, or did they seek a self-image status symbol? Just another ambiguity that made them a curiosity to Alex.

"What if a single *woman* applies for membership?" Lisa asked, obviously irritated.

Garrison shrugged. "She should know enough not to."

Lisa turned to Anne. "C'mon, let's go to the little girl's room."

"Clyde, I'd like you to meet a new partner of mine, Alex Cutter." A scotch and water in hand, Garrison was standing next to the polished oak bar with one foot on the brass rail; it was the first Thursday evening since the enlightening catfish dinner.

A ruddy-faced, overweight man swiveled away from his cronies, recognized Garrison with a smile, then looked Alex up and down. Having sized up the situation, Clyde extended a meaty right hand, his other hand still gripping a tumbler of amber liquor. "You another brain cutter?"

"Guilty as charged, sir." Alex shook hands. *Can't believe I'm actually stooping to this.*

"Where y'all from?"

Nothing like getting straight to it. Alex filled him in on his background. Several of the men were smoking cigarettes, the polished wood bar scattered with heavy, amber-colored glass ashtrays which the black bartender constantly emptied and wiped clean.

"Alex's a squash player," Garrison said. "Been fixing to join the club so's he can play. Got himself a pretty little bride who'd love to run around the tennis courts in one of those short white skirts." After jokingly elbowing Alex, he explained, "Clyde here chairs the membership committee." He gave a wink only Alex would see, Garrison now fully into his back-slapping good-ol'-boy shtick that seemed suspiciously natural for a man who grew up on an Iowa farm.

Clyde introduced him to the man on his right, and then the two began double-teaming him while Garrison faded into the sidelines, letting the little drama play out without him. Alex felt slimy for sucking up to these men but kept telling himself maybe they really were good people. As the conversation continued into right-wing politics, Alex quickly realized he had nothing in common with them. For the sake of obtaining a membership, he played along with the charade.

They were well into their second bourbon when one of the men seemed to scrutinize Alex more closely. "You Jewish?"

The other men's eyes turned to him. Stunned, Alex was at a loss for words.

"How did it go?" Lisa asked, following him into the bedroom. "Will we be allowed the privilege of joining such an exclusive pinnacle of high society?" She still hadn't adjusted to the concept of the men's bar.

Dead tired, Alex wanted nothing more than to go straight to bed, to become horizontal and relax his aching lower back. Days were quickly becoming fuller than he'd ever imagined possible, his caseload exploding, a sign the referring physicians and patients respected his skills. "Take good care of the patients and communicate with the referring docs" had been Waters's two-step recipe for building a successful practice. Alex was impressed at just how simple but effective the strategy—especially coming from a died-in-the-wool academician—turned out to be. But it was like any other business, he supposed; good customer service generates more business.

"We'll see. Jesus, I can't believe I spent an evening sucking up to four flaming John Bircher bigots right out of Two Banjo country. One even had the audacity to come right out and ask if I'm Jewish."

Lisa giggled at that. "What'd you tell him?"

"I asked him if I looked Jewish. They didn't push it after that. How was your day?" He moved into the bathroom to lay out his wallet and keys in case of being called in, despite not being on call that night.

"Great. I'm really getting into working at the thrift store."

He smiled, pleased at the joy in her words. In their prior life Lisa didn't have hobbies or other outside interests, devoting most of her energies to her job. Now she was volunteering for a cause she felt passionate about—animal welfare—and the satisfaction clearly came through in her voice.

35

"Been looking for you," Reynolds told Alex. They crossed paths in the surgeon's lounge, Alex preparing to start two routine craniotomies. Reynolds settled into the couch next to him and lowered his voice. "Friend of mine is on the study section that reviewed your grant. What I'm going to tell you is obviously confidential, and if you repeat this to anyone, I don't care if it's the Virgin Mary herself, I'll deny every word before I drive a spike through your heart. We absolutely, one hundred percent clear on this?"

"We are."

"Two members of that group are big buds with your best friend, Weiner. Seems when your grant came up for discussion, everybody but those two loved it and gave it high enough scores to be funded. Weiner's buddies torpedoed it."

Alex's heart sank. "It won't get funded?"

Reynolds appeared genuinely distressed with the news. "Nope."

Alex sat quite still, not even breathing, his shock morphing to rage. "You absolutely sure about this?"

"Hell yeah. And I'm wondering if this has been the problem with your funding all along."

Before Alex could respond, a nurse stuck her head in the room and made eye contact. "Doctor Cutter, we're ready in Room Three."

"Doctor Cutter?"

Alex glanced up from the heavy Zeiss operating microscope, a twinge of pain shooting down his spine from the sudden change in posture.

According to the twenty-four-hour wall clock, he'd been working in the same position for two straight hours. He arched his back and rocked his neck back and forth in an attempt to loosen it up. "Yes?"

The circulator stood next to Cole, peering over the drapes. "Doctor Berger wants your help. He's across the hall in Two."

Can't you see I'm in the middle of a case?

Alex paused to inspect his gloves, making sure there was no rip, an automatic habit of his anytime he stepped away from a surgery. "What's the problem?"

"Don't know, but he says he needs your help," she replied in an apologetic tone. Because of an increasing surgical caseload, Ellen had taken to assigning the same crew each day. The OR personnel were becoming as tight-knit as family, protecting each other when need be.

Alex handed the suction and Cushing forceps up to Chuck Stevens. He was in the middle of resecting what had turned out to be a glioblastoma. In spite of having suspected the diagnosis from the characteristics in the CT images, it was always depressing when pathology confirmed it. No matter how many times it happened, Alex would never become desensitized to the sadness of that diagnosis. Malignant brain tumors were a deeply depressing fact in an inherently depressing surgical subspecialty. Worse yet, the patients universally seemed to be good people. Not that he'd feel any better about making the diagnosis on a real asshole.

"Lawrence, I want you to sit here and wait for me," he said, draping a damp surgical towel over the craniotomy opening to keep the exposed brain moist. "Chuck, irrigate this every few minutes and don't give Lawrence an instrument unless it's a flaming emergency. And if an emergency does happen, have someone come get me before you dare hand it to him. I'll want to gown and glove again when I get back, so might as well get those ready."

Chuck and Lawrence laughed.

"What's up?" Alex asked, backing through the door into Berger's room to protect the sterility of his gown and gloves.

"Can't find the tumor." Berg stood at an open craniotomy, cleaning his gloves with a wet lap-pad. Alex preferred to sit when operating, elbows propped on a draped Mayo table. This set-up provided superior stability, plus his legs didn't get as tired. He never understood why most neurosurgeons stood to operate, especially considering having foot controls for the cautery and power tools. Steve Stein stood next to Berg, holding a sucker.

Alex stopped at the X-ray view box to read the CT. A mass the size of a nickel lit up about two centimeters below the surface of the right frontal pole, producing a modest amount of edema. The well-defined borders and degree of edema suggested it likely was a metastatic tumor. He noted the patient's name: Yolanda. Age sixty-two. "She right- or left-handed?"

"Right," said Stein.

This put the odds overwhelmingly in favor of the tumor being in the brain hemisphere that didn't control speech, increasing the likelihood of getting away with an aggressive, more complete removal. The bad news was that if the tumor was metastatic, she would undoubtedly have additional ones the CT didn't show. Alex held out his arms for the circulator to strip his gloves. "I'll reglove but not regown."

Carefully, making certain to not contaminate Alex's gown, the circulator peeled off the gloves.

"Lot of pressure in there," Alex said, wiping off his new gloves with a wet lap pad. The increased pressure from the tumor and edema pushed glistening brain surface against the path of least resistance, bulging it out of the craniotomy opening. "Give Ultrasound a call, ask them to join us," he said to the circulator, then turned to the scrub tech. "Blunt-tipped biopsy needle, please."

While the scrub tech searched her instruments for the needle, Alex probed the sterile drapes with his fingers, feeling for the bridge of the nose and the two eye sockets. They would provide landmarks with which to orient the exact skull position, which was obscured by the drapes. Keeping his left index finger and thumb on the bridge of the nose, he studied the CT scan, mentally visualizing the exact relationship of the tumor with respect to those landmarks. He glanced from

CT to skull and back again until confident of his hand in relation with the needed trajectory to the mass. "How deep's that puppy?" he asked Stein.

Before printing a copy of the scan, a radiologist had superimposed a thin white cross-hatched line from the inner surface of the skull to the tumor's center, and this provided an exact measure of the depth. The resident read the number of hatches on the line. Simple enough.

"Five centimeters."

"Mark that depth on the needle, please," Alex told the scrub tech. "Then hand it to me." Turning to Martin he said, "One pass. If we don't hit it, we'll need to ultrasound it." Slowly and gently, using his fingertips to sense resistance, he inserted the needle perpendicular to the brain surface into the soft edematous brain, following his estimated trajectory, and watched the blue Sharpie mark on the needle approach the glistening surface to indicate depth. His fingers felt the blunt tip meet sudden resistance. He'd hit the tumor capsule.

"Bingo! Got it." He drew a deep breath. "Give me that marker." Left hand holding the needle firmly in place, he drew X, Y, and Z axes on the craniotomy drapes with the sterile Sharpie to help guide his approach to the tumor. Handing the needle back, he began a quick dissection straight to the tumor, which shelled out without any additional bleeding.

"Okay, I'm done," Alex said, stripping off his gloves. "Steve, may I see you outside for a moment? You don't mind if I have a word with him, do you Martin?"

"Go on, I'll start closing."

They walked out in the hall. "You still friends with some of the residents at the old place?" Alex was at the scrub sink now, freshening up his scrub.

"We talking Vanderbilt?" Steve, still fully gowned, was careful to avoid touching anything nearby.

"No. My old place." Alex quickly lathered up.

"Yeah, sure. Why?"

Alex kneed off the water valve while continuing to work the lather around his hands. "This conversation stays confidential. I'm dead serious, okay?"

"Yes."

"Dead serious."

"Got it, boss."

"Make a few calls, find out if Weiner is still padding the billings out there."

"Why? What's going on?"

No way he'd tell him, no matter how much he trusted him. "Nothing. Just let me know what you find out."

Alex was laying down sutures quickly now, Lawrence snipping threads. He felt guilty denying Lawrence the job of closing the case, but he needed to make up time for the craniotomy scheduled on the heels of this one. Linda poked her head in the room. "You called?"

"I did, thanks. Any chance you could have someone run across the street to pick up two muffulettas and two diet Dr. Peppers?"

"I'm all over it, Doc."

As soon as Linda left, Chuck said, "We can work straight through, flip the room in fifteen minutes if you want."

"Naw. I appreciate the offer, but you guys need a break. Go grab lunch first. Bob and I'll wait in the lounge. Just give us a shout when you're good to go."

Chuck's dedication impressed Alex. He hadn't encountered a better scrub nurse or tech. "Remind me where you trained?"

"The United States Navy," Chuck said proudly. "When I enlisted, they asked what I wanted to do. Told them I wanted to be a corpsman, so they sent me to scrub tech school instead. Didn't complain none 'cause I figured I was getting a skill I could use when my four years were up."

Alex wondered if some of his drive for excellence was due in part to not having a nursing degree, wanting to show he was as good as the nursing school graduates. Regardless, he was as good as they got.

"Love these things, but man, do they have the salt." Alex held up the second half of his muffuletta. "Makes me as thirsty as hell by halfway through a second case. It happens every time, but I can't stop eating them."

"Yeah, they're a total gut bomb. Expands like a nuclear explosion. Awfully damn good, though," Cole said before taking another bite of his sandwich.

They were on a couch in the surgeon's lounge, a constant flux of scrub-clad personnel coming and going, chatting and joking. Some were using the phones scattered around the lounge for calls or to dictate op reports while, on the large corner TV, Wolf Blitzer was discussing something Alex couldn't make out with the volume low and the ambient noise high. Alex leaned closer to Cole. "I want to ask you something confidential."

Cole nodded, his jaws working over a bite of sandwich.

"You guys"—meaning anesthesiologists—"see just about every surgeon here, right?"

Cole swallowed. "Pretty much. Certainly all you clinic guys. But we're not the only gas-passers here. Some surgeons, Friedman for example, use the other practices. Friedman prefers to use his brother exclusively, surprise, surprise." He wagged his eyebrows Groucho Marx style.

"I didn't realize that. Only other place I've worked was a closed shop. No one but faculty practiced at University Hospital."

Cole swallowed. "What's your question?"

Alex weighed asking. He trusted Cole with his patients, but could he trust him to keep a conversation private? Or should he just keep his mouth shut? "You've seen Martin Berger in action. What's your opinion?" he said, leaving the question open ended.

Cole brushed off a small chunk of olive from his lower lip with a paper towel. "Nice guy. Does a ton of spine work."

A nonanswer answer. Watching Cole made Alex suck a piece of olive free from between his teeth. "Yeah, but would you have him operate on your mother?" That, of course, was the trump-card question.

Cole grinned. "She's dead, so I guess I'd have to say no."

"You know damn well that's not what I'm asking."

Cole considered his answer a moment. "All I can say is, calling you for help doesn't really surprise me if that's what you're asking."

A morbidly obese man in a pinstriped blue suit waddled into the lounge, heading straight for the coffee. Alex watched him pour a cup and stir in sugar and cream while chatting up a nearby surgeon. Alex counted: one, two, three packets of sugar. Same as usual. He'd seen this routine numerous days and it never ceased to amaze him.

"Who is that guy?" Alex asked, voice low. Alex was reminded of college chemistry, how there's a saturation point past which a substance will no longer dissolve in a liquid and just accumulates at the bottom of the beaker. Alex was pretty sure the man's coffee was past that point after the second packet.

"Gene?"

"If that's his name. See him in here least once a day, drinking that supersaturated sugar coffee he loves to concoct. Most mornings he downs one or two maple bars to boot, I kid you not."

Cole thumbed away another morsel of olive from the corner of his mouth. "I know. Hard to watch, given his weight. Name's Gene Roux. If you ever need a hematologist, that's your man. No better blood guy in the area."

"That explains why I never see him in scrubs. What's he doing up here instead of downstairs in the physician's lounge?"

Cole laughed. "Claims the pastry's better up here."

Alex did a double take. "You shitting me?"

Cole wadded up the sandwich wrapping, wiped his fingers, and tossed the ball into the trash. "Dead serious."

"Doctors Cutter and Cole, ready for you in Room Three."

As they passed Ellen Bowen's glassed office, Ellen popped her head out. "Doctor Cutter, got a moment? I know you have another case starting; this won't take long."

"For you, always." He stopped as Cole continued down the hall to start the case.

Ellen smiled. For warmth against the A/C chill she wore a surgeon's gown over her scrubs like an overcoat, the ties dangling down the front, the sleeves rolled halfway up the forearms. "We're all tickled pink about the way your caseload's increasing, and I want to do everything I can to help grow it. Starting today Chuck will be assigned to all your cases. You okay with that?"

Having the same scrub tech for every case improved efficiency. Chuck knew Alex's instrument preferences, so he could quickly set up the packs to be sterilized for the next day's schedule. Chuck was so familiar with Alex's technique, he routinely had the next instrument waiting for him before being asked. Last week Alex had toyed with the idea of asking Garrison to hire a dedicated scrub tech for exactly these reasons. The tech's salary could easily be offset by the improved OR efficiency. Now it was a done deal and at no clinic expense. Better yet—he had to admit—was the satisfaction this validation brought. Without being egotistical—because he objectively knew his complication rate was admirably low—his growth of referrals indicated a regional reputation for excellence. He'd even started flirting with the idea of promoting himself nationally, like Reynolds, by attending more meetings to present his outcomes—a marketing ploy he'd previously frowned upon.

"Ah, that's great. He's wonderful. But as long as we're on the subject, I was planning on asking for priority time on Tuesdays. As of this week, I'm off the out-clinic rotation." Much to his relief. Flying in a private plane hadn't become easier with time. Quite the opposite. Each time they went up, he figured the odds increased against them, that sooner or later they would have a disaster. "Garrison prefers I spend my time here rather than out there." Priority time was a designated OR time the office could count on when scheduling cases. A new surgeon usually was assigned the hours no one else wanted or had to tag cases onto whatever time remained after the big dogs used up their time, often being relegated to late afternoon or even early evening.

"I'll see what I can do. That time's already allocated, but I might be able to steal a room from Ortho. Reckon you want to stay in Room Three?" This would give him not only a stable team but a dedicated room as well. Too good to be true.

"That's my preference." Now, if he could have Cole negotiate a similar arrangement with his group, he'd have a winning team.

The overhead speaker crackled and a voice chirped through. "Doctor Cutter, ready in Room Three."

"Mind if I walk out with you?" he asked Garrison, catching up with him at the stairwell to the parking lot. Both men preferred to take the stairs instead of waiting for the slow-as-molasses elevator.

"I welcome the company," Garrison said, pushing open the horizontal bar to the steel fire door. They started down, footsteps echoing off bare, musty concrete.

"Got a question for you," Alex said after the first flight of stairs.

"Shoot."

Alex debated how best to phrase the sensitive subject. "This is extremely confidential, okay?"

"Okay."

"What's your opinion of Berger's surgical abilities?"

Garrison stopped at the landing to the parking garage. "Why? What's up?"

Alex related being called into Martin's room to help solve what Alex believed to be a simple problem for a neurosurgeon opening a skull. "Given the fact he does mostly spine surgery, I'm wondering if he should still be doing craniotomies."

Garrison pushed through swinging doors into warm evening humidity. "Determining surgical privileges isn't the clinic's responsibility. The hospital credentials committee does that. Every clinic member is Board Certified, meaning they can do spine, intracranial, and peripheral nerve surgery." Clearly, he wasn't pleased with what Alex just said.

"True, but some of us are better at some things than others. Since we share profits equally, there's no reason for each surgeon to do everything. It's exactly the reason some of us subspecialize. You, for example. You're the clinic's go-to guy for aneurysms and AVMs."

"That's different. That takes special skills. I'm good at it primarily because I do all those cases for us."

Alex reached out and touched his arm, stopping him. "Why is that different?"

Garrison opened his mouth to reply, seemed to think better of what was about to come out, and said, "No one's going to stop Martin from doing craniotomies, Alex, so get over it."

Alex shot him a disgusted look. Garrison shook his head. "Which would you prefer he do, plow ahead on a problem or call a partner to help him out?" Garrison's tone and demeanor was one of mild irritation.

"Of course he should ask for help if he's in trouble. That's why I helped him. That's not the point. The point is, I'm not sure he should be doing cases that carry a likely risk of getting him into trouble. He was flat-out lost. Maybe there's a damn good reason he does mostly spine. Maybe he shouldn't be opening people's heads. The clinic's primary concern should be providing the best possible care to our patients, not worrying about hurt feelings." Alex believed they both had points.

Garrison studied Alex a moment. "You looking for ways to expand your turf? Is that what this is all about?"

Aw, Jesus. "No. That's not the point."

"Well, you could've fooled me, 'cause that's the way it sounds."

"Look, I've been watching the schedule. Martin does a hell of a lot of second, third, and forth disk reoperations. How's that justified?"

"Not sure I see your point. He's referred a lot of patients." Garrison's voice had turned steady and cool, transmitting an unstated message: *fuck off.*

He was past the point of no return. "Have you read the L and I statistics"—*L and I* meaning Labor and Industry—"for second, third, and forth reops?"

"Can't say I've stayed up nights riveted to that."

"Each redo has less chance of producing a good result. Certainly, no one goes back to work after the second operation."

Garrison used his thumb to wipe the corner of his mouth. "Getting patients back to work is not our concern. Making them comfortable is."

"That's exactly the point. It doesn't work. But more importantly, why are you defending him so strongly?"

Garrison took a deep breath and began to play with the tie from the surgical mask dangling around his neck. "I'm not defending him. Martin Berger is the clinic's highest producer. Why should I look for ways to kill the golden goose?"

There it was. "In other words, billings trump quality."

Garrison shook his head in disgust. "Right now you remind me of Douglas," he said, referring to his adolescent son. "Everything's black or white, and there's no such thing as gray or middle ground."

Alex's temples tightened. "Tell me the middle ground in this?"

"Berger's Jewish."

Alex recoiled. "What the hell does that have to do with the price of yak dung in Timbuktu?"

"If you haven't noticed, he's the only Jew we got."

Alex still didn't get it. "And your point is?"

"He's our only conduit into that referral pool."

Alex took a step back. "Please tell me you didn't just say that."

Garrison sliced a hand through the air—discussion over. "New topic, now that we're done with that one. Two new topics, actually. We hired your nurse and she just finished her clinic orientation today. She's replacing Linda tomorrow morning."

Alex wasn't listening. Honeymoons typically end with the first argument. Partnership can't exist without occasional discordant views. He and Garrison just crossed that line, leaving him feeling hollow, unsettled, and wishing he could rewind the last ten minutes and start over. He'd always known there was no such thing as a perfect job. Still, he'd worked to stave off this inevitable disillusion, believing that each day without confrontation buttressed his solidity within the clinic. Yet he knew somewhere along the line, a controversial issue was bound to arise. Could he live knowing he hadn't taken a stand once one arose? No. To say nothing would be worse than going on record. His words might not change a damn thing, but he'd feel worse if he hadn't said a word. He vowed that from that day on, the clinic could practice their way, but he would practice his way. As long as he held true to his own professional and moral compass, he'd be okay. Still,…

There was more he wanted to say but decided against it. "Look forward to meeting her, but I'm sure going to miss having Linda around. She's terrific."

"She enjoys working with you. She says you're a good doc."

He sensed their tension dissipate. "What's the other thing?"

"Clinic's adding a new partner."

"Partner?"

"Sorry, I'm getting ahead of myself. He'll start on the same path as anyone new: a probationary year first, then partnership. Good man, you'll like him. Trained here before spending four years in the Air Force. When that obligation was done, he took a job with Randy Clever down in the Gulf for a year, but that turned out to not be a good fit for him, so he called a month ago and I promised to find a place for him here. He's a good person as well as an excellent surgeon. You'll see."

Considering the way this conversation had just gone, Garrison's recommendation didn't hold the same weight as it might have a day ago. Sad. They turned away from each other to walk to their respective cars.

36

"I'd like you to meet Betsy Lou Osborne," Linda Brown said, introducing Alex to an overly buxom woman with a long, plain face that hadn't benefited from either her excessive make-up or her frosted blonde hair. Her white blouse was tucked into tight white jeans. White socks and white running shoes completed the ensemble.

Linda had nabbed him beelining to the stairwell for a quick trip to the hospital to discharge two post-ops. He held his hand out to the new hire. "Welcome aboard."

Smiling, she shook his hand warmly, holding it a few seconds longer than necessary. "Nice to meet you, Doctor Cutter. Linda says you're one of the top docs here. I look forward to working with you." Smiling, she primped her hair.

He felt something off-putting about the way she looked him in the eyes. Wanting to stay on schedule, he shrugged it off. "I'm heading over to the hospital to discharge two patients. Tag along if Linda's done with you."

"I am. As of now, she's assigned to you full-time." Linda glanced from Alex to Betsy and back again before walking away.

Alex headed toward the stairwell. "I prefer to take the stairs. Saves time."

"Typical surgeon."

They started down the stairs to the second-floor sky bridge. "You from around here?" he asked in an attempt at small talk.

"Born and raised in Little Rock, where I attended nursing school. As soon as I graduated, hubby and I moved here. Been here ever since."

He pushed open the fire door onto the sky bridge, Betsy keeping pace. "Where have you worked before here, Betty?"

"It's Betsy. Worked here and there. My first love is pediatrics, so for five years I was with Brett Hoagland. Know him?"

He waved at a referring physician heading in the opposite direction. "No. Don't do any peds, so probably haven't run across him."

"Oh, well, he's been dead a couple years now." She was on his left, matching him stride for stride. "Tragic."

They reached the bank of elevators and Alex punched the "up" button. "Sorry. What happened?"

Another hair primp. "T-boned his Corvette into an eighteen-wheeler while crossing an intersection outside of town. The car's body went right under the rig, completely demolishing the top of the car and decapitating him."

Alex shivered at the thought. "That's awful."

She touched his arm. "But his nurse survived without a scratch," she said with a conspiratorial smile. "How do you suppose that happened?"

Aw, Jesus. He stepped away from her. "She was extremely lucky, I guess."

The elevator arrived, they entered, and he punched "7" while making sure to stand well away from her.

Am I being paranoid?

"Neuro's on seven," he explained. "Except for my ICU post-ops, this is where all my patients are."

As they exited the elevator, Steve Stein stood next to the nursing station writing in a chart. He saw Alex and closed the chart. "Morning, Doctor Cutter."

Alex introduced him to Betsy.

"Got that information you asked about," Steve said.

"Oh?" He knew Steve was smart enough to defer any further conversation on the topic until they could arrange a more private situation.

"The answer is yes," Steve said with a knowing glance.

"Okay, good. We can discuss it more detail later. When you have a minute, drop by the clinic. I'll be there all afternoon seeing patients."

"Let me see your orders," Betsy Lou said, moving next to Alex at the 7 Madison nursing station. He was writing orders in the chart after she had listened to him verbally instruct the patients. The sooner she learned his routines, the more scut work he could begin to delegate while he was in the operating room. Linda was great when she had time, but she was overloaded with covering Garrison and managing the other clinic nurses.

"I close every scalp in two layers. Deep layer with tight inverted subcutaneous Vicryl followed by skin staples."

"I notice the dressing's off and the wound exposed. That seems unusual."

What a relief. She knows a few things.

"A properly closed wound forms a protein-rich seal within 24 hours. Long as the patient doesn't pick at it and break it open, it's better left exposed to air than all covered up with goop that makes a perfect culture for bacteria. Unless there are specific reasons for the staples to stay in longer, I remove them at five days. Produces less scar that way." She seemed to listen closely, which he appreciated.

"Why staples? Most surgeons I know use nylon."

"Less tissue reaction, less inflammation, less scar." He resumed writing discharge orders.

Her right breast pressed against his left arm. "Oh, I see."

Shit. He stepped back and locked eyes with her. She glanced away, flustered and blushing.

Let it go at that. If she's smart, she got the message.

37

"DEEP TENDON REFLEXES NORMAL at two-plus and symmetrical, Babinskis negative." A knock on the open door interrupted dictation. Alex turned from the window to see Garrison's large frame in the doorway.

"I wanted to introduce Clarence Hill." Without waiting for an answer, Garrison stepped into the office, followed by a smaller, round-faced man, hands shoved deep in the pockets of his white coat, which had, like all the clinic physicians' coats, his name embroidered in red above the left breast pocket. Alex was immediately drawn to Hill's intense eyes: two hard marbles behind round, wire-frame glasses. He had the puckered face of a professional lemon sucker. A crescent of close-cut black hair trailed thick stubble down the back of his neck.

Alex came around the desk to shake hands with the new surgeon. "Alex Cutter."

"Nice to meet you." As they shook hands, Alex felt the distinct vibe of being sized up.

"Clarence will be helping with the vascular work," Garrison explained, beaming, his right hand now on the new man's shoulder like a proud father. "Right, Clarence?"

"Absolutely, Garrison." Clarence glanced up admiringly at Garrison as if addressing a general. Then those marbles lasered back at Alex. "You do mostly tumors, don't you." Made as a statement instead of a question. A verification.

Interesting. "I do."

"Building a nice practice of it, too," Garrison added. "Better get you around to meet some of the other new folk. Got a lot of 'em since you were here last."

As Alex watched the two leave, he experienced a vague sense of unease, an off-putting feeling. A forewarning? He stood perfectly still, afraid the slightest distraction would derail his gelling impression before it could be brought into focus. A déjà vu chill snaked down his spine, then, just as quickly, disappeared. He'd been here before. Not literally, of course, but encounter-wise. He wasn't sure where, or with whom, but he knew the outcome hadn't been good.

"What's going on between the new guy and Garrison?" Alex casually asked Dave Ray. They had just finished a tennis match at the public courts a few miles from Alex's house. The courts were located roughly equidistant between their two homes, so it worked well for a quick match. Surprisingly, the courts were never used on Saturdays, the only time Alex could routinely count on being available these days.

After mopping his face with a wadded white towel, Dave asked, "Going on how?"

Alex zipped the cover over his Wilson racket. "They seem very close. In a lot of ways. Even to the point that Clarence does vascular work. Something's going on there, just like there's something between Linda and Garrison—but not the same, if you know what I mean."

Dave wiggled his eyebrows at that remark before dropping onto the courtside bench with a heavy sigh. "Totally off the record?"

Alex sat beside him, towel in hand, mopping the back of his neck. "That's reciprocal, you know."

"Just so it's understood." Dave dried his face again. "You know Clarence was Garrison's golden boy throughout his residency, don't you?"

Alex tossed down his towel and relaxed against the bench. "I'd heard something to that effect."

"Well, it was pretty obvious. He followed him around like a little puppy. People used to make jokes about it, things like how discolored Clarence's nose was. The only surprise came when he took the job at the

Gulf practice instead of coming home soon as Uncle Sam released him. That was pretty much what everyone 'round here expected."

"Why did he take the other job?" Alex inspected his racket grip. Looked about time to replace the sweat-soaked wrap.

Dave shrugged. "Who knows? But getting back to your original question, I suspect he's fixing to be the next CEO come time for Garrison to retire. Do that and he'll have followed him pretty much to a tee."

That explained his impression of Clarence earlier. "How you feel about that?"

Dave snorted. "Day that happens is the day I'm out of here."

"Oh? Why's that?"

Dave leaned back against the bench slats with eyes closed against the waning sun, his wadded towel in hand. "Lots of reasons. Not even sure I can explain all of them, 'cause I'm not sure I completely understand. Gut instinct mostly. But since you asked, guess it all boils down to a serious lack of trust." Dave seemed to weigh his last statement a moment. "Yeah, that about sums it up. A serious lack of trust."

Interesting. "Care to elaborate?"

"Not sure I can. Can't point to one thing and say, 'See!' It's a bottom-line impression, I guess. But there's one thing you should understand about Clarence: he's very spiritual."

"Spiritual? Not sure I follow. What's that mean?"

"Expect you'll understand soon enough." With a tired groan, Dave pushed off the bench, the towel now thrown over his shoulders, white Izod tennis shirt sweat-welded to his hairy chest. "Don't forget we got us a business meeting first thing in the morning. Breakfast will be served as usual."

Alex pushed off the bench, pleasantly fatigued from work and exercise. Towel also around his neck, he shouldered his racket bag and fell in beside Dave for the half-block walk to the parking lot. "Been meaning to ask about that. Five thirty's early. Why? Why not five thirty in the evening?"

Dave laughed and dropped his faded bag on the hood of his sun-baked car before rummaging through it for his keys. "Easy. That's the only way we can make sure these meetings end. And that's only because most the partners have cases to start. We tried evening meetings once, but everyone had something to say, so they took forever. Besides, dinner's more expensive than breakfast."

"I noticed not everyone shows up for those meetings."

"Lotta partners don't. You'd be surprised at how many don't give a flip about how their clinic runs. Alls they want is a monthly paycheck and their share of the quarterly profit. You want to gain power in this clinic, show up at the business meetings and take an active role. You'd be surprised how easy it is. That's the reason I think your new best friend, Clarence, has a shot at succeeding."

38

"Morning, Garrison," Alex said, entering the crowded conference/library room, the walls filled with medical books and bound journals. A thick mahogany table capable of comfortably seating twelve occupied the center of the room with extra chairs crammed in behind the ones at the table. A side-table pushed against a bookcase held stainless steel serving dishes of scrambled eggs, bacon, grits, and a twenty-five-cup coffee urn with a stack of inverted white Styrofoam cups on its right. The smell of salty grease stoked Alex's appetite after having slipped out without waking Lisa. He was famished.

"Morning, Alex. Glad you could make it," Garrison said. Clarence sat directly to Garrison's left, all bright eyed and eager.

Alex spooned eggs, bacon, and two slices of toast—he hadn't been able to develop a taste for grits and doubted he ever would—onto a paper plate and poured a cup of black coffee. He settled into the one unoccupied seat, which happened to be on Berger's right. He immediately speared a fork full of eggs to pop into his mouth.

"Down here, folks say the blessing before they start eatin'."

Still chewing, Alex glanced up to see where the loud voice came from. Hill was sending him a serious dose of laser-eye. The room fell silent, the other partners either avoiding eye contact or simply studying their folded hands. No one else had touched their food, Alex realized. Clarence turned to Garrison. "Isn't that right, Dr. Majors?"

Alex swallowed. He felt betrayed and alienated, as if someone had purposely led him into a social trap. In the meetings prior to Clarence's arrival, no one said a damn thing before eating. Why were things now different? Then he remembered Dave's words: *He's very spiritual.*

He decided to not take the bait and tell Hill to fuck off. Clearly, Clarence's presence was the only difference from previous meetings. Interesting. Even more interesting was that no one seemed up to the task of challenging him. In the next instant Alex intuitively grasped the significance of the moment: a battle line was now drawn. Setting down his fork, he sat back. "Knock yourself out, Clarence."

Head bowed, Clarence reached for the hands of the surgeons to either side of him. "Thank you, heavenly father, for the bounty we are about to receive."

Alex was sorely tempted to bite off a hunk of bacon. *Don't be juvenile.* He glanced at Berger, who simply stared at his plate of bacon and eggs, hands clasped in his lap. Neither he nor Alex held the hand of the partners to either side.

Meeting over, Alex walked with Martin Berger to the sky bridge, the other partners having abruptly dispersed to start their busy days, which, for most, would end sometime after 7:00 p.m.

"Have we always done that?" Alex asked.

Martin shot him a sideways glance. "Done what?"

"Say the blessing or grace or whatever it's called before breakfast business meetings. It wasn't done for the ones I attended." He still hadn't grown used to seeing people pray before meals in restaurants or at the University Club, and certainly not with Clarence's apparent fervor. Did people feel obliged to make these public displays out of deep religious conviction or simply because it seemed the socially expected norm here, making them afraid to be pegged as different if they didn't? A societal lemmings phenomenon. Good question, one he suspected would remain unanswered. The cynical side of him suspected the latter.

Martin scratched the side of his chin. "Do now, now that Hill's back. He used to make a huge point of it as a resident, so I reckon people figure we're back to the way things were then."

"And you're okay with that? I mean, being Jewish."

Martin checked his fingernails. "Makes no never mind to me. Why? Bother you?"

Not the answer he expected. "You bet it does. I don't like being forced to participate in other people's religious rituals. I resent it."

"How come? Doesn't hurt anyone."

Is he kidding? He studied Martin's craggy poker face. "Guess it comes down to what I just said; I don't like people forcing their personal religious beliefs on me. I find that obnoxious. It's saying there's good religion and bad religion and his is the good one. Where does the Christian belief of tolerance come into play the way he's running things?"

"He can believe what he wants. Doesn't bother me."

"To tell you the truth, that surprises me."

Martin shrugged. "Didn't see anyone else object. After all, this ain't called the Bible Belt for nothing."

Alex continued to stare at him. "There's more to it than just religion."

"Like what?"

"You're all empowering him every time you sit back and let him dictate something as trivial as a blessing. The problem is, once a person like him starts to gain that kind of power, it becomes a momentum thing. Next thing you know, he'll have Garrison's job. You happy with that idea?"

"I'll be retired by then." He looked serious.

Fuming, Alex headed to the stairs. "Unbelievable. Catch you later."

39

"Brought these," Alex said, handing four CDs to Cole. One Cal Tjader, two Freddy Kings, and one Albert King. "Some of my prime music."

Cole quickly shuffled through the discs. "Wow, these are terrific. Especially Freddy's *Texas Cannonball* album. And Tjader's 'Doxy.' What order you want?"

"Dealer's choice." He set the mitered wood box for his loupes on the stainless steel counter, freeing his hands to begin sorting CT scans to display. "Love them all. Especially 'Answer to the Laundromat Blues.' Although Freddy's 'Stuck In Lodi' is a close second. Listen the hell out of that one."

"Excuse me, Doctor Cutter." the chief resident popped his head into the OR. "You seen Brett Johnson this morning?" Brett was the first-year resident recently assigned to his service.

Alex set down the scans. "No, I haven't. Why?"

The resident appeared to choose his next words carefully before stepping a bit closer and lowering his voice. "Apparently the paging operator couldn't reach him all night. I was wondering if maybe he'd been working with you."

Alex resumed sorting CTs. He'd recently caught a whiff of grumbling amongst the residents concerning Johnson's performance, but nothing concrete—mostly issues with his availability when taking call. He and Reynolds tended to delegate minor disciplinary matters to the residents in the belief that peer pressure could be more effective than top-down dictatorial rule. "Haven't seen him."

"Okay. I'll have the general surgery resident scrub with you till he shows."

Alex nodded. First-year general surgery residents hated their mandatory rotation on neurosurgery, mostly because they weren't allowed to do much in the OR or were saddled with the scut work the higher-ranking neurosurgery residents sloughed off on them. The reverse happened when the first-year neurosurgery residents rotated through general surgery, so it was a mutual "fuck you" situation. Since surgeons of each specialty needed a firm grasp of surgical theory and principles, the cross-fertilization experience was seen as worthwhile. Besides, you never knew what kinds of situations one might encounter in the real world. Alex once met a general surgeon in Alaska who saved a patient's life by removing an epidural hematoma before air-evacuating him to Seattle. The astute surgeon witnessed a similar surgery as a first-year resident.

Alex was at the scrub sink taping the top edge of his mask to the bridge of his nose when the general surgery resident showed up acting mildly annoyed. Alex felt sorry for him.

Alex and Chuck were draping the patient when Brett Johnson pushed through the doors into the OR. "Morning, Doctor Cutter."

Alex glanced at the wall clock and noted the time. "You're late, Johnson."

"Yes, I am. Sorry about that. Had to finish up a patient over at the trauma center. I'll go scrub."

"You're off the hook," Alex told the surgery resident. "Go see if there's another case you can help on, and thanks for covering."

Without moving his eyes from the wound edge, Alex reached up toward Chuck. "Rainey clip."

Chuck placed the clip applier snugly into Alex's hand. In one smooth motion, Alex had the plastic clip over a small length of incision and released the applier, so the clip now compressed the freshly cut scalp edge to control bleeding. This process would be repeated along both edges of the incision. Out of the corner of his eye, he noticed Johnson push back into the room with his hands up, skin glistening wet. Johnson called to Chuck. "Need a towel."

Alex glanced at the clock. "How long did you scrub?"

"Five minutes. Why?"

"You sure about that?"

"Why would I lie?"

Good question. "Because you only scrubbed for two minutes. I timed it. Go back out and do it right, Johnson, and this time make it a full five minutes. I'm timing you."

"Sorry," Alex said to Chuck once Johnson left the room.

"Don't be. It's those little things, cutting corners, that end up biting you in the ass. Learned that one a long time ago. The hard way, too. Thing I like about working with you is you go by the book and don't shortcut good technique. Keeps us both out of trouble, which actually saves time in the long run."

Alex appreciated that he and Chuck were like-minded. "Thanks. Rainey."

Once Johnson gowned and gloved and stood shoulder to shoulder with him, Alex said, "Since this is your first day on service let me ask you—what do you know about the way I do things?" Alex continued working, Chuck handing him the correct instruments without being asked.

"Don't know a thing."

Bullshit. A universal fiber of every residency culture was the gossip pool, the chatter between members—comparing notes and criticizing attendings. This program was no different from any other.

"Okay then, here are the rules of engagement …"

40

"Doctor Cutter, there's a man outside, says he wants a word with you." Kasey stood in the doorway to his office.

This was his clinic day and Alex was between patients, dictating a note. "From your tone of voice, I assume he isn't a patient." The clinic did not allow drug salesmen access to the physicians.

Kasey stepped in the office and closed the door. "He's an FBI agent."

FBI? Why would the FBI want to talk to me? He glanced at his watch. "He say what it's about?" *Wait. Could it be . . . ?*

She was giving him a questioning look. "No, sir."

"Before you show him in, explain that he gets only five minutes." Alex quickly finished dictating his note.

Kasey ushered in a fireplug Asian, perhaps 5'9", 170 pounds, making Alex think *sumo wrestler*. Kasey shut the door as she exited.

"John Suzuki," the man said, offering his FBI credentials for Alex to view.

Alex returned the wallet. He didn't offer the agent a seat nor take one himself, for it would prolong the meeting and he had a full clinic. "What can I do for you?"

Suzuki slid the ID back into his suit coat. "You are Doctor Alex Cutter?"

"I am."

"Did you contact the Medicare fraud tip line several months ago?"

Aw, that's it. Alex extended a hand toward the visitor chairs in front of his desk. "Here, have a seat." This would take longer than five minutes.

"Can you spare a moment?" Clarence sauntered into Alex's office.

"Sure. What's up?" Alex set the Sony recorder on the chart of the patient for whom he was dictating a note and swept a hand toward the two chairs on the other side of his desk. "Have a seat."

"That's all right; this won't take but a few seconds." Clarence, like Garrison, wore scrubs regardless of whether or not he had a case scheduled that day. Alex figured Garrison routinely wore them as an excuse for not having to decide what to wear. Clarence, on the other hand, wore them to mimic Garrison.

"How do you like being back at the clinic?" Alex asked. Not that he gave a rat's ass; it just seemed to be the right thing to say.

"I'm blessed, truly blessed to be given an opportunity to return home. How 'bout you? You like it here?" Wiry black hairs sprouted over the neck of Clarence's scrub shirt, giving him a feral appearance.

"Love it here."

Uneasy silence followed. Alex waited to hear what Clarence had to say. A moment later Clarence cleared his throat. "I understand you run a journal club."

Ah … "Yes. Faculty are invited, so feel free to attend."

Clarence shifted weight from one to the other foot. "That's what I wanted to talk about. Why did you choose Wednesday evenings?"

Clarence's tone carried a challenging vibe that put Alex on guard. "Seemed the best choice, is all. Why?"

"But why Wednesday? Why not Tuesday or Thursday?"

Obviously, Clarence had an issue with Wednesday. What could it be? How could it make a damn bit of difference? Why was he sounding so accusatory?

"Have to think about that a moment. Let's see … Monday is conference day, so that's out. Fridays are the start of the weekend, so that's out." Alex shrugged. "Wednesdays just seemed to be the best option."

Clarence leaned forward, eyes boring intensely into Alex. "A righteous person would never choose Wednesday. A righteous person would know the difference between right and wrong. This leads me to conclude you're a godless person."

Whoa! His first impulse—to say "fuck off"—was immediately trumped by curiosity. What the hell was he talking about? Calmly, he said, "Excuse me, Clarence, but I have no idea what you're talking about."

"No, of course not. I didn't expect you would, considering where you come from."

That pissed him off. "And where's that?"

"The West Coast." Clarence was standing straight now, white balls of knuckles at his sides.

Alex signaled "time out." "Hey, take a deep breath and explain what it is you're talking about. I'm totally lost."

Glaring, Clarence actually did take a deep breath while shrug-adjusting his white coat. "Folks around here are God-fearing Christians. You understand that much, don't you?"

"Some are, some aren't. Not everyone is Christian."

"That's not the point. Point is, Wednesday evenings are for Bible study. Everybody knows that. You can't just go 'round ignoring these things. That's why I'm telling you to change it to another night. Tuesday's what I think it should be, but Thursday's fine with me, too."

"Fine with you, huh?" Alex mind buzzed with sarcastic replies.

Clarence nodded.

"Tell me something: What happens if I keep things as is?"

"That's your option, but don't expect the residents to be there," he said quickly. "As of this week, I'm requiring the residents to come to my home for Bible study and fellowship."

Alex struggled to control his anger. Clarence had finally crossed a defensible line. "Sorry Clarence, there's no way in hell you can force residents to attend. I won't allow it. This is a neurosurgery residency, not the First Church of Clarence Hill."

Clarence stabbed a finger at his chest. "We'll see about this. Doctor Majors made a commitment to me to attend. He'll be there every week."

Garrison would probably walk on red-hot coals to get away from Anne for an evening.

"Well, have fun. Just don't expect any residents to attend."

Clarence's face was red with rage. "We'll see about that."

"Before you go, let me ask you something."

Clarence cast a wary glance.

"What would you say if I told you Humpty Dumpty was pushed?"

Clarence side-stepped toward the door. "I'm not going to give you the satisfaction of playing your silly games." He wheeled around and stormed from the office.

Fuck!

Pulse pounding his temples, Alex dropped into his desk chair to think. Had there been a better way to handle Clarence? Probably. But the bastard pushed so many hot buttons so rapidly it was impossible to not lose his temper.

Learn to exercise more caution, be more circumspect before reacting. Making clinic enemies will only make your job more problematic.

Sounded good, but realistically, he knew that in an organization this complex it would be impossible to avoid getting into polarizing politics. Besides, for whatever reason, there had been no love between them from the moment of their first encounter. The problem with the present situation was, Clarence Hill seemed too closely allied with Garrison, a person Alex couldn't afford to alienate. On the other hand, he didn't seriously believe Clarence would try to escalate this particular issue beyond their private discussion. Instead, Clarence would be constantly searching for any and every opportunity to subtly erode Alex's cachet within the clinic. In Alex's favor was the fact he was now one of the clinic's top revenue producers, second only to Martin, a point that assured him a layer of political Kevlar in spite of how distasteful Alex found this dynamic. He would prefer clinic stature to be based on more relevant attributes like ethics, decision-making, and patient outcome. Yet he knew this desire was too Pollyanna, too unrealistic. He found it equally discouraging to know this confrontation likely marked the beginning of an escalating power struggle between Garrison's and Reynolds's successors. He hated the thought.

41

THE PHONE RATTLED ALEX awake on the couch. After knuckling his eyes, he checked the clock. 12:03 a.m. Last he remembered, he was sitting there reading a medical journal. Most lights were off, so Lisa had long since gone to bed. He picked up the cordless phone. "Cutter here."

"Doctor Cutter, Harvey Leventhal. Got a GSW to the head over here at the trauma center. Tangential right hemisphere. We're scanning him now, but I'm taking him to the OR soon as he's off the table."

"Be right in." Leventhal was an extremely competent senior resident who Alex predicted would become a dynamite chief resident next year, so there was no need to rush.

He caught up with Leventhal in OR One just as the anesthesiologist finished taping the patient's endotracheal tube securely in place. Leventhal was arranging CTs on the view box, the scrub and circulating nurses flying about in the hurriedly orchestrated pace of an emergency case.

"Got a tangential furrow through the fronto-parietal bone, driving in bone frags here, here, and here," the resident said, tapping obvious bone fragments on the scan.

"What's your plan?" Alex asked rhetorically. He heard the sudden hiss of steam escaping from the autoclave as the circulator unlocked the thick, reinforced stainless-steel door.

"GSW 101. Debride the wound, close the dura, and then play hockey."

Alex laughed. "Yeah, get the puck out of there. Gotcha. Good plan. Let's go scrub up."

At the scrub sink, Leventhal said, "I put in a call for the Baptist resident, but he's tied up at the moment. Soon as he gets here you can head on back if you want." At that point, Alex would have fulfilled his oversight requirements. If he left the OR when Leventhal's assistant arrived, it would signal a vote of confidence in the resident's abilities.

Alex assisted Leventhal by squirting irrigation over the ragged wound edges while he worked at controlling the bleeding. Tangential wounds were often hard to close because the bullet blows out a furrow of skin, producing ragged damaged edges that have to be removed to produce a clean, even closure. This results in less scalp available to cover the same area of skull, making the closure tricky. And unlike a clean surgical wound, these were often grossly contaminated from hair and small bits of skin and other debris. Once the wound edges were cleaned up and the bleeding controlled, Leventhal began carefully picking out bits of contaminants, flicking them off the tips of the forceps onto the floor to keep the operating area sterile. Alex squirted more saline into the field, assisting in the cleaning process as Leventhal worked.

With the superficial areas now debrided, Leventhal placed a self-retaining retractor to spread open the wound so he could get a better estimate of the underlying skull damage. The bullet had made a linear groove high along the left temple, pushing bone fragments through the dura into the brain. Luckily, because the bullet struck tangentially, most of the force had been expended along the bullet trajectory instead of radially into the brain substance. One by one, Leventhal picked out the bone chips with a hemostat. Because the fragments were contaminated with hair and bits of skin, and because bone can't be autoclaved without killing it, he dropped these pieces into a bucket on the floor at their feet. In six months or so, if the wound healed without signs of infection, the scar could be opened and acrylic used to fill in the skull defect for a better cosmetic result.

The junior resident finally walked into the OR just as Leventhal was getting ready to patch the dura and close.

"Go ahead and scrub," Alex told him. "Leventhal, think you can handle the dura?"

"Figure I'll patch it with temporalis fascia," he replied, referring to the heavy connective tissue encasing the muscle to the jaw.

"Perfect." Alex stripped off his gloves. "I'll write an op note."

In the darkened bedroom, Alex carefully slid between the sheets without awakening Lisa, the glowing clock radio now showing 3:41. Sleep would most likely be impossible now, yet he rolled onto his left side to begin his relaxation exercises, hoping to be surprised in the morning by the alarm. He thought about his life, about how differently he lived from the patient just operated on: an unidentified African American male, perhaps mid-twenties, literally pushed out of a moving car in the Emergency Room parking lot, the only witness to the drop too confused and shocked to note even the make of the car, much less who drove or anything else of importance to the police. The kid, of course, had been stripped of all identification. Might be gang related and likely was drug related. No one knew any particulars, not that that information was medically relevant. But the thing was, the patient's history was important because victims of street crimes typically were at higher risk for AIDS and hepatitis, two diseases readily transmitted to a surgeon from an accidental needle stick, especially during a rushed emergency surgery. Alex thought back to Robert Sands, the pediatric neurosurgeon who had been forced into early retirement for exactly this reason. And guess what? In spite of these increased risks, the clinic was likely to receive no reimbursement for this surgery. Or cases like it. The gangbangers and petty criminals, usual patients in the trauma center, didn't carry Blue Cross cards. Although he didn't enter medical school with the goal of making money, he did believe he should be compensated for his services.

Tossing and turning, he watched the glowing digits increment minute by minute. At 4:45, still unable to sleep, he slipped silently into the bathroom and shut the door to begin preparing for another day, another month, another 5:30 clinic business meeting. Thank God he had clinic instead of surgery that day.

42

"JESUS, THAT ONE LOOKED close," Cole said, referring to a missile explosion lighting up the Baghdad night sky on CNN. They sat on a couch in the surgeon's lounge, watching Wolf Blitzer report live from Baghdad as they enjoyed a cup of coffee before they started the first of two cases. Cole was now routinely assigned to Alex's cases. To Alex, Cole and Chuck Stevens were as intimate as family. Residents came and went, but the core group remained intact, each day learning more about each other's lives, tastes, insecurities, and desires.

"Wonder if he gets hazardous duty pay for being there," said Alex.

"Uh-oh, here comes your friend." Cole nudged him.

Alex glanced up just as the TV segued from Blitzer to General Schwarzkopf. Gene Roux, the morbidly obese hematologist, stood at the counter stirring a packet of sugar into a steaming Styrofoam cup. Just one more routine in Alex's life—watching Roux wash down the morning maple bars with sugary, creamy coffee. He watched this little drama with a mixture of morbid fascination and disgust. The guy was killing himself. Surely he must know that.

"There he goes. Maple bar number one," muttered Cole.

Roux's sausage-link fingers made the maple bar seem small and delicate, about the right size for the three bites Roux required to devour it. A lick of his fingers, followed by a second bar, then one more cup of coffee for the road. Done, Roux rinsed off his fingers and left the room.

"Watching this makes me sick," Alex said.

"Yeah, but if you ever need a hematologist, he's your man."

"Assuming he's still alive. I can't imagine what his coronaries must look like. To say nothing of his blood sugar."

"Doctor Cole, patient's ready," a nurse said from the doorway.

Cole slapped his thighs to stand. "We should be ready for you in ten, but feel free to mosey down earlier to select your music. Have a few new CDs for you. You heard the Les McCann and Eddie Harris at Montreaux disc? 'Compared To What' is my favorite on it."

"Know the song, just not that version. It's pretty good?"

Cole was tying his mask in place. "Just wait."

"Doctor Cutter?"

Alex stopped working to peer around the overhead table. Ellen stood just inside the swinging doors, mask held over her mouth and nose.

"Yep?"

"Doctor Reynolds asked if you could drop by his office when you finish this case. Said he wants a few words. Let me know if you want us to hold on your second case."

He shook his head. "No, go ahead and flip the room. Second one's going to take a while, and I want to get done at a reasonable hour today. Whatever it is Reynolds wants to talk about can't take that long. Thanks."

"What's up, Jim?" Alex entered Reynolds's office. Claude wasn't at her desk but had left Reynolds's door ajar, probably out taking a cigarette break now that the university was cracking down on in-office smoking.

Reynolds set down his pen. "Couple things." He pointed to one of the chairs in front of his desk. "Have a seat."

Alex sat.

"Two things for discussion, both important. Y'all got a second case waiting?"

Uh-oh. Sounded serious. "I do."

"All right then, I'll make it short. But before I begin, I just want to say how pleased we all are with your practice. Figured you'd be a success, but never imagined it'd be this successful. I was bragging on you the other day to some friends at the Senior Society," he said, referring to an exclusive neurosurgical organization of program directors and their seconds-in-command. "We should get you into that organization, by the way."

"Thanks." Alex realized how much his priorities had shifted since moving here. Two years ago he would've jumped at the chance to advance his academic career, but that was no longer the case. *What's happening to me?*

Reynolds began polishing his glasses on his white coat. "I received orders to report to Bethesda on account of this Desert Storm business. Don't know how long it's going take, but the way they're talking, it won't be all that long. While I'm gone you're in total charge of the department, which makes me even more thankful for bringing you on. I got the utmost faith in your judgment, but if something comes up and you reckon you need to talk to me, call. Soon's I get there I'll let Claude know how to reach me. Damn! Never reckoned on getting called up, especially at my age, but all's I'll be doing is shuffling some papers behind a desk."

Alex waited, but when Reynolds didn't say anything else, he spoke up. "You mentioned two things. What's the other?"

"That's it. Residency and department. You got 'em both starting tomorrow morning." He seemed to reconsider. "On second thought, we might oughta make that starting at six tonight. Have a problem with this?"

"No problems, but if we're done with this issue, I have something to run by you. Brett Johnson. Heard any rumblings about him from the residents?"

Reynolds haphazardly replaced his glasses and started tapping his steepled fingers together. "Rumblings. Huh. Damn good word for it. Yes, I have. Why d'you ask?"

"He's been late for cases. When I question him, I get the feeling he's lying. I've had a few complaints from the residents about him—not answering pages some nights, forcing them to cover for him. Things to that effect."

This last statement raised Reynolds's eyebrows. "Know this for fact, or is this only just grumblings?"

"Nothing for fact. He's on my service now, so if he is lying to me, I plan to find out soon enough."

Reynolds sucked a tooth. "What you think we oughta do about it?"

Alex hated what he was about to say. "There's no room in the program for liars. If I catch him in a blatant one, he needs to be out of here. I can't believe it would be a one-time event."

Reynolds nodded. "Agreed. Whatever you do, I want to be damn sure we got us ironclad documentation of wrongdoing. I want it in our files. Can't have him coming back at us with some wild-ass wrongful termination suit. In other words, you catch him in a lie that's cause for termination, you better have enough evidence to prove it in a court of law. Understand?"

"Yes sir."

"You get that evidence, you fire his ass. It'll stress the rotation some, but the boys will understand."

Alex checked his beeper. "They're ready for my second case. We good here?"

Reynolds nodded, his attention already back to the paperwork in front of him. "We are."

"… and protect us from harm. Amen."

Alex stopped halfway through the door to one of the small private rooms in the surgery waiting area reserved for families. Clarence Hill stood in the center of room, the family of Alex's patient clustered around him. Taken aback, Alex asked, "What are you doing here?"

Clarence stood with arms outstretched in a pose resembling Christ on the cross. "Leading my brothers and sisters in a prayer for God's benevolent healing. These folk are members of my flock. How's Brother Roland doing?"

My flock? Alex realized the thing he resented most was Clarence's smug self-assuredness. In spite of Alex's ability to control the residents, Clarence knew he could proselytize whenever and wherever he wished. And at the moment, he appeared to savor his ability to rub Alex's nose in it. *The patient comes first,* Alex reminded himself. *Forget it. Let this pass. It's a stressful time for them.* He could think of nothing to do but smile. "Roland's fine. I was able to remove a hundred percent of the tumor. He's in the recovery room and should be waking up soon. Once he does, I'll move him to the intensive care unit for overnight observation. I expect he'll be back to his room tomorrow morning."

Clarence smiled at his flock and lifted his hands like a priest at the altar. "Praise be to God!" The family echoed his words. Alex turned and left. *What goes around comes around, Clarence. Count on it.*

43

"Best way to deal with those rag-heads is to just nuke the hell out of Baghdad," Brett Johnson said. "Drop a big one and turn that damn place into glass. Launch a hundred cruise missiles, that ought to do it."

Alex stopped operating to look at the young man. "Don't joke about that."

Johnson recoiled. "Hell, I ain't joking. I'm serious as a damn heart attack. The Koran tells the Arabs to slaughter all infidels—meaning anyone who's *not* Muslim. We just need to wipe out all them rag-heads before they get the chance and settle the issue."

Alex handed Chuck his instruments and turned to look at the resident. "Where'd you come up with that business about the Koran?" Alex glanced over the surgical drape at Cole. Cole looked up from the latest issue of *Car and Driver* he was reading and nodded, letting him know he was listening.

"Everybody knows that," Brett said dismissively.

"News to me. Then again, I guess I'm not everybody. So tell me, did you personally read those words in the Koran, or is this something you heard from a friend?" The only sounds in the room now were the soft hiss of the suction and the wheeze of the anesthesia machine. The circulator, Chuck, and Cole were all listening. Cole turned down the cardiac monitor to a barely perceptible volume.

Johnson dropped his eyes to the surgical field. "You mean me personally? No, I don't read that Arab shit. But I have it on good authority."

Alex seldom stopped a case to talk, but he wasn't going to let the remark pass unchallenged. "What good authority?"

"Oh hell, I don't remember."

"Have you read *any* of the Koran?"

Johnson gave a derisive snort. "Hell no. Why should I do something like that?"

"Doctor Johnson?" A circulating nurse stuck her head in the door. "You on call today?"

"I am." He sounded relieved to have a distraction.

"Just got called by the ER. They need a resident to come see a patient."

Johnson waved her away. "Tell them I'm busy. Call someone else."

Alex jumped on it. "Wait, don't do that." He looked at Johnson. "You're not really doing much at the moment, and this dissection's going to take me"—he glanced at the wall clock—"another couple hours. Go ahead, scrub out. I'll muddle on without you."

Johnson slapped his sucker onto the overhead table in a snit. "Whatever."

"Doctor Cutter," the circulator said, breaking his concentration, "we just got called again by the ER. Seems they're still waiting on a resident to come see the patient."

Alex handed off the Malis—a forceps capable of cauterizing tissue—to Chuck and rocked his neck side to side, working out kinks. He stood up from the rolling stool and backed away from the microscope so he could flex and extend his spine in an attempt to loosen up the tight, aching muscles. The clock showed him he'd been sitting in the same position for three straight hours.

"Bob, Chuck, please note the time." Then he told the circulator, "Call the lounge and find out which resident is free at the moment. Ask him to come see me. If we don't have one available, find one who's scrubbed."

"You call, Boss?"

Ah, Steve Stein. Perfect. "I did. There's a patient in the ER who needs to be seen. Pop on down there, take care of it, and report back as soon as you're done. Got it?" If Johnson was lying to him—which he strongly suspected—this might be the perfect opportunity to document it.

"I'm on it."

"Note the time?" he asked the moment Stein was out of the room.

Both Cole and Chuck said they had.

"Routine migraine," Stein explained thirty minutes later. "Took care of it and discharged her with instructions to schedule a follow-up with you next week. Anything else?"

Alex thought about it a moment and decided he needed to keep a lid on this incident until he had a chance to sort out all the facts. "Yes. Keep this just between us. Understood?"

After a questioning look, Stein nodded and pushed through the heavy OR doors into the hall.

"Bob, please note the time."

Thirty minutes later Johnson sauntered in, tying his mask in place. "All taken care of."

Alex handed his instruments to Chuck and stood, grateful for another excuse to stretch. *This should be interesting.* "What was the problem?" He tried to sound neutral.

"Routine rear-end collision. Driver was complaining of neck pain. The only reason I needed to be gone so long was I had to get X-rays, and Radiology was backed up as usual. I'll scrub back in." He turned toward the door to the scrub sinks.

"Hold on. Before you do, jot down the patient's name so I can sign the chart when I finish up here."

Johnson appeared at a loss for words. "Uh … that's not necessary."

"Oh? Why not? You signed the chart as my resident, right?" If so, Alex would be required to countersign.

Johnson shuffled his feet. "Not exactly. Thing is, uh, Friedman came in about the time I was finishing up, so I asked if he'd sign the orders. I know he's not on the rotation but thought I'd save you the hassle. So you see, there's no need to bother."

A wave of sadness descended over Alex. Why lie? What could he possibly think he'd gain? Didn't he realize he'd eventually be caught?

"It's no bother because I *do* want to review the chart. Consider it part of resident quality control."

Johnson nodded agreement. "Okay. I'll do it after the case is over."

Alex caught Chuck rolling his eyes. "No, Brett, write down the patient's name *now*. I'm closing anyway. It'll be done before you can finish a scrub. Leave the name on my loupes case. Okay?"

Johnson shrugged. "Whatever."

Alex watched the circulator hand him a progress note to write on. Johnson glanced back over his shoulder at Alex, shrugged again, and wrote something on the paper before slinking out the door.

"Hey, Johnson," Alex called after him. "Two things."

"What?"

"First of all, leave the paper."

"Oh." Johnson reluctantly handed the sheet to the circulator. "What else?"

"What would you say if I told you Humpty Dumpty was pushed?"

As Johnson shouldered his way out the door, he called over his shoulder, "He was probably an asshole and deserved it."

With Johnson gone, Alex asked Cole and Chuck, "You guys catch all this?"

"Hard to miss," Cole said.

"Good. I'd appreciate it if none of this leaves this room. At some later time it may be necessary for you to verify what just happened."

"Uh, uh, uh, Lord have mercy," Chuck muttered. "That boy's in a world of hurt."

With the wound dressed and the patient on his way to the recovery room, Alex—still wearing scrubs—dropped down three flights of stairs to the Emergency Room. Luckily, the nurse who initially called for the consult was finishing up his end-of-shift paperwork.

"The patient you called about, which resident took it?"

"Just a second, let me have a look." The nurse began thumbing through a handful of charts in the "Out" bin. A moment later he slid one from the stack. "Here we go. Let's see … a migraine. Looks like your man Stein took care of it. Why?"

"Brett Johnson show up to see anyone?"

The nurse reached for a log of all the patients seen during the day and by whom, and ran a finger down the list. "Nope. Doesn't look like Johnson's been here today. The list runs from midnight till now. Want me to check yesterday's records?"

"No, that's not necessary. Has a whiplash patient been seen today?"

He checked the log again. "Doesn't look like it."

"Friedman been here to see anyone in the past two to three hours?"

This time he didn't need to check. "Nope."

"Final question: Know of any problems getting Johnson to respond to calls?"

With a sigh, the nurse glanced away, perhaps searching for a diplomatic answer. "Let me put it this way: we've had our issues."

"What sort of issues?"

"Pretty much exactly what we're discussing. Not answering pages. And when he does, he doesn't always come in. Which obviously puts us in a bind, because we then have to turn around and call around for someone else to come see the patient. There've been times when your boys are tied up over at the trauma center so we had to call in one of the private surgeons. They're not thrilled about the idea of backstopping your guys."

Alex closed his eyes and squeezed the bridge of his nose, trying to lessen an impending headache. "Why am I just hearing about this?"

"Supposedly Doctor Reynolds was told about it a while ago, but nothing's been done. Least nothing we've been able to see."

Reynolds was probably too busy at the time and simply forgot. Alex jotted down the nurse's name and other particulars about the incident. "I may need to have you recount this conversation under more formal conditions. Any problem with that?"

The nurse seemed relieved to have the story out. "None at all."

44

"Excuse me, Doctor Stein," Alex interrupted, stopping Steve Stein in the middle of presenting an X-ray during the Monday teaching conference. "I that see Dr. Johnson has elected to join us." The time was 4:16 p.m. All eyes went from Stein to Johnson, who was halfway down the auditorium aisle.

"Dr. Johnson," Alex called, "please tell the group what kept you from being here at the start of conference."

Several residents exchanged knowing glances while Johnson awkwardly slipped into an empty seat behind the group. "Sorry, sir, I was taking care of a post-op."

"Right, patient care comes first." Alex stood up and pulled a blank index card and pen from his lab coat breast pocket. "What's the patient's name?"

More furtive glances between residents.

"The patient's name?" Johnson asked lamely.

"Yes, the patient's name."

"Oh, man … right on the tip of my tongue … give me a second; it'll come. Go ahead, don't hold things up on account of me."

"Okay. After conference you stay and we'll discuss it."

"I'd love to, Doctor Cutter, but I need to get back to my patient soon as we finish. In fact, if my beeper goes off, I may have to leave early."

Alex knew the old beeper trick all too well. Trigger it yourself or have a buddy call you. Who can say you shouldn't leave whatever you're doing to answer the page? Convenient.

"No, you don't. You stay right there," he snapped. "You *will* stay and we *will* discuss this." He addressed the group. "Conference adjourned. Everybody out except for Doctor Stein. Steve, come here please." Alex kept an eye on Johnson as the rest of the residents set a new world record for how fast they filed out of the auditorium.

Stein began quickly repacking the CT scans into a large green Radiology envelope, the green color identifying the films as loaners. Now finished, Stein approached Alex. "Yes, Boss?"

"Wait in the lobby."

Stein glanced from Alex to Johnson, back again. "You bet," he said before high-tailing it out of the room.

Alex approached Johnson, who stood, licked his lips, and started rubbing his thumb and fingertips together, a nervous habit of his frequently displayed when presenting a case at conference. "Okay, Brett, let's go see your post-op."

Suddenly, Johnson went all hangdog on him, shifting his weight, hemming and hawing as he got his act together. He inhaled audibly. "Sorry, sir, but I lied. There is no post-op patient. Actually, I was on the phone to my mother. She's just been diagnosed with breast cancer, and I was trying to talk her through the treatment options. She doesn't understand medical things very well and is frightened to death."

Ah, Jesus. The dying mother routine. Only slightly more believable than the dog-ate-my-homework excuse. "Sorry to hear that." Alex mimed a thoughtful pose. "You know, I bet I could help with that. Why don't we go to my office and call her, put her on speaker phone. I'll be more than happy to explain things to her. C'mon, let's go." Alex motioned to the aisle.

Johnson looked even more pathetic now, complete with a bit of foot shuffling. Another shake of his head. "Aw man … Aw shit … Look, I'm sorry, but that was a lie too. Because, see, I'm too embarrassed to admit the truth. We're having marital problems. My wife … she doesn't understand why I have to spend so much time at the hospital. I was on the phone to her and, well, it's overwhelming … the thought of losing her."

Alex relaxed his fists and extended his fingers, loosening them. “Enough! You just lied twice in less than thirty seconds, and I know you’ve lied to me in the past.” His voice wavered on the cusp of anger.

Johnson snapped from hangdog to righteous indignation. “Lied in the past? Never!”

Alex sliced his palm through the air. “Stop it! I don’t want to hear any more bullshit. It’s all been documented.”

Johnson stiffened. “And just what do you think you’ve documented?” He sounded confident now, as if calling a poker bluff with four aces in hand.

“Fair enough.” Alex nodded and withdrew a card from his white coat. “Let’s start with Friday. You scrubbed out to answer an ER call. I checked on it after I finished my case. You never got within a hundred feet of the place. I ended up sending Stein to cover for you. Then you had the nerve to look me straight in the eye and lie about it. This has been going on all year.” Alex held out his hand. “Hand over your ID card. You’re fired.”

Shocked and stunned, Johnson stared back. “No, don’t do this. Please. I’m serious about my wife. Fire me and she’ll leave me for sure. Please, Doctor Cutter, sir, don’t do this to my marriage and family.”

Alex motioned again for Johnson’s ID. “*I’m* not doing a thing to you. You did it to you. Card, Johnson. I want it *now*.”

“But … I’m on call.”

“No, you’re not. That’s already been taken care of. The paging operators have been notified. You’ve already been removed from the residency roster, and your hospital privileges are revoked.”

They walked from the auditorium, Alex turning right and—to his relief—Johnson veering left, Alex wanting as much distance from him as possible. It’d been harder than he imagined to fire the kid. Stein stood in the main lobby, still holding the green folder of CT scans.

“Steve, sorry for this imposition, but you’re taking Johnson’s call tonight,” Alex said. Of all the residents in the program, he trusted Stein most, probably because of their relationship prior to relocating here.

He and Stein had shared confidential information, so he knew the kid could keep a secret.

"Figured that was what had happened when I got called for a problem on Seven Madison."

"Good. I'll leave it to you and the others to revise the call schedule."

45

"WHAT'S THE BIGGEST RISK of operating with this position?" Alex asked Steve Stein as they opened the bone flap for a craniotomy. Alex had the patient positioned on his left side, the table incline placing the feet a few inches lower than the head.

"Blood loss?"

Alex made the "wrong answer" buzzer sound. "Nope. Try again." Then to Chuck, "Bone wax." Quickly, with the piece of bone detached from the skull and safely wrapped in a saline-soaked sterile towel, Alex began pushing wax into the marrow space of the skull edges. "Why am I using bone wax?" The sterile wax would seal the space, making it airtight.

Steve moved the sucker closer to where Alex worked, clearing away the oozing blood. "To stop bleeding."

Alex packed the last spot, then used a wet cotton sponge to wipe the remaining wax off his gloves. "True, but what else? Why not simply cauterize the space?"

"Don't know. Because cautery doesn't work well with bone?"

Alex placed the unused glob of wax back on the overhead tray. "We want to prevent air from being sucked into the venous system. Doesn't have to be much at any one time, but over time it can add up." He looked to Chuck. "Irrigation."

Chuck placed a blue rubber ball with a short nozzle in Alex's hand. He used this to squirt sterile saline over the exposed dura and bone edges, washing away residual bone dust and blood before proceeding to the next stage of the opening. "Same goes for when we open the dura. We have a major venous sinus running along here," he said, pointing along the midline of the brain surface. "We need to be extremely careful to keep from getting an air embolism. That, Doctor Stein, is our most serious concern right now. And what's the name of this sinus we're trying to avoid?"

"Superior saggital sinus."

"Exactly."

A few minutes later, Alex stopped Stein as he carefully cut open a three-sided flap of dura hinged along the sinus. "Hold on. You're close to the edge of the sinus now. It's not safe to cut any closer. Let me take it from here." Alex stepped over to the wall-mounted X-ray box for a closer look at the CT scans to gauge the sinus width. He heard Stein ask for a pair of surgical scissors and started to turn to tell him again to stop, when, to his horror, blood gushed from the wound. Stein froze.

"Shit!" Alex shouldered Stein aside. "Lap pad, soaked!"

Chuck rammed the sodden cotton into his hand. Alex pushed it against the dura, hoping to stop the hemorrhage and prevent the sinus from sucking air. "What the hell did you do?"

"I ... wanted a bit more exposure. Just a snip."

"I said *stop*. What didn't you understand about that one fucking word?" Alex immediately regretted his tone. "Sorry."

His mind started racing. His gentle pressure on the lap pad was keeping the bleeding minimized but not controlled. He paused to collect his thoughts. It was crucial to glimpse the damage so he could decide the best way to repair it. "Bob, we have a major problem here."

"I can see that," Cole replied, peering over the sterile drapes.

Alex began thinking out loud, talking to no one in particular. "We need to look at the damage. Steve, how much did you cut?"

"Jeez, I don't know. I put the tips of the Metzenbaum in and snipped ... Wasn't much, couldn't been more than a couple millimeters."

Bullshit. From the ooze seeping around the lap pad, Stein had clearly entered the sinus in the upper right-hand corner of the craniotomy. The question now was how much had been opened. Regardless of how much pressure he applied—and he couldn't apply much because he was pressing against brain—the bleeding continued, forcing him to do something quickly to control it before the patient bled too much.

"Okay, I'm going to pull back the corner to get a look. Steve, I want you ready with a large-bore Sachs sucker."

He waited for Chuck and Steve to change to a larger sucker, capable of handling the amount of bleeding.

"Ready?"

Steve put the sucker tip into place next to where Alex would pull back the lap pad.

"Have another soggy lap pad ready, Chuck. Okay, here I go." He tossed the soaked pad blindly behind him then reached for a replacement. Blood gushed at him with such force he couldn't see the origin. "Fuck!" He pressed the fresh pad into place.

"Bob, we've got some *serious* trouble here." He fought to keep gut-wrenching fear from his voice. If he showed the slightest panic, everyone would panic.

"What do we do?" Stein asked.

"Shhh! Let me think!"

Basics. Always default to basics. Knowing there were fundamental rules, surgical principles to follow, gave him a sliver of hope. *Don't deviate from the basic rudiments. Control bleeding and maintain an airway.* He ran a mental checklist of the things he needed. "Bob, how much blood we have on hand?"

"Two units."

"Run out a couple red tops for four more immediate units, then have them set up another four for standby … just in case. We're getting some major blood loss here."

"I'm drawing them as you speak," Cole said.

"And turn off the music."

In the next instant all you could hear were the monitors and mechanicals. Alex bet everyone could probably hear his heart hammering his sternum.

Blood's taken care of, airway's under control. What next?

"Bob. Raise and level the table."

"What do—"

"Silence!" Alex cut Stein off again but this time didn't bother to worry about his tone. Several seconds ticked past as he thought and rethought his limited options. He was sweating profusely as drops slithered down his chest.

"Okay, here's the deal," he explained to no one in particular. "We're in the sinus. That much is clear. The question is how much is cut and how can we control it." All of this was rhetorical, he knew, but it felt better to talk through it out loud. "I need a visual to know that."

"Chuck, load up a big wad of Surgicel plus a wad of thrombin-soaked Gelfoam." Both were agents used to help blood clot. "When you have those ready, let me know and I'll try to take another look. Steve, be ready with two Sachs suckers down here. Soon as I pull the lap pad, get in and clear out as much of the field as possible." He wished for more experienced hands to help him but couldn't afford the time to muster another assistant into the room. He flashed on Reynolds's advice of having seniors with him. Too late for that.

"Want me to bust out Fullager?" the circulator asked, referring to the chief resident. "He's just next door."

"Thanks, but we don't have time." He glanced up and saw Chuck pouring thrombin into a stainless steel bowl, soaking big squares of Gelfoam. Two big wads of Surgicel, a silver mesh, were balled up and ready to go. "Tell me when you're ready."

"Thirty seconds."

Alex checked his own breathing, forcing himself to take slow, measured breaths instead of hyperventilating as he'd been doing. He mentally orchestrated the exact moves he needed to make once he pulled away the sponge. "Speed kills," he muttered, an old axiom learned from Baxter. *Be careful.*

"Ready when you are," Chuck said.

"Okay, listen up everyone. This is the plan. I'm going to pull back the corner of this lap pad while Steve sucks. I figure we have maybe three seconds to look. Chuck, have the Gelfoam ready first." He held up his bayonet forceps so Chuck could load the tips with the foam. "I'm going to stuff this into the corner, then pack it in place with the Surgicel.

Steve, have a cottonoid ready to follow. Soon as I put the Surgicel in place, stuff that cottonoid directly on top of all of it. Then a fresh lap pad." The old pad was already leaking way too much blood. "Okay, we set?"

Chuck, Stein, and Cole said they were.

"On the count of three. One, two, three."

Alex threw the blood-soaked pad off to his left, landing with a sodden plop on the floor, while Stein sucked at the torrent of blood filling the field. "Suck!"

Stein couldn't begin to keep up with the hemorrhage.

"Shit! Gelfoam."

He quickly stuffed the foam into the approximate location, then repacked the field in the order he'd described, holding just enough pressure to keep the blood from seeping around the pack.

"What now?" Cole asked.

Good question.

"Can't see the bleeding site well enough. I want to try one more look, but not until I've held pressure on it for five minutes by the clock." He hoped the thrombin-soaked Gelfoam might slow the hemorrhage by that time. "Start the clock. I don't want us short-changing the time. Bob, raise his head just a bit."

"Why do that?" Stein asked. "Doesn't that increase your risk of air embolism?"

Alex nodded. "Yes it does, but so far we haven't been able to see a goddamn thing. I'm hoping to improve enough venous return to slow the bleeding and see the cut. If we have any chance at all of getting the patient out of here, we *have* to control the bleeding. Forget about going after the tumor at this point."

The room remained deathly silent. Everyone realized Alex wasn't being melodramatic.

"Everyone know what to do?" Alex asked even though he knew they did. "Okay then, on the count of three. One, two, three."

Hands flew. Alex glimpsed the cut sinus. He held out his hand. "Back-handed dural silk. Quickly!" He intended to stitch in a Gelfoam patch, another trick learned from Baxter. If he could just get the stitch in—

"We're getting air," Cole said with urgency.

"Lap pad."

Alex packed the opening as Cole leveled the operating table.

"She just arrested," Cole said.

The pit of Alex's stomach dropped out. The complication just gained more momentum than they could likely handle, and in that instant he knew the patient was doomed.

"Get the overhead out," Alex shouted, kicking off the brake and pushing the heavy table away from the patient just as Chuck jumped off. The sterile field vanished as he dragged drapes over it, but at this point sterility was the least of their concerns. Alex stayed at the patient's head, holding the blood-soaked pad on the wound in an attempt to staunch more bleeding, which he later realized was fruitless because the heart was no longer beating.

With the respirator on full assist, Cole started pumping the chest, the monitors screaming at the flat-line EKG. "Get another anesthesiologist in here!" Cole yelled to the paralyzed, wide-eyed circulator.

She bolted from the room.

"Your call," Cole said to Alex.

Alex used the bloodied sleeve of his surgical gown to blot away tears. He tried to swallow, but the constriction in his throat kept him from doing that. Cole, the other two anesthesiologists, Chuck, Steve, and the circulator waited in the mess surrounding the operating table: syringes, sponges, debris strewn over the floor. He tried to swallow again and wet his mouth with saliva.

"Okay." He glanced at the wall clock. "The official time of death is nine twenty-seven," he said in a weak, cracking voice.

He stripped off his gloves, balled up his gown, and threw the wad into the linen hamper. "I'll go tell the parents." The patient was a twenty-one-year-old single woman.

Cole came up to him and rested a reassuring hand on his shoulder. "I'll go with you."

Alex felt a flood of relief for having his support. Telling the family was going to be difficult enough. Doing it alone, unbearable.

"You don't have to, you know."

"I know, but I should be there with you."

"Thank you."

Alex knocked twice on the door before pushing it open. The mother and father sat side by side in the small room. Styrofoam cups littered the chipped table to the right, and the air smelled of coffee. The mother looked up, saw Alex, and smiled. "That was quick."

Alex entered the room, his mind now completely blank, having lost the words so carefully prepared during the trip there. A flash went through the father's eyes. He knew what was coming.

"I'm afraid I have bad news," Alex said, moving to the mother. "Your daughter had a serious complication and her heart stopped. We couldn't get it started again." She studied his eyes, processing the unfathomable information as her husband wrapped his arm around her shoulders, hugging her to himself. "I'm *so* very sorry," Alex said as she began to cry. Alex knelt in front of her and took her hands in his. "I'm so very sorry."

46

"Fire him," Lisa said.

"Who? Stein? No." Alex waved away the suggestion, his mind endlessly replaying every moment from telling Stein stop opening the dura until he pronounced the patient dead. All the questions reverberating in his brain: What could he have done differently? Wait longer before taking the second look? He kept returning to the bleeding, the volume of it forcing him to act. Could he have worked faster with the stitch? Maybe even …

"Why not? If I understand it, he did the action that resulted in her death."

"He didn't *kill* the patient, Sweetie; an air embolism did." He berated himself for not being more explicit when he told Steve to stop. Was it therefore his fault? It could well have been Alex who cut into the sinus. Well, probably not. He never would've have cut that far. How could he live knowing a patient of his died in the operating room from a preventable error?

"But didn't you say he caused the air embolism? I don't understand your logic; you fire a resident for lying, but you don't fire a resident for a fatal complication? What's wrong with this picture?"

Oh, for Christ's sake. "Can you just drop it? Please? Now isn't the time, okay?"

"I'm just asking."

"Shit. Those two things aren't even comparable. Lying repeatedly is a moral issue, a deeply ingrained personality flaw indicative of future ethical problems. What Steve did was a simple mistake in surgical judgment. Every surgeon is going to make that kind of error sooner or later. It's inevitable. I just hope he learned something from it." He was certain he had. Steve had been devastated, even offering to resign from the residency. Alex had talked him into staying. At the wet bar Alex poured a weak scotch. "Want a drink?" he asked, hoping to distract her.

"Sure. But answer my question."

"I just did." He packed two glasses with crushed ice. "It was a mistake anyone could make, even a seasoned surgeon."

"Know what I think? I think you *can't* be objective about Steve because you two have a history. He's not like any of your other residents. *You* picked him for the program. It's always harder to fire someone you chose."

"Lisa, let it go. Please. I don't care to discuss it. Especially not tonight." He handed off her drink before heading to his desk. He knew trying to read a journal would be fruitless. Never had he lost a patient in the OR, much less from a preventable error. It'd been a point of pride. Somehow, in spite of knowing the risks of neurosurgery, he'd become … what? Blasé? Believing fatal errors happened only to other surgeons, because he was so careful, so tight-assed that he could sail through a career having none? On the other hand, he'd gone so long with so few complications that the odds were stacked against him. No one could practice the volume he did without stepping on an occasional land mine. He was now paying for letting down his guard. He'd always maintained it was the little things that ended up torpedoing you; he constantly drummed it into the residents' heads. It's one thing to have a patient die from a malignant brain tumor, subarachnoid hemorrhage, or head trauma. Those situations carried intrinsically high risks for bad outcomes regardless of any intervention. You felt compassion for those patients but not responsible for their poor outcomes. It was an entirely different matter to have a patient die from surgeon error. Intolerable. If anyone should be punished, it should be him.

But what should he do? Stop operating? Throw away years of training and hard work as penance for one error? After all, air embolism is a well-known complication of intracranial surgery. Isn't neurosurgery a high-risk practice? Can any surgeon be expected to maintain his volume without a death?

Two hours later Alex pushed back from the desk and took the empty glass to the sink. Quietly, to not wake Lisa, he slipped into the bathroom to prepare for bed, having resolved nothing.

Now in bed, he tried to relax, to slip off to sleep. Would God forgive him? If a judgment day did exist, would the good he'd done in a lifetime outweigh the bad? It dawned on him that he thought of God mostly during troubled times—such as now. God. This wasn't a new thought, yet his stormy weather religion disappointed him. It didn't seem fair to seek peace of mind only in difficult times. True believers probably thanked God daily for their lives, like Clarence thanking God for a meal. Perhaps. Yet Clarence's religiosity somehow didn't ring pure, as if he used it as a prop to garner self-worth or social acceptability.

Don't think of Clarence tonight.

Why am I so skeptical?

Well, for one, there was the basic Christian assumption— taken to extremes by conservative fundamentalists—that the Bible is the literal word of God. Alex found it inconceivable that translations of documents and verbal histories generated long after the events they purportedly described and chronicled reflected anything more than hearsay or ecumenical propaganda. He remained leery of the Heaven and Hell concept. Or, for that matter, belief in an afterlife of any kind. In spite of these logic road bumps, the phenomenon of life awed him. He found it impossible to wrap his mind around a time-space spectrum that spanned from an atom to a light year, to say nothing of the incomprehensible vastness of the universe. He was left with a myriad of unanswered questions. What exactly was life? Nothing more than a chemical reaction? And what the hell was consciousness? What had his young patient lost today on the operating room table the moment her heart stopped supporting her brain?

He stared at the barely discernable phone, lit only by the glow of the digital clock. It waited silently two feet from his nose, threatening to ring. He hated the damn thing. Hated how it robbed him of sleep.

Hated being held hostage to it. Because the residents knew he preferred to be kept in the loop for problems with his inpatients, he had only himself to blame for the calls. Each call robbed him of an hour or more of sleep. He'd forgotten how it felt to be completely rested. Did such a state actually exist?

Alex rolled over.

Unable to sleep, Alex checked the clock again. 1:08 a.m. Shit! Six and a half hours until his next case. A complicated one at that. He needed to sleep. And that fucking phone sat there waiting for him to drift off before it would ring, as if it was controlled by some evil intent. Alex closed his eyes and waited for the ring. Had he known how fatiguing neurosurgery practice would be, would he have chosen the same career? Good question. Probably.

He was slowly developing—especially during nights like this—a growing dislike for clinical practice. The harder he tried, the further away research seemed to become. Day after day he removed brain tumors, the majority gliomas, ironically the basis of his research. Would he ever get back on track? Not with his present practice. Not unless he made a major life change. What kind of change, he had no idea.

The good news, he realized, was he and Lisa didn't live large like most of his partners. No new cars, no expensive homes, no fancy trips to Europe. Meaning that once he'd built a nest egg, he could bail.

He squinted at the clock. 2:13. Still no sleep. *Goddamn phone.*

"What time you get to sleep?" Lisa asked, setting out a bowl of oatmeal.

Alex yawned and poured milk over the mush. "Must've fallen asleep sometime after two." The stove clock showed 5:40 a.m. He intended to make fast rounds before heading to the OR.

"Don't forget we're meeting the Canters tonight at your partner's restaurant."

Friday night dinners at the University Club had become an enjoyable ritual for him. Since relocating here, he hadn't made many friends. Mostly, he didn't have time, but he hadn't put much effort into it either, having quickly discovered he shared little common ground with his partners and neighbors. People accepted his practice as a valid excuse that kept them from attending social events. Luckily, Lisa felt the same as he. But Friday evenings with the Canters were different, perhaps because it felt as if they were expats living in a foreign country. Tonight they had reservations at a new Front Street restaurant a clinic partner bought recently as an "investment." Why a neurosurgeon would invest in a restaurant remained a mystery.

"Right. But let's make it a short evening. I'll be dog tired by then."

"Table for four?" asked the maître d'.

The question struck Alex as inane considering only one other table was occupied in the restaurant. He felt foolish for saying, "Reservations for Cutter."

"Yes, right this way." The young man led them ceremoniously to a table at the back of the restaurant. The place had an industrial feel, with two interior walls of exposed brick, a polished cement floor, and a brass rail at the bar. "Your waiter will be with you in a moment," he said, pulling out Lisa's chair.

Once they were seated and the maître d' had left, Andrew leaned into the table and lowered his voice. "It seems ludicrous to have made reservations, the place is essentially empty."

Alex nodded, glancing around the room again. "Pretty pathetic."

"You say a partner owns this?" Diana asked.

"Hi, I'm Michael, your server for the evening. Would any of you like to start with a cocktail or something else to drink—sweet tea, perhaps?"

All four ordered wine, and with the waiter out of earshot, Alex said, "Yeah. Bought it for his wife because she's a good cook and he thought it might be fun to start a restaurant. We never tried the previous restaurant in this building, but from what I hear, it bombed. Charlie claims he picked up the place for a steal. Looks awfully dead for a Friday night, though."

"Have any idea how he's doing with it?" Andrew asked.

"All I know is it's rumored he was forced to pull cash from his retirement account to keep it afloat these past couple months. He claims it takes time to get a new place established, but I imagine he's not doing all that well, especially if tonight is any indication. He's been lobbying the clinic to hold the quarterly business meetings here as a way to generate business, but we haven't done that yet. I think Garrison may be on the verge of caving in on that as a way of throwing him a bone. But wow, this looks bad."

"Your partner, does he or his wife have any experience in the restaurant business?"

"Nope."

She rolled her eyes. "Oh, that doesn't sound good."

"Doctors," Alex added shaking his head, "are notorious for bad making investments and getting into businesses they know nothing about. Another clinic partner poured a ton of money into a racehorse. I mean, what are the chances that's going to pay off? Don't know a thing about the racehorse business, but I can't believe it's a huge moneymaker. Unless, of course, you win the Kentucky Derby."

The waiter served their wine and asked if they were ready to order. Both wives ordered seafood salads. Andrew and Alex ordered filets.

"Why do you suppose you highly educated professionals are so prone to making bad investments?" Andrew asked.

"Good question. Here's my theory. Basically physicians are smart people but tend to overestimate their own capabilities. And it's not just bad investments like this one," he said with a sweep of his hand. "They get themselves into all sorts of trouble. How many times a year do we hear about a physician who crashes his plane in weather conditions commercial pilots avoid?" Alex thought about Garrison flying to out-clinics every week and was glad to be off that rotation.

Alex pulled into their driveway and braked the car. Natalie, their German shepherd, was lying on her side on the asphalt drive, belly distended, half-open glazed eyes staring blankly at the headlights. Alex slammed the transmission into park and was out of the car running to her side. Clearly the pooch was in pain and shock. "Open the back door!" he yelled as he scooped her up in his arms.

"My suggestion is for y'all to head on home," the veterinarian said. "Nothing you can do here, and we'll call soon as surgery's over. This'll take several hours and you'll be better off at home." At this time of night, the only veterinarian hospital open was an emergency clinic several miles from their home. Luckily they knew the location.

"Is she going to be okay?" Lisa asked, in tears.

"Can't guarantee anything, but my assistant's trying to snake a tube down her throat now. Sometimes we can straighten out the problem by doing only that and don't have resort to opening the belly. In any case, she'll have to stay overnight, maybe longer. Now, if you'll excuse me."

"Please tell me she'll be all right."

Alex gently took Lisa's arm. "He can't guarantee anything, Sweetie. The bowel flipped over on itself and is strangling its blood supply. This is an emergency and they need to hurry." He nodded at the doctor. "Let us know as soon as you have something. Please. She's our child."

"I understand."

Alex walked Lisa to their car, the back door still wide open from when Alex scooped Natalie into his arms to carry her into the clinic.

One problem with being a physician was sometimes knowing too much. From his internship on general surgery, Alex knew that torsion of the mesentery could be decidedly bad news, because it kinks the blood supply, causing the bowel to infarct. Once the blood flow is reestablished, the toxins from the dead tissue rush into the general circulation and cause toxic shock. He didn't know the mortality rate for dogs but remembered it to be high for humans if not treated aggressively. But Lisa was a pessimist by nature, so mentioning this to her now would only fuel her emotional turmoil. Besides, there was the chance, although small, that Natalie could survive. In spite of this slight specter of hope, he was already mourning the loss of his beloved shepherd.

The call came at 3:15 a.m., waking Alex from a fitful sleep. He quickly grabbed the phone and spoke softly. "I understand … I know …"

Lisa realized what was happening before he could hang up to give her the awful news. She got out of bed and paced the room, hands pressed against both temples, wailing, "Oh Natalie, Mommy's so sorry!"

Alex tried to hold and comfort her, but she shoved him away. "I shouldn't have given her the extra food," she cried. "It's all my fault. She was such a finicky eater lately. I was so happy when she wanted more. It's *my* fault!"

Alex tried again to put his arms around her to comfort her, but she screamed at him and shoved him away, huge tears cascading down her cheeks. He felt so helpless. This, he knew, would devastate her.

47

"You hear the news?" Betsy Lou asked from the door to his office. He had just finished dictating a note on a patient follow-up visit.

He hated that question because he had no idea what she was referring to. "What news?"

With a conspiratorial grin, she entered the office and half-closed the door. "Dave Ray just got fired. Just now. I saw him escorted out the clinic. We're in the process of getting the locks changed." She gave an emphatic nod. "I saw him leave. It's a big deal, all the nurses are talking about it." Her expression segued to satisfaction at playing the role of clinic newscaster.

For a shocked moment, Alex processed the news. *Could it be true?* Then again, what earthly reason would there be for Betsy Lou to lie about this? None. He believed her. "What happened? What'd he do?"

"No one knows, and I can't get a word out of Linda, no matter how hard I try. It has to be something very sensitive or she'd tell me. I know she knows. She knows everything that goes on around here."

Alex would learn soon enough, having just been appointed to the clinic Board of Governors. "I'm sure we'll all find out in due time. But at the moment, I need to catch up on my dictation." What he really wanted to do was to corner Martin. Martin would tell him.

"Okay, catch you for afternoon rounds."

Out the corner of his eye, Alex saw Martin flash past his door on the way to his office. Alex was up out of his chair and across the secretarial alcove in a blink. "Can I talk to you?" he asked, closing Martin's office door behind him.

"Yep, but I'm already way backed up. That last case took me longer than I reckoned it would. Why, what's up?"

"Caught wind something happened to Dave Ray. Any truth to that?"

Martin's shoulders slumped as his face grew sad and serious. He nodded. "This is for your ears only. And the only reason I'm telling you a thing is 'cause I know you can keep your mouth shut. Yeah, he's gone. Got caught with his hand in the till. We reckon it's something close to a hundred thousand, give or take. Won't be sure until we finish the audit. Might not be a hundred percent sure even after that."

"Aw man ..." The news hit hard enough that Alex had to sit. He and Dave were friends, playing tennis whenever their busy schedules allowed. Small snippets of past conversations came to Alex's mind, Dave saying, "Those of us in administration do everything possible so the docs do what y'all do best, which is take care of patients. It frees you guys from doing what we do best, which is run the clinic." In this new context, the words took on a very different meaning. He never would have suspected Dave of embezzlement.

"Will the clinic press charges?" he asked, wondering what would happen to Dave if criminal charges were filed.

"No. And that's the primary reason we ain't saying nothing to nobody. Reckon it's in our best interest to keep it quiet."

"Why?" Seemed strange to him.

Martin shook his head. "Hell, damn lawyers would probably end up costing us more than fifty grand if we file on his sorry ass. Besides, the clinic certainly doesn't want the negative publicity that's bound to come with it. On top of all that, our lawyer advised us we flat-out might not have us enough proof—I'm talking concrete proof—to win in court." Martin frowned. "Damn shame's all I have to say."

With conflicting emotions, Alex considered Martin's words. Having his money stolen—which is exactly what it boiled down to—incensed him. Yet, Martin made sense—best to minimize their losses. "If you don't mind me asking, how did you catch him?"

The corners of Martin's mouth curled up. "Wasn't me. Jeff caught it," he said, referring to their head bookkeeper, "and slipped word to Garrison. Once we knew what we were looking for, we started digging. Stupid bastard didn't have a clue we were on to him, just kept on keeping on embezzling."

Jeff Strout impressed Alex as the kind of detail-oriented person who would make it his life mission to be damn sure every ledger entry contained two digits to the right of each decimal point. Alex checked his watch and saw he was behind schedule again. "Thanks for the info. I won't say a word about this, not even to Lisa. Better make rounds now."

"Need a word with you, Boss," Steve Stein said to Alex as soon as he walked out of the stairwell on Seven Madison. Steve wore green scrubs under his white lab coat and sky-blue booties over his Nikes, a surgical mask dangled from his neck.

Alex checked his watch. "Sure." He was falling further behind, just like a bad dream. Only moments ago he had run into a referring physician and felt obligated to chat him up a few minutes.

Steve surveyed the hall. "Feel better if we take it down the hall." They walked to a small wheelchair alcove. "I've got a problem and need advice on how best to handle it." He fiddled with the bell of the stethoscope draped around his neck.

"Sure, advice is cheap. What's up?"

Steve lowered his voice. "It's the Rev," he said, using the residents' nickname for Clarence Hill. "He's constantly on my case, pressuring me to have Nancy and I go to church with him. I keep telling him no, that I'm Jewish, but he keeps insisting, claims we're going to hell if we don't accept Jesus in our hearts as the one true God. It's really gotten old, and he's becoming more insistent. He claims his mission is to keep me from graduating unless I—rather *we*, Nancy and I—become Christian. What can I do to get him off my back?" Steve's eyes pleaded as much as his voice.

Alex's temples began pounding. He suspected his blood pressure of spiking too. He sucked a long, deep, calming breath. "Hang tough, Steve. I'll take care of it. Next time he mentions it I want to know immediately. Write down every damn detail: time, place, and exactly what he said. And if there's a witness, I want to know about that too. This is unacceptable."

Steve appeared relieved. "Thank you."

Rounds could wait, this couldn't. Alex took off for the stairs.

Alex found Hill in the surgeon's lounge conversing with two anesthesiologists. Alex interrupted Clarence without hesitation. "I need to talk with you out in the hall."

The moment they were out of earshot, Alex said, "You're to stop badgering residents, especially the Jewish ones, about going to church with you. This is a neurosurgical residency, not a Christian boot camp. I will not tolerate faculty forcing their particular religion on the residents. Understand what I'm telling you?"

Clarence smiled. A smug, self-satisfied smile, his facial muscles expressing more than words. "In all due respect, Alex, being a good Christian carries responsibilities. One very important one is to bring our savior Jesus Christ to those who don't have him in their hearts. Jews are particularly important because they reject Jesus as the son of our one true God. Unless they seek salvation, they're doomed. I can't stand by and see good people like Steve and Nancy Stein destine themselves to eternal hell. Same goes for you, by the way. Consider this my invitation for you and Miss Lisa to join us this Sunday. I'll have my secretary send you the time and address."

Speechless, Alex realized his mouth was hanging open, and closed it.

"You don't seemed convinced," Clarence added. "Too bad. I suppose the best we can do is agree to disagree on this issue. Now, are we done here? I have patients waiting."

Alex wanted to slap that smug, self-serving expression senseless. "This isn't a debate. It's not even open for discussion. I'm giving you an ultimatum. I find out you proselytized a resident, I'll pull your coverage so fucking fast you won't know what happened. I'm serious as hell about this, Clarence."

Well, at least that changed his expression.

"You can't do that. I won't allow it."

"I just did. And I can. I'm vice-chair of the residency, so I control resident coverage. End. Of. Story."

"You haven't heard the end of this, believe me."

"Yes, I have. This discussion is over." Alex headed for the stairs to let Garrison know what just happened before Clarence had the opportunity.

"You need to understand something, Alex. That is Clarence's prerogative. He's very spiritual and believes strongly in spreading the word of God." Garrison stood in his typical, slightly hunched posture, playing with the tie of the surgical mask that was still around his neck in spite of not having a case at the time.

"I don't give a rat's ass how spiritual he is. A neurosurgical residency is not the place to force religious views on people. Certainly not by a faculty member. The power we have over residents makes them vulnerable to coercion. They're in no position to object."

"He's not forcing anything on anybody."

"The hell he isn't. Let me come at this from a different angle. Do you believe a boss should be allowed to demand sexual favors from an employee?"

Garrison waved the question away. "No, of course not. That's ridiculous."

"Why is that?"

"Well … because that's just not right."

"So explain the difference between that and what Clarence is doing."

Exasperation flashed across Garrison's face. "Those are two different things. They're not even comparable. What Clarence is doing is a matter of beliefs and good intentions. He's trying to save a person's soul."

"Bullshit. The common denominator between the two situations is that the person holding power is using that power to manipulate the underling. And I find it all the more reprehensible that Clarence is saying his beliefs are right and Steve's are wrong."

"They're not the same. Clarence is defending his religion. This is something he believes he must do to be a good Christian."

"Bullshit again. He's forcing the residents to accept *his* particular belief. But that's beside the point. The point is he doesn't have the right to force residents—especially a Jewish one—to practice any religion. To do so is an infringement on personal rights."

Garrison shook his head. "You're mixing things up. All I can tell you is he's doing what he feels is the right thing. You can never fault a person for trying to do the right thing. I'm just sorry to see the clinic's future leaders at loggerheads. Both you boys are fixing to be here long after I'm gone. I desperately want the two of you to get along. For the good of all of us."

Alex couldn't believe it. What bond inspired such blind support? Did Garrison actually believe what he just said? Dave Ray had been right. Garrison, and probably the Board of Governors, saw Clarence as Garrison's successor—similar to Reynolds viewing Alex as his eventual replacement. The thought of another decade or so of squaring off against that smug little religious shit didn't seem worth the money he'd make. He continued to stare at Garrison, hoping for a sign of capitulation.

Garrison glanced away. "I'm backed up. Now, if you'll excuse me ..."

Alex had just stopped by the office to finish up some chart work before heading home when his beeper rang. He checked the message and saw it was a page from the exchange. He dialed.

"Yes, Doctor Cutter, we received a call from a Mr. Suzuki. He'd like you to call him. May I give you the number?"

"Yes." Alex slipped an index card from his white coat and readied a pen.

"Doctor Cutter, Agent Suzuki. Thanks for calling back."

Ah, the FBI agent. Now he recognized the name. "What can I do for you, Agent?"

"We're having trouble finding people to corroborate your allegations." Just putting it out there and letting it hang.

"That's not surprising. Weiner rules through intimidation. You spoke to the residents?"

"Yes, we have. And I always come away with the impression they're not being completely truthful. Several of them imply what you've said is correct, but when it comes to being put on record, they shy away. That fits with your suggestion, but at this point, without hard evidence, we're hard-pressed to continue the investigation."

Stalemate. Weiner was going to get away with it.

When he didn't say anything, Suzuki added, "This means, of course, you will not be eligible for a whistle-blower fee."

Alex laughed at that. "That wasn't my motivation for tipping you guys off."

"Anyway, thanks for contacting us."

"Before you go, I have one more idea."

"I agree with you," Lisa said after listening to Alex's story of the encounter with Clarence. They were enjoying a glass of wine before dinner. "Did Garrison give you any reason for supporting him like that?"

"No, nothing other than 'Clarence is following his Christian conscience.'"

She nodded, seemingly considering his words. "Do you think maybe you're too protective of Steve?"

Good question, but irrelevant. "Sure I'm protective of him. He's a good resident. Like you've always said, we go back to a time before we moved here. But whether or not we're friends more than a student-teacher relationship is beside the point. The point is whether or not Clarence has the right to pressure a resident to do something totally unrelated to their job."

"Would you feel the same if one of the other residents complained?" She didn't sound argumentative, just inquisitive.

"Absolutely. The purpose of the residency is to teach neurosurgery. Period. It's not a free pass to proselytize religion. Besides, like I said to Garrison, residents are at the mercy of the professors. Clarence as much as threatened to keep Steve from graduating if he didn't start attending church with them. Is that right?" Okay, perhaps a slight exaggeration of what Steve actually said, but close enough.

"But you have the power to see that it doesn't happen."

"Yes, I do. For Steve. This time. But what happens when I'm gone and Clarence is still here? What's going to happen to a Jewish or Muslim resident then?"

"Then it won't be your problem. Look, you're not going to convince Clarence he's wrong any more than he's going to convince you he's right."

As much as he hated to admit it, she was right.

48

"DOESN'T SURPRISE ME AT all," Martin said between breaths, his stride awkward and flat-footed. For the past three months Alex and Martin routinely jogged five miles every Saturday morning. The course started at Alex's house, continued down Central to the University Club, and looped around a block before heading back again via a zigzag route of side streets.

"What I don't understand," Alex continued, "is why Clarence and Garrison are so tight to begin with. How'd that come about?" He wiped his eyes with his sodden white sweatband, the morning already eighty degrees and as humid as a steam bath. Alex inhaled a floral scent he couldn't identify—sweet and succulent, curiously pleasing.

"What's to understand? He's a suck-up. Garrison is an easy mark for suck-ups. And the truth is, most of us find it hard to be objective when someone's sucking up to us. You know, don't you, that Garrison is godfather to Clarence's children?"

"Sure didn't." Could Martin be right, could it be just that simple? They jogged in silence past the high laurel hedges enclosing the University Club tennis courts, now starting the return route to Alex's house.

"Gotta ask you something," Alex said. "If it's too personal, just tell me to drop it."

"Sure."

"I came here expecting to encounter racial prejudice, so when I did, I wasn't really surprised. But what I didn't see coming was the amount of anti-Semitism. That caught me completely off guard."

Martin blinked sweat from his eyes. "What's your question?"

"How do you put up with it?"

Martin slowed in order to be able to talk in complete sentences instead of gasps. "Same reason the blacks around here tolerate racism: we don't have a hell of a lot of choice. Besides, we have our own community and our own country club. Doesn't mean it doesn't hurt or that I like it when I encounter it, but I learned a long time ago to live with it. When it comes down to it, I suppose I put up with it because I was born and raised here. Went to medical school and residency here; this is my home. If you think about it, that's pretty much Hill's story too. Born, raised, and trained here, so it's his home too. That answer your question?"

Alex wiped his brow again. "Not really. Guess that means I didn't quite ask the right question. It's just so different than what I'm used to. Don't think I'll ever get used to it."

"Well, if y'all plan to live here permanent, y'all better get used to it. Don't reckon things are likely to change anytime soon. Not as long as bigots like Hill live here. Which reminds me, hear what he did right after moving back to town?"

Alex slipped off a sweatband and squeezed sweat from it before slipping it back on. "No. What?"

"Story is he came back to the same church he'd been attending before going into the service. But this time 'round he decided it was too liberal, especially the way the elders interpreted the Bible. Too liberal! Can you imagine that? He quit to join a *really* fundamentalist group. I was shocked to find out there're folks more fundamentalist than the damned Baptists. Boggles the mind."

Alex raised his hand. "Hold up a second."

They stopped, both men leaning over, hands on thighs, gulping deep breaths of steam-bath air. "It may look like I'm about to pass out here, but I am listening," Martin said with a smile.

"You asked why Clarence's proselytizing bugs me so damn much. Well, maybe this will help you understand. I told you, didn't I, that after my birth father died my mom remarried?"

Knees straight, Martin bent at the hips to touch his toes, stretching his hamstrings, and held the pose for several seconds. "Yep."

"My stepdad adopted us. That's how come my name turned out to be Cutter. My birth name was Lippmann."

Martin straightened slowly, a quizzical expression on his face. "Nice Jewish name. What was your mother's maiden name?"

"She was a goy if that's what you're asking."

Martin scratched his crown of salt and pepper hair. "Why'd she have you adopted?"

"She had encountered too much anti-Semitism. She didn't want us to have to deal with it." He paused. "But enough of the true confessions. At Monday conference I'm going to make a point of telling the residents to report any proselytizing."

Martin motioned for them to start running again. "Might want to think on that before you do."

"Why?"

"'Cause it'll just cause more problems than it's worth. You made your point with Clarence, so I think you're good. That is, until Reynolds gets back. After that, well, who knows what the hell's gonna happen."

49

"I'D PREFER IT IF Estella can stay in the room with us," Meredith Costello said preemptively when Alex entered the exam room.

Alex closed the door and plunked down on the rolling stool. "No problem. Hope you don't mind me asking, what's your relationship?"

"She's my life partner," Meredith said with a hint of defiance.

Ah. "No problem." Alex stood up from the stool and motioned for her to sit on the exam table. "Let me take a look at your incision."

As she stared straight ahead, Alex studied the question-mark-shaped wound on the left side of her head and was pleased. Healing well, no more inflammation than normal. "I'm going to remove the staples now."

Staples removed, Alex returned to the stool, hands clasped together. He dreaded this next part and wished there was some way to telepathically transfer the information rather than having to actually say the words. There wasn't any, of course, and he certainly didn't believe in building false hope. After a deep breath, he said, "The pathology report came back and it's not good, Meredith. You have brain cancer. The formal name of it is a glioblastoma multiforme." He didn't add that they're one hundred percent fatal. "The only thing we need to decide now is what treatment you wish to receive to maximize your quality of life." He typically paused at this point to allow the awful news to sink in. Usually, the words didn't fully register until later. Most patients came to this appointment expecting the worst, yet when those fears were realized, they needed time to fully process the implications.

Meredith listened carefully, showing no shock, surprise, or disappointment. She nodded to her partner as if to say, "See, told you so." Then her eyes misted up as she blinked away tears. "How long do I have?"

Ah, so she *did* understand. "Can't say for sure. All I can give you are the broad statistics. With no additional treatment you have perhaps six months to a year. Radiation might extend that by six months. Chemotherapy alone isn't as effective as radiation, but by combining chemo with radiation, you can perhaps eke out a few extra weeks."

"A few weeks?" She snorted a sarcastic laugh. "At what price? I mean, what're the side effects of that combination? I've heard some awful things about chemo. Terrible things." Having anticipated the bad news, she'd prepared the right questions.

Personally, with the present state of the art, Alex wouldn't choose chemo. The only effective drug—if you could call it that—was BCNU, a drug neurosurgeons darkly referred to as "Be Seeing You."

"Well, you can always hold off on the chemo and add it later if you change your mind. But I strongly advise you to start the radiation as soon as possible. The wound's healed enough to be able to tolerate it." Because the objective of radiation was to kill replicating cells, it was not a good idea to radiate fresh wounds that were still laying down fresh scar tissue.

Now came the part of his canned dialog he hated, because it was intended to instill false hope. "A lot of research is being focused on this problem, and several new drugs are in the pipeline. Who knows, maybe tomorrow we'll have one with superior effectiveness to what's now available. What I'm saying is, don't give up hope." He hated himself for saying this, because he knew nothing worth a damn was presently in a clinical trial. And if a new drug did come along, Meredith would most likely be dead by the time it could be used on her.

She looked him straight in the eye. "You really don't believe that, do you Doctor Cutter?"

He hesitated a beat. "Yes, I do believe it."

She nodded as if to say, "I forgive you for lying."

"Don't forget one thing," he added. "A few patients with this tumor *have* survived." But in all likelihood their pathology had been misread. Alex personally reviewed slides of every patient with the pathologist, so he harbored no doubt hers was the real thing. She was terminal and it broke his heart to be the one to tell her.

Betsy Lou poked her head into the room. "Doctor Cutter, see you a moment?"

In the hall, exam room door closed, he asked, "What is it?"

"They want you in surgery STAT. Someone's in trouble."

"Who?"

"Don't know, but it sounds urgent."

"Okay, tell you what. Explain the situation to Meredith. Then schedule her to see Tom Thatcher." Tom was the radiation oncologist to whom Alex referred patients. "Set her up to start radiation ASAP. Schedule another wound check in two weeks." He monitored wounds closely during the radiation treatments.

Alex inspected his left palm. Two months ago the skin in the center had broken down to the point of being continually red, painful, and weeping—on the verge of bleeding. The right palm wasn't as bad but was heading in the same direction. He'd begun to not scrub the area with the disposable plastic sponges, yet during long cases the area would weep, forcing him to double glove.

"What's up?" Alex asked no one in particular as he shouldered through the OR doors, taping his loupes to the bridge of his nose to hold them in place. The operating room chill immediately sprouted goose bumps on his exposed flesh. The surgeon, Dana Cramer, was one he barely knew. She was second banana in a two-person group that kept to themselves and had never been included in resident coverage. If they got in trouble, they relied on the university surgeons to help.

Cramer's body language radiated anger and tension. "What took you so long?"

"Hey, I'm here, aren't I? Had to change into scrubs. What's the problem?"

"Got a real motherfucker of a bleeder. Can't control it." She had stuffed a lap pad into the wound and was holding pressure on it.

Alex stepped in for a closer look, keeping well away from the operative field to prevent contaminating it. "What kind of case is this?" He saw the right side of the patient's neck exposed in the field.

"Carotid endarterectomy." She nodded at the X-rays on the view box. The series of shots had been taken as contrast material was passing through the neck vessels. It showed a severely clogged carotid artery, a bad case of carotid stenosis. "Where's your partner?" he asked out of curiosity.

"You going to help or play twenty questions?"

He did a double take while seriously considering telling her to "fuck off." Instead, he turned to the scrub tech who, being an employee of Cramer's group, wasn't familiar with his routine. "I wear seven and a half browns."

Outside the room, at the scrub sink, he kneed on the water valve and began to wash his hands with Betadine. Because of the palm sores, he didn't bother with the more abrasive scrub brush. It was time to make an appointment with Seth Kaufman, the dermatologist three floors above his office. Garrison had recommended him a week ago, but Alex hadn't gotten around to scheduling a visit because of his busy schedule. Now the sores were becoming a problem he couldn't ignore, and the risk of them contaminating a wound was forcing the issue.

"Let me take a look," he said as he shouldered Cramer out of the way and took control of the lap pad. He asked the anesthesiologist, "What's his pressure?"

"140 over 60."

"How many units we have on tap?" He felt uneasy without Cole on the other side of the drapes to help.

"Four units of red cells. Want his BP lowered?"

"Yeah, take it down to whatever you think you can safely get away with." Lower blood pressure meant less blood pouring out of the bleeding site. "Let me know when you have it bottomed out."

"Harry's out of town," Cramer said, referring to her partner. "That's why I called."

"No problem," he lied. In fact, he resented this group for cherry-picking insured patients and referring all their uninsured to Baptist's "charity" practice, which was covered by residents, which in turn became his responsibility. That wasn't the only issue he had with them.

With the blood pressure lowered and Cramer poised with a large-bore sucker, Alex said, "I'm going to take a peek now," and rolled back the lap pad.

The surgery—to remove cholesterol plaque clogging the artery—requires an incision along a short length of the vessel, directly over the plaque. Once the plaque was scraped off the inner wall, the artery was sewn back together. Although she'd removed the plaque—or at least she claimed to have—she botched the repair. Now the poorly stitched incision was hemorrhaging along the incision line. With a clear idea of the problem, he replaced the lap pad until they had everything set up and ready to go. The problem now was that each puncture wound from each stitch slightly chewed up the two edges of the incision, and replacing the sutures added more punctures. This forced him to plant new stitches slightly further from the edge, narrowing the artery. He withdrew the lap pad again for a closer inspection. It appeared to be repairable, but only if the original sutures were totally replaced.

Satisfied that he now had a plan, he told the scrub tech, "I want two vascular clamps, small pointed scissors, and pick-up. Then load me up a 4-0 Vicryl on a vascular needle." He planned on using one long suture for a running closure instead of individual sutures.

"Change that to nylon," Cramer corrected.

Alex's patience just reached the edge of a cliff. "You want me to do this, or do you want to do it? Be my guest, because I have a full clinic waiting on me."

"I use nylon," she said defensively.

"Fine, but I don't. What's it going to be? Your call."

"Oh, for Christ's sake, go ahead."

Alex removed the failed sutures as carefully as possible to preserve damaging the edges more. With the old suture gone, he quickly sewed shut the incision and removed the arterial clamps, reestablishing blood flow in the vessel. "Okay, bring the pressure back up to normal and let's see how it holds." He glanced at the wall-mounted stopwatch. The amount of time the vessel had been clamped was well within safe limits. Keep the vessel clamped too long and you risk a stroke. The suture held securely.

"Okay, we're golden. Lay down some thrombin-soaked Gelfoam over that and close it up." He stripped off his gloves. "I'm out of here."

"Thanks," Cramer mumbled begrudgingly.

Alex was able to score the one remaining donut from the lounge's morning supply—a plain cake one, always the last to go—along with a cup of coffee. He munched the donut while changing back into slacks and a sports coat. As he was leaving the lounge, "Doctor Cutter to OR Five, STAT," came from the overhead speakers.

Not wanting to change back into scrubs again, he slipped on a "bunny suit" and shoe covers, walked quickly down the hall, and poked his head back in the room. "What is it?"

"Motherfucker's bleeding again."

"Let me see." He stepped closer for a look at the surgical field.

Cramer lifted the corner of the lap pad.

He was stunned. "What the hell did you do? That isn't my closure."

Silence.

"She replaced it with nylon," the scrub nurse muttered.

"You ..." Enraged, speechless, he stared at the mess for a few seconds before turning to leave. "Call a vascular surgeon in here. Someone's going to have to lay in a patch or something, but it's out of my area of expertise now." Still fuming, he pushed open the door.

"We're getting into some clotting problems," the anesthesiologist called after him.

"That's your problem." Then on second thought, he said, "Call Gene Roux."

50

ALEX SNAPPED WIDE AWAKE.

The telephone rang again. He rolled onto his left side, his back to Lisa, and picked up the phone. "Cutter here." The clock digits glowed 2:32 a.m.

"Sorry to bother you, Doctor Cutter. Sam Riddell. I'm covering the trauma center. We just got a GSW to the head in and Kotell"—a clinic partner—"refuses to come in."

"Refuses?" Alex was on the edge of the bed now, knuckling eyes with his free hand.

"Yes, sir."

With Reynolds in Bethesda, backstopping the trauma center defaulted to him, although he doubted Reynolds would have come in. "Be right in."

He drove deserted Central Avenue doing a slow burn. Refused to come in? What kind of bullshit was this? Alex picked up the car phone—a new addition he was rapidly learning to love—and found Kotell's number in the programmed directory, punched "Dial."

Kotell's sleepy voice answered. "Hello?"

"Kotell, Cutter. Did you just get called by the trauma center?"

"Why?" He sounded incredulous.

"Why?" Another spike of anger. "Because I'm the one having to cover your sorry ass. That's why. Why did you refuse to cover? You're on call."

"Damnit, Alex. Can't we discuss this another time? I have a case in the morning and I'm trying to sleep."

"Yeah? Well I was sleeping too, but because you're too lazy to take your call, I have to do it for you. What do you think you're doing?"

"Listen, you sanctimonious ass. Think about it. I bet you a thousand dollars the clinic won't get paid a goddamn cent for that case. Some nigger gets shot at two in the morning, you know chances are overwhelming it's crime related. I'm sick and tired of taking care of 'em. Let 'em all shoot each other and be done with it. That'd be fine with me. Besides, the resident is more than capable of handling a head wound without either of us standing in the OR with our thumbs up our ass." Kotell hung up.

Alex slammed down the phone, almost hard enough to break the handset. A full surgical load—two craniotomies—scheduled for later today, and now he wouldn't sleep until evening. Why did he put up with assholes like Kotell? Easy answer: the pay was too good.

He locked up his Audi in the empty Baptist parking garage instead of using the reserved "Physician On Call" spot at the trauma center ambulance bay. He decided to walk the two blocks between hospitals, because by time he finished the case, it'd be senseless to drive home and shower, only to turn around and come back downtown. His only consolation prize was a full choice of the prime parking stalls just outside the doors to the sky bridge. Still fuming, he trudged down the stairwell to the alley, the muggy night air residually thick with car exhaust from the previous day's rush hour.

4:45 a.m. Alex sauntered out through the automatic glass doors of Trauma Center ER into the brightly lit parking lot. He took the ramp at a leisurely pace down to the deserted street. No sense hurrying now. A layer of clouds hid the stars. Dawn would begin soon. To him, this hour of the morning seemed the stillest of all twenty-four, a transition time between a sleeping city and a city ready to work. Feeling heavy and sluggish from fatigue, he continued the leisurely walk, enjoying the quiet solitude. The cafeteria wouldn't open for another hour and fifteen minutes. His first case didn't start until seven thirty. He wanted nothing more than to curl up and sleep, but that was impossible now.

In the middle of the block, he took a shortcut into the shadowy alley between two large medical center buildings. Glass crunched underfoot and the smell of rotting garbage filled his sinuses. Puddles in the rutted asphalt reflected light from the mercury vapor streetlight at the far end of the alley. For the first time in a week, he thought about his research, about his frustrated attempts to rekindle it and how they repeatedly failed for one reason or another. Yes, he was passing off chunks of tissue to his collaborator in Cell Biology, but their work was pedantic and unimaginative, just barely funded. The longer the gap without solid funding, the murkier his name would become in the minds of NIH. He needed to stay firmly on their radar if his research was going to succeed. He'd debated reaching out to his academic contacts to see what openings might be available, but the thought of packing up and moving and starting over again seemed too daunting. Worse yet, he hated to admit how much he'd become addicted to the quarterly bonuses. Yet he couldn't shake the belief that the key to understanding the horrible disease of glioblastoma resided within the stem cells he saw in the tumors. No one had addressed this particular issue yet, and he still possessed all his lab books and journals from his previous job. Sooner or later, though, someone would come along the same path of research and, Alex believed, make a huge breakthrough. He despised himself for aimlessly floating along.

The surgeon's lounge was empty when he arrived, yet one coffee pot contained what looked and smelled like freshly brewed coffee. He chose the most comfortable of the three couches and stretched out, the heels of his Nikes propped up on the arm. Eyes closed, he rested, knowing sleep would be impossible, but at least he could relax until the lounge began to fill up for the day's schedule.

Sometime later, he heard hushed movement and cracked his eyes. Phil Chapman, an anesthesiologist, was pouring a cup of coffee. Phil glanced at him. "Sorry. I was trying to not disturb you."

Alex sat up, working out a kink in his neck. "Wasn't asleep anyway. You in the bucket or just getting started?"

Phil glanced at his watch. "In the bucket. Just finished a caudal up on OB. What're you doing here so early?"

Alex decided on having a cup to help perk him up, so he poured one while telling Phil about the trauma center case.

First cup of coffee drained, Phil poured a second one. "Want another?" he asked, holding the pot at the ready.

"Naw. Limit myself to one on days I operate."

"Why's that?" Phil came over to sit at the end of the couch at a right angle to him.

"Causes a caffeine tremor in my hands. Never realized I had one until I took Rhoton's microsurgery course in Gainesville. The first lab day we were doing a carotid anastomosis with 10-0 silk"—a suture thin enough to place through a human hair—"and my fingers were shaking too badly to do a good job. I couldn't stop it, so I called over the instructor over, had him look through the observation side of the scope. Didn't take him five seconds to tell me it was a caffeine tremor. Next day I skipped my morning coffee and, voila, the tremor wasn't there. Now I limit myself to one cup when I have to operate." He laughed. "Helps with the bladder issue, too."

Chapman laughed, too. "We're lucky. Our group is big enough to always have a rover who can spell us periodically. You guys aren't so lucky."

Alex stretched out again. "Go ahead, talk. I'm going to relax until the room starts filling up." He decided to take a shower once people started to wander in, just to invigorate him. He kept shaving gear in his locker for just such occasions.

51

"Doctor Cutter? Please follow me." The nurse led Alex past the reception desk and down a short hall to an exam room where he took a chair.

Minutes later the dermatologist entered, shook hands. "Pleasure to meet you, Doctor. What am I seeing you about?"

Alex held out both hands, palms up. "This. It's getting worse and becoming painful. Dermatology was probably my worse subject in med school. Every skin lesion looked the same to me."

He moved Alex's hand into better light, rotating the palm slightly this way and that. "Hmmm … Left looks worse than the right. What about your family? Have any history of similar problems?"

Alex shook his head. "Dad died of a quirk pulmonary embolism when I was five. Mom died of a brain tumor my senior year of high school. My sister believed in naturopathic medicine and died of untreated lymphoma. Other than that, nothing."

"That's quite a lot, actually. Any other skin problems?"

Alex was about to say no when he remembered something. "Yeah, come to think of it, my ear canals itch. Only thing that seems to help is steroid cream."

"Let's have a look."

"It's a mild case of psoriasis, probably exacerbated by the number of hours you wear gloves. The time you spend scrubbing doesn't help either. I'll give you a prescription for a steroid cream. Know what an occlusive wrap is?"

"Actually, I do." Alex laughed. "That was the one part of dermatology that stuck with me."

"Good. Before going to bed apply the steroid over your palms, then put on an occlusive wrap. Use Saran Wrap or a similar product. Try to minimize the brush during scrubs. Considering the amount of surgery you do, a brush probably isn't needed at all."

Alex thought about that. Scrubbing without a brush would seem, well, somewhat ineffectual. But having open sores on his palms would be far worse. And double gloving impeded his sense of fine touch. He'd keep an eye on his infection rate, just to be sure.

He checked the name on the next patient's chart, saw "Meredith Costello," the gliobastoma patient. He pushed open the door to the exam room. "Hey, Meredith. How you doing?"

"We need to talk," she said. "I want a favor from you."

Her serious expression struck him as unusual, not that he expected levity considering her diagnosis. "Sure. What's on your mind?" He sat on the rolling stool, put the chart on the fold-down desk.

"Been thinking a lot. Obviously. You know I'm lesbian, don't you?"

"I did suspect. I met your partner when you were in for staple removal. Why?"

"I want you to understand my situation." She glanced at her hands and swallowed.

"Go on."

"It's hard on us … being, ah, different in spite of there being other gays and lesbians in town. We have friends, but it doesn't mean most folks accept us or our lifestyle. My parents totally reject us as a couple and me as their daughter. Basically I'm facing this awful situation alone." She was fidgeting with the zipper of her coat.

Alex waited a few beats. "Go on."

"What'll happen to me? I mean … how's this … this thing going to end?"

Ah, the big question. He suspected it was the one every patient wonders about but is afraid to ask. Yet he wasn't sure this was her question, so he didn't want to volunteer something until he was certain. It was a touchy subject. "I'm not sure exactly what you're asking."

"Let me try this: I have a brain tumor. True?"

"Yes, you do."

"It's going to kill me."

He nodded. "Eventually."

"How will it kill me? What will happen? I want the details."

He hated this question because there was no one answer—every tumor spread differently. His job at this point was to provide comfort, but this was an impossibility under the circumstances. Alex the surgeon had functioned perfectly, removing as much tumor as possible without damaging function. But Alex the healer was failing miserably. This was the hardest part of his job.

"Please, Doctor Cutter, I need to know."

He searched for a humane answer. "Most likely you'll eventually slip into a coma. Once that happens, I'll make certain you receive enough medication to make you as comfortable as possible, even if you can't communicate with me." *And if a little extra medication helps you exit this life, then so be it.*

She squirmed anxiously in her chair, obviously frustrated with not hearing whatever information she sought. "But what about *before* that happens? What will I be like before I slip into a coma?"

Every brain tumor patient he'd ever dealt with harbored similar questions. Some were just more vocal than others.

"That depends on which parts of the brain the tumor grows into. I can't predict where it will grow and what effects it will cause, exactly."

"A friend's father had the same tumor on the same side as mine. Three months before he died, he lost his ability to talk or move his right side. It was like he'd had a stroke. Will that happen to me?"

Cancer patients became gravitational fields for well-intentioned friends, or friends of friends, who were eager to share advice or relate anecdotal information of questionable relevance, the content of which inevitably provoked more angst than relief. "It's a possibility. But only one of many possibilities. Like I said, it depends on several factors totally out of our control."

She nodded as if this confirmed something. "Then my question is this: Do you believe a patient with a terminal disease has the right to take their own life? To have final control over the disease that will kill them?"

And there it was. "I can't answer that."

"Why not?"

"Because when you say 'the right,' do you mean legally or theologically?"

"I'm asking you as my doctor."

Ah, man ... At this point medical ethics and law collided head-on with Alex's personal beliefs. Like every graduating student in his med school class, he'd sworn to uphold the Hippocratic oath. There were times in his years of practice that he'd read and reflected on the modern translation of the original Greek words. Most of what the oath prescribed was straightforward. However, there were two lines in potential conflict: "I will prescribe regimens for the *good* of my patients according to my ability and my judgment and never do harm to anyone. I will give no deadly medicine to anyone if asked, nor suggest any such counsel." He'd seen too many patients die lingering, demeaning, disabling deaths from this very tumor, their brain being destroyed by tumor while their minds remained intact and fully aware of their awful predicament. How humane was that?

Would he choose to commit suicide if faced with the same disease? Hard question.

"Oh boy, Meredith ... I really don't know."

She looked deeply into his eyes. "Our discussions—doctor-patient relationship I guess you call them—do these stay private?"

"If I don't record any of it into your medical record, it does. There are circumstances in which lawyers can demand to review your records."

"Then this is private, just between us." She swallowed. "Think about this: I'm totally and absolutely screwed. I don't want to die paralyzed and shitting myself as a prisoner in a paralyzed body. I don't know anyone who *would* want to go through their final days in that condition. I want my final days to have some dignity, but I don't have the nerve to off myself with a painful method, like jumping off a roof or slashing my wrist." She paused, as if fighting for the next words. "But if I had some sleeping pills like Nembutal and could down a bottle of them when I reach the point of becoming incapacitated, then that's what I would want to do. Understand what I'm saying?"

He inhaled slowly. "Just so we're absolutely clear, you're asking me to give you the means to commit suicide."

She seemed relieved to have the words clearly laid out. "Exactly."

"What makes you think I could live with the guilt of aiding a suicide?"

"Because I know you care about your patients. And I know you want to give me the option of having at least some control over my disease."

Her words resonated more strongly than she might've imagined. No patient had ever requested this from him, and he wasn't sure what to say.

"Well?" she asked.

"I can't answer you today. That doesn't mean I'll say no, and it doesn't mean I'll say yes. This is a very serious request you're asking of me. I think we both need to take a deep breath and think very hard about this. Are you religious?"

"Yes."

"Okay, then I want you to discuss this with your pastor, rabbi, or whomever that person is. Will you do that for me?"

She nodded, her eyes showing the first sign of hope since hearing the diagnosis. "If that's what I need to do for you to do this for me."

52

"GOT A QUESTION FOR you," Alex said to Martin as they jogged. "I have a glioblastoma patient who wants me to give him"—purposely changing Meredith's gender—"a prescription for Nembutal so he can OD when the tumor starts to incapacitate him." He paused before adding, "This ever happen to you?"

Martin answered immediately. "Nope."

"How would you handle it if you were me?" Strange, who you end up becoming friends with. When he started at the clinic, he never suspected Martin would become the partner with whom he was closest.

Martin slowed for half a block before stopping. He bent over, grabbed his ankles, and held that position several seconds before straightening. He mopped his brow with his wristband. "Why do you ask?"

Stupid question. "Because I want to know your answer."

Feet firmly planted, hands on his hips, Martin rotated right, then left, stretching his spine. "Don't know what the hell I'd do." He started to walk. Alex knew they'd start to run again once they finished this discussion, the day already too hot to talk seriously and jog. Two dogs that routinely barked at them lay panting in the shade of their porch, heads down, watching them pass.

"One thing I sure as hell *wouldn't* do," Martin finally said, "is tell a damn soul I ever discussed it. And I sure as hell wouldn't write anything in the chart."

"Let me tell you a story," Alex said, choosing to open a part of his past that he'd only told Lisa. "Told you my mother died of cancer, didn't I?"

"Yep."

"It was in the era before CT scans, so she wasn't diagnosed until too far along to do much other than biopsy it for a diagnosis. Not that it would've made any difference. She ended up sick as hell. Nausea, partial paralysis, the works. I lived with her at the time, but when she got too sick to live in the apartment, we moved her into her parents' home. She continued to go downhill until it was impossible to care for her there either. She had to be moved into a nursing home. For some reason—maybe because I was her son—I was the one who was given the task of telling her. She knew what those places were like and that this was the end for her. She was already in diapers on a rubber sheet, too weak to even turn herself over in bed. Nothing but a skin-covered skeleton waiting to gasp her last breath. She knew her remaining days were going to be even worse." Even this many years after her death, the memory still misted his eyes.

"The morning the ambulance was scheduled to transfer her, she asked me to bring her her pills. I knew she had a prescription for Seconal. When I asked why she needed them, she said she wanted to OD when she still had an ounce of dignity. I understood *why* she wanted to do it, but another part of me—the son part—couldn't bring myself to give them to her. Not because of any religious or ethical belief; I just couldn't *do* it. Not to my mother. I couldn't give her up." He paused for a deep breath. "I told her no." They walked a half block while Alex reigned in his emotions.

"The nursing home turned out to be exactly what she envisioned and feared. Smelled of urine and feces. You could hear moans and every now and then a screaming sundowner. She lingered in that shithole for three goddamn weeks. It was awful, a real hell. I've never forgiven myself for not giving her the pills."

They started jogging again, Martin silent, waiting for Alex to finish his story. But Alex let it hang. Finally, a half mile from Alex's house, Martin said, "Only one thing I can tell you, and it applies to every patient: do the right thing."

"My spies tell me you did a great job running things while I was gone," Reynolds told Alex the following week, having returned from his Bethesda tour now that Desert Storm was wrapped up.

"Good to hear." Alex tried to hide his disappointment at relinquishing primary control of the residency. He'd been amazed at how quickly he'd taken to managing the residents, segueing the program from Reynolds's dictatorial way to Waters's gentler, reinforcing teaching style. It was gratifying to see firsthand the behavior produced by his changes. Steve Stein—his spy—joked that when residents saw Reynolds approach from down the hall, they dove for the first exit. In contrast, they gravitated to Alex for advice and instruction, eager to learn. Then again, there was always the possibility that Stein was simply giving him a verbal blow job. He hoped that wasn't the case but knew most people tended to suck up to their boss.

"You know, don't you," Alex said without trying to sound too hopeful, "that Dean Turner just announced his retirement."

Reynolds smiled. "Jesus Christ, Cutter, you need to learn to be more subtle. Diplomacy is an art, not a scud missile."

Alex felt his face redden.

53

"Got a sec?" Martin caught Alex returning to his office. "Have a case for you."

Alex veered off to Martin's office. "Tumor?"

"AVM." Martin held up a CT scan and turned on the view box. "Here, have a look."

AVMs, Arteriovenous malformations, are congenital tangles of vessels in which arteries, carrying blood under high pressure, short-circuit directly into thin-walled veins designed to handle low pressure. The major risk of these lesions is spontaneous hemorrhaging that can cause death or brain damage. Luckily, most people with an AVM went undiagnosed and lived completely normal lives, a factor that made surgical removal debatable.

Alex studied the scan a moment. "Garrison seen it?"

"Yep."

Alex shot him a questioning glance. "And?"

"Says he won't touch it."

Made sense. But why was Martin asking him about it? "What about the patient?"

"Yep, that's the rub. He wants it taken out."

"Why? It's a big one, exactly the kind that carries less risk of a bleed."

"I told him exactly that, but he says now that he knows it's in there, he's going crazy worrying about it every damn minute of every day. Says he can't do anything, out of fear it'll explode. Thinks it's a ticking time bomb in his brain. Can't have sex with his wife now because of it. Tried to steer him away from surgery, but he's dead set on having it out."

"Bad choice of words."

"Yeah, guess so. But you get my drift."

Alex glanced at the scan again. "What about Clarence?"

"If it's coming out, I want you to do it. That is, if you think you can do it."

Alex studied the images more closely, weighing the best approach. The trick to removing these things was to isolate and shut down all the feeding arteries first to relieve the high pressure in the thin-walled veins. Once that was done, removing the actual malformation would be similar to removing a tumor. But shutting down the feeding arteries would be extremely difficult for this one. And once you opened the head and started in on it, you couldn't stop until the malformation was completely removed.

"Why *not* Clarence? He's Garrison's prodigy."

"C'mon, Alex, Garrison had the scan for two days before giving me an answer. You know damn well those two conjoined twins looked it over together. If Garrison said no, Clarence will say no. More than that, I just don't want to deal with him if I can help it."

Alex continued to study the images, thinking through strategies. The angiogram clearly showed the feeding arteries. Could he do it?

"If anyone can do it, you can," Martin said, as if reading his doubt.

Alex shook his head, more as a way of casting out doubts than a response. "I don't know. Need to think it over."

"If you don't do it," Martin added, "I know he's going to end up getting cut by someone like Friedman and Cramer. I'd hate like hell to see that happen. With you he gets the best shot of coming through intact."

Alex hesitated, balancing conflicting thoughts of confidence and self-doubt. Why should he think he could successfully tackle a case Garrison went thumbs-down on? Yeah, he was good, but was he that good?

"I want to talk to the patient before I make a decision."

"Figured as much. C'mon, he's waiting on you."

"What? He's in clinic now?"

Alex left the exam room worried that the patient didn't grasp the relative risks of surgery versus leaving it alone. Making matters worse, the patient resonated with him immediately. When this happens, a patient often credits their surgeon with greater skills than is really the case. Alex suspected this just happened. Within minutes of meeting each other, the patient believed Alex was the only surgeon who could safely remove the AVM. Worse yet, Alex knew his own confidence was swayed by the patient's opinion of him.

I really shouldn't touch it. A wise, capable surgeon once told him, "The best case I ever did was the case I didn't do."

On the other hand, I do difficult tumors day in and day out with an envious success rate. Maybe Martin's right, maybe I am the one to tackle it.

Then again, the smart thing might be to leave it alone.

He stopped by the scheduling desk to pass the patient's chart to the duty nurse. "I want Mister Foxx scheduled for surgery, but this isn't a routine case. I want him to be the only case that day, and I want it on a Thursday. That Tuesday I want him admitted for John Stern to do an intervention on him. I'll discuss it with John today." Stern was an interventional radiologist, a new specialty in which radiologists treated various surgical problems using special techniques and catheters. Alex planned on having Stern plug the major arterial feeders before surgery, making his job easier and less risky. More and more surgeons were adopting this strategy to shut down feeders to both AVMs and vascular tumors. In addition, he wanted Stern to do a Wada test to determine if speech was in the right or left side of the brain. "It also has to be on a Thursday when Doctor Cole and Chuck Stevens will be there. I want the A-Team in on this one." With the die cast, a foreboding budded in the very depths of his gut. *Rescind the request. It's not too late. But then what do I tell the patient?*

"Yes, Doctor."

"And make sure the lab types and crosses him for eight units with another eight on standby."

The nurse shot him a look of surprise. "Eight units?" It was unheard of for his cases.

"Eight units," he verified.

CT scan and angiogram in hand, Alex headed for the stairwell. No better time to talk with Stern than right now. The agreement he made with the patient was that if Stern didn't believe he could successfully embolize the feeders, Alex would not do the case. Part of him hoped Stern would say no.

Stern stood at the view box studying the contrast-enhanced CT scans, the contrast lighting up the arteries, defining their lumens. He'd been at it for ten minutes now. Each second that ticked slowly past increased Alex's anxiety. Stroking his chin, Stern nodded to himself. "Yeah, I think I can shut down *some* of those pipes for you." He shook his head. "Shitload of blood going through them. Whole lot of blood. I can see why you want this as a first step."

"I'm scheduling surgery for a Thursday. We'll coordinate with your scheduler so you can embolize him on that Wednesday."

"Smart. Keep me posted."

54

"Hey, are you Alex Cutter?"

Alex sat on his haunches washing the wheels of his Audi with a large sponge and a bucket of soapy water, a typical Saturday afternoon chore he found soothing. So many hours of his days were devoted to precise, meticulous work that a job like this, completely without risk, was a welcomed distraction. He also loved leaving the metallic gray paint shiny, the black leather interior spotless. Lisa's car, on the other hand, was a perpetual disaster he tackled only once a month. Even then he simply washed the exterior, because any interior work would be in vain.

Startled, Alex glanced over his shoulder at the voice. Behind him stood a middle-aged stranger in jeans, camouflage T-shirt, camouflage fishing vest, and aviator sunglasses, wearing a huge, shit-eating grin over his face.

"I am." Alex stood.

The grin enlarged as he pulled a folded paper from inside his vest. He handed it to Alex. "Here." He turned toward the street.

Alex accepted the paper. "What's this?"

"Get it?" the man yelled to a partner aiming a telephoto lens at them from across the street.

The photographer nodded. "Hell, yeah."

The process server said to Alex, "You've been served," then turned and walked away laughing.

Served? What the . . . ? Then it dawned on him. He dried his hands on a rag stuck in his back pocket and carefully unfolded the sheet of paper.

"What do I do now?" Alex asked Garrison. He was on the kitchen phone, the unfolded summons on the counter.

"Nothing for the moment. I'll notify our attorney now and set up a meeting for Monday morning. This being Saturday, there's not a damn thing we can do till then. It ain't going away, that's for damn sure. Just try to calm down." Garrison paused. "But I gotta ask you, any truth to the allegation? You have anything—anything at all—to do with this woman's suicide?"

Alex didn't answer immediately, so Garrison pressed the issue. "Well?"

Alex swallowed. "She had a glioblastoma. I operated on it, then had it radiated. That's it."

"Then you have nothing to worry about. This your first? Malpractice suit I mean."

Alex dropped heavily into a chair. "Yeah. Aw, Jesus, ten million dollars." For the first time since joining the clinic, he wondered how much his insurance covered. What would happen if they won and were awarded the entire amount but he had only five million dollars of coverage? What then? Would they take his house, car, retirement? Why hadn't he been concerned enough to pay attention to these things?

"What else do they want in damages? That is, if you don't mind me asking," Garrison said.

"They want my state license revoked."

"Suspect they're going to have a problem with that one. Can't remember that kind of thing ever happening, especially with this being your first suit. Keep the faith; you'll persevere. What d'ya have going Monday morning?"

"One case. Shouldn't run past noon." He'd purposely scheduled a light week in anticipation of the AVM Thursday.

"I'll be seeing patients by the time y'all finish. Run me down soon as you're free."

Alex was still sitting at the kitchen table, phone in hand, when Lisa came in from the carport carrying a bag of groceries. She set the bag on the counter with a grunt. "What's wrong?"

His mind was consumed by a toxic brew of anger at the process server and the Costello family. Meredith had claimed she was all alone. So why was the family now pressing charges? He held up the paper for her to see. "I'm being sued for malpractice."

She sat in the chair opposite him. "Oh my God! What did you do?"

"Nothing. The patient died from a glioblastoma. A sister I didn't even know existed claims I killed her with a prescription of Nembutal."

"Did you?" Lisa asked matter-of-factly.

Ah, man … "No."

Years ago when they were still learning about each other, he had shared the story of his mother's death in the nursing home, how he regretted not helping her commit suicide. Lisa had been shocked, believing neither a patient nor their doctor had a right to intentionally assist in suicide, regardless of the circumstances. Her belief was based on the simple conviction that life is a gift that no human has a right to take, regardless of how well-intentioned their actions. Alex had argued that a physician's most important obligation to a patient was to relieve suffering, that nothing in the Hippocratic oath stated that physicians should prolong life. He strongly believed that if the final terminal stage of disease increased suffering, it would be more humane to provide the patient the *option* of a merciful alternative. She had found his argument abhorrent.

"I don't believe you. Why? Because I know you," she said in a matter-of-fact tone. "And if I don't believe you, what's a jury going to believe?"

55

"We sure Cole and Chuck are scheduled for the case?" he asked Ellen, the head of surgery.

"They are," she confirmed, but her words didn't do a thing to ameliorate his anxiety.

"How about the type cross-match?" His gut was churning like the wake of a speedboat, causing him to gasp a deep breath every now and then. *Stop freaking out. Calm down. You're going to do fine.*

"Done. Blood bank's sending them over first thing in the morning."

Alex slipped silently into the angiography suite to watch from behind the lead-impregnated glass of the control room. The overhead fluorescents were off, making the glow of the flat-screen monitors feel intense by contrast. Stern, fully gowned and gloved, a lead shield bulking out his gown like a Kevlar vest, stood at the side of the radiology table. He carefully worked the long catheter through the patient's blood vessels, watching his progress on the fluoroscopy screen. A CD played Beethoven softly in the background. Not wanting to startle anyone if they looked up and noticed him suddenly behind the glass, Alex cleared his throat as a warning. Stern glanced up and recognized him, his face etched deeply with concern. Stern stopped what he was doing and walked over to Alex.

"How's it going?" Alex asked, hoping for good news.

"Not well. That thing's the monster that ate Chicago," he whispered. "Each time I plug one vessel, another opens up. Never seen anything like it. You got a tiger by the tail on this one, Bubba."

"What about the Wada test?"

Stern let out a derisive laugh. "Didn't work. The left side is stealing so much blood from the right side we weren't able to get any drug effect. Nothing. I gave up trying so I could put the effort into the embolization. Figured that was more important."

Alex's heart dropped. To properly guide the catheter into the correct vessels, small boluses of contrast agent were injected periodically to show the position of the catheter tip on the fluoroscopy screen. Because the contrast agent was excreted through the kidneys and was slightly toxic, there were limits to how much could be safely injected in one twenty-four-hour period without impairing renal function. And normal kidney function was essential for the long surgery ahead. "How much more can you get away with? I need every bit of help you can possibly give me."

Stern thought for a moment. "I can probably shut down two, maybe three more vessels. After that I don't know. I'm pushing the limit as is."

Needing every possible feeding artery closed, he was tempted to cajole Stern into exceeding the pharmaceutical company's recommended labeling limits. After all, the patient was a healthy male, and manufacturers intentionally erred on conservative estimates when labeling a drug. But with such a high-risk case, any bad outcome or complication might cause the family to sue. If the plaintiff's lawyer discovered any evidence in the chart that Stern exceeded the prescribed limits, he and Alex would be no-contest dead ducks. Up until his pending malpractice suit, Alex never would've considered making such defensive practice decisions. Now things were different. Instead of doing everything possible to increase the odds in favor of his patient, he would choose self-preservation. He didn't dare think of pushing Stern. "Appreciate your help," Alex said.

"You sure you want to go through with surgery?" Alex asked the patient that afternoon. He sat next to the patient's bed, explaining one final time all the things to expect the next morning, secretly hoping the patient or his wife had enough second thoughts to cancel. "We did shut down a lot of arteries, but we couldn't get all of them. This is still a very tough, risky surgery. Never forget, you have the option of delaying. We can easily do the very same thing in a few weeks to shut more of them down. In fact, we can do it several more times before going through with the actual surgery. How does that sound to you?"

"Doc, I know you mean well and all, but the thing is, I just can't live knowing that time bomb's still in there," he said, pointing at his left temple.

Alex placed a reassuring hand on the patient's shoulder. "There's nothing wrong with cancelling. We can always see what today's treatment does over time. Maybe we got more than we thought and you can avoid the surgery entirely," he said hopefully, but he knew that was a lie.

"I want it out, Doc."

Martin's words echoed in his head. *"He'll end up going to someone like Cramer if you don't do it."*

Alex handed him the consent and a pen.

He lay on his side staring at the glowing digits as they passed midnight and continued on toward one o'clock.

Just be careful. Stay cautious and you'll get him through this intact. Now isn't the time to get squirrelly.

Alex prayed to God to watch over him, to get his patient through surgery intact.

Unable to sleep, Alex arose at 5:00 a.m. Bleary-eyed, Lisa dragged herself out of bed to make a bowl of oatmeal and raisins topped with brown sugar, the way he liked it. For some reason the oatmeal seemed to stay with him longer than dry cereal, and he didn't want the grease from bacon and eggs in his stomach. He wasn't sure when—or if—he'd get a chance to eat anything else, because this was the kind of case that, once started, wouldn't allow him to take a break.

"Comforting to see you here," Alex told Cole in the lounge after a quick trip to the waiting room for final words with the family. Family members he'd never met before sat with the patient's wife in a small prayer room off the surgery waiting area, the room already stuffy and warm. The family looked at him with awe, as if he were a god. He wanted to assure them he wasn't, that he could only do his best. On the other hand, this wasn't the time to cast even one seed of doubt. Today, more than any day in his practice, he needed all the positive energy he could muster.

"Big case," Cole said before sipping his coffee, a half-eaten donut in hand.

"Biggest of my career," Alex muttered, then left to change into fresh scrubs. Today would test just how good—or bad—he really was. As he paused to think about that, a rush of guilt and shame overcame him. *Is that what this is all about? A test of my ability? Is this really all about me?*

Shit!

His gut butterflies intensified.

Why not *let Cramer do it? Why do I have to be the one?*

Because I'm better than they are. His chances are better with me.

"Skin knife," Alex said as he eyed the clock, noting the start time: 7:31 a.m. He pressed the scalpel blade into the scalp, officially beginning the case. The initial cut bled more briskly than normal, causing Alex to work slowly and meticulously to control the loss. Every inch of skin he opened took more time than normal. Since blood loss was cumulative, every drop that left the patient became part of the final tally. Let too much slip by and the patient would need a transfusion. With each transfusion came the risk of a reaction. The significance of this abnormal scalp bleeding dawned on him: even the scalp vessels—which usually had no connection with the brain's blood supply—contributed to the AVM. This staggering realization caused him to pause. *Back out? Just close up and tell the patient I can't do it?*

Just pay more attention to every move. Be meticulous. You'll get through.

Steve Stein—who wasn't on his rotation, but who Alex had requested assist him—stood on his right, dutifully sucking the blood and irrigation fluid, keeping the surgical field clean.

9:45 a.m. Alex continue struggling to open the dura. Excessive oozing from all the tissues made progress agonizingly slow. Typically he had a craniotomy open and ready to go in thirty minutes or less, but they were now two hours and fifteen minutes into the case, and he hadn't reached the hard part. He consoled himself by thinking that every vessel coagulated, even the tiniest, was one less he had to deal with. He remained haunted by the reality that this much bleeding this early in the case was a very bad sign.

Stay calm.

"Bob, we're losing more blood than I anticipated. Let's send off a red-top for an additional type and hold. Just in case." As an afterthought, he turned to Chuck. "Why don't you see if we can get one of those doohickeys in that the vascular guys use. The device that recycles irrigated blood. Know what I'm talking about?"

"Roger that, sir. I was about to suggest that."

The sick feeling in the depths of Alex's gut grew more intense.

10:30 a.m. "Chuck and Ethyl, why don't you guys get some replacements in here so you can take a break." This wasn't a question. He purposely wanted to spin them out early for a rest, because it was now painfully apparent the case would take much longer than expected, certainly much longer than his typical tumor case. With the opening completed, he was struggling to discern arteries from veins because, unlike the normal condition in which veins carried blood with less oxygen, these veins carried oxygen-rich blood directly from the arteries. Clip a thin-walled vein under a full head of arterial blood pressure and it could burst, creating a hemorrhage that might be impossible to control. This was the reason all arteries feeding to the lesion had to be closed down first. Now he had to resort to meticulously tracking each vessel back to its origin before slipping a spring-load clip around it. Veins drain to the midline whereas arteries originate from the base of the brain. Each time he passed the jaws of a clamp over a vessel, his heart pounded with anxiety. Would it burst? And each time he did close down a vessel, others seemed to appear or get larger. It appeared that the embolization on Tuesday had accomplished very little. He was sweating now, drops rolling down his chest, soaking the elastic of his shorts.

"Roger that, sir."

Alex glanced at Steve. "Get another resident in and take a break for lunch."

Steve seemed hesitant. "What about you?"

"I'll have someone bring me in a carton of chocolate milk and a straw."

"Call the lounge and see who's free," Steve said to the circulator. "Anyone will do."

2:02 p.m. *Shit!* Alex blinked away a drop of sweat that stung his right eye. He peeked at the twenty-four-hour wall clock. Oatmeal long gone, his stomach growled. He was seeing initial signs of clotting problems from the patient receiving so many transfused units of blood. Cole had resorted to ordering fresh plasma and platelets from the blood bank, and word just came back that the bank was running dangerously low. They had to control the bleeding. Break the bank and they'd be out of luck.

"Hey Ethyl, put in a page for Gene Roux," Alex said.

Cole glanced over the drape and nodded approval. *If you ever need a hematologist, Gene's your man.* Morbidly obese or not, Alex wanted to see him waddle through the door. Immediately, he felt a wave of guilt for ridiculing the fat man's love of maple bars and sugary coffee. He wanted to apologize to someone.

"You call?"

Alex glanced up from the surgical field, sending a sharp stab of pain through his neck. Gene Roux stood just inside the OR doors dressed in green scrubs.

"Boy, am I glad to see you. We got a serious problem."

Now starved and dog-tired, Alex plodded on without any sign of progress. Every artery he clipped seemed to enlarge the smaller neighboring ones. There was no way he could stop and close the case now and no way to predict how much longer it might take before the malformation would be obliterated. He now appreciated why Garrison refused the case. The first wave of panic hit with a dizzying impact, forcing him to stop and take some deep breaths to calm himself. He closed his eyes and willed his mind to not succumb to the terror flirting with him. Every one of the muscles down his spine ached. The palms of both hands were cramping. In a perverse way, he welcomed the discomfort as a form of penance for bringing this unfortunate patient to surgery, believing that if he suffered enough, perhaps the patient would somehow make it through this.

4:10 p.m. "Doctor Cutter, we're rotating out now. Joyce will replace me and Troy will replace Ethyl. Good luck." With that, Chuck stepped off the platform for the overhead table, allowing Troy to take his place. Alex had worked with Troy only once before and had decided that, like Chuck, he'd been well trained in the Navy.

"Thanks, Chuck, Ethyl. Appreciate your help."

He glanced at the clock and realized that both techs had stayed beyond their normal three o'clock end of shift, probably in hopes the case might be finished by now. Not even close. Alex was continually fighting an overwhelming feeling of despair from the creeping knowledge that the case had gotten away from him and that nothing good would come of it. Never before had he been faced with this situation, and he didn't know how to handle it other than to keep on keeping on. He wanted to plead with Chuck or Ethyl—touchstones of normalcy—to stay but felt guilty for even entertaining the thought.

"Before you go, could you call over to the clinic and ask Garrison to come over? Then call my wife and tell her I'm not coming home in the foreseeable future. Certainly not for dinner."

"Doctor Cutter? Clinic says Doctor Majors is tied up and can't come."

Fucking Garrison. He'd never known Garrison to refuse a partner, especially if he was in trouble. It was, after all, one of the reasons he lived in scrubs. *Does he know I'm in trouble? Has to. The whole fucking hospital knows.* He could see pity in everyone's eyes, even staff who entered for various reasons. They knew he was in over his head.

He straightened his spine and rotated his head, working out kinks, stretching sore muscles. The additional pound and a half from the loupes strapped to his forehead was killing him after so many hours, producing the neck ache from hell. Even the bridge of his nose hurt from the pressure of their feet.

5:03 p.m. Alex's left hand had developed a tremor. No matter how hard he tried to suppress it, it didn't ease up. So far Stein hadn't mentioned it, but Alex knew everyone in the room noticed it as the first obvious sign of his mental defeat. A sense of despair was beating him down now. *Don't give up. You can't anyway. You're in this to the end. Be defeatist and the case will go tits up before you know it. Hell, it already has.*

He recognized his lightheaded tremulousness as symptoms of hypoglycemia. He asked the circulator, "Can someone please bring me another chocolate milk?" An hour earlier, the circulator had snaked a straw in from the side of his mask so he could drink a small carton of milk. He'd had nothing else since the morning oatmeal and felt famished, although the thought of eating made him nauseous. He inhaled deeply and pressed on, amazed at being able to garner the strength to do so. There was no alternative.

Why did Garrison refuse to come? His anger toward Garrison pushed him on.

"Hey Alex, want a break? I just finished my last case."

Surprise! Jason Braddock, one of his partners, stood to Alex's right, peering at the exposed AVM. A mirage? He couldn't believe his eyes. "Aw man, would you do that? I'd love to be able to get down on the couch for five, ten minutes and maybe eat something."

"Go ahead, get it ready to babysit. I'll scrub in."

Alex hurried downstairs to the prayer room filled with warm, stale air that smelled of strong coffee and body odor. It was littered with newspapers, empty Styrofoam cups, and plastic food containers. Two young kids played on the floor with primary color toys, every seat occupied by adults of various ages. The wife stared at him the moment he entered. "You look beat, Doc Cutter."

Her words almost brought tears to his eyes. Rather than ask for word about her husband, she seemed focused on his well-being.

"One of my partners spelled me so I could come give you an update in person." Several times during the afternoon he had asked the circulator to call down with a progress report.

He palm-wiped his facial stubble. "This is taking much longer than I anticipated, but I *will* get him through surgery. Can't lie to you: we're in serious trouble with continual oozing. Have been for hours now, but I have a good hematologist working with me. I will bring him though this no matter how much longer it takes." Surprisingly, he felt inspired by his own word.

"We're praying for you, Doc."

"Good. I need all the help I can get. Just want you to know I'm not giving up. I'll be here with him until this is over."

Her eyes glistened with moisture. "I know you will. You're a good doc. We have all the faith in you. But if something happens … well, we know we did the right thing. He said he didn't want to live knowing that time bomb was ticking inside his brain. You're the only one who tried to help him. God bless you, Doc Cutter."

That's because I wasn't as smart as those others.

Ashamed, still fighting back tears, Alex shut the door behind him, relieved to escape the eyes of these people who trusted him blindly. The patient would die from this operation, he knew. Killed by Alex's own hubris.

The cafeteria closed at 7:00 p.m., leaving the vending machine in the alcove next to the surgeon's lounge as his only choice for food. Alex stopped at his locker for change, found enough to buy a Hershey bar. He scarfed down the cloying, sweet chocolate while lying flat on his back on a couch in the lounge. His five minutes had blown past in a blink, and he was relishing the break way too much to return right away. A change into fresh, dry scrubs perked him up slightly. He closed his locker and spun the lock but remained standing with his fingers on the combination knob.

I don't want to go back.

His physical discomfort seemed amplified by the shame and guilt of thinking such a thought.

What if I just walked out of the hospital? Just went home?

What kind of person even thinks such things?

Slowly, he trudged the empty hall back toward the OR, the chocolate making his hunger worse. Every muscle in his back and shoulders ached from hours of sitting tensely on the stool, his fatigue almost overwhelming. His spirits lowered with each step as the OR doors grew larger, but his feet continued forward, as if of their own accord. Then he was poking his head through the doors saying, "I'll scrub back in now. Thanks."

At the sink, water running over his hands, he lathered up Betadine. In a few minutes he'd be gowned and gloved. He knew he wouldn't see this hall again until the case was finished. By now, the other ORs along the long, empty hall were dark and silent, the day's schedule finished long ago, the rooms already cleaned and ready for the start of a new day.

"Thought we were never getting out of there," Cole said as he and Alex pushed the gurney to the empty recovery room. The hospital kept one nurse on duty to monitor the patient until Cole deemed him sufficiently awake from anesthesia to transfer him from the recovery room to the neuro ICU.

"He's going to bleed into that resection cavity," Alex predicted. In spite of his faith in Gene Roux's skills as a hematologist, the clotted edges of the brain would give way within the next twelve hours. "I guarantee it. Probably sometime early this morning." And that would be the end of it.

They continued on in silence, moving slowly up the hall.

Finally, Alex said, "I can't find the words to thank you for sticking with me on this. Without you and Steve I never could've made it through."

Cole patted Alex on the shoulder. "Go talk with the family. I'll finish up the paper work. Go home; get some rest. Seriously. You look like two-day-old dog shit."

Alex veered off from Cole to take the stairs down to the prayer room. The hall clock showed 11:05 p.m.

"I'm on my way home," Alex said over the car phone. "Do me a favor, draw a tub of hot water. All I want to do is soak." Neither Alex nor Lisa usually took baths.

"Want something to eat?"

In spite of an empty stomach, the thought of food made him nauseous. "No, I'm good. A glass of wine might help."

Alex hung up the car phone and continued driving along deserted Central Avenue.

The call came at 3:13, waking him from fitful sleep. Alex knew its significance before even picking up the phone. "Cutter here."

"Your AVM just blew his pupils and is non-responsive to deep pain," the on-call resident said, using doctor-speak for dilated pupils that wouldn't constrict when a light was shined in them, a very dismal neurologic sign.

"Order a CT, I'm on my way."

"Already ordered. The staff's getting him ready as we speak." Moving a patient in that condition required several nurses and a respiratory therapist to breath him while off the respirator.

"Oh, you poor man," the patient's wife said, tears streaming down her face. She hugged Alex as he wrapped his arms around her, unable to hold back his own tears. The rest of the family sat silently, heads bowed in prayer. "I know you did everything you could. You did your very best. This is what he and God wanted."

Alex lay on his favorite couch in the surgeon's lounge, eyes closed, trying to doze even though he knew it would be impossible. No sense driving home just to shower and drive back. Besides, he needed to be alone now. He briefly considered cancelling today's case because of his physical, mental, and emotional condition, but decided the case was so straightforward Steve could handle most of it.

In the quiet of the lounge, he could no longer avoid the thoughts nipping at the back of his mind. *The AVM didn't kill this patient, hubris did. Should've never operated him. Garrison was right to refuse. How dare I think …*

How can I live with this? How can I go on practicing?

56

"THERE IS ALWAYS THE option of settling out of court," Tom Finder, Alex's defense attorney, said.

They'd covered this ground numerous times already, but Alex refused. "I didn't do anything wrong. Settling out of court is equivalent to admitting I did. I can't do that."

Tom exhaled audibly. "I understand your point. But you need to understand what they have. They have a copy of the Nembutal prescription you wrote. Can we agree on this?"

Alex nodded. "Yes. I gave her the prescription. But what about all the other patients I've written the same prescription for? None of them committed suicide. Why does this one have to be my fault?"

"Just listen. Moreover, the autopsy report confirms toxic barbiturate levels."

"Right, I get all that." Alex felt the first twinges of a tension headache. "The question is, how does that prove intent? How does that prove I gave her the prescription specifically to facilitate suicide?"

"The sister gave sworn deposition that Meredith was depressed over her diagnosis and expressed suicidal thoughts, which she claims Meredith discussed with you. She also claims you advised Meredith to talk with her pastor."

This was the point where he had a problem, but short of having an actual recording of that conversation, how could her testimony be anything more than hearsay? "Don't they have to prove that alleged discussion took place?"

"Let me ask you—off the record, of course—were you aware Meredith intended to commit suicide with the Nembutal?"

There it was: The Question. Lie to the man who would defend him in court? Assuming, of course, they went to court. Unfortunately, Tom kept lobbying for an out-of-court settlement.

"Alex?"

"Is there anything I'm not allowed to share with you? At what point does doctor-patient confidentiality come into play?"

"She's dead, Alex. She has nothing to lose by disclosure. Besides, nothing will leave this room. This is your defense attorney you're talking to. Level with me."

Alex blew a resigned breath. "Yes, I knew she was depressed. She had every reason to be. No debate there. She didn't want to end up disabled on a rubber sheet in the back room of a nursing home. I can't blame her for that."

Finder nodded. "In other words you prescribed the prescription so she could end her life."

Alex could no longer look him in the eye.

"This is exactly the reason I recommend we counter with three million and put this unfortunate episode behind us. What do you say?"

"Let me ask you something." Alex explained Meredith's claim of being alienated from her family. "If what Meredith said was true, how did her sister get her medical information?"

"Look, Alex, that doesn't change a thing. My worry is we stand a good chance of losing this case if it goes to a jury. Juries are funny animals, unpredictable, and this is the Bible Belt. They have strong biases, and assisted suicide is one of them."

"I need to think about it. I leave tomorrow for a meeting. I'll give you my answer soon as I return. I still contend there's no way for them to know what Meredith and I discussed in the privacy of my office. I just can't see it as anything more than hearsay."

Tom grunted sarcastically. "You'd be amazed with what juries believe."

"*You* gave her the prescription. You know it, I know it, the family knows it, and every lawyer involved in the case knows it. You knew she wanted to commit suicide with it. My advice? Man up, settle the case, move on." Alex and Lisa were sitting in the TV room watching CNN after dinner, but the volume was turned low to allow them to talk.

Alex grew angrier. "How do you know all that for fact?"

"Because I know *you*. I know your beliefs as they apply to terminal diseases. I know how much you want to do the right thing for your patients. And I believe in my heart you gave her the prescription out of love. I just can't believe you were stupid enough to actually go ahead and *do* it. That's why I think you ought to roll over and admit you got caught with your hand in the cookie jar."

"If I lose this suit, it'll be one strike against me. Two more and I'm finished practicing. At least in this state. I don't want to take that risk."

"But Tom thinks there's a good chance you'll lose anyway. Why submit to the trial?"

"Because I don't believe the sister has anything more than hearsay."

Lisa sighed.

He pushed out of the leather chair and headed for the door.

"Where you going?"

"Out for a walk. I need to think."

57

"What would you guys do?" Alex asked two long-time friends, John and Paul. The three of them had worked as a team throughout one intense year of residency. Three hundred sixty-five days and nights of brutal call in the Dark Ages of residency programs when program directors could exercise unregulated totalitarianism and demand unreasonably long hours. At every annual AANS meeting, the three met for drinks to swap war stories and seek each other's advice. Alex had just explained to them the Meredith Costello case and wanted to hear their opinions.

John leaned back in his chair, hands knitted behind his beefy head. "You gave her the prescription?" It was the first day of the AANS meeting, which was being held in San Francisco; the three of them sat in the hotel lobby bar.

"I did. The lawyers have a copy of the prescription."

Paul set his beer back on the square coaster. "The thing that bothers me is how does the sister have any idea what she did or didn't discuss with you?"

"That's the same thing that bothers me. I can't get it out of my mind. But my lawyer keeps pushing me to settle out of court."

"Fight it," John said, leaving no question in Alex's mind.

58

"Isn't it true, Doctor, that you murdered Meredith Costello?"

And there it was: The Question. Time stopped, as if God pressed "pause" for Alex Cutter's universe. Every courtroom detail suddenly became ultra-sharp: the American and state flags to either side of the judge's black robe, dirt coating the outside windows, the metallic, mold-tinged smell of air conditioning, the jurors' eyes on him, the observers scattered throughout the viewing gallery. Alex's breath caught. Two beats passed before time began creeping forward again.

How did I ever get to this point?

Tom Finder jumped to his feet, saying, "Objection, Your Honor."

"Objection sustained. Mr. Diamond, you've been warned. I will not warn you again."

"Yes, Your Honor," the lawyer said solemnly in spite of flashing a smile at the jury, clearly having made his point.

The witness chair felt like concrete.

"Isn't it true, Doctor, that you wrote Meredith Costello the Nembutal prescription?"

Alex thought back to the endless hours of trial preparation. Tom Finder drilled him repeatedly, approaching each point from as many angles as possible, probing for an inconsistency in answers. "We don't want to be ambushed," Finder had explained.

"Yes."

Diamond nodded at the jury as if to say, "See?"

"And isn't it true, Doctor, that she used this prescription to kill herself?"

"It's possible. I don't know that for a fact—"

"Doctor! Answer yes or no, please," Diamond said, voice raised.

"No. That assumes—"

"Yes or no."

Alex wanted to scream from the frustration and anger boiling inside. "He's going to try to piss you off," Finder had warned. "Don't let him succeed."

"I don't know."

"You don't know?" Diamond's voice was now laced with heavy sarcasm. "You don't know?"

I'm going to lose. Tom Finder had been right to recommend a negotiated settlement. Why had he not followed that advice? Better yet, he should've followed Garrison's advice and refused to operate the AVM. How many times had he criticized physicians for overestimating their abilities—flying planes, launching restaurants and other business ventures—and now here he was, having ignored the advice of his defense lawyer. Maybe he should talk to Tom during the next break and agree on a settlement. Would that work? Or did the shark now smell blood, whipping him into a feeding frenzy? Had he already lost any opportunity to negotiate a settlement? *I'm fucked.*

"No, I don't know that. If the owner of a gun shop sells a customer a pistol, is he then responsible for any murder committed with that weapon?"

Diamond appeared furious. "I want that comment stricken from the record."

"You did just fine," Finder assured Alex during the break. "You didn't let him rattle you, and you remained on point just like we practiced. It's not pleasant being on the stand. I understand that."

Just then, one of Tom's partners passed him a note. Tom read it, smiled, and slipped it into his suit coat.

"What was your relationship with Meredith?" Finder asked Jenny Baker, Meredith's sister.

"We were very close. Like all sisters are." Baker sat with her spine straight. She wore what Alex considered, for lack of better words, a typical southern belle dress: white lace collar and fluted lace cuffs at the wrists. She wore a plain gold cross hanging from a modest gold chain around her neck.

"Does this mean you approved of her sexual persuasion?"

Her smile shriveled immediately as she glanced at Diamond. "Objection," he yelled. "Irrelevant."

"Objection sustained. Restate the question, please."

Finder took his time ambling toward the jury to place his right hand on the dark oak railing. "What I'm asking is this: Did the fact she was a lesbian bother you?"

"Objection."

Jenny Baker squirmed, eyes pleading for Diamond's guidance. She fingered the gold cross around her neck.

"If it pleases the court, I'd like to explain," Finder said to the judge, approaching the bench. The judge turned on the white-noise generator to block the jury from hearing their ensuing discussion.

"The relevance will become clear very soon, Your Honor."

With a stern look, she said, "I sincerely hope so, Mr. Finder."

"Ms. Baker, are you a Christian?" Finder asked.

She hesitated, perhaps looking for a trap in such a simple question, and began fingering the gold cross around her neck again. "Why, yes, of course," she said, as if some things in life should be self-evident.

"I see. Where do you worship?"

She fidgeted a moment before clasping her hands primly on her lap. "Well … I worship every day, throughout the day. I constantly thank our Heavenly Father for his blessings."

Finder leaned in on the jury rail, making eye contact with each juror while addressing Baker. "Yes, I understand that, Ms. Baker. What I am asking is this: Do you attend a specific church?"

"Yes."

He turned to her, her face the picture of innocence. "And what is the name of that church, please?"

Her rigid, prim posture straightened even further, a seemingly impossible feat. "A Christian church, sir."

"I believe we just established that, ma'am. Please give the name and address of the church in question, Ms. Baker."

Eyes straight ahead, she said, "Christ Our King Church on Poplar Avenue."

Finder scanned the jury again. "I see. And is there anyone at this church from whom you receive spiritual guidance? A pastor, a church elder, someone you seek when needing support?"

She shrugged. "Pastor Gilliam, I suppose."

"Pastor Gilliam," Finder repeated. "Have you ever sought the advice of any of the church elders?"

"No," she replied without hesitation.

"Be very careful here, Ms. Baker, and think. I ask you again: Is there *any*one else in that church, especially among the church elders, from whom you've sought advice?"

She clasped her hands tightly together while considering her answer. "No."

"Really? Isn't it true Ms. Baker that Doctor Clarence Hill attends the same church?"

She momentarily froze.

"Your Honor, Mr. Finder is badgering the witness."

"Answer the question, Ms. Baker," the judge said.

"Well, yes, I guess he does."

"And isn't it true, Ms. Baker, that Doctor Hill is one of the church elders?"

"Yes."

"And isn't it also true that you spoke with Doctor Hill on multiple occasions about Meredith's sexual persuasion?"

"Objection," Diamond said.

"Overruled."

"Isn't it also true that you prayed with Doctor Hill for Meredith's conversion to heterosexuality?"

"Objection!"

"Ms. Baker, haven't you just testified that you and Doctor Clarence Hill talked about Meredith several times?"

"I guess we talked from time to time. After all, we attend the same church and are involved in several of the same activities. Bible study is one of them."

"It's more than that, isn't it, Ms. Baker?" Finder stood at the defense table staring directly into her eyes, his voice assertive. Alex expected Diamond to object, but that didn't happen.

"Well, I reckon I've sought his advice on spiritual matters from time to time." She seemed to like that answer, because she added, "But that's all."

"Spiritual matters? You mean like suicide?"

"Objection!"

"Isn't it true, Ms. Baker, that when you learned of Meredith's death, you *suspected* your sister committed suicide?"

She glanced at her tightly clasped hands. "Yes."

Finder nodded. "And isn't it true, Ms. Baker, that you knew she was under Doctor Cutter's care?"

"Yes." Her eyes began to take on a defiant hardness.

"And isn't it true that you knew that Doctor Cutter and Doctor Hill practice in the same group?"

Her defiance began to slump. "Yes, I guess that's true."

"And isn't it true, Ms. Baker, that you are the *sole* beneficiary of Meredith's life insurance policy?"

She was looking at her hands now instead of at the court. "Yes."

"Speak up, please, ma'am, so the court can hear you."

"Yes." She glared directly into Finder's eyes.

"Isn't it true that you asked Doctor Hill to look at Meredith's medical records to see if Doctor Cutter had prescribed the Nembutal?"

59

"Got a second?" Garrison said, interrupting Alex in the middle of signing dictations.

Alex nodded and stood to arch and stretch his back. He also knew if he remained sitting, the conversation—whatever it might be—might be prolonged, and he wasn't in the mood to chitchat.

Garrison closed the door to give them more privacy. "Sorry about the verdict. I know it's tough. But we practice a high-risk specialty. No neurosurgeon I know of has been able to do his job without getting sued several times in a career. Comes with the territory. What with this being your first malpractice suit, I'd to say you're doing pretty damn well. Not that that's any consolation. Doesn't make the loss any easier."

Alex said nothing. He appreciated Garrison's attempt to take the bite out of the defeat, but he still found it difficult to get past Garrison's refusal to help him with the AVM.

"As for the part about your medical license, well, there's no way in hell that one's getting past the state quality assurance board."

"Thanks, but it's still one suit against me. Two more and I'm done practicing. Least, in this state I will be." Alex realized his clenched fists ached from being balled so tightly, so he began to flex and extend his fingers. "Your boy Clarence was the one who was behind the suit. You know that, don't you?"

Garrison shook his head. "No, I don't know that. Neither do you. But even if it was true, we still have the moral issue to consider. You can't go around prescribing depressed patients the means to commit suicide."

"Bullshit. That's *not* the issue. We both know there's no love lost between Clarence and me. He saw an opportunity to fuck me over and took it. Plain and simple."

Betsy Lou poked her head into the office. "Hey, both you docs got patients waiting to be seen."

Garrison waved her off and shut the door again. "Don't blame Clarence for your own actions. End of discussion. We have another matter to discuss."

Alex waited.

"I understand you've been ordering hep C and HIV testing on all pre-ops." Garrison started playing with the loose ties of the surgical mask dangling from his neck, wrapping them around his index finger.

"So? What about it?"

Garrison shook his head. "Can't do that. It's illegal."

"Why not? Shouldn't I know when I'm about to take an extra risk with a patient?"

"I'm telling you, you can't do that. It's an infringement on their rights."

"What about *my* rights? What about Robert Sands's rights? Forced to retire at forty because of hepatitis. Far as anyone knows, he picked it up during a trauma case. Robert is now totally screwed. Can't practice medicine anymore. Think of what he lost from one accidental needle stick. What about his rights?" Alex was fuming now.

"Don't shoot the messenger. I'm just telling you the law."

Still fuming, Alex pulled the patient chart—an Any Doctor—from the wall holder beside the exam room door. He scanned the information, but not a word registered. He calmed down enough to read it again, forcing his concentration to interpret the words. It didn't register this time either, because he couldn't stop rehashing several events in one endless loop: the AVM, the malpractice suit, the preventable fatal air embolism. All reasons to now hate the beloved career he'd worked so hard to obtain. Disasters. He'd killed an innocent man. He'd allowed Stein to kill another patient. How could he continue to do this? Good question.

As a kid, his grandmother had asked what he wanted to be when he grew up. He'd said, "A doctor." Everyone laughed, thinking him cute. But at that moment, his life goal cemented into place. He never wavered or entertained second thoughts, almost like a chick imprinting on its mother. In one unconscious moment, he'd mentally pledged blind obedience to a goal that seemingly materialized from nowhere.

He shook his head and reread the chart. The patient had been initially seen for leg pain two years ago by Martin Berger and had been bouncing back to the clinic for pain meds ever since. Inside the exam room he found a clean-shaven forty-five-year-old male in a white button-down shirt, typical preppy tie, blue blazer, and suntans, the outfit almost a male uniform around here.

"Morning, Mister Bingham. I'm Doctor Cutter." *Murderer.* "What brings you to clinic today?"

"Morning, Doc. Well, see, got me a bad back. Work injury from years ago. Been disabled ever since. Hurts all the damn time. Hell of a pain. Only relief I get's from them pain pills. Don't much cotton to the idea of taking dope all the time, but there's nothing else I can do."

"I see." Alex thumbed through the chart, looking specifically at past outpatient visits. They were all for pain medication, the most recent being the previous week when Martin saw him. He checked the front sheet to see which doctor originally saw him. An interesting red flag appeared. Mr. Bingham had seen only Any Doctors for an entire year and obviously knew the clinic system well.

"What kind of work did you do?" Alex asked.

"Mid-level manager. Retailing."

"How'd you injure your back?" He could easily read the initial evaluation but preferred to hear the patient's own words.

"Was at work when a shipment comes in. Things we need to put on display 'cause of the holidays and all. Bend over to pick up this here box and hear a loud pop in my back, like *bam!* Been hurting like the devil ever since." With a hangdog expression, he sat listing to the right, his left leg extended at the hip, a posture more indicative of hip disease than a low back problem.

"Pain go down your leg, or is it all in the low back?" he asked, motioning toward the patient's left leg.

"Yep, goes down the leg like a red-hot poker."

"On a scale of zero to ten, and ten being the worst pain you've experienced, where would you rate it at this moment?"

He answered immediately. "Eleven."

"In a twenty-four-hour day, how many hours is it there?"

"Every damn minute."

"What helps it?"

"Hate to say this, Doc, but them codeines is the only thing does me a lick of good. Oh, and an occasional Valium." He offered a weak smile. "That seems to help too."

Alex made a show of thumbing through the chart notes. "Seems like you come in a lot on days Doctor Berger's in surgery. Any reason for that?" Alex kept his tone neutral and inquisitive.

"Have I? Huh! Didn't realize it." A smile and a shrug. "Guess that's just the way things happen."

Alex scanned the lab tests, including X-rays. Here, sitting before him, was probably the only back pain patient in the world who Martin Berger hadn't touched with a scalpel. That alone spoke volumes. Martin's threshold for surgery was the lowest of any surgeon he'd known. Finished reviewing the chart, Alex asked, "What happened to last week's prescription?"

The patient let out a short, forced laugh. "Reckoned you'd ask 'bout that. Well, see, my place got broke into last week. Must've been some dope heads 'cause they went straight for my meds. Cleaned me out. Been suffering bad ever since, but I was afraid to ask for more on account of this very reason."

Alex closed the chart. "What very reason?"

That stopped him momentarily. "Well, see, I can hear it in your tone of voice you don't exactly believe me. This is what I feared might happen. Swear on my mamma's grave I'm telling y'all the truth." His hangdog expression morphed into overdone innocence.

Alex had heard enough, his tolerance suddenly worn thin. Aside from the fact that narcotics shouldn't be used for treating chronic pain—if in fact this patient actually suffered from it, something he seriously doubted—he wasn't sure who was more to blame: the doctors who enabled these patients or the patients who connived the doctors. Regardless, he was tired of dealing with them.

"Know what, you're right. I don't believe you. If you hurt as much as you claim, go to Kroger or CVS and buy a bottle of ibuprofen. We're done here." Alex stood.

A shocked expression swept over a reddening face. "Hey, Doc, you shittin' me? 'Cause I don't think you're funny at all. In fact, I think you're gol-darn insulting."

Alex put a hand on the doorknob. "No, I'm not kidding. You can leave now."

The patient stood, left leg functioning perfectly well. "I'll sue your ass, dang nabbit!"

"Yeah? Go ahead, knock yourself out. But deal with the fact you're not coming back to this clinic for narcotics. Have a good day."

Back in his office, Alex was dictating a note when the phone rang.

"Doctor Cutter," the clinic operator said, "a Don Slater from Seattle on line one."

Don Slater? Who the hell?

"… I'm VP of product development with a medical device start-up called Northgate. We just finished a proof-of-principle study and are in the process of planning a feasibility study. I came across several of your papers during my literature search and was interested to see that your research aligns with what we're doing. The reason I'm calling is to find out if you might have any interest in consulting for us."

Kicking the office door shut, Alex dropped into his desk chair. A start-up? Huh. He knew nothing about what that actually meant, although he had a vague idea.

"When you say consult, what are you looking for?"

"We need a physician—ideally a neurosurgeon or neurologist like yourself—to help design the protocol for a clinical trial. Because of your work, you'd be a perfect fit. But, before I get ahead of myself, I need to ask if you have consulting agreements or any formal involvement with any other companies. We have to be sensitive to any possible conflict of interest."

Easy enough to answer. "No, I don't."

"Excellent. Now comes the tricky part. We prefer to discuss this face to face. I could fly there, but it would be preferable if you could come to Seattle for a meeting. I understand you're busy, so we will, of course, reimburse your expenses in addition to a per diem."

Mind racing, Alex leaned back to stare at the ceiling. Here was a possible opportunity to become involved in research again. The glimmer of hope suddenly made him realize how much he missed that aspect of his life. How long had it been since he took the time to ponder theories and to pore over related publications? That facet of professional life had been smothered by practice. Or was this longing nothing more than a by-product of his present funk? Good question.

"I'm intrigued. Intrigued enough to come to Seattle." He glanced at his schedule: surgery booked solid for the next two weeks.

Slater didn't waste a moment. "When? We'll do anything to accommodate your schedule."

"How much consulting time are we talking about?"

"Depends on how much you're willing to be involved. Realistically, we could use as much time as you can spare."

Alex realized he was getting ahead of himself. "I need to think about this. When do you want an answer?"

"The sooner the better. Ever worked for a start-up?"

"No."

"They're tricky, because they're typically forced to move quickly due to limited money. Our entire future depends on getting the clinical trial up and running, then completed."

"I'll have an answer for you by Friday at the latest." Something about Slater's tone—maybe his lack of a southern accent, maybe his directness—resonated.

"Hope it's positive."

"Mind running out to pick up fried chicken and slaw for dinner?" Lisa asked as Alex came through the back door from the carport. She was at the kitchen sink washing dishes. "Got tied up with the fundraiser planning committee and didn't get home until a few minutes ago."

"Sure, just let me change first," he said, continuing through the kitchen toward the bedroom. "Got an interesting phone call this afternoon."

"See if they'll give you thighs and drumsticks instead of breasts," she called after him. "I asked for it last time, but they didn't actually do it. Depends on who waits on you."

He changed from his white shirt and tie into cargo shorts and a T-shirt. "It was a start-up in Seattle. They want me to consult for them."

She wandered into the bedroom, drying her hands on a dishtowel. "What do they do?"

He cinched up his belt. "They're working on a drug delivery system for brain tumors."

She sat on the edge of the bed. "Seriously?"

"Seriously," he said, slipping on a pair of topsiders.

"Now I know you're joking."

Since hanging up the phone, he'd been fantasizing on how it might feel to return to research. The intellectual stimulation between colleagues was something he missed in clinical practice. Although he loved his work colleagues—Chuck, Ellen, Cole—the surgeries were mostly mind-numbingly rote, glorified piecework. Slater's words, "Ideally, we can use as much time as you can spare," continued to echo through his mind.

Don't get ahead of yourself. Take this one step at a time.

"No, I'm not."

"Go get the chicken and then tell me more about it."

He sipped wine, thinking of how best to explain the complex emotions that had haunted him these past months. "I grew up believing all I ever wanted to do in life was be a really good doctor. But having two patients die in surgery because of judgment errors has changed me in ways you can't possibly understand. I'm not sure I can do surgery anymore. Understand what I'm saying?" The disastrous AVM had drained his self-confidence, leaving him edgy and afraid during even the most routine cases at times. As if he finally realized the gravity of his work.

"I think so. Go on."

"Funny how so many things we believe in as children end up being wrong."

"Like?"

"When I was a kid, I somehow thought all policemen were good guys who upheld the law. And maybe most of them are. But then you see videos of cops beating people senseless and you go, 'Wow, that's crazy, that's not right.'" He paused to lick his lips. "For some reason I thought law and justice were equivalent. Ha! How nuts is that?"

He glanced around the kitchen at the hideous wallpaper Lisa's designer had talked them into putting up. The house no longer possessed the same magic for him that it once did.

"Here's another one: I believed doctors were uniformly good people. *Poof*, that one went out the window when Dick Weiner entered my life. He's been cheating the system for years, charging for surgeries he didn't do, bullying residents into covering for him." He wondered if Suzuki had made any progress since their last conversation. How long had it been since they last spoke?

He paused, corralling his thoughts. He wasn't sure where this ramble was headed or if it made sense, but it felt good to talk.

"Waters taught me that teaching residents was a high calling. I enjoyed teaching the kids how to make their first incision or turn a bone flap or remove a tumor. I pushed to allow them to be primary surgeon with the argument that there's no way to acquire manual skills other than doing the actual surgery, that the residents don't have the equivalent of a flight simulator. Then Steve caused that damn air embolism." He shook his head regretfully. "I'm the one responsible for that death, not Steve."

He now realized where this ramble was headed. "But the one thing I know will haunt me the rest of my life is the AVM. I can't believe I allowed hubris to cloud my judgment. There's nothing I can ever do to make amends for that case. It eats at me incessantly. If there's any possibility of creating a job in Seattle, I think I'm going to try to do that."

The next morning Alex walked into the lounge after completing his first case—a routine craniotomy—dropped onto an empty couch, and was immediately struck by the well-worn familiarity of it all: CNN talking heads, scrub-clad surgeons and anesthesiologists milling about, the scent of coffee, pastry, and A/C-tinged air. A homey microcosm of life—warm, inviting, womb-like. He checked the wall clock and calculated West Coast time. From his scrub shirt breast pocket he pulled a folded paper. Using the phone on the end table, he dialed the access number for an outside long-distance line.

60

"How was your flight out?" Harold Levine, Northgate CEO, asked Alex.

Slater had met Alex at the airport, driven him to the hotel, and checked him in. They had just caught up with Levine at a seafood restaurant on the shore of Lake Union.

"Pretty routine. No drama. Exactly the way I prefer to fly."

They sat at a table for four next to floor-to-ceiling windows that featured a stunning view of blue water through a forest of white hulls, masts, and antennas, the clear azure sky darkening to dusk. Alex loved the feel of cool midsummer air in comparison to the constant tangible humidity of where he lived. He also found it soothing to dine next to bobbing white boats, docks, and seagulls.

"Before we start I would like you to sign a non-disclosure agreement." Levine handed him a manila envelope. "Don sent you a copy to read. This is exactly the same."

Alex removed the paper and signed without more than a cursory glance after verifying it was the same as the one attached to Slater's e-mail. He returned the signed paper to Levine.

"Don mentioned you're open to discussing potential employment. Is that correct?"

Alex nodded. "Depending upon various factors."

"Having a doctor and researcher with your stature on our executive team would be tremendously helpful to the company in numerous ways. The position of chief medical officer would be the equivalent of vice president on the reporting structure. This would seem appropriate. You'd be a voting member of the executive team, which makes you eligible to receive stock options as part of your compensation package." Levine glanced at Alex's ring finger. "Where's your wife from?"

"We're both originally from the West Coast."

"Is she agreeable to relocating?"

"We haven't discussed it since I wasn't sure if it was a consideration."

Levine kept his hands folded on the table. "Don said you've not previously been involved with a start-up."

The waiter brought their wine. Because all three of them ordered cabernet, the waiter talked them into a bottle of Sterling Reserve. With glasses poured and the waiter gone, Alex answered. "That's correct. I've been involved only with two universities and the clinic."

"As I believe he mentioned, being with a start-up requires a different mind-set than most environments. It's not for everyone. Our investors give us a fixed amount of money and that's it. We either succeed or we're out of business. In other words, we watch every penny. This doesn't mean we cut corners, but it does mean we don't enjoy various perks as other executives might. We fly coach instead of business class, for instance. Also, executives aren't compensated as well as a Fortune 500 company."

Alex liked Levine immediately. Straightforward, logical, affable—a style that radiated leadership and competence without coming across as overbearing. Qualities anyone would want in the person they reported to.

Alex sat in an overstuffed chair in front of the hotel room window, looking at a mosaic of city lights. He should be sleeping, he knew, especially since his biological clock thought it was past his usual bedtime. But too many thoughts were rampaging through his mind for sleep. Once the rush of being in a real city again began to abate, he could relax. But not just yet. The difference in this environment amazed and invigorated him. The crisper air, the more casual style, the edgy alertness in people. Grating accents replaced by saltwater air and seagull cries. Taken together, this felt strangely like home. Sitting here, he couldn't remember having left the coast.

The engulfing intensity of work that was layered upon his familiar surroundings—the lounge, OR Three, days spent with Chuck Stevens and Bob Cole—had lulled him into a rhythm that burned away days at a mind-numbing rate. Six o'clock in the morning: a quick breakfast, rounds, surgery, more rounds. Seven o'clock at night: pull into the carport. Friday nights at the University Club with the Canters or one of several other couples. Saturday evenings with Lisa. Sunday evenings catching up on journals and preparing for another week. On and on. Was this how he envisioned spending the remainder of his career? On top of the increasing banality of his routine, each day spent in the OR exposed him to the risk of another disaster, the odds unavoidable. Could he live with that threat hovering overhead?

He thought of Meredith. He'd written the prescription with her best interests in mind. Would he do it again? Good question. Probably not. The problem was, he'd refuse not for moral reasons but rather because of the fear of getting caught and sued again. This saddened him.

Time for a career change?

Another good question.

His present life was—for lack of a better term—a sure thing. He'd become a respected member of the Baptist medical staff and a top earner in the clinic. His savings, grown by conservative investing, ensured an eventual comfortable retirement. Finally, Lisa loved the niche she'd made for herself. Leaving a stable, certain life for a risky start-up would mean taking a huge gamble land-mined with massive potential pitfalls. What were the odds the company would succeed? No way to know. Did he believe enough in what they were doing to make the gamble?

Such a move would be in direct conflict to the old school way he'd lived life thus far: minimizing risk by choosing conservative options. He remembered his awe and dismay a few days after high school graduation when his best friend decided to forgo college to travel the world until his money ran out. In contrast, Alex became a poster child of the quintessential goal-directed career: high school to premed to med school to internship to residency, and finally, to his research and surgical work.

Was he now being presented with a one-shot opportunity? Would this chance ever come his way again?

Knowing he might not be able to sleep, he undressed and climbed into bed.

"Sorry I won't be able to drive you to the airport after your last meeting," Levine said. Alex and Levine were breakfasting in the hotel coffee shop. "Any questions for me?"

Several. But he decided to not ask them until he was sure about taking the job.

"Not at this point. The underlying concept and your preclinical data are very exciting."

"Thank you. Don and I are very excited at the possibility of you joining the team." Levine wiped the corner of his mouth with his napkin. "Any inkling of which way you're leaning?"

Alex wanted to be completely honest. "No. It would represent a big change with major repercussions. It's not something I can decide easily."

Levine smoothed his napkin along the edge of the table to rest his forearms on. "Fair enough. Let's say you decide not to come work with us. Would that preclude consulting?"

"I think you can pretty much count on me to be a consultant for the company. But after our discussion yesterday, it's really appealing to have more involvement than that. Your team's energy and excitement is intoxicating. Besides, I may never get another opportunity like this. That alone is a huge attraction. One way or another, I'll have an answer for you Friday."

"How was the flight?" Lisa asked as he slid into the passenger seat. Their routine when he returned from business trips was for Lisa to pick him up outside of the baggage claim instead of leaving his Audi in long-term parking.

"Good. No turbulence."

"I'll drop you at the clinic," she said. "Leave your bag in the car and I'll take it home and unpack it later. We can talk tonight after you get home and have a chance to relax."

"Thanks." Before the flight to Seattle, he'd parked in the clinic garage so Lisa could drop him there now. He planned to catch-up on messages, sort mail, and pre-op the two craniotomies for the following day, both of whom Betsy Lou should've already admitted. He rubbed his tired eyes and blinked away the fatigue that comes with travel. He looked forward to a relaxing evening and an early turn-in. *Thank God I'm not on call.*

61

The next morning, Alex nosed the Audi into a parking spot and killed the engine. For several seconds he sat staring at the drab, familiar interior of the Baptist Medical Center parking garage. As he walked through the sky bridge, he stopped halfway across, gob-smacked by the too-familiar route and his cast-in-concrete routine: cases every weekday except Wednesday, his clinic day, the same schedule every week, almost fifty weeks a year. He never used up all his allotted vacation and sick leave. *Why not? Why work more than I have to?* Well, for one thing, he enjoyed the status of being one of the clinic's top earners, for it validated his worth as a surgeon. If he couldn't be a nationally respected scientist, he would be a regionally respected neurosurgeon.

He thought of the discussions with Lisa about changing career paths. She made a valid point about their present life: What's not to like? Life is good.

I make more money than I dreamed possible.

Yeah, but can I continue now that I know I've killed people?

His heavy caseload raised the odds of it happening again. Accidents are accidents; that's why they're called accidents. If you could prevent them, you wouldn't have them.

He gazed out along familiar Madison Street toward the business district, then in the opposite direction where commercial zoning segued into residential property. This city, flat, drab, and dusty, was made up of two economic poles, the haves and the have-nots. Unlike Seattle,

Portland, San Francisco, or Los Angeles, the minority here was the middle class, producing a dichotomy of country club members and unskilled laborers.

The moment he entered the surgeon's lounge, he paused, acutely attuned to the chatter and the smells of coffee and yeasty sugar from the morning pastry. As he moved to his narrow locker, another thought hit: *I've lived here five years now.* Five years! Hard to believe. Another five could just as easily flash by unnoticed. Then another. On and on until one day he would attend his retirement party at the University Club. What then?

It'd be too late to do anything other than perhaps learn to play golf.

"Doctor Cutter, ready for you in Room Three."

His first case in the recovery room, Alex sat back in the lounge, his muffuletta on a grease-stained brown paper sack, a diet Dr. Pepper on the table to his right. Alex took a paper out of his pocket and picked up the phone, double-checking the digits as he dialed. The connection clicked through, then rang three times. "Harold Levine."

"Harold, Alex Cutter."

"Didn't think I'd hear from you until tomorrow. This mean bad news, does it?"

"Guess that depends on your perspective. FedEx the employment contract to me, and I'll sign and send it back. That means you probably won't get it until Monday or Tuesday, but it's a done deal."

"Wonderful news. The team will be excited to hear this."

"Yeah, I can't wait to join them." At that moment Alex felt more alive than he had for years.

"May I ask how soon before you can start?"

"I'll find out later today when I give notice. The university requires a month, but I'm not sure about the clinic, so I'll be held hostage to my contract. But I never used all my personal time, so there's a ton of days accumulated. Figure perhaps a month before I can leave town, but that doesn't preclude me from working on the trial design and protocol. I'll start winding down my schedule, which will free up more time."

"Don will be happy. You just made our day."

"Likewise."

"Bother you a second?"

Garrison glanced up from the note he was writing in a patient chart. "Sure, Alex. What's up?"

"I'm leaving."

"Okay." Garrison nodded, clearly not understanding. "When will you be back?"

"No, see, that's the thing. I'm quitting. This is my notice." Alex handed him the paper he typed himself, formally resigning from the clinic.

Garrison stared at the paper for several seconds as a collage of expressions flashed across his usually expressionless face. Disbelief, questioning, acceptance. "May I ask why?"

"You may, but I doubt you'll understand. In spite of this being a wonderful practice for me, moving on is something I need to do. Can't tell you how much I appreciate what you did to make a place for me here. For the most part, I've enjoyed being a member of the clinic. But I can't see my future here."

Garrison's brow furrowed. "That's simply not true. You're one of our stars. You've built a phenomenal practice. Why leave?" He held up a hand. "Hold on, let me rephrase that. Guess that means you have another job. You get a chairmanship somewhere? Is that it?"

Alex laughed. Chairmanship. That dream seemed so long ago and foreign now. "No. I'm joining a start-up company. In Seattle."

"A start-up?" Garrison looked totally bewildered.

"I'd appreciate you not saying a word to anybody until I've had a chance to tell Doctor Reynolds. I'm heading over there now before he cuts out for the weekend."

Garrison nodded, resigned to this not being a joke. "Okay. But you never really answered my question. Why are you leaving?"

Alex was torn between dropping the subject or not. Part of him knew he had to say something or he'd always regret it. "That AVM I did? The patient who died?"

Leaning back in his chair, Garrison nodded. "I remember."

"You were in the office that day when I called for help. You sent back word you were too busy. Long as I've known you, you've never been too busy to help a colleague, especially if it's a clinic member. The patient died. I can't help but wonder if he might've lived if you'd helped me. I can't let that go, Garrison. I just can't."

Garrison's shoulders slumped. "That case was inoperable, Alex. He should never have been taken to the OR."

"Maybe. Maybe not. Maybe he died because of being in the hands of the wrong surgeon. But that doesn't change the fact you didn't come to help." Once again Alex felt the sting of that day full-force, his temples throbbing.

Garrison cocked his head, looking at Alex sideways. "You telling me you're fixing to give up a great practice on account of that one case?"

"No. Nothing's that simple. But refusing to help me when I really needed it soured my taste for practice here. And losing that patient is something I'll never forgive myself for. I started medical school with an unrealistic dream of what the practice of medicine was all about. I thought doctors worked for a greater good. Well, I've learned that isn't always the case, that there's as much special interest as we see from politicians in Washington. In fact, I can't think of anything more political than this clinic. The way we court referring physicians, the way you sided with Clarence on an issue I still believe is indefensible. I don't have a clue why you refused to help me that day, but I suspect it was out of some misguided self-interest, revenge for losing a patient to me. That's nothing but pure, unadulterated politics. Want me to keep going, or have you heard enough?" Being rhetorical, Alex continued. "Let me put it this way: Why *shouldn't* I want to leave?"

62

"SORRY YOU'RE GOING, DOCTOR Cutter. I was looking forward to being on your service," a first-year resident said as they prepped for surgery in the OR.

Alex tossed the surgical towel he just dried his hands with into the linen bucket. "I'm going to miss teaching you guys almost as much as I'll miss the muffulettas."

"Seeing's how this is your last case, you get the honor of picking the music," Cole called from the other side of the surgical drape.

He thought back to his first case here at Baptist, the patient with the cerebellar tumor, and remembered the music Cole played. "How about the Bob Seger disc with 'Hollywood Nights' and 'Against The Wind.' That is, if you brought it today." Cole always carried a black nylon CD wallet into the OR with twenty or so discs and his boom box.

"Figured you might want that one." Cole laughed. "You always did like it. Especially the line 'working on mysteries without any clues.'"

Alex finished gowning by knotting the stays around his waist. "Yeah, it's one of my favorites." Then he said to the resident, "Pay attention. Here's how I drape and prepare my field."

Chuck Stevens, gowned and gloved, stood on the step of the overhead table, ready to hand off the sky-blue surgical drape. "All set?"

"I am."

In one fluid movement, Chuck passed the head-end of the drape while peeling off the protective cover of the transparent adhesive barrier. Alex accepted the drape, smoothed the sticky, transparent surface over the incision line he'd marked on the scalp with a Sharpie, and pulled out the wrinkles, funneling the drainage system into the sterile suction bag at the bottom of the drape.

Minutes later they were quickly progressing through the opening, Alex doing it instead of having the new resident muddle through. Besides, this was the resident's first—and only—day on his service, and the standing rule was to observe the first case before being allowed the privilege of taking the scalpel. Chuck and Alex worked flawlessly as a team, having done so many openings together that Chuck had the next instrument ready before Alex asked for it, now wordlessly passing instruments back and forth, Alex's hands moving with deft precision, the only sounds in the room the respirator, the heart monitor, the gurgling suction, and Bob Seger's Silver Bullet Band.

"Where you from, Trevor?" Alex asked the resident.

"Chicago."

Alex bent slightly for a better view before slipping the dural elevator through the burr holes to strip dura from the undersurface of the skull. "Chicago. Huh!" It was a city home to several residencies. "Why come all the way down here?"

"Wanted a change. Grew up there and went to Northwestern."

"Well, you certainly got what you wanted, didn't you?"

"Uh-huh."

"Craniotome."

Chuck handed him the air-powered side-cutting drill. Alex pressed the footplate against the tip of his finger and squeezed the trigger. The drill responded with the high-speed whine of an air-driven motor similar to a dentist drill. Alex let it run a few seconds to make sure the footplate didn't heat up, which would happen if the drill wasn't perfectly seated. Just one more precaution to make sure to stay out of trouble. As much as he trusted Chuck, he always double-checked. Just like Chuck double-checked him.

"Irrigate the blade while I cut," he instructed the resident.

Chuck passed the resident the bulb irrigator filled with saline to squirt over the skull where Alex worked.

As Alex began to cut between the burr holes to lift the square piece of skull away, several emotions surged inside. This, he realized, could very well be his last craniotomy. Ever. After today his surgical career would likely end. He would miss some aspects of practice, the intense camaraderie being one. He felt strong bonds to the OR team, the floor nurses, his colleagues. He suspected this bond was similar to what policemen or soldiers felt toward each other. They shared common stresses and joys and the inherent difficulties and triumphs of their emotionally taxing professions. He could explain a difficult case to Lisa, but she never really understood the daily stress or the complex issues he was forced to deal with. Perhaps this is the reason she had some difficulty understanding his decision to abandon a profession he'd worked so hard to obtain. Fourteen years of training would essentially vanish the moment he walked out the OR door in a few hours.

Also, he was off call now. No sense catching a case if you wouldn't be around to handle the post-op care. At seven o'clock this morning, at the official termination of his last night on call, an incredible weightlessness came over him, as if the soles of his Nikes barely grazed the floor. A chronic burden pressing on him for years simply vanished, leaving him almost giddy with relief. Gone were the anxiety-provoking, sleep-stealing, middle-of-the-night calls about post-op fevers. No more early morning summonses to the trauma center. Yes, he'd miss the camaraderie, but the emotional price he paid for it no longer seemed worth it. He would find similar relationships in his new job, perhaps starting with Levine and Slater.

Suddenly, he realized the music had stopped. Glancing up, he saw Cole smile at him.

"What?" Alex asked. Something wrong? Panic seized his gut.

"Hail to The Chief" filled the room from the boom box, the volume now up.

"What the hell?" he asked, glancing around.

Chuck stood at attention. So did the resident at his side. Then through the swinging doors marched the two chief residents. "Ten hut!" called Chuck.

The two chief residents, Steve Stein and Rene Coumaux, marched to within a foot of Alex and stopped, as if soldiers. "Doctor Cutter," Stein said, "by the powers vested in me by the residents of this university, I award you the medal of the Silver Scalpel for Excellence in Teaching." He paused. "I'd pin it on you, but then you'd have to regown and reglove, so I'll just set it over here next to your loupes."

Misty-eyed, Alex scanned the crowd pouring into the operating room—scrub techs, circulating nurses, Ellen, Betsy Lou, other residents who'd scrubbed out of their cases. A lump formed in his throat, causing him to croak a response. "Thanks … guess I … better get back to work before you guys contaminate the field and this patient gets an infection, 'cause then I'd have to stick around to take care of it."

Two hours later as Alex knotted a suture—a quick instrument tie rather than using his fingers, a final bit of flash to finish the case—he glanced at the new resident. "One last question."

The resident reached in with the scissors to snip the suture tails. "Yeah, what's that?"

"What would you say if I told you Humpty Dumpty was pushed?"

The resident laughed and replied without missing a beat. "Everyone loves a scandal."

Alex glanced toward Cole. Cole's eyes came up over the top of the drape, twinkling. "Goddamn!"

"Knew someone would eventually get it," Chuck added.

Alex shook his head. "Yeah, but it took a goddamn Yankee to figure it out."

63

THE RING OF THE car phone jangled Alex out of autopilot consciousness produced by monotonous miles of interstate. Who the hell would call now?

"Hello?"

"Alex?"

In spite of the hollow cell phone echo, Alex recognized Baxter's voice. How long since they last spoke? They bumped into each other now and then at AANS meetings, but that was about it. "Baxter?"

"'Tis me, 'tis me. Where the hell are you? Had a devil of a time trying to get hold of you. What's this about leaving the clinic?"

Alex glanced at the endless cornfields flashing past, Lisa driving this segment. They alternated hours at the wheel. "Just passed through Omaha, so I guess that puts us somewhere in Nebraska. Why?"

"Omaha? What the hell you doing there?"

"Heading to Seattle." The back of the car contained their clothes and a few personal items, pretty much the same drill as years ago when they drove to the last job. The furniture and household items were somewhere behind them in a Mayflower truck working its way to the Northwest.

"What the hell for?"

"Long story. What's on your mind? Don't know how long this connection's going to hold out here in the middle of nowhere. You're getting scratchy."

"Thought you'd want to hear the news."

Typical Baxter, dangling something enticing out there, forcing him to ask. "What news?"

"The FBI arrested your old pal Dick Weiner."

Alex frantically motioned Lisa to pull to the side of the road and flick on the emergency blinkers. This was just too damn good to drop the call now. "You shitting me?"

"Nope. One hundred percent true."

"For Medicare fraud?"

Baxter laughed. "Better than that. Story is they got wind he was billing cases the residents were doing without him, but they couldn't get enough solid evidence to prove it. Not conclusively, that is. Not unless they followed him around the hospital with a camera."

"What about the nurses and residents? Everybody knew what he was doing. Couldn't they testify?"

"Nope. None of them would risk it. So the feds did the next best thing. They monitored his phone. Caught him threatening witnesses. Word has it, on one call he threatened a resident with firing him before graduation, said he'd make sure he never got into another program. And get this: the dumb shit placed those calls from his office. That's how sure he was of not getting caught. Can you believe that?"

Actually, he did. "How'd the feds find out about the billing issues to begin with?"

Baxter chuckled. "Someone called their tip line."

"No kidding. You wouldn't have had anything to do with that, would you?"

"*Moi*? Course not! Did you?"

Alex laughed.

"Gone full circle now," Baxter said, "and we're back to where we were when you moved. We're looking for a new chairman. Geoff and I, of course, have our hats in the ring. But that's not why I called. We're down a couple people now that Weiner's gone. We need help. You wouldn't be interested in your old job, would you? Your office's still vacant."

"Thanks, Baxter, but I'm out of the game now."

Five years later

The telephone ring jarred Alex from the Michael Connelly novel he was reading. 8:30 p.m. For five years, it had been rare for him to get an evening call from anyone but pain-in-the-ass telephone solicitors.

"Hey Alex, Steve Stein. How's it going?" Stein, now practicing in San Francisco, occasionally called to chitchat, still motivated, Alex suspected, by Stein's gratitude for being given a residency slot.

"Good. What's up?"

"Just got back from the AANS. Ran into several of the old gang. Heard some pretty interesting gossip involving your old pal, The Rev."

Ah yes, Clarence Hill. Hard to remember the last time he thought of him. "And?"

"You remember, don't you, that shortly after you left, Garrison divorced Anne to marry his nurse Linda?"

He'd heard about it, probably during an earlier installment from Stein, but in truth he really didn't care to keep track of Garrison or any of the other partners except Martin. Neither he nor Lisa was surprised; you'd have to have been a flaming idiot to not see that one coming. "I do remember."

"Well, here's the kicker. The clinic has a mandatory retirement age for the CEO position. Soon as Garrison hit sixty-five, he was forced to retire but could stay on as a surgeon. There was some discussion about changing the by-laws, but guess who led the charge against it?"

Alex laughed at the irony. "Clarence?"

"Bingo. But here's the really good part. The moment Clarence assumed the throne, he fired Garrison. Claimed it was because of the divorce from Anne, that divorce is against God's will as stated in the Bible. Perfect irony, isn't it." Not making it a question.

A tinge of sorrow tapped Alex's heart. Garrison, after all, had championed Clarence, grooming him as his successor. "Ironic, yes. Perfect, no. Still, I believe in the old saw—what goes around comes around." The random thought of Garrison flying his Pitts in aerobatics competitions flashed through his mind.

"Still content to not do surgery?"

Alex weighed his answer. What should he say to a friend who still practiced? How could he describe how different and relaxed life was now in contrast to the pressures of neurosurgery? He was still haunted some nights by the ghost of his mistakes. Steve—his assistant on the AVM case—would never understand the impact the patient's death dealt him, because he didn't shoulder the full weight of responsibility. Then again, perhaps Steve had learned from both the air embolism and AVM cases and would never make such mistakes. If so, Alex had taught the younger man something worthwhile.

"I still miss teaching you clowns, but I don't regret the decision to quit."

ACKNOWLEGEMENTS

Thanks to the following friends who read the initial draft of the manuscript and provided feedback:

William Dietrich
Simone Bruyere Fraser
Astor+Blue Editions editorial staff
Mary Osterbrock